The sun glinted off something down the steep hillside, drawing her eye to her right. Her heart skipped. Now what? She edged down a few steps, trying to get a better view through the pine, hemlock and naked birches and oak. She squinted, wondering if the sun had just caught a rock with a lot of mica at the right angle.

No, there was something there.

Metal for sure—a lot of it—in a compact heap amidst the tumble of rocks and half a dozen pine trees. If not for the sun striking a bit of metal at just the right moment, Penelope would have gone past it.

She held her breath. *No.*

She stared at the heap of metal. It was unquestionably a plane. Anyone in New Hampshire would be thinking just what she was thinking—this was the spot where Colt Sinclair and Frannie Beaudine had gone down.

Her pulse pounded in her ears, and she didn't move as she absorbed the impact of what she had stumbled upon.

Carla Neggers's "knack for blending wonderfully eccentric characters with passion, humor, and suspense makes her novels a pure joy to read!"
—*Romantic Times*

Coming soon from MIRA Books and
CARLA NEGGERS

ON FIRE

Available November 1999

CARLA NEGGERS

KISS THE MOON

MIRA

ISBN 1-55166-485-2

KISS THE MOON

Copyright © 1999 by Carla Neggers.

Printed in U.S.A.

AUTHOR'S NOTE

I have people to thank! First, my brother Jeffrey and sister-in-law Janine for their help with researching Lake Winnipesaukee, and to Grace Steward and her husband, the late Baldwin Steward, for introducing us Neggers kids to the beauty of the lakes region of New Hampshire. Next, Robyn and Jim Carr, for talking to me about planes (and Robyn, about everything), Christine Wenger for talking to me about police procedures and writing and just for being a pal, and Janet Evanovich, for the tuna fish at Lou's and the cheese soup at Simon Pearce.

It's time, finally, to thank the people on Elm Hill for being such great neighbors for seven years: Pam and Paul Hudson, Frances Flanders, Russ and Mary Moore, Bob and Sue Fogg, the Kendalls, the Harringtons, the Lawrences, Larry and Mandy Traineanu, and Michelle, Zachary, Jereme and Crystal—we miss you all.

Dianne, Amy, Meg—this is already such fun! Thanks.

And Joe, Kate and Zachary...you're the best family a writer could have.

To Kate and Zachary

PROLOGUE

Frannie Beaudine had the intelligence of a Katharine Hepburn and the sexiness of a Marilyn Monroe, and he couldn't believe she was his. That such a woman had fallen for him, Colt Sinclair, a skinny twenty-one-year-old, filled him with a pride and contentment he'd never known.

She paced in front of the tall windows of his family's sprawling apartment on Central Park, Manhattan glittering at her feet. Her long, dark hair was swept into an elegant twist, and she wore diamond studs at her ears—fake diamonds, for she couldn't afford real ones. She'd even borrowed her gown, a swirl of black velvet that barely contained her breasts. Her lips and nails were painted a deep red, sexy, vibrant.

Colt said nothing about the thrill he felt just watching her. Complimenting her appearance would only irritate her, add to her already heightened state of impatience. Frannie despised being beautiful. She believed it distracted people from noticing her other attributes—her skills as a pilot and art historian, her independence, her spirit of adventure. She wanted *everything*, she'd told Colt last summer in New Hampshire, when she still regarded him as a gawky Dartmouth graduate, a pampered rich boy. She was already something of a legend in her hometown, a poor girl from the hills who'd become an accomplished and daring pilot while simultaneously studying art history, not at a college, not with a tutor, but on her own, at the public library.

Colt, who'd been born with the "everything" Frannie wanted, knew she would get her wish. But he also knew her beauty wouldn't be a hindrance, it would be an asset. And it was.

She'd asked him to fly tonight. Just six weeks ago she'd seemed so remote and unattainable. He fell short as a Sinclair. His father had told him as much less than an hour ago.

But now he was with Frannie, and all things were possible.

Her eyes, a deep, almost navy blue, were vivid, shining as they focused on him, and she stopped pacing just for an instant. He could feel her urgency. "You're sure there won't be a problem with the plane?"

"I'm positive. Everything's ready, Frannie. Unless you change your mind, we'll be on our way before midnight."

She nodded, taking in a sharp, shallow breath. They had everything planned almost to the minute. First they would make an appearance at the reception honoring the donation of the Sinclair Collection to the Metropolitan Museum of Art. Colt's father had offered Frannie a job last fall as an assistant curator for the collection, and she'd seized it as her chance to live in New York. Colt had been barely aware she was in the city. She worked exhaustively all winter, seldom emerging as she catalogued, picked, chose, examined, checked and rechecked the history and authenticity of every painting, sculpture, artifact and bit of treasure that the Sinclairs had collected over the past century and stored in their warehouse on the lower east side. His family's trips to South America, Central America, Africa, Asia, Russia, Australia had all yielded their prizes. Frannie worked without a break, and Colt had to admire her dedication even as he worried about how pale and weak she was from overwork, even now, six weeks after he'd spotted her at the museum and she'd turned his life upside down.

She would want to collect her kudos tonight for the brilliant work she'd done. Colt understood. Frannie Beaudine was a woman consumed with the need for recognition and affection.

In the second stage of their plan, they would make their apologies and leave early, separately, within a decent interval of each other. They had warm clothes waiting in the hangar north of the city, and Colt's Piper Cub J-3, ready to fly. A grand adventure. That was what he and Frannie were embarking on. It wasn't a lion hunt in Africa or an attempt at Mount Everest, but it was, finally, an adventure Colt felt the courage to undertake. He loved Frannie with all his heart and soul. That she wanted to run away with him, now, tonight, didn't have to make sense, didn't require a five-year plan, a vetting by a menagerie of Sinclair advisors. It required only faith, trust and the willingness to take action. All his life, one of those had been missing. Not now.

"Then there's nothing more to do but get on with it," Frannie said. "Your father and mother are already at the reception. We should go."

"I'd just like to say goodbye to Brandon." Colt observed a rare flash of nervousness in her eyes. She knew if anything could give him cold feet, it would be his baby brother. "He's asleep."

"Hurry."

Colt had rehearsed this moment a thousand times in his mind. He hurried down the hall, hardly making a sound on the thick carpeting, his heart racing, his hands clammy. He passed portraits and photographs of uncles and great-uncles, cousins, his grandfather, on various adventures. There would be no photographers to record his adventure. He didn't want notoriety or adulation.

He just wanted Frannie Beaudine, he thought, his pace slowing as he approached his brother's half-closed door.

He pushed the door open, and his throat caught at the sprawl of boy and stuffed animal in the bed, the city lights silhouetting his bony figure. He wore pajamas with little cars and trucks on them.

Unexpected, unrehearsed tears stung Colt's eyes. He doubted he would see his brother again for months, perhaps a year. He would have given up Bear by then, lost his boyish imagination and possibility. Sometimes Colt longed for his own boyhood, when he had liked nothing better than to roam around in the Museum of Natural History. His father had assumed his mind was filled with fantasies of becoming a Sinclair. Instead he'd memorized the form and the colors, the shapes, the essence of the birds and animals and tools on display. In dark corners, where no one would find him, he would pull out scraps of paper and a nub of charcoal and try to capture what he'd memorized.

Sinclair men did not become artists.

If Frannie hadn't fallen in love with him, Colt was certain he would have thrown himself off the Empire State Building by now. And then he would never have seen Brandon again. Now, at least, there was a chance.

He gave his sleeping brother a mock salute and tiptoed down the hall, where Frannie was waiting for him. She had no brothers and sisters. She couldn't know the agony of what he'd just done.

Ten minutes later they were at the museum. They made small talk and drank champagne and pretended not to be in love, and Colt thought Frannie was the most beautiful and alluring woman in the room. She seemed at ease with everyone, scholar, rich donor, journalist, poor art student, and she talked knowledgeably and passionately about the collection of art and treasure she'd helped put together even as people asked her when she would again climb into a cockpit. She was unique, and Colt could hardly contain himself at the thought that she loved him.

He avoided his father, fearful Willard Sinclair would penetrate his older son's mind and find out what he was planning. When the time came, Colt had no intention of telling his father goodbye. His mother, either. She would be impossible to extricate from her friends and her champagne.

Across the room, he saw Frannie, impatient, unable to stay still, slip down a dark corridor past indulgent guards. Colt followed, stifling a surge of panic. What was she doing? They were to make their apologies and separate exits in minutes. He glanced at his father, who was regaling eager listeners with tales of his latest expedition up the Amazon. If only he could give his two sons as much care and attention, Colt thought bitterly, and tried to ignore the tug of regret for his brother, who would no longer have a buffer between their father's increasingly domineering temperament and Brandon's zeal to take him on. After tonight, Brandon, just eleven, would be on his own, at least for a while.

Colt shook off his sudden melancholy and followed Frannie into the bowels of the museum, where she had been granted a closet-size office to continue her work on the Sinclair Collection. She used her key to open it, moving quickly. He could hear her rapid breathing. She left the door ajar, but he remained in the dark shadows, trying to ignore a sense of foreboding. This wasn't in their plan.

Seconds later she emerged from the tiny room, and he heard her check a laugh.

In her hand was a black, hard-sided case the size of a small artist's painting case.

Colt took a step forward, and she stopped, her already pale face going paler still. "Colt, good heavens, you startled me!"

"Frannie?" He pointed. "What's in the case?"

She caught him by the arm and pulled him down the corridor. "It's no time for questions," she whispered fiercely, "or for the fainthearted. You're in, Colt. You're in all the way."

"Frannie..."

"We have to go."

He didn't move. He didn't speak.

"*Now.*"

Wisps of hair dripped from their pins, her dark blue eyes shone even in the shadows, and her chest heaved, not from fear but breathlessness. Excitement. She was so certain. Always so certain. He hadn't asked about how many men she'd loved. She was twenty-six, and she was Frannie Beaudine, beautiful, intelligent, spirited.

Her expression softened. "Colt...I can't do this without you."

Still he didn't move. "What's in the case, Frannie?"

Her lower lip quivered, the red stain gone, and he could see uncertainty creep into her eyes.

"It's something from the collection," he said.

"Of *course* it's something from the collection. Diamonds, Colt. Valuable, perfect diamonds of an uncertain provenance. No one but me even knows they exist. God knows how long they sat in that dusty warehouse."

"Frannie, I can't."

Irritation set her jaw. "It's the only way for us to be together. You know that as well as I do. Colt—please, we have to go. If the guards catch us now, it won't be Canada we'll be seeing at dawn, it'll be the bars of the jailhouse."

He followed her out. There was nothing else he could do. They would take a cab to the airfield where his Piper Cub was waiting. She'd asked him to fly it. He'd been so stupidly pleased. Now he knew he was a romantic, idealistic fool, just as his father had told him.

In the cab, Frannie covered his hand with hers. "I do love you, Colt Sinclair."

Maybe she did. He stared out the cab window as they crossed the bridge. It was a cold night for flying, but they had a full moon. It was so huge, and it seemed so heavy and big that even the night sky couldn't hold it. Colt pretended he was on it, looking down at the shiny cab, at the beautiful aviator, the rich twenty-one-year-old and their stolen diamonds. He had fancied them living by their skill and wits in Canada until his family accepted them and what they'd done. But Frannie had wanted it all, and she'd wanted it now.

For six weeks, Colt had deluded himself into thinking he was enough.

He remembered reading *Treasure Island* aloud to his little brother under a full moon last summer, and he wished he could be with Brandon now, poking him in the ribs and sneaking him into the kitchen for hot cocoa.

Wouldn't their father be surprised, Colt thought. He was a Sinclair, after all. He had given up the love of his brother for a misguided, wild adventure, and in so doing, he had given up himself.

It was, of course, the Sinclair way.

ONE

Five hours after she'd headed onto Sinclair land to check out sugar maples for tapping, Penelope Chestnut sank onto a granite boulder and admitted she was lost. The sun had sunk low in the sky, the temperature had already started to drop, she was down to the last of her water, and she didn't have the vaguest idea where she was. New Hampshire, in the woods above Lake Winnipesaukee, probably still on Sinclair land. More specifically than that, who knew?

Her parents were expecting her for Sunday dinner at six. If she didn't show up, they'd worry. Given her history, they'd worry all of ten minutes before calling out a search party. Dogs, snowmobiles, helicopters, men on snowshoes with flashlights. They'd all join in the hunt. Not one would be a stranger. And not one wouldn't be just a little pissed at her for taking them out on a chilly March night.

It was galling. She'd rather spend the night in the woods. She could make a little fire, boil snow if she couldn't find a stream, survive quite nicely until daylight. With the clouds pushing out, the temperature would drop overnight. Not that she minded—the cold nights and above-freezing days of early March made the sap run. Her current predicament notwithstanding, Penelope was an accomplished hiker. She wouldn't freeze.

Maple-sugaring season was what had ostensibly brought her onto Sinclair land in the first place. A tiny corner of their vast tract of central New Hampshire wilderness abutted the ten acres she'd inherited from her grandfather, and she'd wanted a few more maples to tap. So she'd set off for an hour survey, with anorak, gloves, a hip pack of water, a Granny Smith apple and two Nutri-Grain bars. One thing had led to another—through a clearing, up a hill, over a stone wall, across a stream—and pretty soon she was sitting on a rock in the middle of nowhere.

All because she didn't pay attention. She'd spotted a woodpecker fluttering among the hemlock, an osprey nest high in a tall half-dead pine, followed the sound of a waterfall newly formed by the melting snow, thought about tea and warm scones with her cousin Harriet tomorrow afternoon, when she would return from ferrying two businessmen to Portland, Maine. Provided her father let her carry passengers. He didn't like the way she'd been flying lately. A wandering mind was a dangerous thing on foot in the wilds of northern New England, but in the air, it could be fatal.

Which, Penelope decided, didn't bear thinking about while she was lost in the woods with dusk encroaching.

She had hoped to find something on top of the hill to orient her. A view of the lake, a stream, a stone wall, smoke curling from the chimney of a nearby house, *something*. But below her was just another steep, narrow, dry ravine. There were no landmarks.

No promise of a way out. She had to go down this hill and up the next and just keep hoping for the best.

"I need another Nutri-Grain bar," she said aloud in the stillness and silence that seemed to envelope her. But she'd consumed her last one an hour and several over-hill-and-over-dales ago.

She blinked back fatigue and the eye strain that came with hours on snow-covered hills without sunglasses. She hadn't brought a compass, either. Or her wilderness medical kit. If she tripped and fell, she'd just have to lie there until someone found her. She'd tried following her trail in the snow, but it wasn't good snow for tracks, and the two times she did pick up her trail, she found herself back where she'd started. So she'd given up, figuring that even if she could follow her tracks, there were five hours worth of them. They wouldn't exactly provide the shortest, most straightforward route home. And she figured she had no more than ninety minutes of daylight left.

She was doomed. A search party was inevitable.

The sun poked through gray clouds that had been hanging over the lakes region for three days and were due to move out tonight. Everyone's mood seemed to have suffered because of them, including her own. Heading into the woods by herself had seemed like a damned good idea five hours ago.

She scooted to the edge of her boulder and looked at the steep, tree-covered, rock-strewn hill. The going certainly wasn't getting any easier. It was a north-facing hill, still encased in snow and ice, with small patches of wet, slippery leaves where the snow and ice had melted in circles around trees and rocks. She was sweating from temperatures in the upper forties, exertion, frustration. She'd worn none of her specially designed hiking clothes, just jeans and an anorak over a red plaid flannel shirt she'd been maple sugaring in since she was seventeen.

"Might as well get on with it," she muttered, the silence and stillness almost eerie.

She lowered herself off her boulder, and her foot slipped on a patch of wet, brown leaves. She caught herself before going down on her butt, her heart rate jumping at the close call. A broken ankle and hypothermia were just what she needed. She scooped up a handful of snow and stuffed it down her back. It melted instantly on her overheated skin, cooling her, soothing her. There were worse things than having her parents call out another search party on her. She just needed to stay focused and make their job as short and simple as possible.

She wished she'd brought her cell phone. Flares. Even a book of matches would be welcome.

The sun glinted off something down the steep hillside, drawing her eye to her right. Her heart skipped. Now what? She edged down a few steps, trying to get a better view through the pine, hemlock and naked birches and oak. She squinted, wondering if the sun had just caught a rock with a lot of mica at the right angle.

No, there was something there.

Penelope took another couple of steps to her right. The snow was wet and slippery on the steep hillside, and getting a good purchase in her day hikers wasn't that easy. She grabbed the thin trunk of a birch for balance and leaned over as far as she could for a better look.

Metal for sure, a lot of it, in a compact heap amidst the tumble of rocks and half a dozen pine trees. In summer, ferns and brush would leaf out and make the pile even harder to spot. If not for the sun striking a bit of metal at just the right moment, Penelope would have gone past it even at the end of winter with the landscape at its starkest.

And for the sun to glint off it, it wasn't completely rusted, and that meant it was aluminum.

She held her breath. *No.*

The frame of Frannie Beaudine and Colt Sinclair's Piper Cub J-3 was aluminum tubing. Its fabric covering would have rotted away by now, forty-five years after it had disappeared in the skies above Cold Spring, New Hampshire, last seen by a half-dozen locals out on the clear, chilly night. Penelope wouldn't expect to find much more than a crumpled heap of struts and trusses, rusted engine, bits of wing and tail assembly, whatever hadn't succumbed to the crash and decades of exposure to the harsh weather of northern New England.

But she hadn't expected to find Colt and Frannie's plane *here*. According to her own pet theory, they'd faked a crash in New Hampshire and made it to Canada. Whether they'd crashed there or were living happily ever after was open to question.

Except it wasn't anymore. This had to be Colt and Frannie's long-missing Piper Cub. Penelope suddenly shivered as she stared at the wreckage. What else could it be?

A leap of the imagination, brought on by fatigue, low blood sugar, her own fascination with the ill-fated flight of the two lovers. Even as a kid, she would wander the woods with one eye searching for a downed Piper Cub. Later, she'd started collecting information—newspaper and magazine articles on the weeks-long search, headed by Willard Sinclair himself, then articles on the Sinclair Collection and Frannie's role in pulling it together, turning it into a magnificent, coherent whole instead of a mishmash of stuff generations of Sinclairs had picked up on their various expeditions. In the past year, Penelope had started interviewing local residents who remembered Frannie Beaudine as a little girl and a young woman, who had known the Sinclairs from their years of mountain climbing, fishing, hunting and boating in the lakes region. The men were all Dartmouth alumni. Colt was barely a year out of Dartmouth when he disappeared.

The intensive, exhaustive search for the missing plane had turned up nothing, not one clue beyond the separate, positive sightings of it in the sky over Cold Spring. It was possible it wasn't Colt's Piper Cub J-3—but who else's could it have been? When the news came out of New York that he, his plane and Frannie Beaudine were missing, the search was mounted, focusing on the New Hampshire lakes region.

After a while, people stopped looking. If the plane turned up, it turned up. Most believed if it was in New Hampshire at all, it was at the bottom of a deep part of one of its many lakes. Sections of Winnipesaukee, a clear, glacial lake, were ninety feet deep—nobody could see that far down. If the plane was ever to be found, whether in water or on land, it would have to be by accident.

In the forty-five years since Colt and Frannie had

disappeared, not one Sinclair had set foot in Cold Spring.

Except for Harriet, of course. Penelope grimaced in anticipation of her cousin's reaction to what she'd just found. But Harriet was another matter. Penelope couldn't concentrate on scoping out plane wreckage, finding her way out of the wilderness *and* the oddities of Harriet Chestnut.

She squinted at the heap of metal. It was unquestionably a plane. Anyone in New Hampshire would be thinking just what she was thinking—this was the spot where Colt Sinclair and Frannie Beaudine had gone down.

From her position, Penelope couldn't make an educated guess about what had happened to the plane, why or how it had crashed into the steep hillside. She imagined the Piper Cub coming in low on that dark night, in trouble, possibly clipping trees before slamming into the hill. Colt and Frannie saying their goodbyes, guessing their fate. Penelope wasn't a romantic, but the image of the two young lovers plunging to their deaths brought tears to her eyes.

Her pulse pounded in her ears, and she didn't move as she absorbed the impact of what she had stumbled upon. To get to the wreckage, she would have to climb over icy rocks and big boulders, fallen trees and limbs, patches of slippery leaves covered in thin, clear ice and rough, snow-covered, nearly vertical ground. It would take time she didn't have, and it would involve risks she didn't need to take. Given that Frannie and Colt's plane had lain here for forty-five years without being discovered, Penelope didn't like the odds of what would happen to her if she fell and couldn't get up again.

Not that anyone in Cold Spring would appreciate her reining herself in. Being lost in the woods at dusk was enough for them to assume she was back to her old tricks, taking unnecessary risks, not thinking, not considering who might have to strap on snowshoes to come fetch her on a cold, dark night.

She frowned, preferring not to think about past transgressions. She was thirty, after all, not twelve. She hadn't been *this* lost in years.

Naked deciduous trees stood outlined in sharp relief against the gray sky, every twig sharp and clear and black. Soon pinks and lavenders would streak across the horizon, and they'd seem so bright and vibrant against the grays and whites of the late winter landscape.

Darkness would fall rapidly, and the temperature would plummet.

She had to get back. Tearing her gaze from the wreckage, she crawled over another boulder, then carefully made her way through young trees and stick-like brush, through more wet, dense sugar snow—not the light and fluffy snow of January—to the bottom of the steep, narrow ravine. There was no stream, there were no trails, no stone walls, no hunter's lookouts—there was no reason for anyone to have stumbled on the wreckage in the past forty or so years.

Colt and Frannie's bodies.

Penelope came to a sudden halt, imagining the skeletal remains of the two lovers above her on the hill. This wasn't merely the solution to a forty-five-year-old mystery. It was a tragedy. Two people had died up there.

She shook off the morbid thought and started up

the opposite hill, her legs aching, her stomach begging for a Nutri-Grain bar. She needed home, food, water and rest. Then she'd figure out what to do about Colt and Frannie and their Piper Cub.

A twig—something—snapped, and she stopped. Went still. Listened.

Had she heard anything? A squirrel, birds prancing in the branches of a nearby tree? She couldn't be sure.

"You're tired."

Her voice seemed to go nowhere in the quiet, still, late afternoon air. Maybe she'd heard a deer or a moose, even a bear venturing out of hibernation.

Yep. Best to get on home.

Her water-soaked socks squished inside her day hikers. No blisters yet. She was lucky. She hadn't bothered with boots or snowshoes, never imagining she'd end up lost. A little lost was one thing. That she could manage. But she was a lot lost.

Then, there in front of her, at her feet, was a melting trail of footprints. Not moose or deer or even bear, but human prints. And not her own. They were big. Probably male. She pivoted and stared toward the opposite hill, unable to make out the wreckage from her position. The snow, the gray rocks, the gray trees, the gray sky. The heap of plane tubing was gone, as if it had been a mirage.

The footprints ran down the hill to the left of the way she'd come, weaving among maple and oak and hemlock, even, unhurried. They had to be relatively fresh prints. The warm temperatures had barely melted them, and the last snow had been just two days ago, four inches that freshened the landscape and heartened the skiers who loved to see March stay a lion for as long as possible.

But who could have ventured out here, possibly have seen the wreckage and not mentioned it?

"Bubba Johns."

Of course. He would have no interest in a lost plane.

Penelope could feel some of the tension ease out of her. She wasn't afraid of Bubba. He was the town hermit, a recluse who had a shanty on the edge of Sinclair land—technically *on* Sinclair land, but no one had made an issue of it in the twenty years since he'd set up housekeeping there.

"Bubba!" she called, her voice dying in the ravine. There was no echo. "Bubba, it's me, Penelope Chestnut!"

She could almost feel his ancient, some said crazy, eyes on her, a frosty gray that went with his unkempt white beard and scraggly white hair, his tall, rangy body. Sinclairs or no Sinclairs, it was Bubba who owned these hills and had for years. Penelope's parents had warned her as a child to stay off Sinclair land, not because she was trespassing, but because she might run into Bubba Johns. But at ten years of age, she'd found herself out in the hills, exploring on her own, pretending, fantasizing, not realizing until it was nearly dark that she was lost. Bubba had materialized out of nowhere and silently led her home. She had been terrified, and her active imagination had conjured up images of Little Red Riding Hood meeting up with the big bad wolf. She half expected Bubba to drop her over a cliff or toss her onto a fire even as she'd followed him home, chattering at him as if she'd known him all her life. Without ever speaking, he'd left her at the end of her parents' driveway and disappeared, not waiting for thanks or an invitation for coffee and cake. Her parents hadn't seemed too sure they should believe their only daughter's story about the silent hermit who'd seen her home.

Bubba Johns was as much a part of the landscape as the moose, deer, hawks and chipmunks, and like everyone else in Cold Spring, Penelope left him to his chosen life of isolation and solitude.

She turned and continued on her way, feeling the sun sinking in the west even as the sky melted into a pink so deep and dark and beautiful it made her want to lay on the snow and stare at it. But she kept walking, her head spinning, her legs leaden, her mind full of thoughts of Colt Sinclair and Frannie Beaudine buried in their twisted metal grave and Bubba Johns out there in the gathering darkness, waiting, perhaps, to see if once again he needed to lead her home.

Wyatt Sinclair gave up on sleep and kicked off his blanket sometime before dawn. He didn't know the exact time because Madge, his ex-lover, had insisted on removing the clock radio from his nightstand. It was bad chi, she'd said. Apparently he was a walking time bomb of bad chi. That was spooky enough, but then she did his astrological charts using some computer program. She'd plugged in the date, time and place of his birth, and out popped stuff that had compelled her to pack up.

"I have to move out," she'd told him, whipping things into her suitcase. "There's just too much negative energy around you. You're—well, to be very straightforward with you, Wyatt, you're one scary son of a bitch."

He'd grinned. "You needed a computer to tell you that?"

Ten minutes later, she was out the door. She'd left the cat. Allergies.

He stumbled out to his living room, tripping over the cat en route. It got up and did its cat-stretching thing. It wasn't much of a cat. Short gray hair, yellow eyes, lean. Bad tempered. Madge called him Sarsaparilla, but Wyatt thought that was a hell of a name for a cat and just called him Pill.

A New York apartment, a cat, an ex-lover like Madge. No wonder he had sleepless nights.

He flipped on lights, put on coffee, poured some orange juice and clicked the remote. "Headline News" came on. He flopped on his couch, noticing on the TV clock that it was four-eighteen. Early, especially for New York. The city was strangely silent at this time of day, at least from the vantage point of his fourth-floor upper east side apartment.

He liked New York on and off. His mother, the first of Brandon Sinclair's three wives, had raised him there through eighth grade. Then the Sinclairs had taken over, and it was off to prep school, Dartmouth and Wharton. He'd endured, struck off on his own for a while and returned to the city of his childhood eighteen months ago. Who'd have ever thought.

If Hal hadn't died, Wyatt supposed he might still be tallying new bird and plant species in remote parts of Australia and South America. But Hal had died, and Wyatt had come home.

He stared at the reporter on the screen and

yawned, not out of fatigue, he realized, but boredom. Stress was not a factor in his intermittent insomnia. He had money, food, lodging and—dear God, it was true—a good job. He would be at his desk on Wall Street in another five hours.

His office had a view of the harbor. It was something.

He watched a commercial pushing laxatives, then a report about the latest scandal in Washington, and he was about to flip to "Nick at Nite" when the anchorwoman started in on her next news item.

"The solution to one of the more tantalizing mysteries of the past half-century may be at hand. A New Hampshire woman claims she's found the small plane adventurers Frannie Beaudine and Colt Sinclair were flying the night they disappeared."

Wyatt sat straight and turned up the volume.

The woman was named Penelope Chestnut, she lived in Cold Spring, and she had stumbled on the wreckage while she was out hiking on Sunday, the report continued. She would be leading local authorities to the crash site today, Tuesday, for verification.

Contacted at his vacation home in St. Croix, Brandon Sinclair had declined comment.

Wyatt wasn't surprised. His uncle's disappearance was the most enduring and mysterious scandal involving a Sinclair, if hardly the only one. Or the most recent. Hal's death and Wyatt's near death—and presumed culpability—in Tasmania had garnered their share of headlines. His father maintained his only son was a throwback to previous generations of Sinclairs, who had been adventurers and daredevils since Roger Sinclair had taken on the

English as a privateer in the American Revolution. Naturally, he'd made a fortune, pissed off friend and foe alike and died young.

"Headline News" put up the famous picture of Frannie and Colt taken the night of their ill-fated flight. Wyatt was struck by how young they looked. Frannie was from Cold Spring, a captivating mix of daring pilot and self-taught art historian whose exploits, intelligence and beauty had drawn her rich lover's eye. They'd cut out of a reception at the Metropolitan Museum of Art, took off in Colt's Piper Cub and were never seen again. No trace of them or their plane was ever found.

Until Sunday, Wyatt thought, wishing they'd put up a picture of Penelope Chestnut instead of his uncle and Frannie Beaudine. He was generally an excellent judge of character, and if he could see what she looked like, he would be better able to assess if this was a hoax. But there was no picture, no footage, even, of Cold Spring, New Hampshire.

He debated calling his father. Colt's disappearance was still a raw wound that infected everything Brandon Sinclair did, including raise his only son. He seldom talked about his brother, brushed off questions Wyatt would ask. Wyatt wasn't sure whether his father's reticence stemmed from the lingering pain and grief of losing his only brother or from embarrassment. Even after forty-five years, Colt could still attract national headlines.

To his credit, Brandon had worked hard to change the Sinclair way of doing things. He wanted to preserve their spirit of scholarship, exploration and adventure but without the penchant for scandal and premature death. He was determined his brother's example would not extend to another generation. Colt would be the last Sinclair whose recklessness and zest for adventure would leave behind mourning parents, wives, children—and younger brothers.

Not that Brandon had ever told Wyatt he'd loved his older brother, missed him, felt hurt and betrayed because he'd abandoned him for Frannie Beaudine. But if he knew nothing else about his family, Wyatt knew that love was never enough for a Sinclair. That was their abyss. It was impossible to fill with money or adventures. No matter how many lions they shot or mountains they climbed or discoveries they made, the abyss remained unfilled.

He wondered when his father had realized his only son was that way, too. Another Sinclair destined for notoriety and adventure.

But no more. After the disaster in Tasmania, Wyatt had opted for the safe path. A desk, a suit, a job putting his MBA to use. He'd already thrown his trust fund in his father's face, so there wasn't that. But there was plenty of money. Even a disinherited Sinclair was good at making money.

The cat jumped up on his lap and started pawing, and Wyatt shut off the television and listened to Manhattan awaken on a dreary March morning. Garbage trucks, cabs, dog walkers, hospital workers, a siren off in the distance. He patted Pill, although he didn't much like cats, and he told himself that Penelope Chestnut and her discovery in the woods above Lake Winnipesaukee weren't his problem. His only problem was scrounging up enough energy and interest to get to work for nine o'clock.

By nine-fifteen Jack Dunning was standing in front of Wyatt's office window high above New

York harbor. Jack was a tall, rangy, sandy-haired man dressed in cowboy boots and jeans. Wyatt regarded him without comment. A Brooklyn native gone Texan. He'd worked as a private investigator in Dallas for years, apparently wore out his welcome and was back in New York. His chief client was Brandon Sinclair, a man not only very rich but also very suspicious, determined to protect himself, his wife, his two ex-wives, his son and his two young daughters from scoundrels, kidnappers, con men and lunatics. Jack seemed perfectly willing to oblige. As soon as he made enough money, he always said, he planned to buy a ranch in west Texas and retire. New York made him itch, and the women wore too damned much black.

He glanced at Wyatt. "Nice view."

Wyatt smiled. "The Statue of Liberty reminds me of the virtues of tolerance."

"Reminds me of the dangers of being a sucker."

Wyatt couldn't tell if he was serious. In his eighteen months back in New York, he'd come to believe Jack Dunning was a man not nearly as uncomplicated as he liked to pretend. His angular features and dead gray eyes made him difficult to read. He could be fifty—he could be sixty. It was impossible to tell. And Wyatt had no real desire to know. Jack worked for his father. If he was here, it was because Brandon Sinclair wanted him to be here.

"You heard about your uncle's plane?" Jack asked.

"I caught it on the morning news." Wyatt didn't say how early that morning. Dunning would regard a sleepless night as a weakness and file it away as something he had on his employer's eldest child.

"Then you haven't heard the latest. The woman who said she found the plane—this Penelope Chestnut—she's changed her mind. Says it was a mistake. She was hypoglycemic and on edge because she was lost."

"Lost?"

"That's how she found the site in the first place— she was out hiking on Sunday afternoon and got lost. Her folks were organizing a search party when she found her way out on her own. Claims she went back yesterday afternoon and saw it wasn't a plane but just an old dump site, probably from the turn of the century."

Wyatt rolled that one around in his mind. A mistake. Not what he'd expected from Penelope Chestnut, although he had no reason to expect anything. "So no Colt and Frannie, after all."

"That's what she says. Here's the thing." Jack turned from the window. There was no indication he felt out of place in the elegant wood-paneled Wall Street office, which Wyatt had leased furnished, down to the brass lamps and slate blotter. If he were to play the venture capitalist, he needed a robber baron office.

Dunning stayed focused on his reason for being there—Penelope Chestnut. "Now she's also claiming she can't find the dump site again," he said.

That tweaked Wyatt's interest. "How's that possible?"

"She says she was able to follow her tracks in the snow yesterday, but it was tough even then because of all the daytime melting. Says she planned to take people up today to prove it, but it snowed last night and covered what was left of her tracks. She got up at the crack of dawn this morning and says she can't find the site. Says she wandered around and just can't find her trail or figure out how to get back there. Maybe she can find it in the spring."

Wyatt tilted in his buttery leather chair and considered this twist. At first blush it sounded like bullshit. "What do you think?"

"I think it's hogwash. This girl's lived her whole life in those woods. She can find her way back, snow or no snow. I'd bet my molars on it."

"What does my father say?"

Jack gave a small grin. He was a striking man, but not handsome. Wyatt sensed he liked his employer, despite the vast difference in their manner and sensibilities. "Your daddy's more diplomatic than I am. He asked me to go up there and check out this girl's story. New Hampshire in March. Just where I want to be. But I'll do it and see what's what."

"And why tell me?" Wyatt asked.

The grin turned to a smirk. "Because your daddy asked me to."

As Wyatt had expected. "Okay. Thanks for the report. If you need my help for anything, let me know. You have my number."

Jack winked. "I have all your numbers, Sinclair. See you around."

Thirty minutes later, Wyatt was still staring at the same printout. He'd had his secretary hold his calls. He got up from his desk and walked to the window, the Statue of Liberty shrouded in a sudden fog. He agreed with Jack. Penelope Chestnut's story didn't wash.

He called his father, knowing already he was making a futile effort. His father would tell him nothing, possibly less than he'd told his personal private detective. Jack was a professional. He could be controlled.

"Wyatt—good to hear from you. How's the weather in New York?"

"Foggy. Jack Dunning was just here. He told me you've sent him to New Hampshire to check out this woman's story about Colt's plane. Anything I need to know?"

"It's just a precaution. If she made a mistake and is doing what she can to save face, so be it. But if she's lying, I want to know why. And, of course, if she's lying, I want to find my brother's plane." He paused, no chink in his self-control. They might still have been discussing the weather. "After all these years, I'd like to know what happened to him."

"You trust Dunning?"

"I'm paying him well enough."

Wyatt didn't comment. As far as he was concerned, money and trust had nothing to do with each other. "I guess that's your call. Anything else?"

His father was silent for half a beat. "What else would there be?"

"I don't know. I've just always had the feeling there's more to Colt and Frannie's disappearance than you've said."

"There's nothing more, Wyatt. If you can, come down this weekend. Ann and I would love to have you, and you know the girls would be thrilled to see you." Ann was his third wife; they had two daughters together, Ellen, nine, and Beatrix, eleven. "March isn't my favorite month in New York."

"Thanks for the invitation. I'll let you know if I can wiggle loose."

"It's best I sent Jack up to Cold Spring, Wyatt. The people there tend to blame Colt for what happened. Frannie Beaudine was one of their own."

"No problem."

When they disconnected, Wyatt didn't hesitate. He told his secretary he needed to go out of town and asked her to keep her finger in the dike for a few days, possibly longer. He caught an elevator to the lobby of the 1920s building and hailed a cab to take him to his apartment. He fed the cat and called Madge. "I'm going to be out of town for a few days. Can you tend to Pill?"

"You know I'm allergic."

"Wear gloves and a mask."

"You're a heartless bastard, Wyatt. Just because you can climb a rock wall with your bare hands doesn't mean the rest of us are weaklings. My allergies are serious."

"If you can't take care of Pill, say so and I'll get someone else."

"Can I stay at your place while you're gone?"

His apartment was bigger and in a better location than hers. "Sure."

"I'll take medication for my allergies," she added quickly.

Within the hour, he was on the Major Deegan Expressway heading toward New England.

No Sinclair had ventured to Cold Spring, New Hampshire, since Colt and Frannie had disappeared—unless his father had lied about that, too. Because something—maybe a lot, maybe not a lot—was missing in Brandon Sinclair's rendition of the events of forty-five years ago. Wyatt had believed that for years, but hadn't pushed, hadn't confronted his father out of respect for the loss he'd suffered. Some things, he'd decided, just weren't a son's business.

But as he drove north against a hard wind, he wondered if he and his father could ever make their peace if he didn't learn, finally, the truth about the night Colt Sinclair and Frannie Beaudine took off into the darkness.

TWO

Penelope tried to ignore the clicking of a camera three yards behind her. Another reporter. Most of the swarm of reporters—print, television, radio, tabloid, mainstream—that had flocked to Cold Spring had gone home after hearing the discovery of Colt Sinclair and Frannie Beaudine's plane was a mistake. A few lingered, angling for whatever news and gossip they could find while they were there. Penelope didn't know what good a picture of her preflighting her Beechcraft would do anyone.

It was a breezy, chilly morning, and she couldn't wait to get into the air. She'd pulled her hair into a sort of braid, put on a functional flight suit that always, rather ridiculously, made her feel like the Red Baron and packed herself some cheddar cheese a friend had made on her own farm, an apple and a bit of this season's maple sugar. Decadent. In twenty minutes she was saved. No more questions, no more doubting eyes.

"You know, Penelope," the reporter called, using her first name as if they were pals, "I drove all the way up here from New York to cover this story. Colt and Frannie are, like, icons on the upper east side. Rich, good-looking, adventurous, intellectual, fucking doomed. Now, here I am, and what do I have? A dump. A fucking dump."

Penelope ignored him. A turn-of-the-century dump was the best she could do. It was lame, and it wasn't sexy at all, but it explained the metal. She had decided pegging the whole thing on a mirage was just too much to swallow.

The reporter didn't quit. He was lanky, bearded and obnoxious. "You should get your facts straight before you go to the media."

She turned from her plane. She was at the tail, trying to concentrate on her checklist. "I didn't go to the media. They came to me. Look, stop at Jeannie's Diner on Main Street for pie, or if you want to hang around until three o'clock, wait and stop at the Sunrise Inn for tea and scones. My mother and my cousin Harriet make the best scones in New Hampshire. The inn's on the lake. Just take a left off Main."

"I didn't come to fucking New Hampshire for pie and scones. Jesus. This weather. You know, we have daffodils in New York."

"Send me some when you get back."

He let go of his camera and let it hang from his neck. It was a small, cheap camera on a thin black cord. He was probably freelance. He certainly wasn't from *Newsday* or the *Times*. "You're not very contrite," he said.

"I made a mistake. You guys jumped all over this thing before anyone could verify what I'd found. It's not my fault you got the cart before the horse."

The guy went red. Penelope thought he might throw his camera at her, but then she saw her father marching toward them. He had on his work pants and wool work shirt, and he didn't look as if he knew as much about airplanes and flying as he did. People underestimated Lyman Chestnut all the time. He was the quintessential hardheaded Yankee, a gray-haired, craggy-faced man of sixty who was the law at Cold Spring Airport. It was a small, uncontrolled airport with three hangars, one runway and three full-time year-round employees: Lyman, his sister Mary and Penelope. What they couldn't do they hired part-time help to do or contracted out. Winter and early spring were their slow seasons. Come summer and autumn, the place hummed.

Lyman jerked a thumb toward the parking lot. "Out. Let Penelope do her job."

"I was just—"

"You're compromising safety."

The reporter sputtered, then gave up and retreated.

Penelope grinned at her father. "Why didn't I think of that?"

"You've done enough thinking for this week, I expect."

"What's that supposed to mean?"

"Nothing. Finish your walk around."

He about-faced and returned to the office in a corner of one of the hangars. Penelope watched him in frustration, then resumed her preflight. She knew what he meant. He meant he didn't believe her dump story, either. *No one* believed her dump story.

But this morning when she woke before dawn, she realized she had no choice. She had to undo what she'd done. Brandon Sinclair, contacted in St. Croix, was sending his own investigator to represent his family's interests. It was a Sinclair plane found on Sinclair land, and it had been a Sinclair in the cockpit. As Penelope had said yesterday afternoon to Andy McNally, the local police chief, "Who's looking after Frannie's interests? What if Colt killed her before the plane crashed? Then we have an unsolved murder. There's no statute of limitations on murder, you know."

Andy had calmly told her, yes, he knew, and she should mind her own business. The story was out, reporters were on the way. That was when Penelope realized she had no control. She'd been booted to the back of the raft, and someone else was negotiating the rapids.

Except for one thing. *She* knew where the wreckage was. No one else did, besides Bubba Johns, who presumably wasn't about to talk.

Late yesterday, when she'd found reporters skulking around on her land discussing getting shots of her sap buckets and hunting up "that hermit," Penelope had realized the extent of her folly. If she didn't do something fast, dozens of reporters, the police and Brandon Sinclair's investigator would descend on poor Bubba Johns. Even if by some miracle he had never noticed the plane wreckage, he was a colorful addition to the story. A wild-haired hermit living on Sinclair land. It was a nice contrast to the scandal and tragedy of the missing daredevil heir and his beautiful, intelligent, adventurous lover.

And then there was Harriet. Only humiliation and embarrassment awaited for her.

So Penelope had made up her mind. The wreckage became a small, turn-of-the-century dump, and she couldn't find it again. She pretended she'd made her way to it late yesterday and tried to thrash her way back first thing this morning. The light covering of snow gave her a touch more credibility, although apparently not enough for her father.

"Well," she said to herself, "first things first. The heat's off Bubba for now."

She climbed into the cockpit and took a breath, focusing on the task at hand. She was transporting a time-sensitive package to Plattsburgh, New York, from a management consultant who worked out of his home on Lake Winnipesaukee. It had to be there this afternoon, not tomorrow morning. Her father had canceled her passenger charter yesterday. He didn't like the way she was flying, hadn't for weeks, and getting herself lost in the woods on Sunday proved she was distracted and bored. She'd had a few semi-close calls in a row, and he'd decided she wasn't taking her job seriously enough. He couldn't put his finger on what was wrong, but he wasn't happy. And finding a forty-five-year-old plane wreck that turned out to be an old dump hadn't done a damned thing to get her with the program.

She hoped by the time she returned, Brandon Sinclair's investigator and the last of the reporters would all have turned around and gone home. Then she could take her time and figure out what, if anything, to do about the downed Piper Cub J-3 in the hills above town.

There were no bolts of lightning and no men with tar and feathers to greet Wyatt when he crossed into Cold Spring, New Hampshire. It was late afternoon, and the landscape was bleak. Pretty, but bleak. The White Mountains looming in the distance, rolling fields, winding roads, stark, leafless trees, lots of pine and fresh, clean, white snow clinging to everything. The snow was melting rapidly in the above-freezing temperatures, and the roads were clear. The only signs of spring he could see were the potholes and frost heaves.

The sun was out intermittently, and a persistent breeze made the temperature seem colder than it was. Wyatt had pulled over once to consult his map. Damned if he'd give the locals the satisfaction of seeing him get lost his first day in town. He had climbed the White Mountains, including the infamous Mount Washington, during his four years at Dartmouth, but at his father's request, he'd avoided Lake Winnipesaukee. He'd had other things on his mind at twenty besides the fate of an uncle he'd never known. He'd never seen his family's land in New Hampshire and couldn't understand why they hadn't sold it or donated it as a nature preserve.

A two-lane road led into the village of Cold Spring, a few picturesque streets nestled along the western shore of Lake Winnipesaukee. Twenty-seven miles long, Winnipesaukee was the largest lake in the state, formed by glaciers and famous for its crystal-clear water and three hundred islands. At this time of year, it was still an expanse of snow and ice, although only a few ice-fishing shanties dotted inlets close to shore. Winnipesaukee, Wyatt had learned from his map, was Abenaki for "beautiful water in high places."

Like most of the other villages on the lake, Cold Spring was busiest in the summer and fall, but from the mix of shops on its maple-lined Main Street, Wyatt guessed it had a strong year-round population. Signs were discreet, storefronts neat and pretty even on a dreary March afternoon. Wyatt noticed shops that sold antiques, vintage clothing, quilts, gifts and the like, which the tourists would enjoy, but he also saw a pharmacy, a diner, a photo and print shop, a clothing store—the sort of shops one needed when a mall wasn't close at hand.

He pulled into a parking space in front of the diner, fed the meter and went in for a very late lunch and whatever local gossip he could pick up about one Penelope Chestnut. So far, no sign of Jack Dunning, not that Jack would willingly share his findings with his boss's son.

The diner was crowded for four o'clock on a bleak Tuesday afternoon. A plump waitress with perfect mauve nails was moving down the counter with a pot of coffee. Five booths lined the opposite wall, three of them filled. Reporters, Wyatt guessed. They'd be up from Boston and New York and God knew where else to check out the sighting of Frannie Beaudine and Colt Sinclair's plane. The story had probably evaporated before they'd arrived, and now they were having a bite to eat in a country diner before heading back to the city.

Wyatt slid onto the one unoccupied stool at the counter and listened.

"Of course she's lying," a middle-aged man at the other end of the counter said. "The question is why."

A skinny woman yawned. "No one gives a shit, ace. The people don't care about Penelope Chestnut. The people care about the fate of Frannie and Colt."

"One of these days I want to meet 'the people,'" an older woman grumbled, "because I don't give a rat's ass about Frannie and Colt, either. I just care about that last piece of coconut pie sitting over in that case." She raised her voice. "Miss, you earmark that pie for me, okay?"

Wyatt managed to get in an order of grilled ham and cheese on rye and coffee while listening to the reporters grouse and catching the locals—two men in flannel shirts at one of the booths—grinning at the wild-goose chase Penelope Chestnut had put them on. From what he gathered, she'd done this sort of thing before. Maybe not this precise thing—crying wolf about a famous long-missing plane—but stirring up trouble in her small lakeside village.

Then he got it. A scrap of conversation, a link between what was being said on one end of the diner and the other.

Miss Penelope was a pilot.

Wyatt smiled. Pilots he understood. He wasn't one himself, but he'd hung out with them, used their services and appealed to their sense of adventure for most of his twenties and the first two years of his thirties. Now he was thirty-four, a suit behind a desk. He grimaced and drank his coffee and ate his sandwich. When he paid his tab, he got directions to the airport from the waitress.

"Penelope won't be there," she said. "She's flying today. And she's not talking to reporters."

Wyatt didn't disabuse her of her notion that he was a reporter. As instructed, he followed the main road the way he'd come, turned left at a flower shop, followed that road—its massive potholes and frost heaves required bright orange warning signs—until he came to a perfunctory green sign that said Airport. Bingo. He turned onto a barely paved country road, bounced over it until he came to a precious stretch of flat land. The Cold Spring Airport. It wasn't much of an airport, but he hadn't expected much. The one runway and three small hangars fit with his image of the woman who said she'd found Frannie and Colt's plane, then said she didn't.

He rocked and rolled over the undulating dirt parking lot and did his best to avoid the huge holes that had opened up with the warming temperatures. They'd filled with water that, presumably, would ice overnight and melt again tomorrow. Leaves on the trees, flowers and green grass all seemed a long, long way off.

Wyatt parked next to a mud-spattered hunter green truck. It had four-wheel drive. So did the SUV next to it. His car did not. The air was damp and cold, the kind that got into the bones. He picked his way through water-filled holes to a small, squat building with a crude sign indicating Office. People did get to the point around here.

A sixtyish man stood out front, glaring at the gray tree line. Without even glancing at Wyatt, he said, "If you're from the press, the story's over. You can go home."

"I'm not a reporter."

He turned, but Wyatt sensed his mind was still on whatever he expected to find on the tree line. "What can I do for you?"

"I'm looking for Penelope Chestnut. As I said, I'm not a reporter, but I would like to talk to her about what she found in the woods."

The older man's eyes narrowed slightly. "You're a Sinclair."

His tone hadn't changed. He fit the stereotype of the naturally stoic, taciturn New Englander. Wyatt checked his surprise. "Yes, I'm Wyatt Sinclair. Colt was my uncle."

"You're Brandon's boy."

It wasn't a question, but Wyatt said, "That's right."

A heavy, fatalistic sigh, as if he should have expected a Sinclair to wander into town. "Your father sent his own investigator, you know. Jack Dunning. He's flying up—he's taking a detour over your family's land first. I suppose he'll try to spot Penelope's dump."

"Jack's thorough. I'm here for my own reasons."

"I see. Well, Penelope'll be coming over those treetops in about three minutes. She's low on fuel. Not paying attention. Too damned much going on. I never should have let her fly today." He bit off an irritated sigh. "I'm her father, Lyman Chestnut." He put out a hand, and they shook briefly. "I knew your grandfather, and your father and uncle."

Wyatt nodded. His father had never mentioned Lyman Chestnut.

"I was fifteen when Colt disappeared," the older man went on. "Tough break. It happens. We had a plane go down about an hour west of here a couple years ago, and it still hasn't been found."

He stared at the horizon, and Wyatt got the message. Whatever he might believe about what his daughter had found on Sunday, Lyman Chestnut was on her side.

The office door opened, and a heavyset woman thrust her hands on her ample hips and said, "Jesus Christ, Lyman, I can't believe that girl! She says she's running on fumes. She's going to land. You want me to get the ambulance and fire department up here?"

"Get the police, because when this is over, one of us is going to be arrested. Her or me. I've had it, Mary. She's crossed the line."

Mary snorted. "Now, how many times have I heard that?"

A small Beechcraft materialized above the treetops, and Lyman Chestnut held his breath. Wyatt thought everything looked just fine. It seemed to have good speed. A normal descent. It landed smoothly on the single paved runway without a hitch.

Lyman breathed out with a whoosh, but his relief only lasted a moment before he clenched his teeth. "Goddamn it, this time she's grounded." He turned to the gray-haired woman, who still had her hands on her hips and was shaking her head in disgust, whether because Penelope had landed safely or didn't have the close call she apparently deserved Wyatt couldn't tell. Lyman pointed a thick finger at her. "Mary, you hear that? I'm grounding her. I own the goddamned plane. I'm her goddamned boss. I can goddamned ground her."

So much for stoic and taciturn. Wyatt judiciously kept quiet.

"For how long?" Mary asked.

"Thirty days."

"She'll go crazy. She'll drive all of *us* crazy."

"Three weeks, then."

Wyatt stood between two dripping icicles and watched Lyman march up to the Beechcraft. He moved at a fast, determined clip. He wasn't a big man, a couple inches under six feet, and his granite-like features didn't bode well for the woman in the cockpit, given that they were related.

By the time he arrived, Penelope Chestnut had jumped onto the runway, beaming, no indication she'd given herself a scare.

"Well, well," Wyatt said under his breath.

He assessed her from a distance. Gray flight suit that would have done NASA proud, dark blond hair in a fat braid that had long since gone wild, athletic body, height just an inch or two under her father's—and attractive. Not cute or elegantly beautiful, but striking. Unless the package all fell apart a few yards closer, Penelope Chestnut was not what Wyatt had expected. On his way north, he'd developed two different images of what he'd find. Both were older than he was. Neither had her flying planes. In one, she was the stereotypical pinch-faced New Englander with no makeup, faded turtleneck and tweeds, sensible shoes. In the second, she was the dairy farmer and earth mother. Cows, kids, land, gardens, dogs, cats, maybe a few chickens.

Obviously he'd been way off the mark.

Lyman Chestnut started in on her, pointing a callused finger, and Penelope about-faced and walked off as if they'd done this all before. Her father hollered so half the state of New Hampshire could hear. "I don't give a good goddamn if you were in control of the situation, you're still grounded!"

She stuck her tongue out at him. Without turning around. That bit of prudence was the only point Wyatt had seen so far in Lyman's parenting favor.

"I saw that, Penelope Chestnut," Mary said from the office door. "You're lucky you have a father who cares about you. You've scared the bejesus out of him more times than any daughter has a right to and still live."

Penelope took a breath. Up close, Wyatt saw that the last few minutes had taken their toll on her, after all. She was a bit paler and shakier, he expected, than she wanted anyone to see. He also saw that she had green eyes, greener even than her father's. She said, "I've scared the bejesus out of myself a time or two."

"Ha. The day you're scared, I want to be in the front row. Do I need to call the FAA?"

"No, Aunt Mary. Good heavens. I didn't crash. I just didn't get an accurate fuel reading before I left Plattsburgh. I never should have told you."

Mary sighed loudly. "Your father's right. What you need is a break, and a break's what you're going to get. I still have the paperwork from the last mishap, before Lyman softened. He won't this time. I won't let him."

"Damn it, Aunt Mary, this is collusion. I have rights—"

"Not here you don't, missy."

Mary withdrew into the office, and the door banged shut behind her. Wyatt thought he saw a glimmer of humor—and affection—in Penelope Chestnut's eyes. Then they focused on Wyatt, and he could see the wariness come into them—but no hint of embarrassment over the scene he'd just witnessed.

Before Wyatt could introduce himself, Lyman caught up with his daughter and, containing his obviously still-boiling anger, jumped in ahead of him. "Penelope, this gentleman wants to see you about the junk you found in the woods. Talk to him. Then come talk to me. Wyatt, this is my daughter, Penelope Chestnut. Penelope, Wyatt Sinclair. Brandon's son."

He stood back as if expecting fireworks. Penelope tilted her head, slightly, studying Wyatt with a frankness that somehow didn't surprise him. Boots, jeans, black shirt, black leather jacket, no hat, no gloves. She seemed to take in all of him with that one appraising look, no problem shifting from her troubled landing and her quarrel with her father to a Sinclair on the premises.

"I drove up from New York this morning," Wyatt said.

"I see. Well, I'm sorry you've wasted your time, but I don't have anything to tell you except that I screwed up. Low blood sugar, bad light, an overactive imagination." She shrugged, matter of fact. "I didn't find your uncle's plane. I found an old dump. That's all there is to it. Look, I have to see about my plane—"

"*I'll* be seeing about your plane," her father broke in. "You might as well have a cup of coffee with Wyatt here. You're going to have three weeks to kill. And that's just for starters. If I don't like what I see in three weeks, you'll have another three weeks to cool your heels."

"I don't need a break. I need to fly *more.*"

"You don't fly to get your head together. You fly *when* your head's together."

She turned to Wyatt. "Never fly for your own father."

It was the wrong thing to say. Wyatt saw that immediately, even if Penelope didn't. Her father swallowed his anger and allowed his natural stoicism to reassert itself. He said calmly, making it impossible to be misunderstood, "I am not acting as your father right now. I am acting as a responsible owner of six charter planes and a flight instructor for the last thirty years who has the right and the duty to ground an unfit pilot. And you, Penelope Chestnut, are unfit to fly."

"Fine," she said without missing a beat, "then I'll boil sap."

Wyatt would have throttled her right then and there.

"Have coffee with Sinclair here," Lyman said, teeth gritted, patience spent, and headed to the runway and his daughter's plane.

His departure left Penelope alone with a Sinclair, which made Wyatt wonder if his family's reputation was as bad in Cold Spring as he'd been led to believe. Then again, Lyman Chestnut could simply believe a Sinclair would insist on talking with his daughter and best get it over with.

With one hand, Penelope stuffed stray hair behind her ears, missing even more than she captured. She had a face that was all angles and straight lines—except her mouth, which was soft and full. Some color had returned to her cheeks, and she wore tiny silver hoops on her ears. Her green eyes narrowed on him. "I'm sorry you had to witness that little spat. Pop worries too much— I don't know, maybe I should go easy on him. It's been a crazy couple of days. Do you really want to go for coffee? I don't have a thing to tell you."

No question in his mind she had a lot she could tell him—if she would. "I'd love some coffee."

She shrugged. "As you wish."

He made a move to go into the office, but she shook her head. "Not here. Aunt Mary's into flavored coffees. I think today's is raspberry. Blechh. My mother and cousin own an inn on the lake—they serve coffee and tea in the afternoon. And they make the best scones in New Hampshire, maybe all of New England. I think today's are currant."

"Sounds fine."

"You're not the investigator your father sent up here, are you? I had the impression it was someone he'd hired."

"That would be Jack Dunning. He's supposed to arrive soon—he's flying up from New York, scoping out the landscape. He has his own way of doing things."

"Does he know you're here?"

Wyatt shook his head.

"Your father?"

"No."

"Well, I guess you're a big boy and can do what you want to do. Let's go. We can take my truck."

So the truck was hers. Here was a woman who flew planes, drove a truck and was off to have tea and scones at a lakeside inn. Definitely not what he'd envisioned—never mind the wild, wavy blond hair, the green, green eyes, the tight, sexy body, the flight suit, the keen wit.

She stopped abruptly in the middle of the parking lot, tilted her head at the sky and took a deep breath. She held it a moment, then exhaled. "It's a fine spring day. I'm glad I didn't crash."

Yep, a pilot. She liked life a little on the edge. Maybe a lot on the edge.

And suddenly Wyatt could see how she might

have made the leap from old dump to Frannie Beaudine and Colt Sinclair's plane. A missing plane was more exciting to find in the woods when you were lost and tired—and this woman would hate to be either—than an old dump.

Which meant his trek to New Hampshire could be for nothing.

"I'm glad you didn't crash, too," he said dryly, "but this isn't spring."

She grinned at him. "Technically, no. But the ice is melting and the sap is running—it feels like spring to me."

THREE

A black-haired, black-eyed, suspicious-minded Sinclair in a leather jacket. Just what she needed. Still jumpy from her mishap in the air, Penelope waited for Wyatt Sinclair to climb into her truck. "Whoops—hang on a sec." She whisked a little blue calico bag off his seat onto the floor. "Rose petal potpourri. I let Pop drive my truck and it came back smelling like an ashtray. He's taken up smoking cigars. Disgusting."

"You have strong opinions."

"About cigars. Anyway," she said, starting her truck, "opinions are by definition strong. Otherwise they're not opinions."

She backed out over the rutted, washboard lot, which seemed even worse this year than usual. On the main road, she drove faster than was necessary, swerving around potholes, braking hard for frost heaves. She knew just where the worst ones had formed in the freezing, thawing, refreezing cycle of late winter and early spring that wreaked havoc on the roads yet made the sap run sweet.

Beside her, Wyatt Sinclair didn't say a word. He was *exactly* what she'd expected of a Sinclair. Suspicious, probing, good-looking. He had a natural arrogance that she didn't find as off-putting as she'd anticipated. It was just so...*easy* for him. Her research into Frannie and Colt had led to facts about the entire Sinclair family, including this first of his generation. He was well-educated, he spoke four languages, he was an expert mountain climber and outdoorsman, and he came close to killing himself every year or two.

Two years ago, his luck ran out and tragedy struck during a climbing expedition in Tasmania, when bad weather and bad judgment combined to leave him bug-infested, dehydrated, infected, with three broken ribs, a broken leg and his hiking companion and best friend dead at his side. Penelope had read about the incident in the papers. Even the *Cold Spring Reporter* had picked up the story.

She didn't notice any obvious lingering effects of such a terrible ordeal. Maybe he'd gnashed his teeth and pushed, pulled, argued, rebelled and thrown himself into enough danger over the years to have established a certain peace with himself. Except he didn't look peaceful, either.

It was way too early, she reminded herself, to draw any conclusions about what Wyatt Sinclair did and didn't feel. Indeed, she'd probably do herself a favor not to go down that path at all. She heard he'd moved back to New York to become some sort of money type on Wall Street, possibly because of his experience in Tasmania. Then again, sooner or later, all Sinclairs made it back to Manhattan to prove they could make money and didn't need the family fortune.

Of course, she also heard his father had disinherited him. Rumors were forever circulating around town about Sinclairs, and Penelope had learned not to believe everything she heard.

She glanced at him. The black eyes were squinting as he stared at the landscape, the square jaw set hard. For sure, getting lost in the New Hampshire woods for a few hours and running out of gas in a small plane would be nothing to Wyatt Sinclair. A pop fly to Plattsburgh and back to deliver a package would bore him silly—he'd probably dump fuel just to liven things up.

But Penelope loved her work, and she couldn't believe she'd screwed up again. Damned near running out of fuel. How *stupid*. She wanted to blame the reporters, the hoopla over her discovery in the Sinclair woods, the anticipation of having to explain herself to Brandon Sinclair's investigator—but that wasn't it. This sort of thing had been happening before she'd wandered into the woods and found a forty-five-year-old plane wreck. She and her father had been at loggerheads for weeks over her inability to concentrate.

Maybe it was just spring fever, she decided.

Whatever it was, she was grounded and off to town with a Sinclair—and at the Sunrise Inn, no less. And it was *her* suggestion. Lord, what a day. But the only cure for it was tea and scones, despite the risk of running into Harriet, who'd wanted to meet a Sinclair her whole life. Considering her impulsiveness of late, Penelope supposed she should never mind Harriet and worry about herself instead. With that black Sinclair gaze probing her from across the table, she could blurt out everything. Clearly, he'd come to Cold Spring to find out if she was lying. If he concluded she was, he'd have the truth from her.

It was that quiet, natural arrogance, she thought. She could sense it, even as they roared down Main Street in her truck. He'd simply get her to tell the truth, and he knew he would.

The Sunrise Inn was tucked onto a point that jutted into the lake just off Main Street. Harriet and Penelope's mother had bought it twelve years ago and painstakingly turned the relatively simple Queen Anne into a charming, popular lakeside inn. It was painted deep brown and had a curving porch that overlooked the lake and a smaller screened porch that looked out on one of the inn's many stunning, award-winning gardens. Of course, at this time of year all the gardens were covered with mulch and melting snow, and the porch furniture was in storage.

"I'd appreciate it if you didn't mention you're a Sinclair," Penelope said as she lurched around a pothole. "It'll just complicate things—and for heaven's sake, don't mention that episode at the airport to my mother, if she's here. She hates planes. If I come home alive, that's all she needs to know. She's still having fits about having to call a search party on me this weekend."

He turned to her. "Do you like living life on the edge?"

"I don't *like* it. It just sometimes turns out that way."

She led him up a brick walk. Since the house faced the lake, the inn's main entrance was at the back, up a set of stone steps. A spring grapevine wreath graced the door, its pretty dried tea roses, larkspur and pepper berries a colorful contrast to the snow, mud and patches of sopping, grayish grass. Inside, stairs curved up to the right, and the wide entry opened into a sitting room with a fireplace and the front desk. Immediately to the left, off the entry, was an elegant parlor, almost completely Harriet's doing with its dark wood and damask fabrics. She'd added an 1893 rosewood upright piano, a dozen needle-point pillows, even an easel for drawing.

Penelope immediately felt the heat of the sitting room fire and smelled apples and cinnamon and something faintly tangy—oranges, perhaps. Harriet always liked to keep something fragrant simmering, and if there was snow on the ground, there was a fire in the fireplace. She was convinced her guests wanted fires.

In borderline temperatures like today's, that meant it got toasty fast. Penelope unzipped her flight suit about six inches. She'd worn a black T-shirt underneath, a mistake on a day filled with lies, reporters, a flying screwup and Wyatt Sinclair. She groaned. "It's hot in here. I can't believe Harriet has a fire going. It's almost fifty degrees outside."

Sinclair cut her a quick smile. "Downright balmy, isn't it?"

"Compared to the eighteen degrees it was two weeks ago, *yes*. I'm suffocating."

She grabbed what was left of her braid with both hands, let it drop and undid her zipper another inch.

Out of the corner of her eye, she noticed Wyatt twitching. With a white-hot jolt, she realized he wasn't her father or one of the guys from town. He was a *Sinclair*, and he would be attuned to everything physical in his surroundings. Including her. Especially her, because she was the reason he was here. He wanted to know about his uncle's plane.

That he was obviously aware of her meant nothing. She didn't have to be his type or even particularly attractive—she had only to be breathing for him to scope her out. It was simply the nature of the beast.

Scones, she reminded herself.

Fortunately, neither Harriet nor her mother—in fact, no one—was at the front desk. Penelope led Sinclair down a short hall to the left, past the wood-paneled bar and up another short hall to a cheerful octagonal room that served as the inn's dining room. It jutted from the main house, with views of both the gardens and the lake. With nothing in bloom, the tables and windowsills were decorated with pots of narcissus, paperwhites, daffodils and hyacinths. They were a cheerful touch that complemented the white linens and blue willow china.

Penelope greeted Terry, the manager of the Octagon Room and sole server of afternoon tea, and quietly asked, "Is Harriet or my mother around?"

"Harriet's upstairs, and I think Robby's at the sugar house."

Penelope couldn't hide her relief. She was pretty sure Sinclair noticed. He was in observational mode, keying in on every nuance. Best to remain on guard, no matter how good the scones, how tired she was after her long day.

"Do you want me to tell Harriet you're here?"

"No—that's okay. We're just having tea and scones."

"Of course. Any table's fine. We were crowded yesterday and this morning, but I think all the reporters have checked out by now."

Terry was clearly curious about the man at Penelope's side, but Penelope had no intention of introducing him. She wanted to convince Wyatt of her sincerity and honesty and hurry him back to New York. She chose a table in front of a window with the best view of the lake and a blue pottery dish brimming with daffodils.

"My mother does sugaring in the spring—the sap's running like crazy," she explained to Wyatt, just to say *something*. She wanted to distract him from coming to judgments she couldn't control, like the certainty that her turn-of-the-century dump was made-up. "She and Harriet use the syrup at the inn and sell the surplus to guests."

He settled into a chair opposite her. Even in black leather, he didn't look out of place. He had an obvious ability to make wherever he was his space. The New York financial district, the Tasmanian wilderness, a charming New England inn. "Is Harriet your cousin on your mother's side?" he asked.

Already they were on dangerous ground. Penelope shook her head. "No, Harriet and my father are first cousins. She's between my mother and me in age—they've just always gotten along." And that was all he needed to know about Harriet Chestnut.

"Are you related to everyone in town?"

"Not quite."

Terry brought two individual pots of tea, two small plates of warm currant scones and two little crockeries, one of soft butter, one of raspberry preserves. Penelope smiled and thanked her, then said to Wyatt, "After nearly dying today, I'm putting jam and butter on my scones."

"I didn't realize it was that close a call."

"It wasn't, but anything to justify butter and jam."
She split open a scone, spread a generous amount of
butter and checked her tea. "Another minute." She
settled in her chair, trying to ignore a flutter in the
pit of her stomach. Lying to the national media was
one thing, to a Sinclair another. "I'm sorry I got your
family all stirred up about your uncle's plane."

Wyatt broke off a piece of his scone, smeared on a
bit of butter. "I'd like to hear your story from start to
finish, if you don't mind."

"Not at all."

He smiled. "Is that the truth?"

She smiled back, her stomach twisting—damned
if she'd let him ruin her afternoon tea. "Okay, so it's
awkward and I'd rather not. But I'll oblige you.
How's that?"

"Better."

"Are you going to pick apart every sentence?"

He shrugged. "Only if I sense you're...
dissembling."

"Dissembling's just another word for lying. It's
that Dartmouth education showing, huh? Well,
sense away, Mr. Sinclair."

"Wyatt," he said smoothly.

She poured her tea, relieved her hand didn't
shake. "Wyatt Sinclair," she said. "The only son of
Brandon Sinclair, who was just eleven years old
when his older brother and Frannie Beaudine
slipped out during the reception honoring the donation of the Sinclair Collection to the Met." She
sipped her tea. "Rumor has it Colt stopped to say
goodbye to his little brother before heading to the reception."

"You've done your research."

She waved a hand. She wanted to establish a measure of control over their conversation but saw no need to get into what she knew about Frannie and Colt—and him. "That much everyone around here knows. It's printed on diner place mats. Frannie Beaudine's sort of a local heroine."

"And the people of Cold Spring blame Colt for sweeping her off her feet and to her doom?"

"Pretty much."

Wyatt poured his tea, adding a bit of lemon, no sugar or cream. "It's been forty-five years—"

"Around here, forty-five years is the blink of an eye. I mean, it's not like we're in England or Greece, but still. My father remembers both your uncle and Frannie—and your grandfather, too."

"He told me."

"He was fifteen when they disappeared. He helped search for their plane. It's not so long ago."

"I suppose." Sinclair leaned back, watching Penelope as she ate her scone, which was feathery light and just perfect, but she resisted the temptation to wolf it down. "So, tell me how you mistook a dump for plane wreckage."

She'd been explaining that point since morning. On her trip to Plattsburgh, New York, and back, she'd worked out the kinks in her story. "Well, I did and I didn't. I just *thought* it was plane wreckage—I realized I wouldn't know for sure until I went back. Because of the conditions, I only saw it from a distance. It was on a steep, icy, rocky hillside, and I didn't want to risk climbing over to get a closer look. It was late, and I was out in the woods alone."

The dark, almost black eyes settled on her. "And you were lost."

She gave him a self-deprecating smile. "I wasn't lost-lost. Lost-lost is when the search party has to find you. I made my way back while they were still arguing over who got to ride the snowmobiles."

The eyes didn't move from her. Wyatt Sinclair wasn't going to be easy to roll. He had more at stake. It was his uncle—his flesh and blood—in that plane. Feeling a twinge of guilt, Penelope poured her tea. "Anyway," she went on, welcoming the steam and the smoky smell of Earl Grey, "I said I thought I *might* have found Colt and Frannie's plane, and next thing it's all over the news that I *did* find it. So before things got too far out of hand, I slipped off on my own late yesterday to check out what I'd found for myself."

"What time did you leave?"

"I don't know, about four, four-thirty."

"And when did you get back?"

She slathered jam and butter onto another piece of scone. "What're you going to do, get out your compass and map and calculate my coordinates?"

His gaze darkened enough to remind her that she was dealing with a man who hadn't exactly driven six hours for tea and scones. "Maybe I'm just pinning you down."

He said *pinning* in such a way that her stomach rolled over and a prickly, all-over awareness settled in. "Pin away," she said lightly, making it a challenge. "I got home after dark. I didn't look at the clock."

His gaze remained steady, probing, all the more disconcerting because she had the distinct feeling he knew he'd gotten to her with that last remark. No doubt it had been deliberate. Part of his strategy.

Make the woman quiver with thoughts of your hard body and dark eyes and then pounce—prove her a bald-faced liar.

"You must have some idea," he said mildly.

She had no idea because she'd never made the trip. She'd tramped to the edge of her property, tossed snowballs against trees for a while and tramped back by a different route, careful not to let any enterprising reporter spot her. "I guess it must have been around seven. I took a shower, ate dinner, checked my e-mail and went to bed."

"All right. And you say what you found this time was a dump."

"What I found last time was a dump, too. I just didn't know it."

"Isn't it unusual to find a dump, even an old one, that far out in the woods?"

"Unusual but not impossible. Most of New Hampshire was denuded by logging and farming a hundred years ago. A lot of reforestation has occurred over the century. The woods—even the Sinclair woods—are crisscrossed with stone walls, old logging trails, cellar holes, wells. Dumps. We see trees and like to think we're stepping on virgin ground. But we're not." She sipped her tea, feeling calmer. "You went to school up here. You must know this stuff."

"I was more concerned with climbing mountains and surviving for another semester than with local yore." He settled back, his attention focused intently on her. He would want to be absolutely certain she was telling the truth before he left Cold Spring. If not, she had no idea what he'd do. "What made you think you'd found plane wreckage? Initially. Before you went back and learned otherwise. You're a pilot. Something must have made you think it was a plane, specifically a Piper Cub J-3."

So much for working out the kinks in her story. Being pelted with questions from a reporter was one thing—from Colt's only nephew quite another. But Penelope saw no point in backing down. Telling Wyatt about his uncle's plane would only bring on chaos. "It was a weird day. I don't know if there was anything specific or not. And what I thought I saw on Sunday is irrelevant—what I did see yesterday was an old dump."

"Which now you say you can't find again."

His tone wasn't neutral. If he'd meant it to be neutral, it would be neutral. But it wasn't. He didn't believe a word she'd said. And he meant her to know it. "Mr. Sinclair, I get the distinct impression you don't believe me."

He shrugged. "I didn't come here to put you on the defensive. I just want to know the truth. You tried to follow your footsteps to the site this morning but they'd been covered with snow?"

"That's right."

"Where's the snow now?"

"There was more in the higher elevations. Four inches in some spots. We hardly got any along the lake. Microclimates."

"There was enough snow to obliterate your tracks?"

"My tracks were hard enough to follow yesterday with all the melting and refreezing this time of year. And I wasn't really paying attention to landmarks. It was lousy light, and I was focused on my tracks. I suppose I *might* be able to find my way back, given enough time, but I don't see the point. It wasn't Frannie and Colt's plane I found, it was a dump."

The dark gaze stayed on her. "That's your story?"

Penelope popped the last of her scone into her mouth. "That's what happened."

"The press buying it?"

"Sure. They're not going to traipse through the wilds of New Hampshire in March and risk finding out I'm not lying after all. They'd look like idiots. Beside, they won't find it—it was a miracle I found it myself."

Wyatt said nothing.

"I'm sorry you wasted your trip north," Penelope said.

He leaned forward, gave a roguish wink that called up all her images of eighteenth and nineteenth-century Sinclairs—the adventurers, the privateers, the reckless men who'd lived hard and too often died young. "Your story's bullshit, Penelope. I doubt anyone believes it. I sure as hell don't."

In hindsight, she should have said she'd hallucinated the Piper Cub. She could have blamed stress, the trouble she was having concentrating in recent weeks, cabin fever, her general restlessness and malaise. Her father would have believed her. He'd have immediately grounded her, of course, but he'd ended up grounding her, anyway.

The dump story hadn't worked. Now it was too late. She had no rewind button, no chance to revise it and start over.

And damned if she'd give the skeptical man across the table from her the satisfaction of witnessing her admit her folly. If he was naturally arrogant, she was naturally defiant and stubborn—faults, at times, to be sure, but occasionally, too, virtues.

"Well," she said, "there's nothing I can do to make you believe me. That's your problem."

"At the moment, yes. In a day or two, if I've found anything that casts doubt on your story—then we'll have to have tea again." He grabbed the check. "Allow me."

Damned right she'd allow him. He'd ruined her tea, he could pay for it. He slid to his feet, calm, knowing just how much he'd rattled her. "This looks like a decent inn. I expect they're not booked solid this time of year."

"You're going to stay here? Why? There are hotels in Laconia—"

"I prefer to stay in Cold Spring."

Penelope nearly choked. Harriet, her mother and Wyatt Sinclair. *No...*

He paid Terry and walked to the front desk, leaving Penelope to sputter, recover her senses and follow. How could she explain her cousin to him? The dump in the woods was enough to swallow.

Harriet was at the front desk. Tall, plain, blue-eyed, sensitive Harriet. Penelope felt a rush of emotion. Although her cousin was fifteen years her senior, Penelope was the one who was protective, who did what she could to allow Harriet her illusions of gentility and refinement. When she was small, Harriet would read her L. M. Montgomery, Jane Austen and Louisa May Alcott, and she let Penelope thumb through her scrapbook of pretty houses and gardens she clipped from magazines. They'd had tea parties, trimming the crusts from their sandwiches, and they'd played dress-up with clothes from the church attic, Edwardian dresses, feathered hats, impossible shoes. With unwavering patience, Harriet had tried to teach Penelope crewel embroidery and needlepoint, but their lessons usually ended with blood all over everything. Penelope had found ways to prick her fingers—and often Harriet's—with even the bluntest of needles.

Sunrise Inn was perfect for Harriet. It took all her yearnings and all her skills and put them together in a profitable business. She had a suite of rooms on the third floor, as precious and perfect as she could ever want. If she longed for marriage and children, she never said. Certainly no one in Cold Spring expected her to take a husband—who would it be?

She wasn't naive, innocent or stupid. There was a core niceness to her that people tended to respect, and perhaps, as a result, she brought out the best in them. *That* was what Penelope found herself wanting to protect. Harriet wasn't cynical or bitter about anything, including the guests who stayed at her inn. She wouldn't become one of those businesspeople who griped about the tourists.

But the thing was, Harriet was also just a little odd.

"Penelope, I don't believe you. I just got off the phone with your father. He said he's grounded you. All I can say is it's about time. A wonder you haven't given that man a heart attack."

"Harriet, Pop's going to live to be a hundred. Look, I've got to run—"

But Harriet's brows drew together, and clear, blue eyes—easily her best feature—focused on the tall, dark man next to her cousin. She expected an introduction. Penelope *knew* she expected an introduction, and she silently cursed her father for not mentioning there was a Sinclair in town. It was the coward's way out. He knew damned well she'd find out.

Before Penelope could sort through this latest dilemma, Wyatt stepped forward, playing the gentleman. "You have a lovely inn, Miss Chestnut. I was wondering if you might have a room available for tonight. My name's Wyatt Sinclair. I drove up from New York this morning."

Penelope groaned inwardly.

Harriet gawked, turning pale. She fumbled around on her antique desk, trying to find something to do with her hands, her fingers finally closing on a pen. Penelope felt for her. This was the day Harriet had waited for her entire life, when she would stand face-to-face with a Sinclair. "Um—are you related to the Sinclairs—the Sinclairs who own the land up above the lake—Colt—"

"Brandon Sinclair is my father. Colt was my uncle. I never knew him. He disappeared before I was born."

"Oh." She breathed out, her lower lip trembling. "Oh, dear."

Wyatt glanced at Penelope, who was making a show of pretending she wasn't listening. Damn him for being so smooth. She snatched up a jar of maple syrup from a display of goods the inn had for sale and held it to the light. "Harriet, I wouldn't call this Grade A. I think it's Fancy."

Sinclair wasn't giving an inch. Instinctively suspicious, he was probably wondering why she didn't want him staying at the inn. "Do you have a room?" he asked Harriet gently.

She nodded, clutching her shirt. She favored cotton button-down shirts and skirts or jumpers, sensible shoes. She didn't dye her graying, mousy brown hair, just kept it parted in the middle and pulled back, occasionally pinned up. "Yes, yes, of course. I'll freshen it up myself. We've had reporters here the past two nights..." She took a breath, steadying herself. "But they've all left now that Penelope changed her story."

"Well," Wyatt said, "I won't be leaving for a while."

Penelope thumped down the jar. "What do you mean, a while? A while could be a week. There's no reason—"

"I came all this way, I might as well check out the land my family owns." He glanced at Penelope, his dark eyes unreadable, his mouth neutral, neither smiling nor unsmiling. She had no doubt—not one—that he knew he was getting under her skin. "I've never seen it."

She was beside herself. "It looks like all the other land around here. Steep hills. Trees. Rocks. Brooks. Stone walls."

"Turn-of-the-century dumps," he added without detectable sarcasm. Unmoved by her protest, he turned to Harriet. "I'd like to reserve a room for three nights, perhaps longer."

"As long as you wish, Mr. Sinclair. This is our slow time."

"I rode with your cousin from the airport. I'll check in after I've picked up my car."

"You can check in whenever you want."

He smiled, laying on the charm. "Thank you, Miss Chestnut."

"My pleasure. Penelope—"

"I'll talk to you later, Harriet. The scones were spectacular today, as usual."

Penelope had no intention of chitchatting with her cousin. Couldn't she *tell* she wanted Wyatt Sinclair out of town? Not Harriet. There was a simple reason she could deal with the public with such genuine good cheer—Harriet was oblivious to the undercurrents between people. She took them at face value, and that was that. Which was why she'd missed Penelope's frustration with Sinclair, the phoniness of his charm and how much he was enjoying thwarting her. If she was going to stick to her story, he could at least do something she didn't want him to do. Jerk her chain. Rattle her.

As if the black leather jacket and the strong, lean build weren't enough, Penelope thought grimly.

She started for the door, assuming Sinclair would follow. To her relief, he did. She glanced at Harriet. "Oh, and if Mother calls, I'd like to tell her myself I've been grounded, not that she won't have heard it from half the town by now."

"Your father already told her. She's staying out of it."

Just as Penelope had expected. If Robby Chestnut was anything, it was laissez faire when it came to her husband's relationship with their daughter, especially if flying was involved.

Penelope charged through the door and into the chilly, damp air. She never should have picked the Sunrise Inn, except that during the crisis, thinking about Harriet's scones had helped her stop berating herself for not properly preflighting her plane.

Her *father's* plane, she amended, suddenly feeling quite grouchy.

When she finally had Wyatt Sinclair in her truck, she gripped the wheel and took a deep breath. It had been one hell of a day. And it showed no signs of improving.

"What's the matter?" he asked mildly, knowing damned well he'd struck a nerve. "Is Harriet the crazy cousin who snuck out of the attic?"

"No, she's the crazy cousin we should *lock* in the attic." Penelope shook her head, debating how much she should tell Sinclair about her cousin before he spent the night under her roof. Tears rushed to her eyes. Damn. That was all she needed, to start crying. *Harriet, Harriet. What am I going to do with you?* She took one last look at the Sunrise Inn, shook her head and started the engine. "You knew I don't want you staying there."

"Why not?"

"Harriet's—she's—" This wasn't going to be easy. "You're the first Sinclair she's ever met."

"I'm the first Sinclair you've ever met. It hasn't seemed to affect you."

"You don't understand."

"Then explain."

She thrust her truck into gear and let out the clutch. "It's not my place, but if you're intent on sticking around town for a few days, you'll find out anyway. If no one else tells you, Harriet will herself." She exhaled slowly, refusing to imagine the results if that happened. Would Sinclair laugh hysterically? Threaten her? Call in the men in white jackets? "Look, she's a sweet soul."

"And?"

"Well, she thinks she's one of you."

Wyatt frowned. "You're right. I don't understand."

Penelope bit her lower lip. "Harriet is convinced she's Colt and Frannie's long-lost daughter."

FOUR

That was all Wyatt could get out of her. The plain, sweet-souled woman at the inn thought she was Colt and Frannie's daughter. It was a harmless fantasy, no one believed it, end of story. Just like the turn-of-the-century dump was the end of that story.

He was beginning to think Cold Spring was one weird little town.

He headed for his car. The temperature had dropped noticeably, the sun long gone. Penelope had driven him to the airport, given him a tight-lipped smile and charged off in her truck.

"Sinclair—wait a second."

It was Lyman Chestnut. He crossed the rutted lot at an unhurried pace, wiping his thick fingers with a black rag. Wyatt waited for him. His patience was at a low ebb. Tea, scones, lies—and those green eyes and flushed cheeks, sexy, challenging.

"Harriet called," Lyman said. "Says you're staying a night or two."

"I might."

"Penelope tell you her story?"

Wyatt noticed the careful wording. He nodded.

"She was in rough shape when she came out of the woods Sunday night. She was lost most of the afternoon. It was dark—we'd organized a search party and were just about to get started after her. She has a way of losing track of what she's doing and getting herself in trouble. She's been doing it since she was a little kid."

He wiped his fingers on the rag, pretending to concentrate on the task. Wyatt could see he was frustrated, preoccupied, awkward. Having the daughter he had would have its ups and downs. "Mr. Chestnut—"

"Lyman. I make my flying students call me Mr. Chestnut, but that's about it. Look, Penelope's been fantasizing about finding that plane since she could walk. Everyone around here has. I'm guessing once she realized she didn't find anything up in the woods after all, she just tried to figure out a way to save face. She hates to be wrong."

That Wyatt could believe. "What about this dump story?"

"There are plenty of old dumps around here."

He wouldn't counter his daughter, not to a Sinclair. Wyatt acknowledged his statement with a curt nod. "It's hard to believe she can't find her way back to whatever it is she found."

Lyman shrugged. "Maybe she's just embarrassed."

"Excuse me, but your daughter doesn't strike me as a woman who embarrasses easily."

"That's the God's truth." He almost managed a smile. "Here's the deal. I don't want any trouble. Penelope's a good kid. Her mind hasn't been on her work lately, but that's got nothing to do with you Sinclairs."

"What does it have to do with?"

Lyman inhaled, shaking his head. "Damned if I

know. Boredom, I think. She needs—well, hell, I'll
just get myself into trouble if I start talking about
what she needs. It's getting around town, you being
here. You know, I searched for your uncle's plane
myself. I walked up and down these hills for weeks,
never saw a thing, not one sign a plane had gone
down. We all did everything we could, but..." He
broke off, shook his head. "What's done is done."

Wyatt finished Lyman's thought for him. "But my
family wasn't satisfied. My grandfather didn't think
you'd done enough. The people of Cold Spring, I
mean, not you individually."

Lyman leveled his frank gaze on Wyatt and nodded. "I guess that's right. I heard he died—your
grandfather. He and my father used to go hunting
and fishing together. Well, I guess old Willard
thought of my father as a guide. But that's not how
my father saw it."

He stopped, looking faintly embarrassed, as if he
hadn't strung that many sentences together at one
time in years. Wyatt couldn't tell if this little visit
was a shot across the bow, a fishing expedition or
just a father not knowing what to do about a daughter he feared was in over her head.

"By the way," Lyman went on, "this Jack Dunning character's decided to park his plane here.
Mary's renting him a car." He paused, his gaze settling on Wyatt. "You'll go easy on my daughter?"

Wyatt grinned. "I left my thumbscrews in New
York."

He chose not to mention the crazy cousin who
thought she was a Sinclair or to stick around for
Jack's arrival. Instead he drove to town, hitting
every damned frost heave and pothole in the road,

mostly because he kept thinking about Penelope un-
zipping that flight suit in the heat of the Sunrise Inn.
He hadn't expected any attraction to her. But there it
was, impossible to ignore.

Harriet Chestnut, still flustered, put him in something called the Morning Glory Room. She gave him
his key—a real, old-fashioned key, not one of those
card things—and told him his room rate included a
continental breakfast. Nothing about her reminded
him of either Colt or Frannie. Coloring, build, features. It wasn't that it was impossible she was their
daughter, just not readily apparent. He thanked her
and headed upstairs.

Morning glories, indeed. They were on the wall-
paper, a needlepoint pillow and a print above his
four-poster bed. It was all tasteful, pretty, elegant,
just the sort of room a husband tolerated on a weekend getaway with his wife. A side window looked
out on snow-covered gardens, a front window on
the lake. In addition to the bed, there was a marble-
topped bureau, a writing desk and an antique wash-
stand that served as a night table. Wyatt figured
he'd gotten off easy, because he'd passed a rose
room on his way down the hall.

He dumped his bag on the floor and tried not to
think about what in hell he was doing, or why. He'd
never known his uncle. His father hadn't asked him
to come here. Now he'd rented a room at a charming
country inn for three nights.

But he knew he wasn't staying because of Colt or
Frannie—he was staying because of Penelope Chestnut. She intrigued him, and he had an odd, possibly
unreasonable sense that she was in trouble, perhaps
more than she knew. It was the sort of sixth sense

he'd come to rely on before his ignominious return to New York and a desk on Wall Street. He could be dead, flat wrong, just as he had been when he and Hal Strong had embarked upon their most exciting and ultimately final adventure, no sixth sense telling him they never should have left Melbourne, that danger and death awaited them in the mountains of southwestern Tasmania.

"So, you could be full of shit," he said aloud, breaking the spell.

He could. Penelope Chestnut's only trouble might be him.

The energy required to weave her tale about the turn-of-the-century dump and the snow obliterating her tracks had probably led her to miss her fuel check in her preflight. She was distracted. The truth was seldom simple but at least it was easier to remember.

He wandered into the bathroom, where the morning glory theme continued. Thick, soft white towels and a big, gleaming tub beckoned. He settled for splashing cold water on his face. He noticed little blue soaps and bottles of locally made lotions. When he traveled, he was used to pitching a tent.

The phone rang. Grateful for the distraction, he returned to the bedroom and picked up.

"You're in Cold Spring," his father said. "Why?"

The abrupt tone didn't offend Wyatt. His father prided himself on his self-control and would bury any strong negative emotion under an abrupt, even cold manner. "Jack must have arrived. Obviously he's reported back to you."

"I like to know where my son is."

"Well, you've found me."

His father inhaled sharply. He wouldn't yell at his son the way Lyman Chestnut had at his daughter. Open confrontation wasn't the Sinclair way. "How long are you staying?"

"I don't know." He decided, at that moment, not to tell his father about his dealings with Penelope Chestnut and his sense she was in over her head. "Father, Colt was your brother—"

"Yes, he was. I knew him, Wyatt. He was a person to me, not an adventure. This woman has withdrawn her story. Let Jack figure out why. He'll tie up loose ends and make sure her story checks. That's his job." *Not yours*, was the unspoken rest of the sentence.

No more details were forthcoming for the meddling son. Wyatt said hello to his stepmother, and to Ellen and Beatrix, who begged him to fly down for the weekend and take them snorkeling. They were on school holiday, and he promised to see them when they got back to New York—he'd do whatever they wanted. The rascals were his soft spot, and they knew it.

When he hung up, he stood in front of the window and looked across the lake toward the mountains. It was dusk, quiet, still. His father and uncle had roamed this area as boys with their father, the imposing, exacting Willard Sinclair, who'd died when Wyatt was fourteen. They'd gone swimming, fishing, mountain climbing, camping. He knew from his father that, despite their age difference, the brothers had been close, relishing their time together.

After Colt ran off with Frannie Beaudine, Willard Sinclair refused to let his younger son return to the

New Hampshire lakes region. Willard became increasingly difficult in his grief, his surviving son never able to make up for the loss of his firstborn, never able to be the bright spark in his father's life that Colt had been.

Wyatt had sensed all this, pieced it together over the years through observation, overheard fights between his father and one wife or another, his own conversations with his dying grandfather. Always, always he came away with the unshakable conviction that his father and perhaps his grandfather were holding back on him—not just feelings, not just their private grief, but information, possibly even vital information.

As Penelope had said, forty-five years meant nothing. Colt was still real to his younger brother. The loss, the questions, the scandal still resonated in Brandon Sinclair's life and the lives of his family. This wasn't some damned lark. This was *real*.

She had to understand the consequences of her lie. If she'd found Colt and Frannie's Piper Cub in the woods on Sunday, she had to admit it and take Wyatt there.

No, he thought. Penelope Chestnut's pretty eyes and whatever trouble she might be in weren't what he was doing in New Hampshire, weren't why he was staying. A missing brother, a lost son, an uncle never known—that was what he was doing here, why he was staying. He couldn't let himself be distracted from what was a clear, uncomplicated mission.

But while he unpacked his bag, Wyatt wondered where Cold Spring's green-eyed, hot-headed pilot lived, and when he finished, he headed downstairs to see if he could get directions out of her cousin.

Penelope was relieved to be home, a fire crackling in her wood stove, a robin investigating her deck. She'd changed into a soft fleece shirt and drawstring pants and sat at her kitchen table, watching the robin through her sliding-glass doors. The snow had melted off her deck, another sign spring was on its way.

She'd inherited her grandfather's winterized, lakeside cabin when he'd died three years ago. It was on a narrow dirt road well-removed from the village, and her lake frontage was the bare minimum. The cabin sat atop a steep bank with stairs down to the water, a dock and the little shed where she kept her canoe and kayak. But she also inherited ten acres on the other side of the road. Her woods eventually bled into Sinclair woods, which was how she came to be hunting maples suitable for tapping there in the first place.

The cabin still had a seasonal feel to it. It consisted of a living room and kitchen across the front, overlooking the lake, and two small rooms and a bath across the back. She'd kept her grandfather's mismatched dishes, his red-and-white checked vinyl tablecloth, his moose head on the wall above the fireplace. His ugly lamps and the vinyl recliner had had to go.

No one had expected her to move here. She'd had a nice apartment in town where she could walk to the Sunrise Inn and have tea and scones with her mother and cousin every afternoon. The idea, of course, was for her to get married before she moved into a real place of her own—at least, that was the idea of most of the women she knew. The men didn't seem surprised at all by her choice of a home. They showed up to use her dock, invited her hunting and fishing, tossed trout on her grill, shared their six-packs with her on her deck. One of the guys. It wasn't that she *looked* like a guy. She wore dresses and makeup and did her hair. She polished her nails.

"They don't think of you as one of the guys," Harriet had told her. "They think of you more as a surrogate sister."

And you didn't date your sister.

Not that Penelope wanted to date any of *them*. She shuddered. They were her friends. She couldn't envision sleeping with them any more than they could her.

Her social life had taken a sharp downward turn in recent months. For a while there'd been a man in Bangor she'd see whenever she flew in that direction. Another pilot. Then she realized he never made the effort to get to New Hampshire to see *her*, and if she knew anything about herself it was that she didn't want a one-way relationship. So, exit the pilot. Enter no one to replace him.

Well, she wasn't pitiful. She had her place on the lake, her flying, her friends, her family. If this was it, this was it. She liked to fantasize about tearing down her grandfather's cabin and building her own place, with lots of wood and glass. She'd hire an architect to design a house especially for this piece of land.

But that all seemed a long way off. Right now, she was grounded, and she had a Sinclair out to prove she'd lied about Colt and Frannie's plane.

Which, of course, she had.

She shrugged off a sudden wave of uneasiness. She could almost feel the smooth leather of Wyatt Sinclair's jacket as he'd sat next to her in her truck. She'd never touched him, but she might as well have.

This was just the sort of effect Colt must have had on Frannie Beaudine. And look where that weakness had lead *her*. Right into the side of a hill.

At least Wyatt wouldn't be on the loose in Cold Spring, not if he was staying at the Sunrise Inn. Her cousin had been madly curious about Sinclairs for as long as Penelope could remember. The two of them had even wandered through the Sinclair Collection at the Metropolitan Museum of Art on a trip to New York. Harriet would keep a close eye on the first Sinclair to step foot in Cold Spring in her lifetime.

Penelope went into the second bedroom, which she'd converted to a study, and turned on her computer. While it booted up, she stared at the framed front page of the *Cold Spring Reporter* from the first day of the search for Colt Sinclair and Frannie Beaudine. On her bookcase, she had scrapbooks of articles and cassettes of recordings she'd done of interviews with locals who remembered the crash and the ensuing search. She hadn't developed such a hobby just because Colt and Frannie were pilots, because they'd disappeared in one of her favorite planes or because her father and grandfather and Aunt Mary had participated in the search. She'd come to it because of Harriet, because of the years she'd listened to her cousin fantasize—at first tentatively, then with more certainty—about being the daughter of the handsome, adventurous couple.

Wasn't her cousin entitled to her fantasy? It was harmless enough. But Penelope pushed such thoughts aside and got on the Internet, going straight to one of the sites devoted to the missing Piper Cub. There was an amazing amount of information, gossip, speculation and junk about Frannie and Colt on the Internet, most of which was useless. Theories about their disappearance ranged from elopement to kidnapping by aliens with a thousand scenarios in between. They were alive and living in Canada, they were Communist spies, they were thieves, it was a suicide pact, it was murder-suicide. Colt was the foppish un-Sinclair, the impressionable college grad, the innocent. Then he was the quintessential Sinclair, the rake, the daredevil, the instigator. Frannie was the beautiful innocent, the bookish refugee from the wilds of New Hampshire, the vixen, the gold digger. Every possible theory from the nutty to the sublime was there.

News of Penelope's false alarm had reached the enthusiasts. Debate was raging about why she'd changed her story. Had she been forced? Had she found something in the wreckage she wanted for herself? There were, of course, conspiracy theorists. But most believed she'd simply made a mistake, even if her turn-of-the-century dump was an awkward cover for that mistake. They didn't want to give up their Frannie-Colt fantasies any more than Harriet would want to give up hers. Not every mystery begged for unraveling.

How had she ever thought finding their plane would help her cousin? Seeing her flush and stutter over Wyatt Sinclair this afternoon was unsettling, and now Penelope wished she'd never started down this path. She should have kept her big mouth shut about what she'd found in the woods.

But, as her grandfather would remind her, there was no point crying over spilled milk.

She decided she'd have supper by the fire and read until she fell asleep. The aftereffects of her mishap in the sky and tea with Wyatt Sinclair were taking their toll. She couldn't think straight.

An instant message flashed on her screen. She jumped, startled, then was pleased for the diversion. She had plenty of friends in faraway places.

Frannie Beaudine was a sweet young thing not unlike you. Yet her bones lie bleached by the elements, her flesh no more, her body and spirit dead and gone. Do you want to share her fate? Behave yourself, Penelope. You know what you've done wrong.

She stared at the screen, paralyzed. She didn't breathe. She didn't blink. The words blurred, and her eyes stung until tears formed. Finally she hit the key to reply. But the person on the other end was no longer available. She jotted down the user ID. It would be useless, she knew—who would send such a message if it could be easily traced?

She typed a reply, deleted it. Maybe she should pretend she hadn't received the message, hadn't read it. Just ignore the thing. Don't do anything to stir the pot.

Her hands shook, and suddenly her whole body was shaking. She gulped for air, felt the bile stinging her throat.

"Well, Aunt Mary," she said, "you should have your front row seat." Because she was scared. There was no other word for it.

She returned to the great room, where the warm

fire of the wood stove helped to calm her. She could call the police. Andy McNally would roar out here. But what could he do?

It was a kook, she told herself. The Internet was full of kooks. No one took instant messages seriously. She'd once had one asking her if she liked to skinny-dip in Lake Winnipesaukee. The whole *world* knew she'd claimed she'd found Colt and Frannie's plane. She should have anticipated such harassment. Andy McNally would tell her as much.

Her stomach ached, and she had to fight dizziness, a pulsing pain behind her eyes. She was Penelope the Fearless, the woman who could live on the lake in her grandfather's cabin, who loved adventures and thrills and action and scoffed at things that went bump in the night.

Yet as the sky slowly went black and the fire crackled in the stove and she couldn't even hear the caw of a crow, she couldn't shake her fear. The reporters, Wyatt Sinclair, a Sinclair investigator, her mishap in the air, her own lie—and now a creepy message on the Internet. It was all too much.

She made herself go out to her woodpile and bring in wood, five trips, five full armloads, until her wood box was overflowing, because she had no intention of letting the fear get to her. She hadn't this afternoon when she'd realized she was low on fuel. She wouldn't now.

She dumped the last load into the box. A log rolled off and narrowly missed her toe. She jumped back, out of breath from exertion and too much adrenaline pumping through her system. There were more logs on the floor—five at least. She'd tossed in one load after another, not concerned about neatness, only about the need to force herself to keep moving.

Hearing a car negotiating the pits and ruts of her spring-ravaged dirt road, she prayed it would continue past her cabin.

It didn't.

She groaned. "Now what?"

Picking sawdust off her fleece shirt, Penelope went to the side door off the kitchen. Maybe it would be her father, telling her he'd changed his mind and she wasn't grounded, after all.

But there on her doorstep, as if he'd *known* his timing couldn't be any worse, was Wyatt Sinclair.

FIVE

He wasn't wearing his leather jacket, as if he expected to go straight from warm car to warm house. Penelope could feel him taking in the bits of sawdust and wood on her shirt, her difficulty in getting a decent breath. "Your road's nothing but mud," he said. "I sank up to my hubcaps."

"It'll freeze overnight. Of course, it'll be all mud again by noon."

"What happens if you have to get out of here in a hurry?"

"I use my four-wheel drive."

Wyatt paused, studying her. She wondered if she was pale, if she had a wild look in her eyes. He said, "May I come in?"

Just what she needed. "Sure. I'm a little out of breath from filling my wood box."

He glanced past her into her front room. "Looks as if it's plenty full."

She raked a hand through her hair, ignoring the snarls, the bark chips. "I kind of just dropped the last two loads. I'm more tired than I thought." Changing the subject was her only hope. "Have you eaten yet? I was just about to heat up some chili."

Wyatt didn't move. "Penelope, are you all right?"

"Yes, of course. Why wouldn't I be? Here, come inside before we let the cold air in."

He came in without comment, and she shut the door behind him. The quiet thud made her heart skip. What if he'd sent her that instant message and now he'd come to see the results of his handiwork? Except he seemed more direct, more the type to tell her straight to her face that she'd lied.

You know what you've done wrong.

She didn't know! Was it telling about the plane in the first place? Or changing her story? What was so wrong about trying to keep the spotlight off an old hermit and her crazy cousin. They were alive. Colt and Frannie weren't.

But Colt's family was, she reminded herself. She shook off the thought. The message was from a nut, someone intent on upsetting her after she'd dashed expectations of ending the mystery of what happened to Colt Sinclair and Frannie Beaudine. Well, mission accomplished. She was upset.

"I'll fix your wood box," Wyatt said, his gaze on her, narrowed, wary. "You can heat the chili."

"Don't feel obligated to stay."

He smiled. "Already regretting your invitation?"

She didn't know if his steadiness was a tactic to throw her off guard or if he was simply trying to be nice. Either way, she found his presence reassuring. Suddenly she could feel the warmth of the fire, and her breathing was less shallow. Wyatt got to work arranging the overflow logs still in the wood box. Penelope caught herself watching him, then quickly pulled open the refrigerator for the quart of chili her mother had given her yesterday. She scooped it into a bowl and heated it in the microwave while Wyatt continued his work.

"Did Harriet give you directions?" Penelope asked.

"Don't skewer her, but, yes, she did."

Her cousin would never give such directions to a guest she didn't know, but if most people in Cold Spring demonized the Sinclairs, Harriet romanticized them. Penelope couldn't blame her for telling Wyatt where she lived. She chopped onion and grated cheese, got out bowls and spoons, and when the microwave dinged, she put everything out on the table.

Wyatt had the wood box straightened, the extra logs neatly stacked in front of it. He joined her at the table. The hissing and crackling of the fire, the sudden darkness outside, the scratch of her chair on the floor all made her aware of how isolated she was, how far from any help if Wyatt Sinclair was a nastier son of a bitch than she thought he was. She was on her own with him.

"Was there something I could do for you?" she asked, keeping her tone formal and distant.

A darkness came into his eyes that hadn't been there before, and she took a quick breath, realizing the multiple ways he could interpret her question. But he, too, maintained an outward level of formality. "I'd like you to tell me about your cousin and why she thinks she's Colt and Frannie's daughter. It's not something she made up out of thin air, is it?"

Penelope shook her head. She sprinkled cheese on her steaming chili. She would have to tell him something. If she didn't, he'd find another source, perhaps not one as devoted to Harriet as she was. "Not out of thin air. Out of a coincidence."

"Tell me," he said softly, not making it an order.

"My great-uncle and great-aunt adopted Harriet around the time Colt and Frannie disappeared. Uncle George was a minister here in town forever. He's my grandfather's younger brother—he's almost eighty now. He and Aunt Rachel have retired to Florida."

"Aren't there adoption records, some way to disabuse your cousin of this notion?"

"It's not that simple." She tried the chili, which was spicy and packed with vegetables. Her mother did like her hot peppers. "Look, this is none of my business or yours. Harriet didn't ask for any trouble."

"I'll be discreet."

A Sinclair discreet. Penelope almost smiled. "What about your father's investigator? Are you going to tell him?"

"Jack doesn't report to me, I don't report to him."

"I suppose you'll find out anyway. Everyone in town knows the story." She paused, added chopped onion to her chili, saw that none of what she'd said so far had affected Wyatt's appetite. She forced herself to think, examine her options. They weren't good. "Okay. Uncle George found Harriet on the church doorstep about forty-eight hours into the search for Colt and Frannie's plane. The doctors figure she was between six and eight weeks old. She was wearing a diaper and a sleeper, and she was wrapped in a blanket. She'd been placed in an apple basket."

Wyatt straightened. "Good Lord."

"I know. It's right out of a Dickens novel."

"There must have been an investigation—"

"A thorough one. The authorities didn't find a thing, not a single clue as to who her biological parents were, who'd left her there. My aunt and uncle stepped in and adopted her. They were thrilled—they have an older son, but Aunt Rachel couldn't have any more children after him."

"They treated Harriet well?"

"They're a wonderful family. They love her, and she loves them. That didn't stop her, though, from creating this kooky fantasy."

"I don't know," Wyatt said, "maybe it's not so kooky."

"It's much more likely someone took advantage of the hoopla over the missing plane. Chances are she's the result of some incestuous or otherwise illicit relationship. But it's a lot more fun to be Colt Sinclair and Frannie Beaudine's long-lost daughter."

"The timing—"

"There's a narrow window of opportunity. Say Harriet was six weeks old. The Piper Cub disappeared in mid-April. That would mean Frannie would have given birth around the first of March. Right?"

Wyatt nodded, motioning for her to continue. She had his complete attention, every fiber of him focused on her and what she had to say. She felt energized, the fear and creeping exhaustion of an hour ago gone. Yet at the same time, she was keenly aware she was walking out on thinner and thinner ice. Telling this man *anything*, even something he could find out on his own in two minutes on the streets of Cold Spring, could be a mistake. She couldn't assume she was in control. He had climbed dangerous, difficult mountains. He was used to capitalizing on whatever foothold opportunity offered him.

Penelope took a breath and continued. "The most visible part of her pregnancy would have been during the winter months, when she worked on the Sinclair Collection."

"From what I understand, she worked night and day."

"That's what I've heard, too. I suppose it's possible she could have been concealing a pregnancy."

"Or she was just obsessive about her work. It was an enormous opportunity for her."

"There are a thousand reasons this scenario doesn't work. That's just one of them. Frannie and Colt didn't officially start seeing each other until a month or so before they disappeared. For her to turn up pregnant, they'd have had to have some sort of relationship the previous summer."

Penelope paused for more chili. Discussing a sexual relationship with Wyatt under the best of circumstances would be awkward, but alone in her cabin, at night, with him already convinced she was a liar, with him so focused on her every word—it was impossible.

He finished his chili and waited for her to continue.

"I hope you don't think you're prying this information out of me by being so patient."

He stared at her, then smiled suddenly, devastatingly. "Penelope, I doubt anyone could pry anything out of you that you hadn't already decided to give freely, if grudgingly. As far as my patience—what gave you the idea I'm being patient?"

Her mouth snapped shut, and instantly she knew there was no good way to answer that question. She went on quickly. "Frannie and Colt were both in Cold Spring that previous summer."

"Simultaneously?"

Penelope nodded.

"You seem to know a number of details," he said.

"Only because of Harriet." She didn't want him thinking she'd been eaten up with curiosity about his family. "We've always been close. She used to baby-sit me, and she'd tell me all kinds of stories. They were fascinating to a little kid. I ended up doing some investigating on my own." She'd done a lot of investigating, but somehow she thought that would only add to Wyatt's suspicions. "It's farfetched, but technically it's possible that Frannie came back to Cold Spring, had a baby, and returned to New York—"

"With or without the baby? Was Harriet in the plane that night? If not, where was she? Who put her on the church doorstep? Did Frannie have help here in town? In New York? Did Colt know about the baby?" Wyatt shot out the questions rapid-fire, then exploded to his feet. "It's damned far-fetched."

Penelope nodded. "I know. We've all indulged Harriet. Please don't embarrass her. She's a lovely person, and she's never hurt a soul—she never would."

He grabbed up his chili bowl and set it in the sink, his movements abrupt, his frustration palpable. Penelope could feel her mouth going dry as she watched him pace her small house. Without his leather coat, she could see his slim waist, his flat stomach, and she tried not to think about all the things she knew about him—the triumphs, the tragedies, the rebellions—lest he read her mind and decide he was entitled to the mental files she had on him, too.

"It's not as if Harriet plans to come after your family's money or anything," she said calmly. "She's no threat to you."

He stopped. He turned to her, his black gaze narrowed, suspicious, probing. Her stomach burned. She wished she'd heard him in her driveway in time to lock her doors, turn out her lights and hide under her bed.

Finally, he said, "Is your cousin why you changed your story about finding the plane?"

Back to the plane. Of course. Wyatt Sinclair would have a one-track mind. He was driven, relentless. Penelope got quietly to her feet and cleared her dishes, then flipped on the water in the sink. No dishwasher. Her grandfather didn't believe in them.

Finally she turned to him. "You know, it's wrong to accuse a woman of lying in her own home."

His grin was so sudden, so unexpected, so *sexy* she could have melted onto the floor. He stood close to her, invading her space. "You're right. I'll wait until we're on neutral ground."

"There is no neutral ground, not around here. You Sinclairs might own the biggest tract of land in Cold Spring, but damned if—"

He touched one finger to her lips, silencing her mid-sentence. "I'm not 'you Sinclairs.'" She could hardly breathe. The dark eyes, the half smile, the strong line of jaw, neck and shoulder fired her mind and senses with a kaleidoscope of images and possibilities. It was like getting sucked into some dangerous imaginary world. She jerked back and turned off the water, breaking the spell.

If Wyatt was aware of the effect he was having on her, he gave no indication. "I'm not my grandfather. I'm not my father. I came here for my own reasons. I want to know why you're lying, but not at any price." He paused, and when she said nothing, he added, "And I want to know why you're afraid."

She spun around. "I'm not afraid."

He smiled, not pleasantly. "You lie persistently if not terribly well, Miss Chestnut."

"Oh. So you've been in town an afternoon and already you can tell when I'm lying."

"Some things are obvious." He started for the door, a breeze gusting outside. He glanced back at her. "If you're afraid of me—"

"I'm not."

"I didn't think so. You'll be all right here alone?"

She nodded.

"Good night, then. Thanks for the chili."

After he left, she stood at the sink, up to her wrists in hot, soapy water, and didn't move until she heard his car out on her dirt road. Then the tears came, and she did the dishes and cried until she'd just had it with herself and Sinclairs and the whole damned mess. It wasn't just Harriet, it wasn't just Bubba Johns—she didn't know what all it was, but she'd *had* to change her story.

"Damn it, Sinclair, I had to lie."

But Colt Sinclair had been Wyatt's uncle, his father's only brother, and she had the power to put to rest the mystery of his death.

Yet deep down, on a level beyond reason and calculation, she knew the Piper Cub J-3 in the woods was meant to be where it was. Its discovery would only bring heartache and pain to those who, unlike Colt and Frannie, weren't past suffering. It was an understanding she wished she'd come to sooner, before she'd blabbed to the world. But she hadn't, and now she had Wyatt Sinclair to deal with.

Harriet settled onto a stool at the bar and sipped a glass of house Chardonnay, as she did at the end of each day. Robby, Penelope's mother, had chosen the inn's wine list. Harriet couldn't wait to see her in the morning. They would make apricot scones in the inn's tidy, warm kitchen, and they'd laugh and work and talk. Harriet would tell Robby everything. Robby was a good listener, and she never judged. She would caution and worry—she had her opinions—but she wasn't one to pass judgment. That was what Penelope didn't understand about her mother, which was a problem for another day. Harriet had enough on her mind.

Wyatt Sinclair was everything she had imagined a Sinclair would be. Tall, dark, good-looking in an unpretty sort of way. She smiled, *knowing* they were related. The Chestnuts were her family, but the Sinclairs—they were different. They were blood.

Absurdly, she'd found herself wanting to touch him when he'd come down to ask directions to Penelope's house. It was as if touching him would make the connection between them more real. A Sinclair here in Cold Spring, in her house.

Then there was Jack Dunning, Brandon Sinclair's private investigator.

"Lord," Harriet breathed, feeling like a faint-hearted heroine of Victorian stereotype instead of the capable, independent businesswoman she was. But what fun to have two such men under her roof. Jack Dunning wasn't at all handsome, but he radiated strength and sexuality and a raw intelligence one would be loath to underestimate.

And the black cowboy boots, the cowboy hat, the put-on Texas accent. In New Hampshire in the dead of March. Harriet suppressed a giggle. She hadn't expected *that.*

Andy McNally eased behind the oak bar and helped himself to a bottle of Long Trail beer, his nightly custom. He smiled at her. "Evening, Harriet. You're looking like you swallowed the canary."

She waved a hand. "Oh, it's nothing. How are you this evening?"

"Not too bad." He opened the bottle and poured the beer into a tall glass, letting it foam to a perfect head. "We pulled in extra speeding tickets thanks to your cousin."

"She didn't speed—"

"No, she wasn't *caught* speeding." Andy didn't have much use for Penelope, which she and Harriet and everyone else in Cold Spring knew. "It was all those reporters she lured into town with that cockamamie story of hers."

"It was an honest mistake, Andy."

He frowned, and she could see the fatigue in his light-colored eyes, the strain of a long day. He was a big, burly, gray-haired man, born and raised in Cold Spring. He had lost his wife in a car accident five years ago. He'd almost died himself. A jagged, fearsome scar ran along his hairline from the top of his head to his neck. Now he was raising two teenage daughters on his own and seeing to a small town as its police chief. He liked the image of Cold Spring as a quiet, safe lakeside village.

He drank some of his beer, sighing into the glass. "Penelope makes too many honest mistakes, Harriet. One day they're going to catch up with her. I don't care how optimistic and brazen she is."

He wasn't the only one in town who shared that opinion. But Harriet didn't want to let go of her bubbly mood. "You're tired. Drink your beer and relax."

He narrowed his eyes. "You're not going to tell me why you're about ready to chortle?"

She could feel her cheeks warming. For once, she wasn't turning red simply from embarrassment or standing over a hot stove. But she said coyly, "It's been an interesting day, that's why."

"You've been making money off those reporters." Andy came around with his beer and sat on the stool next to her, as he did most nights. He would walk from his house in the village, taking a half hour from his roles as chief of police and widower father of two. "Nothing you like better than a positive cash flow, except you won't admit it. You sit there pretending to be the lady of the manor when you've got that calculator mind of yours working up figures."

"You think you know me so well."

"Nah, Harriet." He grinned at her, looking less tired. "I don't know you at all."

"Oh, Andy."

He swallowed more beer, his steady presence helping to calm her happy jitteriness and anchor her in reality. "That nut cousin of yours has asked Rebecca and Jane to help with her sap collecting to-morrow after school. I hope things have settled down enough. I don't want them involved in this plane wreck business."

Harriet smiled reassuringly. "Penelope corrected her mistake as soon as she could. You can trust her with your daughters, Andy. You know that."

"Lyman grounded her today. You heard?"

"Of course."

"It's long overdue, if you ask me. The thought of that woman in the skies above this town scares me to death."

"Andy, she's a fine pilot. You think of her as the twelve-year-old you pulled out of the lake."

He grunted, a gruff man who was all bluster. "It's not something I'll ever forget. Ungrateful little snot. She was a skinny hothead, kept yelling and kicking because she could have rescued herself. She was half a second from freezing to death, her skin was blue, her teeth were chattering, but it didn't affect that mouth of hers."

Harriet smiled. "I remember. That's what kept her alive, you know. That sheer willpower of hers."

"It's also what got her into trouble in the first place. She acts, then thinks." He sighed heavily, fin-ished his beer. "You know, I was just a kid myself when that plane went down. I helped my father comb the woods for it. I wanted to be a hero. We looked everywhere. The Sinclair family wouldn't rest until we'd covered every square inch of those hills. If Colt's Piper Cub was up there, we'd have found it."

"Maybe not," Harriet said. "If it was tucked on a hillside amidst rocks—"

"That's another thing." He leveled his cop's gaze on her. "Who'd put a dump on a steep, rocky hillside? Doesn't make sense."

Harriet felt her heartbeat flutter. "Andy..."

"If she's lying, I don't want to know about it. Honest to God, Harriet. My opinion, Penelope didn't find anything in the woods on Sunday. She just can't admit she was seeing things entirely." He eased off the stool. He looked tired again, as if the pressures of life were too much for him. Then a spark came into his eyes, a touch of the wry humor Harriet had seen in him for as long as she could remember. "Did I hear a Sinclair was in town?"

She giggled into her wineglass. She couldn't help herself. Andy McNally knew about her fantasy. Everyone in Cold Spring did. Most didn't believe it, of course. That was to be expected. It didn't matter to her—it was her fantasy, her life. Her parents had never discouraged her from finding a way to make sense of being left on a church doorstep on a chilly April night. "Yes," she said primly. "Brandon Sinclair's son, Wyatt, came up from New York today."

"He talk to Penelope? Think he believed her?"

"I didn't ask."

"Ask," Andy said. "Last thing I need is a Sinclair stirring up trouble in town. Bad enough we've got Penelope. Look, Harriet—" He took a breath and shook his head. "Never mind."

She smiled. "It's okay, Andy. I won't make a fool of myself. I promise."

"It's not that," he said, awkward.

But it was, and they both knew it. He asked her to put his beer on his tab, as he did every night, and she told him to tell Rebecca and Jane hello, as she did every night. When he left, she poured herself another glass of chardonnay—an indulgence—and sat in the empty bar, sipping her wine and imagining.

SIX

Penelope was up, dressed and ready to go by seven o'clock. At 7:05 it hit her that she had nowhere to go. Her father had called last night and told her not to show up at the airport for a few days. "Take a break. Get used to terra firma. Then you can reacquaint yourself with washing planes and sweeping out hangars."

She turned on the "Today" show, turned it off again. She still had plenty of wood after last night's panic. She built a nice fire in her potbellied stove and listened to it crackle for a few minutes before she was climbing the walls again.

What was she going to do for three weeks?

She didn't want to get on her computer. Maybe the weirdo would be there again. She'd reassured herself overnight that her nasty message was a simple prank from some nutcase. She would dismiss it. She needn't mention it to anyone.

She walked onto her deck. It was cold this morning, maybe not even twenty degrees. Twenty-degree nights and forty-degree days were perfect for sap. It'd be running by midday. At least she had Rebecca and Jane McNally coming over this afternoon to help her boil sap.

What to do until then?

This part of the lake was still, silent, motionless beneath the layers of snow and ice, which glistened in the bright sunlight. Here, there were no fishing shanties and few other year-round houses. She breathed in the cold air, imagining summer, boats humming on the water, kayakers and canoeists paddling along the shoreline, neighbors opening their camps for the season.

She envisioned herself in her kayak on the cool, clear water, staring straight down to the sandy, rocky bottom. There was plenty to do in the lakes region during the summer. Even in the dead of winter, she could ski and snowshoe. Now her options were more limited. Maybe she could talk her father into postponing her grounding until warmer weather.

"Fat chance," she muttered and went inside.

She checked the weather channel. Yes, it would get into the forties this afternoon. Satisfied, she flicked off the television.

It was seven-forty.

She contemplated her options. Spring clean her house. She glanced at the simple furnishings, peered into the kitchen, her bedroom, her study. Well, yes, she could spring clean, but it wasn't a spring kind of day, not with the thermometer stuck at nineteen Fahrenheit. And who could spring clean with a fire in the wood stove?

She could drive into town and offer to help Harriet and her mother at the inn. There was always something to do. They'd put her straight to work. She could clean, paint, water plants, help in the kitchen.

She could spy on Wyatt Sinclair.

That settled her down. She flopped onto her

couch and pictured his black eyes and skeptical frown, the shape of his chest and shoulders under that black leather jacket. He must have chosen the black shirt and jacket deliberately, to square it in the minds of the people of Cold Spring that, indeed, he was a Sinclair. Possibly he'd done it to square it in her mind in particular.

Spying on him didn't seem like a bad idea.

"Good God, you'd better do something before you get yourself into real trouble."

She popped off the couch, energized. Ten minutes later she had her hair up in sticks her mother had given her and was crossing the frozen ruts in the dirt road to check her sap buckets. The air was bright and cold under a cloudless blue sky.

Huge, old maples lined the road, looking picturesque and majestic with their galvanized buckets hanging from their taps. Farther into the woods, she used plastic milk jugs, cheap, efficient, not as high a capacity as the buckets but quite workable. She was meticulous about not drilling too many taps—the trees could easily replace the small amount of sap she took. Gravity tubing would be more efficient, but she wasn't making syrup commercially, just for the fun of doing it.

She checked a few buckets, the void of the next three weeks yawning before her. She *needed* to fly. Didn't her father understand? She loved Cold Spring, but it couldn't contain her.

But she'd run out of gas. "I'd have grounded you, too."

She climbed over the stone wall that ran alongside the road and checked a few more taps, noticing footprints and trampled brush. Possibly Bubba, more

likely reporters. They'd wanted footage of the landscape for their reports. They didn't need to go onto
Sinclair land—this was good enough.

Penelope pushed her way through whiplike leafless brush, the snow shin deep in places, barely up
to her ankles in other spots. It had melted to the
ground around many of the trees. Before long, she'd
be out cutting pussy willow.

She heard a movement and stopped, listening. A
squirrel? A bird?

Silence. That made her suspicious.

"Bubba?" she called softly.

No answer. If it was Bubba, there wouldn't be
one.

She wondered if he knew she'd changed her story,
if he knew she'd told about the plane in the first
place. She hadn't been to his shack. For all she knew,
he'd packed up and left before the reporters could
find him, before she could renege.

In a day or two, she would go and check on him.

She started back, the cold air and exercise improving her spirits. When she climbed over the stone
wall, a man emerged from behind a maple and
stood in front of her. She yelled, startled.

He held up both hands, palms forward. "Easy,
there. It's okay. My name's Jack Dunning—Brandon
Sinclair sent me up here."

She recovered quickly, nodding, as her heartbeat
settled down. He was a fit, sandy-haired man in a
shearling-lined jacket and a cowboy hat, and if he
didn't fit in the New Hampshire landscape, he
didn't look as if he gave a damn, either. If Wyatt
would give her little benefit of the doubt, this man
would give her none.

"You're Penelope Chestnut?"

She nodded again, feeling faintly self-conscious. Had he deliberately snuck up on her? How long had he been out here? She shook off the rush of questions. "I was just checking my taps."

"Nice little hobby, maple sugaring. I'm kind of partial to the fake stuff myself. You mind if we talk?"

His accent was a curious mix of southern—Texas?—and New York. Penelope tried to relax, not look as if he'd caught her doing something wrong. "No, of course not. I explained to Mr. Sinclair's son—"

He leveled flat, colorless eyes on her and said patiently, "Wyatt doesn't represent Brandon Sinclair. I do."

"Okay. Fine."

She walked onto the road. The sun was hitting it, the temperature steadily climbing, and the frozen ruts were already softening. Jack Dunning followed her. His rented car was parked behind her truck in her short gravel driveway. She wondered if he'd just arrived or if he'd heard her calling Bubba. If it suited his purposes to tell her, presumably he would.

"I can see why it's been so hard to find that plane. It's rough ground up here, lots of rocks, trees, undergrowth, steep hills." He eyed her, and she decided she'd rather have a thousand reporters tramping through her woods than to deal with Brandon Sinclair's private investigator and his only son. Dunning added, "Of course, that's if it crashed here."

"I've always thought they made it to Canada."

"I understand you've made a hobby of the crash," he said.

She wondered who'd told him, instantly hated the idea of him snooping among her friends and family. "I wouldn't call it a hobby. That trivializes two people's deaths. It's an unsolved mystery here in my backyard. I've taken an interest in it, that's all." No point in mentioning Harriet. He'd probably know everything about her, too, before long. "Look, as I told Wyatt, you're wasting your time. I'm as sorry as I can be for jumping the gun, but it was a dump I found in the woods, not a plane."

Jack Dunning studied her with open suspicion. The naked trees cracked and groaned in a gusting wind, and Penelope wished she'd thrown on more than her fleece jacket. She didn't want Dunning to think she was shivering because of him. "Let me be clear," he said. "I don't care what you found. I represent a man who wants to know what happened to his only brother. It's that simple. I don't intend to leave here until I'm satisfied you didn't change your story under outside duress or for your own personal reasons."

"And how will you be satisfied? I assume you won't take my word for it."

A small, humorless grin. "I don't take anyone's word for anything. You'll know I'm satisfied when I get in my plane and fly south. Now, why don't you give me a general idea of where you found this dump."

"Out in the woods. Probably on Sinclair land. On a hill."

He inhaled through his nose; otherwise there was no change in his expression. "Well, Miss Chestnut, that leaves a lot of options."

"I'd work harder to pin myself down if I'd found a plane wreck instead of an old dump."

"You've been grounded for three weeks. You've got time on your hands. Why don't you and me take a walk up on Sinclair land this afternoon and see if we can refresh your memory?"

"I'm boiling sap this afternoon."

He grinned at her, winked. "You're living up to your reputation, darlin'." He continued across the road toward his car, glanced back. "I'll come by another time and you can show me your research into Mr. Sinclair and Miss Beaudine."

"Call first," she said. "I'll put on coffee."

"You're a pistol, all right. I'll be in touch."

Penelope gave Jack Dunning a fifteen-minute head start before she jumped into her truck and raced to town. She had no plan in mind. She knew she couldn't stay in her house another minute, not with a private investigator skulking around town. As if a Sinclair weren't enough.

She found Harriet and her mother in the inn's gleaming, spotless, sun-filled kitchen, chopping vegetables for their famous curried chicken salad. During the off-season, they served a limited lunch menu in the Octagon Room. When the tourist season kicked into high gear, they'd hire more help.

Robby Chestnut carefully chopped a rib of celery at the butcher-block table. She greeted her daughter with a curt nod. Penelope had anticipated her mother's mood. It was only Wednesday, and so far this week, her only child had gotten lost in the wilderness, brought on the national media and the Sinclair family and earned herself a grounding after one episode too many of inattention. Her mother, Penelope knew, would prefer she do just about anything but fly planes and wander around in the woods by herself. She would rather she chop vegetables and bake scones, help design the inn's gardens and choose new furnishings and incidentals, learn how to do needlework or just sit in front of the fire and read a book. It wasn't that Penelope had to take up inn keeping. She could be a doctor, a lawyer, a teacher, an accountant—anything that didn't involve her running out of gas at five thousand feet and getting lost on snow-covered hills.

Penelope pulled up a chair at the table. Her mother was two inches shorter, rounder, attractive in a more delicate, feminine way. Her hair was a tone lighter than Penelope's, liberally streaked with silver these days and kept short. She wore zero makeup. Soap, water, moisturizer, and Robby Chestnut was ready for the day. She'd had two miscarriages before her only daughter was born, and one after. The miscarriages, Penelope often thought, helped her tolerate the natural fight in her daughter. Otherwise she and her mother would probably have butted heads even more often than they did.

"He came down for breakfast an hour ago," Harriet said from the counter, where she was running carrots through the food processor.

Penelope feigned ignorance. "Who?"

"Wyatt Sinclair. Isn't that why you're here?"

Robby continued chopping celery without comment. Some things she didn't want to know. When they could, her husband and daughter spared her those things. For example, there was absolutely no point in Penelope telling her mother about last night's e-mail message or this morning's visit from Jack Dunning. It wasn't that she would meddle. Robby fully recognized and accepted Penelope as an adult. She'd fret, retreat into paralyzed worry or go out and buy yarn and knitting needles with the hope her daughter would find an alternative to scaring the living daylights out of her poor mother.

"I'm here to help," Penelope said. "Pop won't let me near the airport today, and I'm already stir-crazy. I thought I might clean rooms or wash windows or something."

The two women exchanged knowing looks. They were no fools, their expressions said.

Penelope wondered if her mother had met Sinclair. Best not to ask. "Look," she said, "I'd be here even if you didn't have a Sinclair under the roof. But it's occurred to me—well, what if he's not really who he says he is? If I clean his room, maybe I can…I don't know, verify his identity."

Harriet spun around, paring knife in hand. "Penelope, good heavens! You plan to snoop!"

"Of course, she does," her mother said, unsurprised. "You don't believe Penelope would voluntarily clean a man's bathtub without ulterior motives, do you?"

Penelope snatched up a rib of celery and bit off the end. She hadn't fully thought this through. Snooping in Sinclair's room was one thing. Cleaning his tub was another. Still, she couldn't accomplish one without enduring the other.

Harriet and her mother called her bluff and sent her to the cleaning closet. There were two other guest rooms occupied, one by Jack Dunning, the other by a businessman from Massachusetts who,

Robby Chestnut said, had never even heard of Frannie and Colt. Penelope would have to clean their rooms, too.

Well, she told herself, there was no shame in an honest day's work.

Penelope was almost as interested in Brandon Sinclair's private detective as she was in his son, but she approached the idea of snooping through Dunning's things with a bit more trepidation. She wondered if he'd come armed.

She gritted her teeth and did Dunning's room first. Naturally, he hadn't left so much as a pair of socks as a clue to the scope of his intentions in Cold Spring. He struck her as the kind of man who trusted no one, including the local chambermaid. She made up the bed, scrubbed the bathroom, vacuumed, dusted and was finished in no time.

Wyatt's room was just down the hall. Key in hand, Penelope tucked her ear against the closed door before knocking. He was in. She could hear him talking in a low voice on the phone. Sounded like business. She didn't want him to know she was the one scheduled to clean his room, so she headed to the Massachusetts guy's room. He'd checked out. No tip. She flipped on the radio and did a thorough cleaning job to a political talk show that set her teeth on edge.

She lost track of time, her mind racing with thoughts and possibilities about the unintended consequences of her lie about Colt and Frannie's plane. When she stood from wiping down the TV, dust rag slung over one shoulder, furniture polish in hand, Sinclair was in the doorway. He had on a charcoal gray shirt that somehow made his eyes seem blacker than yesterday. And he looked taller. She had no idea how long he'd been standing there.

A corner of his mouth twitched in amusement. "I see you're a woman of many talents."

"I'm just helping out Harriet and my mother."

"With the hope of searching my room, I presume."

She scowled at him. "You know, I've always hated a know-it-all."

"Some things are obvious."

"I woke up this morning thinking you might not be a Sinclair, after all. I take it back."

"Who did you think I'd be?"

"An impostor of some sort. A reporter. I don't know."

He stepped into the room, making it seem immediately smaller, more intimate. "Well, I'm not an impostor, although there've been times my family's wondered, I'm sure. I was just heading out to take a look at my family's land. Since you seem to know your way around it fairly well, maybe you could point the way."

"You mean go with you or draw a map?"

"Go with me," he said.

Go with him onto Sinclair land. She glanced around the pretty Victorian room with its rose theme. It was pure Harriet, but Penelope had it gleaming. A beam of sunlight penetrated the frothy curtains, inviting her outside. "You have proper attire? If you get lost, you could freeze out there."

"I'll be fine."

Of course. He was Wyatt Sinclair, outdoorsman extraordinaire. His Tasmanian tragedy notwithstanding, a little trek through the New Hampshire wilds wouldn't intimidate him.

She thought of Bubba Johns and wondered what he'd do if Wyatt stumbled onto his shack. What *Wyatt* would do. The Sinclair land would be criss-crossed with Bubba's melting footprints. Wyatt could even stumble on remnants of her prints from Sunday, and if he did, he might end up finding the plane. Then she'd be back to Go. Reporters, investigators, Bubba's life never the same. Harriet's never the same. Her own. With a pang of fear, she thought of last night's instant message. What if it hadn't been a nut?

It was a long shot, but Penelope didn't want to risk Wyatt stumbling on the crash site. She preferred to show him around herself. There were risks there, too. She remembered the crackling atmosphere between them last night. Well, it was too cold and windy for those kinds of urges.

"Okay, sounds good," she said, maybe a little too brightly. "I'll be your guide. I'd be more efficient than a map, anyway."

He eyed her, instantly suspicious.

"What?" she asked.

"I'm trying to figure out your motive for being so agreeable."

"That's simple. I'd rather be out in the woods than polishing furniture and listening to Harriet and my mother try not to be obvious about lecturing me on my flying, my love life and where I live."

"In that order?"

Penelope ran her dust cloth along the footboard of the cherry bed. Just as well he hadn't caught her in his room. This was dangerously intimate enough. "In that order today. Other days, maybe not."

"What's wrong with where you live?"

"Dirt road, cabin, too far out of town."

"I see. Your flying—"

"Mother doesn't like it that I fly at all. It's not that she thinks flying's unsafe. She thinks *I'm* unsafe."

"Ah."

"And my love life is no one's business," she added quickly, before he could ask.

The dark eyes sparked, but whatever he was thinking he kept to himself. "Of course. Shall I wait downstairs while you search my room? It really doesn't need cleaning."

This wasn't a man who rattled easily. He was self-controlled, self-possessed—he'd kept his wits when he and his friend lay dying on a Tasmanian ledge. That he'd survived and his friend hadn't wasn't his fault, despite lurid headlines that had intimated the contrary. Yet beneath the calm Penelope sensed a cauldron of emotions that made her not want to be around when he lost patience. "I can just leave fresh towels and call it a day."

"Do that."

She started toward the door, feeling as if Sinclair had won this round—as if he'd planned it all before he'd appeared in the doorway. He might have spotted her in the supply closet or cleaning Jack Dunning's room. It was unnerving to think he'd figured out how her mind worked.

"By the way," he said behind her. "Just for the record, no one around here believes your story."

She glanced at him. "Which part?"

"Any part. They think you either found the plane

or didn't find anything and made up the dump to save face."

"If I found the plane, why wouldn't I say so?"

"That's the question of the hour, isn't it?"

Penelope refused to squirm. "It was late, and the light was funny, and I had low blood sugar. I could just have easily thought I'd seen a yeti out there that turned out to be a deer. *I* was there. No one else was. Are you going to pester me with questions and watch me like a hawk in the woods or just relax and enjoy yourself?"

He settled on his heels, eyes narrowing, mouth twitching ever so slightly. "Maybe I can do all three."

SEVEN

Once Wyatt mentioned he was heading into the woods for a few hours, Harriet insisted on packing him a lunch. When he said Penelope was going with him, she grudgingly packed her one, too—cob-smoked ham, sharp cheddar cheese, French bread, Granny Smith apples, grapes and a stack of warm chocolate chip cookies. She put both lunches into a hip pack and warned him not to let Penelope carry it, because she'd forget and everything would end up getting squashed.

Penelope was into the cookies even before she and Wyatt reached her dirt road. They'd decided to take her truck, and she used one hand to lurch around potholes and frost heaves and the other to rummage through their lunch. "That Harriet. She gave you four cookies and me just three."

"How do you know?"

"She marked one bag with a big black *W*. I expect that means you."

He grinned. "I like Harriet."

"Well, she must think I'll expend less energy climbing hills than you will. Do you want to stop and rent snowshoes or will you be okay in those boots?"

He was wearing water-resistant hikers. Nothing fancy, but adequate for the conditions. "I'll be fine."

"It could be rough going in places, but I guess you're used to hanging from cliffs by your fingernails. A little snow down your ankles'll be nothing."

At least, Wyatt thought, whatever had scared her last night no longer seemed to be troubling her. He'd decided not to disabuse her of her ideas about him. The more the devilish Sinclair she thought him, the more on her guard she was. And the more on her guard, the easier, oddly, she was to read. This was not a woman accustomed to having to play her cards close to her chest. Whether she appreciated or even realized it, she was accustomed to living her life fully and openly, saying her piece, arguing with those who loved her and in general getting away with murder.

On the other hand, the people in her life did exactly the same with her. They had no practice in hiding, dissembling, keeping secrets and out and out lying. Which was about all that gave Wyatt any hope of his job getting even the slightest bit easier.

They drove a half mile beyond her tiny lakeside house and parked alongside the dirt road in front of a small field, the sun bright on the smooth, stark white snow. Penelope had put on sunglasses, and she gestured with one hand. "Your land's across that field, to your right and left as far as you can see and up and over the hills—you just keep going until you get to state land. It's enough land to keep you busy for a while. For the most part, nobody's touched it since your father and grandfather gave up the search for Colt and Frannie and left town."

"What do you mean 'for the most part'?"

She grinned at him. "Well, I've tapped a few maples and got lost up there a few times. You might get a hunter or two, but most people just leave it alone. We don't want to push our luck and have your family sell it to developers."

Wyatt let that one go. "You have a proposed route?"

"I tapped about a dozen trees up just beyond the field. I thought we could loop around and catch them on our way back. You can help me bring down the buckets. There aren't that many." She cocked him a look, her eyes impossible to read behind the dark lenses. "Or are you going to make me untap the trees?"

He'd noticed a blue plastic holding tank in the bed of her truck. A hell of a hobby. He knew it was, by her measure, un-Sinclair of him, but he said, "I hardly feel I have the right to make you pull your taps. And I can help empty the buckets."

She gave him a mock bow. "Thank you kindly."

"Presumably this route won't take us anywhere near your dump site?"

That took a bit of the cockiness out of her. "Even with one of Harriet's lunches, we're not prepared to go that deep into the woods—provided I could find that particular ravine again, which I can't."

"You weren't prepared on Sunday."

"I was *lost*."

That much Wyatt believed. "Lead the way, then."

She started through the field, where the sun had melted the snow to just a few inches deep, and there were wide patches of sodden, gray-green grass. Wyatt noticed the shape of her bottom, the length of her legs. She'd pulled an anorak over her rugby shirt but hadn't bothered with a hat or gloves. She was fit, athletic and strong in a hundred ways and places that were all female, plenty to give him pause. From his brief conversations with people in town, he'd deduced they regarded her with exasperation and affection and had little hope she'd ever find a man who could take her on her own terms—and damned if she'd go flitty just to get one.

She turned, impatient. "Are you coming?"

Wyatt grinned. Yep. This was a woman who wanted her share of the cookies.

She led him onto an old logging trail at the edge of the field. It took them through a young forest and up a gently sloping hill that offered stunning views of Lake Winnipesaukee. It was beautiful country, Wyatt acknowledged. Out of nowhere, he remembered hiking Mount Washington with Hal on a bright, clear autumn day. What had they been, nineteen, twenty? Now Hal was gone. Penelope had a point. He was as difficult and dangerous as she believed, if not in the precise ways she believed.

They walked down that hill and up another, and eventually the logging road narrowed to a wide path that gave the feel of being deeper in the woods than Wyatt knew they were. It ran parallel to the field and dirt road on the edges of Sinclair land. This wasn't what he'd had in mind, which he suspected Penelope knew—and could mean she was deliberately keeping him away from something.

When they came to the top of another hill, she paused, breathing hard, and looked at the landscape of gray trees, white snow and blue sky. She was obviously in her element. "You can see so much this time of year. Gorgeous, isn't it?"

Suddenly Wyatt understood how she'd come to be lost on Sunday. It wasn't because she didn't know her way around in the woods or because she was out looking for the Piper Cub or even maple trees for tapping. She hadn't paid attention. She'd let things distract her—the prospect of a better view of the lake, anything that caught her eye—and she'd wandered off until eventually she realized she didn't know where the hell she was.

He could picture her looking around, and all of a sudden there was no trail, there were no familiar landmarks, and no matter how adept she was in the woods, how skilled a hiker, how mortifying it was, she was lost.

It was a damned dangerous way to live.

Still, he was confident that once she found her way home, Penelope would be able to find her way back to where she'd been.

"I'm starving," she announced. "Do you want to eat lunch out here or wait until we get to the truck? We could always go to my place and sit by the fire."

She spoke matter of factly, apparently unaware of any romantic overtone to her suggestion. She pushed her sunglasses onto the top of her head and raked her blond curls with both hands, surveying the possibilities of lunch in the woods. Wyatt pointed to a boulder just off the trail. "I like that rock there, myself."

She unzipped her anorak. "Perfect."

It was a good-size boulder, tucked between two hemlocks, about five feet tall with a broad, flat top. The side closest to the trail sloped gently, with a straight, steep drop into brush and pine on the other side. Penelope grabbed a thin birch, climbed onto the boulder and plunked down. Wyatt followed. All he needed to do was fall on his ass, but he managed to settle beside her without incident. His climbing skills were getting rusty. A two-year hiatus and a New Hampshire rock gave him pause. He shuddered, could hear Hal's snort of laughter mixed with disgust. Get on with it, he'd say. Live your life. Take risks. It's who you are.

"Well, this is a nice spot," Penelope said, pushing up the sleeves of her anorak and rugby shirt. She had great hands, with long, feminine fingers and short, well-kept nails. "Rock's a little cold on the behind, but otherwise we're in good shape."

Wyatt didn't say a word. There's your risk, he thought grimly. Having lunch on a rock in the middle of the New England woods with a woman who was oblivious—beyond oblivious—to her own appeal. Maybe she figured she wasn't a Sinclair's type. Or maybe, right now, he was just a hiking buddy. He wasn't supposed to be thinking about her fanny on the cold rock and everything else he was thinking. If she knew the twists and turns his mind was taking, she'd summarily boot him headfirst in the snow.

Then again, it might be fun if she tried.

He shook every stupid thought out of his head. Yes. It was a cold rock.

"The temperature's warming up nicely," she said, handing him his plastic bag of cheese, ham and bread. "At least the sap won't be frozen in the buckets. It's about all I have to keep me from going nuts over the next three weeks."

"Three weeks isn't so long."

"It's *forever*. Another eleven hours and I'll have

made it through day one. I'm hoping I can wear Pop down, get him to ease up. A week should do the trick." She dug into her lunch, eating the bread first. "Maybe I'll buy a jigsaw puzzle. That ought to help me pass the time."

With the warm curve of her hip against his, Wyatt thought of a variety of ways he could help her pass the time. He quickly bit into the crusty bread, faintly squished from its trek into the countryside. Wall Street felt very far away. He breathed in the crisp, clear air, smelled the damp moss and pungent hemlock, and with Penelope so close, the scent of her hair, citrusy, clean.

Enough, he told himself. "Are there any Beaudines left in Cold Spring?" he asked, needing a distraction from his dangerous train of thought.

"No—her father died when she was four, her mother when she was ten. They were hard, poor hill people with lousy health and no health care. Her grandparents tried to raise her, but they weren't much good. They've been dead forever—they both died several years before she disappeared. She had no reason to come back here. In fact, she had more reason *never* to come back. But I guess this was her home, and people say she always meant to come back to stay."

"No brothers and sisters?"

"Just her. She'd always been bookish, sneaking off to the library to read everything she could. An art teacher at the local high school took an interest in her and helped her get books, taught her what she knew. Supposedly Frannie just gobbled information. She took up flying when she was fifteen and became quite the sensation, then headed off to the big city. She was beautiful, daring, smart, and people just loved her."

"You seem to have a good sense of her."

"I don't know, sometimes I don't think I have any sense of her at all. I've talked to all kinds of people who knew her. I drove down to Concord to the nursing home where her art teacher is living, and she remembered every detail about Frannie—I think she just had that kind of effect on people."

Wyatt nodded. "It's a shame she died so young."

Penelope returned her leftovers to the plastic bag, got out her cookies and handed him the plastic bag with the W. "That mix of art historian and pilot fascinates me. I guess it's because of my own situation. I've been flying for so long. For years it's pretty much all I wanted to do." She shrugged. "Well, you're not here to talk about my problems. My personal theory is that what Frannie wanted more than anything—more than flying, more than being an art historian—was to be loved."

"Why?"

"That's what comes out when I talk to people who knew her. She was desperate to love and be loved. She ached for it. In a way, that could be why she excelled at two such seemingly disparate disciplines, flying and art."

Wyatt tried one of the cookies, also squished. He was intrigued by how a woman she'd never known had captured Penelope's fancy. "In what way?"

"I'm just speculating, but I think when she was flying, she could love herself—she could experience the thrill of being the star. Her old teacher says Frannie brought an emotional sensibility to her art studies that would have embarrassed or terrified someone else. She didn't overthink or overanalyze. She trusted her instincts, turned her vulnerability into strength."

"Until Colt came along," Wyatt said.

She nodded. "Frannie was ripe for someone like him to come along and sweep her off her feet. He was rich, good-looking, just as daring as she was. And he wanted love as much as she did." She popped her last chocolate chip cookie into her mouth. "Sex, too. I mean, I'm not naive."

"He was five years younger than Frannie."

"Ah, but he was a Sinclair."

As if that explained everything. Wyatt glanced sideways at her, watched her lick chocolate off her lower lip, felt a jolt of pure, unabashed lust and wondered if she didn't have a point. "He was a twenty-one-year-old kid."

"You think Frannie swept him off his feet?"

"I think they saw in each other what they wanted to see."

Penelope gave that some thought. "They were in love."

"And you think that's why they ran off together? Because they were in love?"

She seemed mystified. "Why else?"

"Because that's not enough," Wyatt said, looking into the snow-covered woods, the silence and isolation settling deep into him. "Love's never enough reason for a Sinclair to do anything."

"Well, that's a heck of a legacy."

"So it is."

She seemed to realize his seriousness and started to speak, but he stuffed the remains of their lunch in the hip pack Harriet had supplied and shot off the boulder. "We'd best get to your sap buckets."

She nodded. "Sure. I think I just gave you the introduction to *The Biography of Frannie Beaudine*, which, by the way, I have no intention of writing. But I don't mean to imply that your uncle's death was any less a tragedy. They were both so young."

"That they were."

He could see her reluctance to drop the subject. She pushed her sunglasses on her nose and climbed off the rock, slipping slightly in the snow. He caught her elbow, and she thanked him politely, formally, which told him she hadn't been unaffected by her talk of sex and the Sinclair nature.

With visible effort, she started along the path, looping to the field and the series of maples she'd tapped. She explained that she'd stuck to buckets instead of gravity tubing because it was old-fashioned and she didn't have a big operation, not like her mother, whose sugar house apparently attracted scores of tourists on weekends. Maple sugaring occurred during the off-season for the inn, so it worked out well.

Wyatt helped her consolidate the various buckets into two buckets, one for each to carry to her truck. Some of the trees had two taps, some four, and she explained the number of taps was determined by the size and age of the tree. "You really shouldn't tap a maple until it's about forty years old."

He was learning more about maple sugaring than he'd ever imagined knowing.

On the far side of a fat, way-older-than-forty maple, he spotted distinct footprints in the dense, wet snow. "Whose are these?" he asked, pointing.

Penelope came next to him. "They must be ours."

"We didn't come this way." He squatted and examined the prints. "They're a different kind of boot."

"Then they're mine from the other day—"

"Foot's too big."

She wrinkled her face at him. "I would get a flatlander who knows footprints. It's probably just someone out walking. Tourists like to take pictures of sap buckets."

"There are dozens of buckets close to the road. They wouldn't have to traipse all the way up here."

"Maybe it's a reporter or your investigator, Jack Dunning. He was sneaking around my house this morning."

"He's not my investigator, he's my father's. What was he doing sneaking around your house?"

"Actually, he just came by to talk to me. I don't want you reporting to your father and getting him fired. Spooky guy."

"Penelope..."

She stared at him, the sunlight catching the ends of her blond hair. "Hmm?"

"Whose prints are these?"

She thrust her hands onto her hips, feigning indignation. "You know, it must be a pain to be as suspicious-minded as you are. You make life a lot harder on yourself than it needs to be."

"That's the pot calling the kettle black. I can't imagine the effort it must take to keep all your lies straight."

Her mouth snapped shut, and she spun around, huffy.

Wyatt shot to his feet, grabbed her by the elbow

and turned her toward him, firmly but not harshly. He stood very close. Too close. Way, way too close. He wished he could see her eyes behind her sunglasses. But her wisps of blond hair, her mouth, her throat were distractions enough. He should have stayed in New York. But he was here, and so was she. "Before I leave town, you'll tell me the truth."

Her brow furrowed, but there was no fear in her, unlike last night—something else that still needed explaining. "Is that a threat?"

"No. It's something I know." She licked her lips as if his mouth was on hers, as if she were thinking about it. He lowered his voice. "I don't know why you're lying, Penelope, but you have no reason to hide anything from me. I only want to put my father's mind at ease about a brother he lost a long, long time ago. That's all. I have no other interest in being here."

"I'm not hiding anything."

"Look, people up here are closemouthed. I understand that. They don't like strangers, and they particularly don't like Sinclairs. I understand that, too. But just because you all don't like to talk out of school doesn't mean you're any damned good at lying."

"I'm not closemouthed. I blabbed one little thing about thinking I might have found Colt and Frannie's plane, and I end up with half the planet's media and a Sinclair on my case. *And* a private investigator. Why on earth would I want to look like an idiot to the entire world? Why would I want you and Jack Dunning breathing down my neck? If I were lying, I could do a better job."

Wyatt shook his head, seeing it now, understanding. "That's not it. The truth is, you don't give a damn what the entire world thinks. You care about Cold Spring. You care about your family and your friends."

"Are you kidding? I've spent most of my life figuring out ways to get out of here. Why do you think I fly?"

"I'm right," he said with certainty.

She sputtered. "So you know that much about me already?"

"I do."

She couldn't get the buckets down the hill and poured into her holding tank fast enough. Wyatt helped, but she was like a whirling dervish. Finally, she grabbed the two empty buckets and marched through the snow. He waited at the truck, figuring she'd run out of steam. But she was still charging when she came across the field, the buckets presumably back on their taps.

Wyatt leaned against the truck, watching her, his hands warming in his pockets. He could see hers were freezing. Her nose was red, and her hair was flying around in a light breeze. All that restless energy, all that movement, just to keep from thinking about what she was going to think about no matter what. Which was him, and those footprints she didn't want to explain.

But she pretended to be all business. "Rebecca and Jane McNally will be at my house any minute. They're the chief of police's daughters." A warning. She gave him a second to get it. "They're helping me boil sap."

"Good. I'll help, too. I'm not in a hurry. You can

take me to town after you're done with your sap boiling."

She exhaled at the sky and raked her fingers through her curls, pushed up her sunglasses, chewed on her lower lip and finally fastened her gaze on him. "I want rid of you, Sinclair. Damn it, I don't need you staring at me with those doubting black eyes."

"Doubting black eyes. I like that. You do have a flare for the dramatic." He eased his hands under hers, which were red and cold and stiff, and she immediately curled her fingers into tight fists as if steeling herself against him. "You don't believe in gloves?"

"I didn't think I'd be emptying sap buckets. I just—"

"Relax," he said softly, her hands slowly warming in his, "I'm not going to force you to do anything or say anything."

"There's nothing—"

"There's something, Penelope. Something had you spooked last night, and something's got you into a whirlwind right now."

She shut her eyes, breathed. With his thumbs, he massaged her hands, feeling the heat come into them, some of the stiffness ease out—feeling a certain heat and stiffness of his own, which he pushed way, way to the back of his mind. He concentrated on the creaking and groaning of the naked trees in the chilly breeze, the twittering of chickadees, the drilling sounds of a woodpecker.

Finally, she looked at him and swallowed, calculating, debating. He could see her mind working out her options. She eased her hands from his, shoved them into the pockets of her flimsy anorak. "The footprints—"

"You don't have to tell me now," he said.

She stared into the field. "They belong to Bubba Johns."

"And Bubba Johns would be?"

She looked at him, bit on one corner of her mouth as if not sure she should tell him. "Bubba's the local hermit."

Wyatt absorbed her words, then shook his head and gave a short laugh. "Well, hell. I should have known a hermit would turn up somewhere in this mess."

But that was it. She would say no more. She muttered about having to get to her house to meet the police chief's daughters and boil sap, and she went around the front of her truck and climbed in behind the wheel. Wyatt glanced at the snow-covered field. A hermit. A baby found on a church doorstep.

And Penelope Chestnut, blond, green-eyed, energetic and on edge.

He would do well to stay alert and at least a tad suspicious. Beware, he thought, of going soft. He was an outsider, he was a Sinclair, and these people weren't about to trust him. That included Penelope, no matter how much he'd wanted to kiss her with the snow melting and the mud softening under them.

"Bubba's harmless," she said.

"That's what you said about your cousin Harriet."

"They're both harmless."

"Is Bubba the reason you withdrew your story?"

She took in a sharp, shallow breath. "I didn't *with-*

draw my story. I was wrong about what I saw, and I corrected my mistake. Harriet and Bubba don't have anything to do with the dump I found in the woods."

"So why didn't you want to tell me about this hermit?"

"Because—because of the way you are."

He settled in his seat, and she negotiated the muddy road with skill and determination. "Well, then, being the way I am, I should have gone ahead and kissed you while I had the chance."

That got her. The truck sank into a mass of mud, and she muttered, "You're impossible," as she downshifted and roared onto firmer ground.

Yep. No question. She wished he'd gone ahead and kissed her, too. Wyatt smiled to himself. It wasn't finding Colt and Frannie's plane, but it was something.

Harriet slipped into the private half bath down a short hall from the front desk and locked the door. She shut the toilet lid and set her bag of goodies on it. She'd spent so much money! Twenty minutes in the drugstore, and she'd come away with gobs of stuff. Tubes and bottles and special sponges. She had foundation in two different shades, both very pale, and *three* shades of lipstick, but just one mascara. She'd stood paralyzed in front of the eye shadows for at least five minutes, finally settling on a collection of four different shades of taupe. She'd put an eyeliner pencil in her basket and took it out again several times before finally deciding, no, that was just too much. She'd smear it all over her eyes and end up looking like a raccoon.

Methodically, she ripped open her treasures, discarding cardboard and plastic packaging into her drugstore bag, which she would take upstairs and throw out in her room. Her hands shook, and her heart raced. Robby didn't wear makeup. She didn't oppose it, just didn't think it was necessary. And she was so attractive without it.

Harriet glanced in the oval mirror above the small pedestal sink. *Not me.*

Before she let negativity get the best of her, she picked up one of the bottles of foundation and shook it. It wasn't a top-of-the-line brand, so she couldn't try it on in the store—she'd had to match the color to her skin as best she could. She felt thirteen again. She couldn't remember why she'd never really started wearing makeup. At some point, it had suddenly seemed vain and stupid, and she'd always felt so ridiculous, gobbed up with creams and powders.

She poured a few drops of foundation into her palm, dabbed it with two fingertips. She looked closely at her reflection in the mirror. The fine lines at the corners of her eyes had been there for several years, the more recent creases at her mouth and in her forehead. She was forty-five. Halfway to ninety. *Halfway to Kingdom Come.*

She touched the foundation to her cheek and blended the way she'd seen on infomercials. She stood back. *There.* Her freckles had disappeared. The reddish spots had evened out. Otherwise she looked the same.

The eyeshadow was harder. At first she couldn't tell she had any on. Then there were big brown blotches on her temples. She used a tissue to get rid of them and tried again, awkward with the little sponge applicators that came with the eye shadow collection. The mascara was a relief to put on, and the lipstick—a soft, pretty shade of plum. But it seemed too garish on her, and she opted for one of the nude shades.

"Better," she said, giddy.

But her hair. She ran her fingers through it, seeing the gray, the shapelessness of it. Penelope could get away with quick trims and finger combing, could roll her blond curls and pop in those hair sticks and look fabulous. When Harriet had tried the sticks, they'd ended up on the floor. Barrettes and covered rubber bands she could manage. She'd never dyed her hair, although she sometimes fancied herself going copper.

Well, there was nothing to be done about her hair right now. She brushed it, pulled it into a wooden barrette and quickly shoved all her goodies into her handbag, which, of course, was sensible, like everything else about her. If she didn't feel as beautiful and daring as Frannie Beaudine, she at least felt less dumpy and plain. She grabbed her trash and scooted back out to the front desk.

Jack Dunning was there, having emerged from a late lunch. He gave no indication of noticing Harriet's transformation. She said, "Good afternoon, Mr. Dunning," so he'd say something and she could hear that deep, gravel-rough voice with that delicious half Texas, half New York accent.

"Afternoon, Miss Chestnut. Mind if I have a word with you?"

"Not at all. Is everything all right?"

"Everything's just fine. Come on and sit by the

fire with me. Wind's kicked up, clouds're rolling in. I do believe we're in for a storm."

"Yes, they're calling for snow tomorrow."

She came around the front desk, and he sat on the couch facing the fire. The only other seat was a ladder-back chair. Harriet remained standing, feeling the fire hot on her back. He patted the seat beside him. "Sit down, Miss Chestnut."

"Please, call me Harriet."

He smiled. "And I'm Jack."

She almost blurted something stupid about loving the way he talked, but instead said primly, "What can I do for you?"

He had one booted foot on the other knee and held his ankle, casual, at ease with himself—and with her, she thought. He made a clicking sound with his tongue, thinking. "Well, I tell you what, Harriet. You can tell me what you know about this hermit. Bubba Johns, I think his name is."

"Bubba?" It wasn't what she'd expected. Something about Penelope, perhaps, or background on the town, but not Bubba. "He's just an old hermit who lives in the woods."

"On Sinclair land."

"That's possible. I don't really know for certain. He's been up there for years—since I was in college, I believe. He keeps to himself. Occasionally he comes into town to barter."

"You ever talk to him?"

"About once or twice a year, I'd say. He brings us fiddleheads in the spring."

Jack's brow furrowed. "Fiddleheads?"

"It's a growth stage of ferns, in early spring when they're just coming up out of the ground. They're a little curlicue shape, and they taste rather like asparagus. They're a favorite here at the inn. Around Christmas, he'll bring us balsam and princess pine. He never says very much."

"Is he crazy?"

"I don't think so. Eccentric, perhaps. But not mentally ill. People around here generally leave him alone."

Jack grinned, winked. "I'm not from around here."

Harriet paled. "You're not going to throw him off Sinclair land, are you? That wouldn't go over well here at all. He's an old man. He won't live forever. He—"

"Easy, Harriet. I don't care about an old hermit. If my boss cares, that's another story. Me, I kind of like the idea of living out in the middle of nowhere in a shack. Nobody bothers me, I don't bother anybody. Sounds awfully damned peaceful."

"I don't know, I suppose I'm more of a people person."

His gray eyes, ordinarily so difficult to read, took on a warmth she hadn't noticed before. "The world needs more of you. I guess I've just been wallowing in the flotsam and jetsam for too damned long. I like the idea of sitting on a hillside watching the squirrels."

"Your work must be trying at times," Harriet said, feeling inadequate.

"That it is." He got to his feet, and she saw that he was as rangy and fit as her first impression of him had led her to believe. He had on jeans, a denim shirt, his boots. He must have left his hat and shear-

ling-lined coat in his room. "Well. I've taken enough
of your time. Thanks for the information."

She wanted to ask him if he intended to go to
Bubba's, but she didn't. Penelope would have. She'd
have told him to leave Bubba alone. She wouldn't
understand Harriet's reticence in dealing with a private investigator hired by Brandon Sinclair. That she
was attracted to him, too, just made it more impossible. She didn't want Jack Dunning thinking ill of
her before he'd even really noticed her.

So she told him he was welcome, and she sat on
the couch, staring at the fire, listening to his footsteps on the stairs. In a few minutes, he came down,
hat on, coat in hand. He waved goodbye and promised he'd be back in time for dinner, that voice of his
curling right down her spine.

When he'd gone, she ducked into the half bath
and tried the plum lipstick again. This time, she
didn't think it looked garish at all.

EIGHT

The smell of maple syrup sweetened the air, and the sunset—swirls of vibrant orange, deep lavender, the palest of pinks—filled the sky, despite the ominous clouds gathering to the west. The McNally girls had finally left. Wyatt suppressed a sigh of relief. They were talkative, hard workers and nice enough teenagers, but they'd come along at an inopportune time. As he and Penelope had arrived from their hike, a tall, white-haired, white-bearded man was retreating into the woods. Wyatt had volunteered to go after him, but Penelope had touched his hand and said, "No, don't. That's Bubba Johns." Then Rebecca and Jane McNally showed up, and Wyatt was sucked into sugar making and not asking questions.

The girls obviously adored Penelope. She was something of a mentor for them, a capable and independent woman even if she did have a search party called out on her from time to time. Wyatt suspected he'd inhibited their conversation. He'd sensed the sisters' mad curiosity about him and twice he'd caught Rebecca, the older of the two, silently mouthing questions to Penelope.

The sap was bubbling, still clear and watery, in a big tub, set on a roaring fire they'd built on the edge

of the gravel driveway. When it boiled down sufficiently, Penelope had said she'd transfer it to a canning pot and finish the process inside, hoping, ultimately, to get a gallon of syrup from the forty or so
gallons of sap she'd collected. She'd explained backyard maple-sugaring techniques in excruciating detail, presumably since she and her helpers couldn't
talk about him.

Before they'd started, she'd had to change into an
old plaid flannel shirt, some sap-boiling ritual. She
tossed another log on the fire, her face flushed from
heat and exertion. "I know you're chomping at the
bit to ask me about Bubba," she said.

Wyatt stood close to the flames, feeling the heat
on his face. "How far is his place from here?"

"About a forty-minute hike, depending on conditions."

"Does he visit often?"

"No. Never."

Wisps of blond curls framed her face, softening
her features, stirring in him things better left undisturbed. As much as she'd claim she wanted to be flying, she wasn't unhappy with her bubbling cauldron. Wyatt struggled to keep his mind on the
business that had brought him north. "Tell me about
him."

"What's to tell? He's a hermit. Most people think
he's from northern New Hampshire, maybe Canada. Some say he's a Vietnam vet, but I think he's
too old. Korea, maybe. He just keeps to himself. He
doesn't talk to anyone and he doesn't hurt anyone."
She poked the fire with a long iron rod. "He's your
basic, old-fashioned hermit."

"Why do you think he was here at your place?"

"I have no idea."

"But he's never stopped by before."

"That's right." She laid her iron rod on the ground and held her palms over the fire. "It doesn't mean it's all that weird he would. Usually he takes another route to the main road, then walks in to town. He made himself a wooden wheelbarrow, and he pushes it with whatever stuff he plans to barter. He empties it, fills it up with new stuff and pushes it home. He manages to live on next to nothing."

"How well do you know him?"

"I don't know him at all, really. We first met when I was ten and he led me out of the woods."

Wyatt grinned, picturing her as a preadolescent. "I'll bet you were a blond-haired hellion at ten. You were lost?"

She nodded, unabashed. "That was the first time I had a search party called out on me. I chattered away at him, but he never said a word. In those days, people were kind of nervous about him. But now we all let him live his life the way he wants to."

The fire popped, and a gust of wind blew ashes and hot coals onto the driveway. Penelope jumped back, the clear sap boiling wildly. "I guess we should shut this down for the night," she said. "I'll just let the fire die and the sap cool off, then I'll bring it in. I think it'd fit into my canner, don't you?"

Wyatt didn't think he'd ever seen a canner. "We can dump whatever doesn't fit into the lake."

She grinned at him. "You're offending my Yankee sensibilities."

The sunset was fading rapidly, the naked trees outlined in sharp relief against the darkening sky. Wyatt could feel the night settling in, the quiet seeping into everything around him. The nights would be black up here. There were no city lights to ease the isolation, none, either, to blur the moon and stars. He considered Bubba Johns. At times over the past two years, the life of a hermit was one Wyatt could imagine for himself. Simple, with no one else to hurt.

He recognized the danger signs and shook off the melancholy before it could take root. "Do you think Bubba Johns can find your turn-of-the-century dump?"

"I don't know. I could ask."

He smiled, probably a little nastily. "I think I'd better do the asking."

It wasn't the answer she'd expected. She gave an impatient hiss, snatched up her iron rod and leaned it against her woodpile. Wyatt wondered if she chopped her own wood. He would like to see her swing an ax. She was an intriguing mix of independence, kindness, vulnerability and capableness. From tea and scones to hauling sap. He had to struggle not to be too intrigued and concentrate instead on the pack of lies she'd told him.

"Bubba doesn't talk much to locals," she said. "I can't see him talking to a stranger—and it wouldn't go over well around here if you upset him. People tend to be protective of him."

"No burning bamboo shoots. Promise."

"Good." She dusted off her hands, obviously eager to change the subject. "It's getting windy. I can smell the storm coming, can't you? I think I'll take a hot shower and call it a day."

She started across the driveway. Something in her walk made him think maybe she was fighting off the same thoughts and urges he was. He scooped up a stray piece of kindling, tossed it on the fire. What was he supposed to do now? Say good-night? The evening stretched in front of him, dark and quiet. He supposed he could sort through what he'd learned today. And what he hadn't.

"Do you lock your doors?" he asked.

That got her. She stopped in the muddy driveway, spun around to him. "What?"

"Maybe Bubba Johns decided to help himself to your larder. Have you checked to see if anything's missing?"

"No, and I have no intention of doing so. If I have something Bubba needs, he can have it." She sauntered over to him, hands on her hips, eyes an even deeper, darker, sexier green at twilight. "You know, Sinclair, you're starting to piss me off."

He grinned at her and before he could talk himself out of it, he tucked a finger under her chin, gave her that half second to tell him he was *really* pissing her off, and kissed her. Hard, quick and with no plans for regret.

"Well, I—you've your nerve," she said, pretending to be stunned.

He laughed. "Don't tell me you've got all the men around here too afraid to kiss you."

"I'm not telling you anything."

She sniffed, straightening her ragged flannel shirt, which, he noted, he hadn't had a chance to unstraighten. He wanted that chance. Now. He'd have taken her right there next to the fire, in the mud, with the wind blowing and the storm coming, if she gave him the slightest inclination she wouldn't pull the hot sap down on him should he try.

All the coolness had gone out of her eyes, and he could see that a part of her—however unacknowledged—was thinking about making love in the mud, too.

"You're awfully kissable for a crank pot, hard-headed New Englander," he said. "Come on, jump in the shower and put on a dress. I'll take you to dinner at the inn."

She didn't move. "I should resist."

Like she was Scarlett O'Hara. "Why?"

"Because you're dangerous and you're irritating."

"Jesus, you sound like my father. Look, you have to drive me back, anyway. We came in your truck, if you recall."

She licked her lips. He wondered if she could taste him. "All right. I'd probably just open a can of soup if I stayed here. You can douse the fire and cover the sap—if you don't mind. I'll bring it in after it's cooled."

He did as she asked. It only took a few seconds, and even from her driveway, he could hear her shower running. He couldn't resist. There was no point in wasting time *trying* to resist. He slipped inside, surveyed the kitchen and living area with a more clinical, neutral eye than he had last night. It was a curious mix of an old-fashioned, rustic lake camp and a young woman's home. Most disconcerting was the musty moose head on the barn board wall. A leftover, Wyatt suspected.

He moved quickly, silently, with very little premeditation to her study. Fluorescent lights glowed over a trestle table of sprouting plants, all neatly marked with Popsicle sticks. Foxglove, delphinium, petunias, marigolds, Canterbury bells, coleus, pansies. She had a small yard, but he could imagine her filling her deck with pots of flowers and greenery— and giving away the excess.

But he hadn't ventured in here to check out her plants. He turned his attention to another, larger trestle table desk with its jumble of computer, printer, fax, telephone, jars of pens and pencils, file folders, notebooks. A prosaic metal shelving unit overflowed with books, scrapbooks, photo albums. One shelf was devoted to flying, planes, helicopters, flying in wartime, flying in peacetime, everything from technical to coffee-table picture books. Another offered books on New England, history books, guides to its trails, flora and fauna, birds, inns, mountains, coastlines, waterways, cities and attractions.

On the bottom shelf were two loose-leaf notebooks marked Colt and Frannie and a box of cassette tapes, each neatly hand-labeled. Penelope's research. Obviously this was a more consuming hobby than she was willing to admit to him. But Wyatt didn't risk a closer look, although he could still hear the shower running. He tried not to imagine Penelope under its steaming spray.

On the wall were two framed prints, one of a golden, romantic Piper Cub J-3 against a clear blue sky, the other a page of the local paper announcing the disappearance of Frannie Beaudine. There was a big picture of her, smiling, young and so beautiful. There was no picture of Colt. Even Wyatt had seen few pictures of his uncle, remembering him vaguely as a dark and handsome man—and young. He and Frannie had both been so damned young.

He pulled himself away from the study and took a

quick peek into Penelope's bedroom, in case she'd squirreled away an obvious clue to why she was lying. He surveyed the small, cozy room from the doorway. Double bed with a billowing down comforter, lots of colorful pillows, white curtains, a small television, an antique oak bureau. Her sap-boiling clothes hung over a wooden chair painted a bright yellow.

"Just who's dangerous here," he whispered, his mouth dry, his throat tight, and headed stiffly outside.

A few minutes later, Penelope emerged in an ankle-length black knit dress and black boots. She'd put on makeup, pinned up her hair, her blond curls damp from her shower. "I put on lip gloss," she said, smacking her raspberry-colored lips together. "I've never met a man who likes to kiss a woman with goop on her lips."

Wyatt said nothing. If only she knew.

She grinned at him, her green eyes sparkling. "That ought to keep even a fearless Sinclair at bay."

While she waited for Wyatt to dress for dinner, Penelope had a glass of chardonnay in the kitchen with Harriet, who was arranging dinner salads at the other end of the butcher-block table. Her mother, thank God, was at the sugar house. It was a slow night at the inn. Penelope tried not to gulp her wine. "I think the bastard searched my place while I was in the shower."

Harriet almost dropped a handful of sliced radishes. "That's appalling! How could you even think such a thing?"

"That's how guys like Sinclair operate."

"Did he have good reason?"

"*Harriet.*"

Her cousin slipped the radishes onto the perfect shreds of lettuce and started on pitted black olives. "Well, you haven't been yourself lately—"

"That's because I'm grounded. I always get antsy when I can't fly."

Harriet pursed her lips, her critical, knowing gaze falling on her cousin. "You were already antsy, Penelope. That's why you were grounded."

"Then it's because it's March." She sipped her wine, noticing something different about Harriet. Makeup? Her freckles were gone. "I need leaves on the trees."

"Winter's never bothered you before." A half-dozen salads set, Harriet moved to the dessert tray. Maple cheesecake, apple crisp, Indian pudding. Penelope's mouth watered. After hours and hours with Wyatt Sinclair at her elbow, waiting for her to crack, she was starving. Harriet worked quickly, not looking tempted by her array of sweets. She said, "Robby and I have always thought flying keeps you from getting cabin fever. You're restless enough as it is."

Penelope stared at her cousin. After years of practice, she could fill in the blanks between what was being said and what was deliberately not being said. "You don't believe me, either!"

"About what?"

"Mistaking a dump for Frannie and Colt's plane."

Harriet dusted off her fingers. She had broad hands with blunt, clean nails, but her movements were gentle, deliberate, always patient. "I've seen old dumps, Penelope. I've seen planes. How anyone, especially someone with your expertise, could mistake the two—"

"Well, I *did*."

Harriet didn't respond. That was her modus operandi when she disagreed with someone. To avoid confrontation, she clammed up. It was a handy trait as an innkeeper—she didn't yell at her guests—but it could be frustrating for her family and friends, who sometimes never knew when Harriet was carrying a grudge.

Robby Chestnut breezed into the kitchen, humming happily. "Keep your fingers crossed—I think we're in for one of our better sugaring seasons. Not too cold, not too hot." She smiled. "Like Goldilocks's porridge. And how are you, Penelope?"

"Just fine. I survived day one of my grounding."

"So far," her mother amended.

True. She had dinner with Wyatt yet to go. But like everyone else in town, Penelope had learned to spare her mother the worst of her excesses. She had no intention of mentioning Jack Dunning, tramping through the woods with Sinclair, boiling sap with him, kissing him—and suspecting him of searching her place while she was in the shower.

It wasn't that her mother wouldn't care. She would, and did. She just didn't necessarily want to know details. Her laissez-faire approach to child rearing had left Penelope to do as she pleased, which had its advantages. On the downside, she couldn't count on her mother putting her neck on the block to spare her daughter. Of course, Penelope was, after all, thirty years old. If she wanted to hang out with a Sinclair, especially one who damned well knew she was lying, that was her call. Her mother wasn't about to interfere. She was a kind, generous, talented woman, but she let Penelope fight her own battles—and Penelope suspected she had a major one ahead of her.

She filled her wineglass and slipped to the front lobby. Wyatt was coming down the stairs. He had changed into a dark sweater, and he looked as rakish and devil-may-care as any of his lion-hunting forebears. It was a good reminder that she was dealing with dangerous genetic material. He smiled at her. "You look as if you could run right across Lake Winnipesaukee."

"I feel that way, too. I'm about ready to jump out of my skin. You were right. *No one* believes my story. Even Harriet doesn't."

"Even your father doesn't."

"It's a damned conspiracy. Nobody believed a thing I've said since I was a little kid." She started down the hall in a huff, stopped, glanced sideways at Wyatt. "How do you know what my father believes?"

"He told me as much yesterday after you dropped me off at the airport."

"Just like that?"

"No, not exactly. I got the impression he didn't like telling me anything."

"He's not your basic blabbermouth," Penelope said, resuming her course to the Octagon Room. With Wyatt looking so damned devastating, it was just as well she'd seen the salads and dessert tray and knew that grilled rainbow trout was on the menu. Otherwise she'd have been totally insane to stay for dinner. This way, she had an excuse.

"You could tell the truth," Wyatt pointed out, his tone neutral.

"I could move to California. I left once, you know. After college. I moved to North Carolina for eight months and worked at the Charlotte airport."

"What brought you back?"

"My father decided to let me fly for him, after all. Before that, he'd hire any scumbag with a pilot's license before he'd hire me. We've started talking about a partnership."

"That would be after your three week grounding's up," Wyatt said.

She smiled, refusing to let him get to her. "Pop's a little ticked at me these days. He blames me for every gray hair on his head."

They came to the Octagon Room, and Terry showed them to the same table they'd had at tea yesterday. A white votive candle flickered in a brass holder, the flame reflecting in Wyatt's dark eyes. Penelope took a big sip of wine and sat down. Wyatt requested a beer from a local brewer.

"Did you miss Cold Spring while you were in North Carolina?" he asked.

"I missed the lake—and a proper winter. I have the soul of a New Englander, I guess. I've tried to beat it out of me, but it's just there. I need cold winters and fog on the lake in the summer."

"And mud season?"

She grinned. "I love mud season. One year, I got so stuck on my road I thought I'd have to get a wrecker to pull my car out. That's when I bought my truck. Most people hate late winter and early spring in northern New England. They'd spend March and most of April in the Bahamas. Not me. I like all the subtle changes that say spring is upon us. The sap running, the tiny buds on the trees, the change in the snow, the longer days—the mud."

Wyatt's beer arrived, and he poured it into the frosted glass. Penelope watched his movements, noticed his long fingers, the muscles in his wrists.

"You did seem to be in your element today," he remarked.

"Yes, all in all it was a good day—since I couldn't fly. Of course, I'm not counting that kiss by the fire. I'm chalking that up to your Sinclair genes. A woman's a woman, and there I was. It's an impulse, a natural reaction to stimuli. Like a frog on a lily pad when a mosquito buzzes by. You just couldn't help yourself."

He smiled, tasted his beer. "And I suppose you just couldn't help yourself when you kissed me back."

"Anymore than the mosquito could when the frog swallowed him."

"Penelope..."

A change in subject was necessary. "So, tell me about snooping in my house while I was in the shower. Did you find anything that confirms I'm lying about not finding Frannie and Colt's plane?"

He leaned over the table and narrowed his black eyes. "If I had, I'd have presented it to you in the shower."

She refused to picture *that* particular scenario. "You have no shame, Sinclair. One minute I think we're building a little trust between us, next minute you're pawing through my stuff."

"I didn't have enough time to do much pawing."

He settled in his chair, smug and amused with himself. "I like the moose head."

"That's Willard."

"My grandfather was named Willard. I presume there's a connection?"

"He and my grandfather, who built my cabin, used to hunt and fish together. Your grandfather shot the moose and had him mounted—this was many years ago, before I was born. He presented him to my grandfather as a gift. When I inherited the cabin, I got the moose head. I was going to put him in a yard sale, but I kept him."

"And named him," Wyatt said.

"I had a nightmare one night shortly after I'd moved in, and when I stumbled bleary-eyed into the living room, here's this moose glaring at me from the wall. I almost dropped dead of a heart attack. I'd forgotten all about him. So I named him Willard. It seems to fit."

They ordered their dinners, grilled rainbow trout for both, and had warm dill bread while they waited. Jack Dunning entered the dining room. He didn't look as out of place as Penelope would have expected, with his close-cropped, graying sandy hair, his jutting jaw, his precise, military bearing—not to mention his cowboy boots on the polished wood floors.

"Aren't you two worried about stepping on each other's toes?" Penelope dabbed butter on her warm bread, aware of Wyatt's gaze on her. "I mean, you're both here for the same thing, namely figuring out whether or not I'm a liar."

Wyatt shrugged, shifting his gaze to the investigator across the room. "Liar's fairly harsh. You could have changed your story for a lot of different reasons. I just want to make sure you didn't find my uncle's plane, after all. I assume Jack does, too."

"Does your father approve of you both being here?"

"I didn't ask. Jack's here because my father sent him. I'm here because I decided to check out your story myself. If my father doesn't approve, that's his problem."

"Unlike me, you're not your father's employee as well as his offspring. That gets complicated, and I suspect being Brandon Sinclair's son is quite complicated enough. Whoops. Here comes our Jack Dunning now."

Wyatt turned, and Penelope smiled as the investigator came to their table. They greeted each other politely before Dunning got to the point. "I stopped by your house again about one-thirty, two. I saw an old man sneaking around—the hermit, Bubba Johns."

So he already knew about Bubba. "Wyatt and I saw him, too. I expect he wanted to barter some maple sap. He does that sometimes."

"He comes to your house often?"

"Well, no, usually he does his bartering in town. With all the hoopla this week, maybe he wanted to avoid town." It was certainly possible, but not likely. Bubba's trips to town were well-planned, thorough and infrequent. He wouldn't just pop over to her house instead.

"You should lock your doors," Dunning said, "just in case."

She gave him a sharp look. "How do you know my doors weren't locked?"

"I tried them. The side door and the sliding-glass doors on the deck. I didn't go inside."

"I'd have caught you if you had."

His back remained ramrod straight, his gaze unflinching. "I expect I'd have scared you more than you'd have scared me. If it's convenient, I'd like to come by in the morning and have a look at your research into the Sinclair-Beaudine matter. Ten o'clock okay?"

Penelope glanced at Wyatt, but he was letting her handle his father's private detective by herself. She doubted Dunning would answer to his boss's son. She smiled. "Ten's fine. I hope you're not expecting professional research. I'm strictly an amateur."

"I'd like to see whatever you have." He smiled, but his eyes had gone cool, making his smile seem forced, even unpleasant. "Consider this my call in advance, Miss Chestnut."

She remembered their earlier conversation, but refused to let him intimidate her. "I'll have the coffee on."

Wyatt casually reached for the breadbasket. "I'll stop by, too. I'd like to have a look at Penelope's research myself." He glanced at Dunning, and Penelope sensed he was being deliberately irritating. "I'll bring the doughnuts."

The detective's eyes cooled even more. "You do that."

Penelope expected him to retreat to a table, but instead he left the Octagon Room. She tried to contain her relief. "Well, he's a barrel of laughs."

Wyatt spread a thin layer of butter on his bread. "Jack's a serious man, and he's being paid well for his efforts."

"Does that make him more determined than you or less?"

"His motives aren't mine. Neither are his methods. But I wouldn't underestimate his determination."

"Or yours?"

He smiled. "Never underestimate me, period. Penelope—if you want to tell me about Bubba and Harriet and what you found on Sunday, now's a good time. Jack doesn't believe your story any more than anyone else around here."

"I've told you everything," she said quickly, before she could change her mind. Acting on impulse with Wyatt Sinclair wasn't a smart idea. She'd decided on her story, and she'd stick to it until she'd examined all her options.

"You've told me everything you want to tell me. You haven't told me everything." His smile vanished, and his dark gaze was probing, searching. "Something has you scared."

"Scared? I don't think so. Stir-crazy because I can't fly, yes. Unnerved because I've got a Sinclair and a New York private investigator on my case, yes. Agitated because nobody believes me—sure. But I'm not scared." She sat back, almost believing herself. "Right now, I'm just hungry."

He sighed. "I wish I could wave a magic wand and make you trust me."

"Well, I wish I could wave a magic wand and make you go back to New York."

He laughed, and in spite of the tight spot she was in, Penelope laughed, too. Their dinners arrived, the trout fresh that day and beautifully prepared, and she and Wyatt ate and talked of other things. The work required to restore the inn, the plants she'd started for the inn and her deck overlooking the lake, the passion she had for flying. She tried to draw him out, but beyond agreeing he was lucky he had the kind of life that allowed him to take a few days off to skulk about the New Hampshire woods, he told her nothing about himself she hadn't already read in the papers or heard in local gossip. The man was on a mission, and everything he did and said was in service to that mission. Including kissing her. Including asking her to dinner. Soften up the prey. Then pounce.

She winced at her unfortunate analogy and started for her wallet, ready to get herself home before his strategy worked. He shook his head. "Let me pay for dinner. It was my idea. Otherwise you'd be having soup in front of the wood stove with Willard the moose."

"Willard never accused me of lying." She smiled. "Thanks for dinner. I've almost made it through the first day of my grounding."

"Glad I could help."

She ignored his amused undertone. "I'm sure I'll see you around."

The dark eyes sparked. "You won't be cleaning my room in the morning?"

"Very funny. If you decide to check out—"

"I won't."

"Then I won't see you until you and Mr. Dunning show up to look at my materials on Colt and Frannie. Unless I change my mind." She started across the dining room. "Don't forget the doughnuts."

She left him to pay and slipped down the hall, stopping in her tracks when she saw Harriet tucked in a candlelit booth in the bar with Jack Dunning. Her heart sank at her cousin's smitten look. There was no other word for it. Harriet was smiling dopily, her eyes doe-like, and Penelope wanted to march in there and shake her.

Of course, who'd been kissing a Sinclair out by the maple-sugaring fire?

She bit her tongue and continued on her way, trying to shake off the rush of doubts and questions and possible courses of action for herself. All she had to do was tell Wyatt and Dunning about the plane. They'd go off and find it, do whatever they needed to do and quit pestering her about lying. But they couldn't control the media, the attention that would focus on Bubba and Harriet. And what about the subtly threatening message on her computer?

Besides which, she didn't like the two New Yorkers' tactics. Jack Dunning was deliberately charming Harriet to get information out of her. If she felt comfortable, safe, *understood,* Harriet would tell him her theory about her birth parents. He might already know—he might not. But if he could use the information, or anything else she told him, to put the screws to Penelope, he would. She hated being so cynical, but she knew she was right.

She groaned. "Oh, Harriet. Why couldn't you fall for someone like Andy McNally?"

Because Harriet wanted her Scarlet Pimpernel, her Scaramouche, her D'Artagnan, her Spiderman. She didn't want a scarred widower with two daughters, a small-town guy she'd known all her life, any more than she wanted to be the child abandoned by some unknown teenager. She wanted to be Colt Sinclair and Frannie Beaudine's daughter.

Penelope gave herself a mental shake. Who was she to criticize Harriet?

As if to prove her point, Wyatt caught up with her outside. The light from the back door glowed softly, making his eyes seem blacker, but also less menacing, less as if he were a man who'd do anything to get his way. "I just wanted to make sure you know you can call me if your hermit shows up tonight."

"Bubba doesn't scare me."

"Okay. But you know where to find me."

She nodded. "Thanks."

He adjusted her scarf, letting one knuckle curve along her jaw, featherlight. "I'm not imagining things. I know something's not right with this whole plane story." She started to answer, but he touched her lips. "No, I'm not trying to put you on the spot. I just want you to trust me if you get to the point of feeling you're in over your head."

"I'm not—"

He smiled, cutting her off. "I know you're not. You're in command of the situation."

"I don't know about that. You're here. Jack Dunning's in there wooing Harriet. I'm not in command of much. But I'm not worried about spending the night alone in my cabin."

"Not even a little?"

"Nope. Frankly, I'd be a lot more worried about sleeping here."

He laughed, and when she laughed, too, his mouth found hers. She shut her eyes, soaking up the feel of his lips, the heat of a quick taste of tongue. She wondered if she should be less worried about Bubba and Harriet and threatening messages and more worried about her attraction to this man, this

Sinclair, with all his complexities and layers and built-in determination. All she wanted, right now, for the rest of the night, was his hands on her body, the chance to explore and taste and—

And you're crazy!

"I've got to go," she whispered. "Harriet, my mother—if they see us, ten to one I'll end up grounded from flying for a million years. Pop won't think I have a lick of sense left."

"Caught kissing a Sinclair in the parking lot. You'd have to be out of control." He eased one hand into her hair, kissed her again, hard, deep, fast. Then he stood back, winked with a mix of amusement and sexiness that would haunt her all night. "Question is, do you want to be out of control?"

"Wyatt—"

He shook his head, his gaze suddenly serious. "Just say good-night and thanks for dinner."

She nodded, her body quivering with a desire that rocked her to her core. "Good night. Thanks for dinner."

Her truck was cold, dark, so damned quiet. She flipped on the radio and headed out the winding main road, making the turns that took her to her dirt road, its squishy mud already hardening in the falling temperature. When she came to her house, she locked her truck and ran up the steps, imagining Bubba Johns lurking in the darkness, wondering if her judgment about him was wrong.

She locked her door behind her, made sure the sliding glass doors to the deck were locked. She ran around the house and flipped on all the lights, every one, even the one on the stove. She breathed, trying to relax. It was that kiss, of course. She *was* out of control.

Her tiny house was bright. Quiet. Light gleamed in Willard's glass eyes. She could never shoot a moose. Never. But here was a moose head mounted on her living room wall. Next she'd sprout bushy eyebrows and turn into her grandfather, an old curmudgeon who'd never discussed his relationship with the Sinclairs. He'd known Colt, he'd known Frannie Beaudine. He had steadfastly refused to expound on what he might know or surmise about their love affair, their personalities, their hopes and dreams. He'd say to people, "I don't know how that's going to help find their plane."

Whatever Sam Chestnut knew about Colt and Frannie went to the grave with him. His younger brother, the Reverend Mr. George Chestnut, had come out of his retirement in Florida to bury him. George's idea of recreation in the lakes region was more in tune with Penelope's—canoeing, kayaking, hiking, occasionally fishing. If her great-uncle had asked for the moose head, she would have given it to him.

She sighed heavily, still feeling restless, agitated. She unlocked the sliding glass doors and slipped onto the deck. The clouds were gathering over the still, snow-covered lake. She leaned over the rail, the cold seeping into her and the sounds of the night calming her. Yet she could feel, in a way she seldom let herself feel, how isolated and alone she was. She'd moved out here more or less on an impulse, another example of Penelope Chestnut operating on instinct, everyone in town thinking—telling her—she was crazy.

"And now," she whispered, "here you are."

An engine started. Up the road, down the road—she couldn't tell. She stood up straight, listening. Not in her driveway. Not that close. She went still, wondering if whoever was out there knew she was outside.

The engine didn't rev. It was as if the vehicle—car, truck, SUV—was trying to slip off quietly into the night without her noticing.

A spy?

She was getting paranoid.

But she shot inside without making a sound, locked the door behind her. She didn't have bars or bolts or fancy locks, nothing that would stop anyone determined to get in. She ran to the study, ducking low as she approached the window, then creeping up, peering into the night.

Half expecting someone in the window, she almost screamed at her own reflection. Running out of gas at five thousand feet she could handle. Things that go bump in the night, forget it.

She couldn't see the vehicle. She could hear it rolling down her dirt road, without lights, not fast, coasting.

Why? Why not turn on the lights and lay on the gas?

Was the driver deliberately trying to scare her? Trying to avoid being seen? Or just having car trouble?

What if he stopped past her house and snuck up for a peek in her windows?

"What ifs will drive you nuts," she warned herself.

For the first time in her memory, Penelope found

herself wishing simultaneously for good locks, a gun and maybe even a man she trusted. For all she knew, that could be Wyatt on her road. But she didn't think it was.

She gave herself fifteen minutes to calm down. This was no time to go crying wolf. When the fifteen minutes passed and her heart was still pounding, her hands still shaking and clammy, she dialed Andy McNally at home. It was the most sensible course of action. They'd had their disagreements in the past, but he knew his daughters looked up to her—and he had a soft spot for Harriet. Plus, he was a responsible chief of police.

"Penelope? What's up? I was just heading over to the inn for a drink."

"I'm a little spooked, Andy." A lot spooked, but she was trying not to overdramatize. Andy had been saying for years that one of these days her zest for drama, in his words, was going to bite her in the ass. "Someone drove down my road without lights about fifteen minutes ago. I'm still spooked about it, even though I know it's probably kids or some straggling reporter—"

"I'll drive up there myself and have a look. Penelope—hell, this must be a first, but you even sound upset. You telling me everything?"

She didn't know if she should mention the weird e-mail message. It wasn't overtly threatening. It might not even be a police matter. She'd have Jack Dunning and Wyatt Sinclair down her throat about what she *really* found on Sunday. Not that she didn't already, but they didn't need more ammunition. And what if the message was their doing, to try to scare her? "Just drive by. If you see anything suspicious, let me know."

"Damned right I'll let you know. I'll be knocking on your door." He paused, going cop on her. "You sure there's nothing else?"

"Andy, if it was bad guys on my road, they could be doubling back here now with shotguns and knives—"

"Nah. They'd have already napalmed your place by now. Next time don't wait fifteen minutes before you call."

He hung up, and Penelope paced until, ten minutes later, he drove past her house and up the road, turned and drove back, tooting his horn.

The all clear.

Relieved, she went into the study and turned on her computer to check her e-mail. She noticed a paper in her fax machine, and as she pulled it out, she automatically looked for the ID line at the top. There was none. That was illegal, though perhaps an oversight if one of her friends had just bought a fax machine, an unlikely event.

The message was one line, in a large, easy-to-read font.

Don't show anyone what you really found in the woods.

Her hands shook. Her stomach lurched. She crumpled the fax and threw it against the wall and dialed the inn's number. Harriet picked up. Penelope fought an urge to jump up and tear out of her house. "Harriet? It's me. Tell me—where are Jack Dunning and Wyatt Sinclair right now?"

"I have no idea. I don't keep tabs on my guests."

"Don't tell me you're not keeping tabs on these particular guests. Please, Harriet. I need to know."

"You sound awful. What's wrong?"

"Nothing's wrong. I just—I just have the feeling things are spinning out of control. Are they there?"

"No," Harriet said. "They went out after dinner. Separately. Jack first, then Wyatt. Jack said he was going to the airport to check on his plane. I don't know where Wyatt was going."

Penelope bent and picked up the crumpled fax. Neither Wyatt Sinclair nor Jack Dunning had made any pretense they believed she was lying about Colt and Frannie's plane. How low would they stoop to get her to change her story? Like the instant message, the fax wasn't overtly threatening. Probably Andy McNally would blame the national media coverage and tell her to forget it, let the dust settle. Without an actual threat, there was probably little he could do.

"Penelope?"

She could hear the concern in her cousin's voice. "Thanks, Harriet. I'm just tired. It's been a long day. I'll see you tomorrow."

"Call me if you need me."

Penelope smiled. She could always count on Harriet. After they'd hung up, she folded the fax into a tiny square and stuck it in her lingerie drawer. Was Bubba Johns capable of sending a fax? She shook off the question, shook off *all* her questions and fixed herself a cup of lemon chamomile tea. She drank it sprawled on the couch with a fleece blanket pulled to her chin and Willard, silent and composed, on the wall, as she had countless times as a kid on a rainy day with her grandfather puttering around his small cabin. The wind had picked up, and she listened to the trees creak and groan. She thought about a Sinclair and a Sinclair investigator on the loose in her dark, quiet little town, and she wondered if she could trust both of them, one or neither.

"Neither, if you're smart," she said.

And she thought it was a hell of a life she lived, in an old man's lakeside cabin with no one to talk to but a dead moose.

NINE

Wet, fat snowflakes covered the roads and fields and clung to power lines and tree branches. Penelope's windshield wipers turned the snow to ice as she drove out her dirt road, wishing whoever had spied on her last night had gotten stuck in the deep ruts. She almost did, even with four-wheel drive. She stopped at the airport en route to town and found her father up to his elbows in engine parts.

"Your mother wants me to keep you busy," he said. "She thinks you'll get into less trouble here than at home. It's the lesser of two evils."

"Does that mean I can fly?"

"It means you don't have to cool your heels at home, you can come in and sweep, wash planes, help your aunt in the office—"

"I can't this morning," she said, as if she were her own boss. "Wyatt Sinclair and this Dunning character are coming to my place at ten to check out my research into Colt and Frannie. If I'm not around, I have a feeling they'll help themselves."

Her father nodded, climbing heavily to his feet. "You probably have a point there. It won't be any comfort to your mother." Little was, and they both knew it. "I won't mention this meeting to her. Just don't make the mistake of thinking you can handle those two."

By "handle" Penelope suspected he meant "lie to." She adjusted the sleeve of her anorak. She'd pulled it on over a fleece shirt, along with jeans and her day hikers. It was March, and she refused to wear a hat and gloves if she was driving around town. She told her father, "It's not as if Colt and Frannie disappeared yesterday. They've been gone for forty-five years. Wyatt wasn't even born yet, and Jack Dunning—why would he care?"

"It's his job to care. And Wyatt—"

"I know, I know. He's a Sinclair, and that explains it all."

Her father grabbed an old rag and wiped his greasy hands, studying his only child in a manner that made her think he really could read her mind. "I know all the media attention caught you by surprise—I know you worry about Harriet. You wouldn't want her ending up in the tabloids, a laughingstock." When she started to protest, he held up a hand. "Harriet's stronger than you think. She can take care of herself. You just do the right thing."

"I'm trying to do the right thing, Pop. What about Bubba Johns? Is it right his life should be turned upside down and inside out? Reporters were already tramping around on my land. It was only a matter of time before they found him."

"Reporters aren't your worst problem—or Bubba's. Wyatt Sinclair and Jack Dunning are, and they aren't going anywhere until they're satisfied you're telling the truth." He tossed the rag onto the floor. "You might think about that."

She'd thought of little else all night. She shoved

her hands in her pockets. It was chilly in the hangar, and the snow hadn't let up. Grounded or not grounded, she wouldn't be flying today. "Pop, if you were me and you *had* found Colt and Frannie's plane, would you come clean?"

He shrugged. "I'd do what I thought was right. I wouldn't let Sinclair and Dunning intimidate me—but I wouldn't let fretting about Harriet and that old hermit influence me, either."

"Then on what grounds do you decide what's right?"

"Your own grounds," her father said simply.

Penelope nodded. "Of course, this is all theoretical."

"Right. You didn't find the plane."

On her way out, she stopped at the office to say hello to her aunt, who was griping about the weather as if it never snowed in March. The office was small, cluttered and purely functional. Her aunt didn't even keep a picture of her family or a vase of flowers on her desk.

Penelope asked her about Jack Dunning's plane, and that perked her up. "It's his personal plane," Mary said. "It doesn't belong to the Sinclairs. What a beauty it is, too. You should peek inside—it's a custom interior."

"I might just do that. Aunt Mary, what're you doing?"

"Oh—I'm programming my fax machine. It was a mess this morning. Must have had a power surge or something, I don't know. I've had to input our identification. It's a pain. I'm almost done."

Penelope twisted her hands together and stifled an urge to pounce on her aunt's fax machine, trying instead to stay calm and not jump to conclusions. "Did anyone break in last night? Did you let someone use the fax machine yesterday? Jack Dunning came by after dinner to check on his plane. I'll bet he's good with locks. He could have broken in and—"

She stopped abruptly, but her aunt prodded her. "And what? Penelope, people don't break into offices to use a fax machine. That's insane."

"Did you forget to lock up last night?"

"I didn't do the locking up. Your father did. When I got in this morning, everything was perfectly normal. I'd have Andy McNally up here if there had been any sign of a break-in."

She frowned at her niece, her hands on her hips, suspicion etched in every line and feature of her round face. Aunt Mary had four kids of her own, all older than Penelope, all convinced she'd give their mother a heart attack one of these days. Yet they understood the special affection their mother and cousin had for each other, never mind that it was tried on a near-daily basis.

"Honestly, Penelope," Mary Chestnut Feeney said. "You've been grounded for one day and you're already acting crazy. This is an old machine. Sometimes it goes haywire. That's all there is to it. For heaven's sake, if you want excitement, I'd hope you find it somewhere besides a fax machine on the blink!"

Penelope smiled lamely. "You're right, Aunt Mary."

"It's having these two New Yorkers in town. Harriet told me they're watching you like hawks, thinking you found that plane on Sunday. I'll bet they think you've looted it or you're planning to write a book—"

"They can think what they want to think. Look, I just wanted to pop in and say hello. See you later. Don't mention this fax machine thing to Pop, okay?"

"As if I would. I tell him this one, and I'll be lucky he doesn't fire me for talking him into grounding you for three weeks instead of four."

"Pop can't fire you. You're partners."

"Like you, Miss Hot Shot, he can find a way to get done what he wants to get done."

Before she could paint herself firmly into a corner, Penelope made her exit. She drove straight to town and bought a jigsaw puzzle, milk, juice and bullets for her grandfather's rifle. If common decency didn't keep a New York Sinclair and a private investigator at bay, maybe a loaded gun in the kitchen would.

Wyatt arrived at her cabin first. He tossed his leather jacket over the back of a kitchen chair, his dark gaze taking in her birds of the northeast puzzle and her Winchester leaned against the table. She hadn't loaded it yet. She said, "That's my grandfather's old rifle. He taught me how to shoot."

He ran a finger over her new box of cartridges. "When's the last time you loaded this thing?"

"About a year ago. We had a convicted murderer escape from the state prison. It can get creepy living out here, especially in the winter. There are more people around in the summer." She dumped scoops of coffee—regular Colombian coffee—into a filter. "I don't hunt, but I like to keep up my shooting skills. Figured I'd do some target shooting while I'm grounded."

"And build a puzzle," Wyatt said.

"There's only so much shooting and sap boiling I can do. Television reception stinks out here, and I don't have a dish."

"I see."

Controlled, watchful, taking in everything around him. Penelope was afraid he did see. Wondering how obvious she was, she shoved the filter into the coffeemaker, poured in water and flipped it on.

"I think I'll get the sap boiling again while you two look over my research materials. I hope you're not expecting a smoking gun—it's mostly old newspaper articles and transcripts of interviews I had with people around town who remember Colt and Frannie or helped search for their plane. I have the original cassettes, too, if you want to listen to them." She glanced at him, cool. "Of course, you already know that from your little look-see last night."

Jack Dunning arrived, not looking like someone who relished digging through research materials, but Penelope supposed the job of private investigator involved plenty of dull, routine work. She sat the two of them down at the kitchen table, where she'd stacked all her materials. She removed her rifle to the study. Dunning hadn't commented on it, and she wondered if the only point she'd made was that she was a lunatic. She set the cartridges on the kitchen counter and got her canner of sap bubbling, the steam and sweet maple smells soothing her nerves, making the place seem cozier, as if the two men at her table were playing cards or clipping coupons, not trying to catch her in a lie.

Twice she almost told them to strap on snowshoes and she'd take them to what was left of Colt and Frannie's Piper Cub J-3. Just get it over with. What had seemed the right thing to do on Tuesday no longer was clearly so right on Thursday.

But she resisted—if only because the two men at her kitchen table were so obviously *not* interested in her research materials. Jack was there to scope her out, Wyatt to scope out her and Jack. Newspaper articles from the 1950s and interviews with old people weren't going to do them any good. She was the one who'd found the long-missing plane. They were the ones looking for it.

As she busily stirred the syrup—it was looking like syrup now—and washed canning jars, Penelope speculated about what Jack knew that Wyatt didn't know and vice versa. Or what each *thought* the other knew, whether in fact he did or didn't.

She frowned. She was getting way ahead of herself. They could just be two frustrated men stumbling their way through a problem not of their own making. They suspected her of lying, and they were trying to get her to feel comfortable enough to change her story back again.

Which didn't explain the fax. Maybe she should ask them who'd messed with Aunt Mary's fax machine.

Jack Dunning sat her at the table and asked her several questions about interviews she'd conducted. Then, calmly, he asked her about several glaring omissions. "You didn't interview your father, your aunt or your grandfather. The newspaper articles indicate they were all actively involved in the search efforts, particularly your grandfather."

"I didn't get started on the interviews until he was sick. As for my father and Aunt Mary—I haven't asked."

The flat, almost colorless eyes narrowed on her. "Why not?"

"Family protocol, I guess. They know about the interviews. If they want to participate, they'll say so. Now that I have three weeks to kill, I might make it clear that even if they don't think they have anything to offer, I'd like to get their perspective."

"Going to write a book?"

Maybe Aunt Mary had been on to something. "No."

She glanced at Wyatt, saw he was absorbed in a transcript of Uncle George's memories of those first weeks after Colt and Frannie's disappearance. Her uncle had been careful, she recalled, not to say too much about the baby he'd found in the apple basket on the church doorstep. Penelope hadn't asked, but she assumed he didn't want to draw any more attention to the unsettling coincidence of Colt and Frannie's ill-fated flight and the mysterious appearance of an infant.

"This dump you say you found," Jack Dunning said, segueing into the subject that really interested him. "Would there be any record of it?"

Penelope shook her head. "It'd just be stuff an old farmer hauled off into the woods from time to time."

"Then why isn't it on a trail or old logging road?"

"I don't know. When I was a kid, I used to pick through some of the old dumps in the woods for bottles. I had a collection."

"But you never ran across this dump before?"

"Not that I recall."

He got to his feet, his gaze more amused than challenging, as if he really didn't care if she lied to him or not. Either way, he'd get to the truth. "It's been interesting. Thanks for your time."

"You're welcome. Will you report to Mr. Sinclair today and head home?"

He smiled. "Not yet."

Penelope followed him to the door and shut it hard behind him, then spun around to Wyatt. "Why doesn't he give up and go back to New York?"

"Same reason I don't."

"Because you're both waiting for me to miraculously drop Colt and Frannie's Piper Cub in your laps." She groaned, frustrated, the thought of the fax folded in her underwear drawer and the car outside her house last night interfering with her thinking, her mood. So was being alone with Sinclair. "Can't you fire him?"

"He's not my employee." Wyatt brought his and Jack's mugs to the sink, checked the bubbling syrup. Without looking at her, he said, "I want to know what's going on here, Penelope—and I'm not talking about Colt and Frannie's plane. I'm already fairly confident you found it."

"Then what are you talking about?"

He stirred the syrup with a long-handled wooden spoon. "You didn't buy ammo and clean the Winchester because I came on a little strong."

She said nothing. She stood in the middle of her kitchen, watching Wyatt stir her syrup. Her life wasn't spinning out of control. It had already spun.

"Penelope..." His voice was low and seductive, but not patient. "Something's going on."

"Nothing may be going on. I just—" She plopped on the chair he'd vacated, her Colt and Frannie materials neatly stacked around her. When she'd started, she'd fantasized about discovering their fate. She'd fantasized about meeting her first Sinclair. It just wasn't Wyatt she'd expected. She shut her eyes briefly, tried to calculate the consequences of giving in to her impulse to tell him everything, then blurted, "I've been receiving unsettling messages. They're more odd than anything else. One came by an instant message while I was on-line, the other by fax. And last night someone spied on me. I think. I'm not positive. It could have been kids."

"One at a time. Stick to the basics. When, what, where, how. The why is fairly obvious. You said you found a famous missing plane and then said you didn't."

"Yes, but this guy's motive...I don't know."

"The instant message came first?" When she nodded, he said, "Tell me about it."

His tone was encouraging and even tender, not the least bit dictatorial. But his eyes—those black, incisive Sinclair eyes—gave him away. Inside, she knew, he was pulsating with the urge to take her by the shoulders and shake the information out of her, syllable by syllable if necessary. It was just the warning she needed. Wanting to slip inside this man's soul for a look around was crazy and dangerous— like doing a preflight check, discovering mechanical problems and going up anyway, even when she knew the plane wasn't airworthy. Some things you just didn't do.

But she told him about the instant message, the fax, the car. She focused on the facts and didn't mention flipping on lights and ducking under windows and sleeping on the couch. Fear had always been a private issue for her. When search parties had found her, when Andy McNally had pulled her out of the lake, she'd never admitted her terror.

When she finished, Wyatt set the spoon down and returned to the table. The snow was piling up outside her cabin. March snows were often wet and deep, but not long-lasting. Penelope imagined her deck brimming with summer pots of flowers, herbs, tomatoes. Everything changed. Nothing lasted forever.

She said, "You should know I'm not operating under the assumption that you're not responsible. I don't think either you or Jack Dunning has an ironclad alibi, should I report these incidents to the police. You both have motives for wanting to spook me into showing you the dump—or the plane, seeing how you both think I lied."

His jaw was set tight, controlled. "Fair enough. But we're hardly alone in thinking you changed your story."

"Who else cares about finding the plane? You care because Colt's your uncle. Jack cares because it's his job."

"Frannie's from Cold Spring, and she and Colt most likely went down in this vicinity. There could be parties unknown with motives unknown who want to manipulate you. The fax said *not* to show anyone what you found in the woods."

"That could be reverse psychology."

"It could be a lot of things. You still have it?"

She nodded. "I'll get it."

With sudden energy, she shot up from the table, but stopped halfway to her bedroom. She turned, saw he was watching her. She forced herself to concentrate. "Aunt Mary's fax machine was messed up this morning."

The black eyes showed no emotion. "And you think it was our mad faxer?"

"Why not? He could have snuck in last night and popped off the fax to me. There was no sign of a break-in, but he could have had a key, stolen a key, picked the lock, snuck in when Pop and Aunt Mary weren't looking. The airport office isn't exactly Fort Knox."

"He—or she—could have seized the moment."

"Right. I know it's hard to swallow, but so's a threat by fax. I suppose whoever sent it could have used his own machine and messed up Aunt Mary's just so I'd think it came from hers. But that's getting labyrinthine."

Wyatt thought a moment. "It's always possible your aunt messed up her fax machine without any help."

"I guess. A few years ago, you could count the number of fax machines in town on one hand. Now, I wouldn't be surprised if Bubba Johns had one." Before Wyatt could jump in, she added, "And no, I don't suspect him."

She darted into her bedroom, located the fax, returned to the kitchen, and handed it to Wyatt. While she paced, he unfolded it, read it, and pinned his gaze on her.

"You should have Jack take a look at this. He's an experienced investigator. My father wouldn't have him on retainer if he weren't discreet."

Penelope shook her head. "I think this is a case of the more you stir it, the more it stinks. There's no overt threat. It could be a reporter trying to goad me into changing my story—it could be Jack Dunning for all I know, or you, or some idiot relative of mine having a laugh at my expense. Look, I've already had a search party formed to come after me, turned an old dump into a plane wreck and got myself grounded. This time I'm looking before I leap."

Wyatt smiled. "You do have a reputation for putting people around here through their paces. But what do you believe right now? What do your instincts tell you?"

Her instincts had already told her not to get into an alliance with this man, and a fat lot of good that had done her. "My instincts told me to get out Granddad's Winchester and buy bullets. Just in case."

"You could move in with your folks for a few days," Wyatt suggested, "or take a room at the inn with your cousin."

"Are you kidding? I'd never live it down. You just said you know my reputation. Something happens in Cold Spring, New Hampshire, people look around to see where I am. They're still ticked about the search party the other night."

"That shouldn't matter—"

"It *does* matter."

"You don't strike me as the type to worry about what other people think."

"I have to live in this town. I don't get to go back to a life of anonymity in New York." She snatched up her wooden spoon and stirred the syrup, smelling the maple, feeling the steam on her face. It was almost time to pour it into a smaller pot. "This is my house, and I'm staying here."

"At least get a friend to stay with you."

His tone was neutral, but he joined her at the stove, standing close, and she could feel the fear welling up, her uneasiness about him, her attraction to him. A swirl of conflicting questions and emotions had her head spinning. Outside, the wind was gusting off the frozen lake, whipping icy snow against her cabin windows.

She kept stirring the syrup. It still had a ways to go. If she cooked it too much, it would crystallize. "I'm just trying to make the best decisions I can and not give in."

"Not give in to what?"

"I've always been restless, I've always needed a lot going on in my life—the adrenaline, the excitement. I do impulsive things. I get distracted and forget what I'm doing and—and..."

"And pretty soon you're lost in the woods or plunging through thin ice."

"But I'm *capable*," she said. "I know what I'm doing. I don't need to be hovered over and protected. I'm not an idiot, and I'm not reckless. And damn it, it's not that I'm looking for drama, that I need that kind of rush."

He smiled, and this time it reached his eyes. "You sound like a Sinclair."

She grinned. "Horrors. But Sinclairs aren't hovered over and protected and told they should just sit home. Not the men, at least."

"No, we die prematurely instead. Or others die in our place."

She remembered his friend, the awful circumstances of his death. A fall, bad weather, no help. Accomplished hikers, he and Wyatt had underestimated the Tasmanian mountains, the potential for extreme changes in climate, and their hubris had cost Hal his life. Penelope could only speculate about the effects of Wyatt's ordeal—his guilt—on him. His experience could have colored his move to New York, his decision to come to New Hampshire, his reaction to her messages and the idea of someone spying on her. It could even muddy how he saw her. If he saw in her the same qualities that in him had led to tragedy, he could go all self-controlled and distant and fight any attraction to her—or he could want her all the more. Either way, he was looking at her through a clouded lens, not seeing her for who she was.

Of course, she was doing the same to him. He was a Sinclair, and she knew Sinclairs. She sighed, wishing she could stop trying to sort everything out. "I suppose I should keep in mind that you Sinclairs are human beings, not just the sum of my prejudices. We have ideas about you here because of the past. In any case, I've hardly had the kind of adventures you've had—I've just had to be pulled out of the lake a few times too many."

"You get in over your head."

"At times. We all do. I'm not now," she added quickly, and if he'd asked, she couldn't have told him if she meant in over her head with him or with the story she'd told about Frannie Beaudine and Colt Sinclair. But he didn't ask, and his mouth found hers as he brushed the tips of his fingers along her jaw and into her hair until she thought she'd melt right into the sap pot.

She moaned softly, their kiss deepening, his arms around her, drawing her against him. He was all hard muscles and warm, soft fabric, and when his hands slipped under her shirt, she could have crawled right inside him.

But he drew back, said, "We all get in over our heads from time to time. The trick is to know when we need help and when we're just having fun, pushing the envelope but still in control."

She didn't feel in control at all. Her nerve endings were on fire, and she had no clear notion of whether the kiss was to prove a point or—or just a kiss. With a quick tug on her shirt, she got the spaghetti pot from a low cupboard. "I think I should strain the syrup once more when I switch pots."

"Sounds like a plan."

She glanced at him. "What're you going to do?"

"Poke around, talk to Jack."

"You won't tell him about the messages—"

He shook his head. "Not my place. But I think you should at least tell your parents, your aunt Mary—someone besides me. I'm an outsider, an automatic suspect." He walked to the table, and if he was experiencing any residual effects of their kiss, they weren't apparent. He pulled his leather jacket off the back of the chair. "If this thing escalates, you'll want someone on your side you can trust and who trusts you without question."

She smiled through her sudden uneasiness. "That wouldn't be you, huh?"

"Honey, we both know I don't trust you." He opened the side door. The wind was howling, but the snow was subsiding. "However, you can trust me."

"I don't know that."

He grinned. "But I do. That syrup will be ready

later? I'll come back. I make great pancakes, you know."

"I can see how you ended up scaling tall mountains. You just don't give up."

"Something to remember while the snow flies and the sap boils."

Harriet was surprised anyone showed up at the inn on such a miserable day, much less Andy McNally. He brought Rebecca and Jane for afternoon tea—an hour early. They'd been let out of school because of the storm, and Andy had a meeting at three. "You can heat up yesterday's scones if you don't have any fresh."

"I just pulled apricot scones from the oven."

He grinned at his daughters. "Didn't I tell you we could count on Harriet?"

They ordered scones and individual pots of English Breakfast tea, and the girls asked Harriet to join them. She did, gladly. Andy wasn't fond of tea, and scones he could take or leave. The girls, who both favored their mother, loved the elegance and indulgence of afternoon tea and would often stop by on their own when they didn't have after-school activities or some adventure scheduled with Penelope.

"Anything from your cousin today?" Andy asked.

"No, I haven't seen her."

He'd told Harriet about the false alarm last night. She reminded him that he should be relieved, not annoyed. One, because he found nothing. Two, because Penelope had had the sense to call him instead of charging out into the night herself.

Rebecca, a junior in high school, said, "The sap won't be running today. It's too cold."

Her father grunted. "Just what we need, Penelope with too much time on her hands."

"Lyman's not going to rescind her three-week grounding—"

"No. God forbid. The only thing worse than Penelope with time on her hands is Penelope distracted in an airplane."

Jane, a freshman, giggled. "Oh, Daddy, you're so hard on her!"

"She's hard on us. Now drink your tea and let me talk."

"We're right here. It's not as if we can turn our ears off—"

Andy silenced her with a quick look, then turned to Harriet. "Smart alecks, both of them. It's Penelope's influence. But—they can hold their own and think for themselves. I guess she's been a help there, too. Look, I'll be straight with you, Harriet. I'm worried about her."

Harriet nodded, pouring tea, which she liked dark and strong with just a drop of cream. "I know. We all are."

"Why doesn't she just say she found that goddamned plane and be done with it?"

"Because she's stubborn and because she can't control the consequences."

"What consequences? It wasn't any of her relatives in that plane. Besides, the thing's been missing for forty-five years. Except for the Sinclair family, who cares? Frannie Beaudine doesn't even have any family left."

"There might be other, less direct, unintended consequences."

Andy frowned. He was a concrete man with a good, incisive mind, but he lacked imagination and had a cop's reluctance to charge too far ahead of the facts. "Such as?"

"Well...the reporters. Many of them checked in here at the inn, and it wouldn't have been long before they heard about Bubba Johns and—and me."

"You? What the hell—oh." His mouth snapped shut, and he quickly buttered a scone. "You mean your notion—your claim—"

"It's neither a notion nor a claim, Andy. It's a hypothesis."

Harriet sipped her tea, welcoming the heat. She was sounding so much more controlled and sensible than she felt. Most people in Cold Spring, she knew, considered her hypothesis kooky. She couldn't blame them. She felt kooky. Her. Sensible, plain Harriet Chestnut. She'd applied makeup twice already today, scrubbing it off each time, feeling ridiculous. Jack Dunning had left early and hadn't returned. Silly to think she could interest such a man. She felt like Rebecca and Jane with their high school crushes.

"And Bubba," Andy said, awkwardly changing the subject. "What's he got to do with anything?"

"Oh, you know Penelope. She'd hate to see an old hermit's life disrupted because of something she did."

"She didn't do anything. She found a missing plane. Now *her* life's being disrupted—she's got Wyatt Sinclair and a PI on her case." He bit off a hunk of scone, and out of the corner of one eye, Harriet saw Rebecca wince at her father's lack of delicacy. He might have been eating a pastrami sandwich. "If those two do anything against the law to get her to talk, I'm nailing their hides to the wall."

Harriet paled. "They both strike me as professional and quite decent. I can't imagine either would harass Penelope..." She stopped, aware of Andy's sharp gaze on her. She added quickly, "That's just my impression."

"Don't let what you want to be cloud your view of what is, Harriet."

She noticed the girls studiously drinking their tea, pretending not to be listening. "Just you do the same, Andy."

His easy grin caught her off guard. "I'm a cop. I'm always looking for the dark side."

He turned to his daughters, and they changed the subject, luring Harriet into a discussion of their various teachers, many of whom she'd known since childhood.

After the McNally family left, Harriet did paperwork in front of the parlor fire. She found herself listening for the door, anticipating Jack Dunning or Wyatt Sinclair's return. Finally, she gave up all pretense of concentrating and stared at the orange flames. Wyatt could be her cousin, her blood. He was so rich, so accomplished, so self-controlled—so much of what she wasn't. It gave her hope, just thinking they might be related.

And Jack Dunning...she almost didn't dare picture him. It had been years and years since she'd had such a blatant, intense crush on a man. Maybe never. He was good-looking, sexy, charming and surprisingly kind. They'd sat up last night, drinking wine and talking about the inn, Cold Spring, the lake. He hadn't pried into her family or asked a single question about Penelope. Certainly he hadn't mentioned the tantalizing coincidence of her arrival on her father's church doorstep and the disappearance of Frannie Beaudine and Colt Sinclair. He had to know about it.

"Harriet—I thought I saw you in here."

His voice. She jumped, papers flying off her lap. "Oh! Jack, hello. I was just doing some work."

"Sorry to interrupt."

"Oh, no—no, you're not interrupting."

He squatted, picked up the papers and returned them to her clipboard. He smiled, eased effortlessly up. "The snow's stopped. I thought you might like to take a short walk, unless you're busy."

"I'm not busy. With the weather, it'll be a slow night."

She got to her feet, feeling a fat lock of hair fall loose from its bobby pin. She wished she'd tried again with her makeup. As she held her clipboard against her chest, she noticed the nicks and scars in her hands from years of remodeling the inn. She could feel the extra pounds around her middle, imagined the kind of women Jack would attract in New York. She was a plain, middle-aged New Englander without style or sex appeal.

Self-delusion, she thought, had never been one of her faults.

But she found herself tucking her hair behind her ear and smiling. "I'd love a walk, if we can be back in a half hour."

"A half hour it is."

"Did you see Penelope this morning?"

"Yep." He grinned, shrugged. "I won't mince words, Harriet. The woman's a pain in the ass."

She laughed. "Yes, but she's *our* pain in the ass."

"I love how you people think. When I was acting up, my daddy'd give me a cuff to the ear and that'd straighten me out. If it didn't, there'd be more where that came from."

"Oh, my. What a difficult way to grow up!"

He shook his head, grinning in amazement. "It was a great way to grow up. I knew my limits. Your cousin, in case you haven't noticed, has no idea of hers."

"But isn't that to the good?"

"Everyone has limits, Harriet, even Penelope Chestnut."

She bit back another laugh, feeling almost giddy at his openness, his irreverence. Nothing bothered him. "You won't tell her, will you?"

"Not a chance. Shall we?"

TEN

Penelope breathed in the clean, cold air. She could smell a hint of smoke from Bubba Johns's wood stove. His shack was just ahead through the woods, around a bend and down a gently sloping hill. After finishing the syrup and shoveling her driveway, she'd strapped on her snowshoes and headed through the freshly fallen snow. Hers were traditional wooden bear paw snowshoes, a gift from her grandfather when she was in college, and although the snow was wet and fairly compacted, the going was still tough. In hard, out easy. That was the old saying. She could follow her tracks on the way back.

There was no marker indicating she'd crossed onto Sinclair land, no thick black line, no No Trespassing signs. She knew only because she was familiar with the boundaries of her own land. When the old logging road went through a gap in a stone wall, she knew she had left her land. The road narrowed to a footpath, and the stone walls that had once marked off farmland, long overgrown, gradually disappeared. The forest thickened and darkened, the hills were steeper, and there was a greater sense that this was wild land, left to the deer and moose, the occasional bear and Bubba Johns.

Penelope spotted his crude, rustic one-room

shack, nestled amid pine and hemlock on a hillside above a sparkling, winding brook. The winds from the storm had subsided and the only sound was the water rushing over the rocks. The landscape, even the sky, was a soft white, broken only by touches of evergreen and the gray branches and trunks of leafless trees. The heavy, wet snow clung to the trees, weighing them down. A stand of thin gray birches bent almost to the ground.

The trail twisted along the top of the hill, then wound to Bubba's shack, a combination of logs, tar paper, plywood and tin. It had two small, mismatched windows he must have scavenged from cast-offs. He'd constructed a simple outhouse and a tiny garden shed, and he'd put up homemade bird feeders, dozens of them, in the trees, on poles, stuck to his windows. They were quiet, the birds waiting to make sure the storm was over.

On the opposite side of the shack was a small garden enclosed in chicken wire. Animals would be a major menace to gardens this far in the woods. Bubba Johns might not be entirely normal, but he'd fashioned a comfortable subsistence life for himself out here.

"Bubba?" The snow absorbed her voice, and she tried again, more loudly. "It's me, Penelope Chestnut."

No answer. Just the stillness, the steady flow of the brook.

She moved forward on the path. There were no other fresh tracks in the new snow. Her snowshoes had left clear, definite tracks that anyone could follow. She couldn't turn around and sneak home— Bubba would know she'd been here. She peeled off her hat, damp and frozen, the ends of her hair glistening and stiff from an icy drizzle early in her trek. She didn't have much time. It was already after four, a good hour's hike back to her place in these conditions.

Why had she come, anyway? To ask Bubba if she could tell Wyatt Sinclair the truth? To get his permission?

He'd never asked her to lie in the first place. She was the one who'd decided to change her story. She didn't even know Bubba. No one did. He was an old man who lived alone, nothing more—or less.

She stood in the silent, picturesque woods, imagined dozens of reporters and investigators, Colt and Frannie hobbyists, locals and sightseers rushing to the crash site to get the first pictures of the wreckage, the first trinkets from the famous, ill-fated flight. What if they photographed Colt and Frannie's remains, looted the wreckage, brought back stuff for auctions and tabloids? It was voyeuristic. Wrong. She thought of the tangled heap of metal tucked among the rocks, trees and brush. Undisturbed. Quiet. Peaceful. A grave.

Her father had talked to her about doing the right thing for the right reasons. Well, she had. The possible consequences for Bubba and Harriet were only part of her reasoning. There were also the consequences to the two people who'd died in that crash forty-five years ago.

Two scruffy mutts charged from the shadows toward her, barking and snarling. Penelope stood still, heart pounding. Should have brought Granddad's Winchester. But a voice from inside the shack hollered, "Back off!"

The dogs obeyed instantly, trotting to the shadows of the shack. Penelope felt her knees go out from under her, and if not for her steady, wide snowshoes, she'd have gone down. Dogs. She'd forgotten Bubba had dogs. They were old and didn't always travel with him, and he never brought them on his rare trips to town.

The old hermit emerged from the shack, pulling stretchy suspenders over a frayed brown plaid flannel shirt. His gray and white hair stuck out, and his beard hung to his chest, untrimmed, not particularly clean. He wore black boots with buckles from her grandfather's era. Maybe they'd even been her granddad's boots. Bubba Johns wasn't known for his vanity.

His gray eyes leveled on her. "What do you want?"

"I was just—I was out walking—" She took a breath, reminding herself she had no reason to fear this man. She was young, strong, fast. Even if he did go wild on her, she could defend herself. If she had to, she'd take a rock to the dogs. "I was lost on Sunday. I think you saw me. At the plane wreckage."

He was silent, eyeing her. He was a tall, rail-thin man. His gray eyes seemed even frostier in the March landscape.

Penelope didn't back down. "You know about the wreckage. You know I found it. You were out there—you came to my house yesterday."

"What of it? Your business doesn't concern me."

"I wanted to tell you that I changed my mind and withdrew my story about finding the wreckage. I don't know what you know about it, but it's a famous wreck—it's been missing for forty-five years.

The two people who died in it—'' She stopped mid-sentence, frowned at his obvious disinterest. ''Well, I guess I decided to let them rest in peace. I realized what it'd be like for you, having people crawling through the woods.''

''There's a plane out there?''

She sighed. Maybe this was how Wyatt and Dunning felt talking to her. ''Yes. I saw it on Sunday when I was lost in the woods.''

No reaction. He stared at her without expression.

''If anything in the wreckage has been disturbed in any way—if dogs dragged off the bodies or someone looted their belongings and kept quiet about it—the media and the authorities would be all over you. You'd be their prime suspect, at least at first.''

''Is this what you came to tell me?''

She nodded. ''I thought you might be worried.''

''I don't care about any plane wreckage. I can leave here if people come.''

''Leave?''

He shrugged, matter-of-fact. ''I don't have much. The dogs and I can pack up and go anytime.''

''But you've lived out here for years. You shouldn't have to—''

He cut her off. ''Anything else you want to say?''

''Wyatt Sinclair's in town. His family owns this land. I don't think he'll bother you. But I thought you should know.''

Bubba didn't seem interested. ''Okay.''

He turned and started toward his shack. Penelope felt dismissed. But she said to his retreating figure, ''Bubba, that *was* you in the woods on Sunday, wasn't it?''

He didn't answer. She didn't know if he hadn't

heard her—he was an old man—or if he was ignoring her. She pushed back a wave of queasiness and turned, suddenly eager for pancakes, ham and hot syrup. She'd eat salads tomorrow. Her second day of grounding, snow, a suspicious PI and a Sinclair in her kitchen—kissing a Sinclair. She deserved to indulge.

She waited for Bubba Johns to change his mind and come back and chat with her a while longer, explain when he'd found the plane, how, why he'd never mentioned it to anyone. But he said something to his dogs, and they all went inside his shack. He shut the door.

Dismissed.

Reminding herself their conversation had gone better than she'd expected, Penelope pulled her hat on and followed her packed tracks along the ridge, and down, then over a low rise, moving fast, getting her rhythm and more flotation than on the way in.

The path widened, and as she made her way down the last steep hill, she stopped and listened, uncertain what had put her on alert. A soft breeze stirred, whistling in the trees, bare branches clicking. She stood very still, aware of how alone she was. Twisting from her waist to one side and then the other, she managed to do a three-hundred-sixty-degree scan of her surroundings.

A distinct movement several yards behind her. A shuffling sound in the snow, detectable only because she'd held her breath. It wasn't an animal. She couldn't explain why, but she knew it was human. Someone was out there in the trees and freshly fallen snow, watching her. She glanced around for tracks but saw only her own.

Had someone followed her to Bubba's shack?

Was Bubba spying on her?

She shuddered at the possibilities and used the jolt of fear to propel her through the snow.

She moved as quickly as she could on her snowshoes, careful not to lose her balance or go head-over-teakettle or run out of steam. When she got to her land, she broke into a trot, pushing herself hard and fast, sucking in the cold air, her lungs burning, her face numb, her legs dead.

She was running when she reached her dirt road, and Wyatt was there, standing in the shadows of a thick maple. She accosted him feeling wild, out of control. "Have you been following me? Damn you, Sinclair! I hate being spied on. I *hate* sneaky men. If you've got something you want from me, you say so. You don't goddamned do an underhanded, slippery thing like that."

"Penelope, stop." His voice was calm, serious. "I just got here. I saw your tracks and thought I might catch up with you. Which I did."

"You didn't follow me?"

"No."

"Then who—" She took in shallow breaths, panting from her mad race through the woods. "Do you see other tracks? Is Jack Dunning's car here? Did you see it down the road anywhere?" She stopped herself, peeled off her hat and gloves and shoved them in her anorak pockets. God, she needed to get a decent breath! She could feel Wyatt's dark gaze on her, probing, assessing. She had to calm down. "I suppose it could have been anyone. Someone else on snowshoes, enjoying the fresh snow."

Wyatt watched her silently as she unstrapped her

snowshoes, clogged with wet, icy snow. Her fingers, shaking and stiff, had turned red with the cold, and if she'd had her jackknife, she'd have hacked off the damned bindings.

She looked at Sinclair. "Well? Aren't you going to demand answers?"

"There are no other tracks here. Just yours."

"So you think I'm jumpy enough I made up someone following me?"

"I don't know. Did you?"

She kicked off one snowshoe, then the other, and picked them up. She had to be a mess. Red face, runny nose, ice in her hair, wild-eyed. But she nodded, certain. "Yes. Someone was out there. I'm sure of it. But I'm not positive I was actually being followed."

He tilted his head, no snow in his dark hair, no wildness in his dark eyes. He was steady, controlled, not even breathing hard. His mouth was straight, neither smiling nor unsmiling.

In two seconds, Penelope had had enough. "Okay, don't believe me. I don't give a damn. I'm sorry I ever let you get under my skin. I mean, it's not like I didn't know better. If you'll excuse me—"

He bit off a sigh, took her snowshoes from her and tucked them under one arm. "Okay. I believe you. You have no idea who followed you?"

She shook her head. Her teeth started to chatter. It was humiliating, but she couldn't stop them. She wasn't that cold. It was nerves. Fear. Running through the snowy woods like the demons of hell were after her. "I suppose I could have imagined the whole thing. My imagination is running amok these days. It was probably Bubba."

"But you don't know for sure."

Everything about him—his narrowed black eyes, his rigid stance, his self-control—served as a warning. She needed to remember he was a man of determination and energy, that even his obvious physical attraction to her would not deter him from his mission.

Penelope attempted a smile, her heart rate slowly normalizing. "Right now I'd have to say I don't know much of anything for sure, except that homemade maple syrup hot off the stove sounds good to me."

Just the barest ghost of a smile. "Maybe it's a truth serum."

"Watch out. That's a sword that cuts two ways."

Wyatt might have gotten all kinds of things out of Penelope if her parents hadn't descended on them within minutes of her turning on the heat under the syrup and dashing into her room to change. Nothing was going on, they said. They'd just stopped by to say hello. Wyatt didn't try to explain his presence in their daughter's house. When she emerged from her bedroom—in dry clothes and remarkably calm—she gave them a bright smile and invited them to stay for pancakes. "I'll just double the recipe."

Wyatt wasn't fooled. Anything to avoid being alone with him. Robby Chestnut didn't look keen on the idea of pancakes, but Lyman accepted immediately. Four people in the front room were at least two people too many. Wyatt could feel the walls closing in on him. The three Chestnuts hovered over the boiling syrup, debating its grade and quality, and Penelope got down dented measuring cups and spoons, a mixing bowl from the thirties, a chipped crockery of flour, and pretty soon she was spooning pancake batter onto an ancient griddle, and her father was frying ham in a cast-iron pan.

As she laid mismatched plates on the kitchen table, Robby gave Wyatt a tentative smile. "When Lyman's father was alive, the three of them would spend a lot of time together up here. It felt more isolated in those days. It's bad enough now—but Penelope seems to like it."

"It must be beautiful here in the summer," he said diplomatically.

"Oh, it's gorgeous."

Wyatt considered telling her that her daughter had just been followed in the woods—or thought she had—and that Robby should ask her to show her the mysterious fax and tell her about the instant message she'd received. He would guess neither parent had a clue what was going on in Penelope's life. Then he reminded himself why he'd come to Cold Spring. He wanted to learn his uncle's fate, not get caught up in the schemes, troubles and charms of a blond-haired pilot.

Dinner was good, not as interminable as he'd expected, and involved an exacting analysis of Penelope's first batch of maple syrup and discussion of Robby's projected yield at her sugar shack. Wyatt had never imagined so much could be said about syrup. He didn't pay close attention, instead observing the dynamics of the nuclear Chestnut family. Robby and Lyman indulged their only daughter. No question about it. But she, in her own way, indulged them, granting them their need to be with her for whatever instinctive reasons, understanding their protectiveness.

Her life was so unlike his. Syrup, pancakes, cob-smoked ham, parents in for dinner on a blustery March night. He would have chosen from a dozen favorite restaurants, possibly met friends or taken in a movie. He had no idea where the nearest movie theater was to Cold Spring. What did people do here? Boil sap. Get lost in the woods. Make up stories about famous missing planes.

Once her parents had cleared the driveway, Wyatt stacked dishes in the sink, squirted in detergent and turned on the water. He said, "They don't have a clue you're receiving threats."

Penelope was wiping off the kitchen table. "I hope not. My mother sometimes can divine these things, but she didn't this time—I think it's just way more than she wants to know."

"Your father?"

"He'd want to know, but he's not intuitive about anything except flying. If I were flying today, he'd have figured out something was up." She shrugged, joining him at the sink. "Of course, he did on Tuesday, and that's why I'm grounded."

"You won't confide in them?"

She shook her head. "Not about this. This morning Pop told me to do what I felt was right, and that's what I'm doing."

Wyatt swished a wet rag over a plate. No dishwasher. He hadn't bothered to look, just assumed a place with a moose head on the wall wouldn't have a dishwasher. "I don't think it's a good idea for you to spend the night here alone."

"Who am I going to get to come up here? Harriet?

She'd tell Mother. Rebecca and Jane McNally would tell their father, and all my friends have kids or have to work or both—and it'd get around town and to my parents by ten o'clock." She rinsed the frying pan in the other half of the sink. "I'll just load the Winchester and keep it next to my bed."

"I'll stay."

She gaped at him. "Oh, sure. That'd be around town by eighty-thirty."

"I can pretend to go up to my room for the night and sneak out."

"Under Harriet's nose?"

"It can be done," he said, whipping through the dinner dishes.

Penelope frowned. "What about Jack Dunning? He must be suspicious as it is."

"I don't care if he's suspicious or not, and I don't have to explain my actions to him."

She wiped the frying pan with paper towels and set it on a hook above the stove. "Well, it doesn't matter. I don't need a Sinclair looking after me. My grandfather used to tell me that your grandfather had enough nerve to get himself killed a dozen times over. Half the time, it'd be someone else doing the killing. The other half, he'd just get himself killed through his own recklessness."

"It's not a ringing endorsement," Wyatt admitted.

"No, it's not."

He drained the dishwater. "I remember my grandfather as an old man who loved to read Rex Stout and tell stories about his adventures. He particularly enjoyed his archaeological expeditions in South America. He fancied himself an amateur ar-

chaeologist, but he had enormous respect for the
real thing."

"I suppose most people have more than one side
to them. My grandfather could be a cheap, rigid old
cuss. It's not like I'm saying he was a saint and your
grandfather was a devil."

"You're just saying you don't want me spending
the night."

She didn't answer.

"Penelope," he said, "we can make up the couch.
I'm not trying to rush you into anything."

Her eyes, so green even in the dim light, fastened
on him, and he could see the whirl of emotion behind them—fear, uncertainty, determination, no
small measure of desire. She said, "If you can sneak
past Harriet, do it. If not, I'll be fine tonight. Really."

"Give me an hour?"

She nodded. It wouldn't be easy for her to admit
she wanted company. She was used to not needing
anyone, or at least presenting that image to town
and family.

When he left, Wyatt wondered if she noticed the
quiet, or if that was the way, deep down, she liked
her life—quiet, simple, alone. Just her and her mismatched dishes, the stars, the woods, the lake.

And whoever was trying to scare her.

He found Jack Dunning in the Sunrise Inn bar,
nursing a beer. The private investigator studied Wyatt and shook his head, for once a gleam in his gray
eyes. "Nope. I don't see it."

"See what?"

"A resemblance to Harriet Chestnut."

Wyatt sat opposite Jack, motioned for the bartender to bring him a beer. "Did she tell you or did you find out on your own?"

"She told me, which is a variation of my finding out on my own. If I don't make the contact, I don't get the information."

"You should go home, Jack. I should go home. These people don't need us here. Colt's fate has kept for this long. It can keep a while longer."

"If that plane's out there, I'm going to find it."

"The plane and Harriet Chestnut don't have anything to do with each other. She's a sweet woman. Don't belittle her fantasies."

"Fantasies, hell. She's convinced she's a Sinclair. Knows it in her gut. She told me so." Jack drank more of his beer. His cheeks were rosy from the alcohol, the warmth of the inn, the long, snowy day. "If she can prove it, she'll have her hand out for her share of the Sinclair trust. Mark my words. I don't care how sweet she is."

"I'd hate to be as cynical as you are."

"You *are* as cynical as I am, Sinclair. Otherwise you wouldn't be here."

Wyatt sighed. His beer arrived. He didn't bother with the glass. A beer on top of pancakes and ham. He'd have to run a million miles tomorrow to burn it all off. "If Harriet's a Sinclair, she deserves her fair share. I just don't see how she can be. We don't know for sure Colt and Frannie were lovers when they ran off, never mind that they had any kind of physical relationship before then."

"They were in Cold Spring at the same time for a few weeks the previous summer. If you do the math, it could work. You're pregnant so you squirrel yourself away in some dank basement and catalogue bones, art and shit. Wear baggy clothes. Stay away from people you know."

"That's pure speculation."

Jack shrugged. "Of course it is. I'm just saying that Harriet's little fantasy isn't as far-fetched as people might want to believe."

"Have you told my father?"

"No point yet. As far as he's concerned, Frannie Beaudine seduced his big brother and caused both their deaths—not to mention a family scandal. He's not going to want to hear about a love child."

Wyatt drank his beer. The inn was quiet, and he could hear the fire crackling down the hall and the wind gusting against the windows. In changing her story, Penelope had undoubtedly hoped to spare her cousin the scrutiny she was under. A proverbial case of shutting the barn door after the horse had already fled.

Finally, he said, "Maybe Harriet just wants answers about her birth, validation—"

"Horseshit. She wants money." Jack leaned back and folded his hands on his flat middle. He wasn't being argumentative, just stating the facts as he saw them. "Frankly, I don't blame her. I'd get every damned penny I could out of you Sinclairs. Jesus, it's not like she'd have to fight you for it."

Wyatt smiled without humor. "True."

"How's our Miss Penelope? Any closer to telling us the truth?"

"It seems to me she's bit off more than she can chew."

He'd decided not to tell Jack about the messages or the incident—real or imagined—in the woods. Jack grunted in agreement. "She'd have been a lot smarter if she'd said she'd created a Piper Cub out of nothing when she was lost, tired and hungry. She could have taken us all out to a pile of rocks and said, *See?"*

"Would that have satisfied you?"

He grinned. "Not a chance. Either way, her goose is cooked. Her only option is to tell the truth."

"You aren't helping her to see that, are you?"

Jack's gaze sharpened instantly, a reminder that he was a professional, experienced investigator, not a wannabe Texas good ol' boy doing Brandon Sinclair a good turn. "I'm doing my job. Why? What's going on?"

Wyatt shook his head. "Nothing. I'm probably seeing things myself."

"Well, if you get in over your head, ace, you know where to find me. Your daddy'd have my ass if I let something happen to his boy."

"Is that what he said?"

"Some things don't need to be spelled out."

"This does." Wyatt leaned over the table and said in as clear and straightforward a manner as possible, "I am not your concern. You do what you have to do on my father's behalf with regard to my uncle's fate. You do nothing on my behalf. I don't need your protection, and I don't want you breathing down my neck."

Jack had no visible reaction. He drank the last of his beer and got to his feet. "Fair enough. So let me be straight with you. If you get in my way, I'll mow you down. And when it's all over, your father will believe my version of events, not yours. I'm the pro. You're the black sheep son." He straightened abruptly and grinned at Wyatt. "Seeing how you're a fucking Sinclair, you can buy me my beer."

Jack walked out of the bar as Andy McNally walked in, and Wyatt began to wonder how in hell he was going to sneak out. McNally got himself a beer and pulled out a chair at Wyatt's table.

"You mind?" Not waiting for an answer, he sat down. He looked tired, gray around the eyes, and his scar was more prominent, almost seeming to pulse. "I heard you and the Chestnuts all had pancakes and fresh syrup at Penelope's." He grinned at Wyatt's surprise. "No secrets in a small town. I stopped by a few minutes ago. Damned near gave her a stroke. I don't know if I've ever seen her this jumpy."

"Too much syrup," Wyatt suggested lightly.

"I hope you and that PI aren't trying to get under her skin. I've known Penelope Chestnut since she was in diapers, and she's not going to do anything she doesn't want to do. Trying to intimidate her is just going to get her back up that much more."

"I'm not here to intimidate anyone. I don't speak for Jack."

The police chief drank some of his beer, his exhaustion hanging on him, dragging down his big shoulders. "I ran into Harriet in the hall. She looked a little shaken up, too. She's a good kid, you know. She has some odd ideas, but she's one of the nicest people you're ever going to meet, here or anywhere else." He leveled his cop eyes on Wyatt. "You and that private dick know, don't you? That she thinks she's Colt and Frannie's daughter? It's nothing we make fun of around here."

"I would hope it's nothing anyone would make fun of, anywhere."

"If she meant to make a claim on your family, she'd have done it by now. She just wants—" He paused, searching for the right words. From what Wyatt had observed, extensive analysis of people's deepest feelings didn't come easily to the naturally stoic population of Cold Spring, New Hampshire. McNally finished, "I guess she just wants to know who she is."

Wyatt shrugged, wishing he'd skipped the beer. The snowstorm must have made everyone morose. "I suppose that's what we all want."

The chief grinned unexpectedly. "Not me. I've known who I am since my mama slapped me on the behind and said, 'You're Andrew James McNally.' No mystery. The last year of her life, she didn't know who I was. That was tough." His eyes went distant, and he inhaled sharply through his nostrils. "But there are tougher things. She was old. It was her time."

He drank his beer, and Wyatt had the feeling the chief was waiting for Harriet to come into the bar. When she didn't and his beer was finished, McNally got stiffly to his feet. "Hell of a day today. The storm snuck up on us. We had a lot of ice on the roads. A dozen stupid little accidents—but no deaths." He pushed a big palm through his gray hair, struggling, it seemed to Wyatt, to shake off his melancholy. "You know, they can do a lot with DNA these days. Christ, you leave an eyelash at a crime scene and we'll nail you."

"Amazing," Wyatt said.

"I expect a real Sinclair could put Harriet's mind at ease."

"If that's what she wants."

McNally nodded. "Yeah. If that's what she wants."

An hour later, Wyatt managed to sneak out the side door. The roads were plowed, but there were icy patches. Penelope's road was a nightmare. It alone would deter spies and cretins.

By the time he knocked on her door, she had the couch made up with an ancient wool blanket and white sheets that had to be forty years old. More leftovers from the dead grandfather. She'd put away the excess maple syrup, sanded her steps and cleaned and loaded the Winchester.

"Harriet didn't see you?"

"No, but I ran into your mother at the front desk. Not to worry, I told her I was a throwback to a Victorian Sinclair who wasn't a scoundrel—"

"That's not even a little bit funny."

He laughed. "Your mother was nowhere in sight. Nor were Harriet, Jack Dunning, the police chief or anyone else who'd care that I might be sneaking off to sleep on your couch."

She didn't look relieved.

"Penelope," he said, "you need a friend tonight. Let me be that friend."

"We're not overreacting?"

He didn't hesitate. "No."

She seemed tense, agitated, and he suspected it had more to do with the very real and immediate threat he presented to her peace and stability than with the nebulous threat of some mad faxer. "I hope this isn't a case of the wolf guarding the henhouse."

He shrugged, smiled. "You're armed."

She pushed at her blond curls with both hands. "I've had a long day. I'm going to bed. And I think I will keep Granddad's rifle in the bedroom with me."

"No problem. If someone tries to break in, Willard here and I will handle it."

"I've thought about getting a dog—"

"Who needs a dog when you have a moose and a Sinclair?"

That elicited a smile, and Wyatt decided it was enough. For tonight.

After she slipped into her bedroom, he peeled down to his underwear, fed the wood stove and climbed under the musty blanket and old sheets. This was willpower. This was honor. This was courage. Damned if he'd prove himself a Sinclair scoundrel.

He listened to the fire crackle and pictured Penelope snug in her bed, no doubt in his mind that she wanted him as much as he wanted her. He sighed at Willard. The blanket smelled like mothballs, the couch was lumpy, and the moose—well, he thought, the moose had been dead a long time.

ELEVEN

Harriet watched the stars disappear and the sunrise lighten the sky. She had slept fitfully, first unable to fall asleep, then unable to stay asleep. She would catch herself obsessing and throw back her covers, change positions, anything to stop the endless stream of thoughts and images. At four o'clock she gave up. She had three rooms on the third floor of the inn. Sometimes when sleep eluded her, she would wander down to the kitchen and clean, whip up muffins or sit with a pot of tea and a book.

This time, she didn't dare. She would die if her footsteps woke up Jack Dunning or Wyatt Sinclair, if either man checked on her.

Instead she sat in a wing chair in an alcove overlooking the lake. She'd tried doing needlepoint, but she kept making mistakes, her hands shaking, her vision blurring. She'd stabbed her finger twice, which, even with the special blunt needle, hurt. So she put aside her latest project, a pillow for the sofa in the parlor. The design was of maple leaves in a fiery autumn red. She was in the mood for pastels, spring colors, Easter eggs and baby bunnies.

"You're a sap, Harriet," she whispered to herself. "A sentimental fool."

Negative self-talk. Damaging. Degrading. She

knew she should stop. She had read a dozen self-help books that all said not to talk that way to yourself. She should do affirmations. Tell herself positive things. *I'm a wonderful person. I'm smart and kind and capable.*

Except she didn't believe it.

Using her fingertips, she wiped the tears on her cheeks. Her skin was rougher and drier than it used to be. She was forty-five years old. Unmarried. Childless. She lived in three rooms on the third floor of an inn. She looked at her sitting room with its pretty, feminine decor. She'd shopped flea markets and yard sales for many of the furnishings, which she'd sanded, refinished, reupholstered herself, not wanting to spend money on rooms her guests would never see. The result was charming, enchanting, entirely her, and yet at dawn, it struck her as pathetic. An old maid's quarters. Forty years from now, she would be sitting here by the window, her life the same, her body older, frailer, more wrinkled. If she didn't act, she would wither away here.

But you like your life.

The positive words tricked her, coming out of nowhere. It was all those books. They'd indoctrinated her. She couldn't even feel sorry for herself without perky little phrases popping into her mind.

She had a right to feel miserable. Of course, she was lucky in many ways. She was healthy, she had a wonderful family—Lyman, Robby, Penelope, her parents in Florida, her brother in Boston, her cousin Mary and her family. She did work she loved, she enjoyed her guests. She wanted more, but what?

In her heart of hearts she knew she hadn't really

wanted children. She adored her friends' babies, her little nieces in Boston, Mary's brood—but herself?

Harriet smiled sadly as she stared at the frozen lake. In her twenties and early thirties she'd deluded herself into thinking children would fulfill her, give her life purpose, be fun. She thought she'd make a wonderful mother, and perhaps she would have, but did she *want* children? She was so introverted, so awkward. She liked her simple life, her quiet nights reading by the fire, the guests who came and went. Children would have changed everything, complicated everything.

And she would have had to have a man.

She shuddered, pushing back thoughts of the few men with whom she'd tried to have a relationship. Tentative, self-conscious, prudish—she always turned into such a simp around men. She'd had sex exactly six times in her life, the last time ten years ago. It was true what they said—use it or lose it. She didn't care if she ever fell into bed with a man again. In fact, she couldn't bear the thought of anyone seeing her without clothes. Even her annual mammogram sent her into days of anxiety.

You're overstating your case, Harriet. You're a woman full of life and love. You just haven't had a lot of luck with men.

And you're trying to pretend you're not attracted to Jack Dunning when you are.

She shot from her chair. Jack wasn't attracted to her. He was the type of man who went for blond bombshells and big-haired tarts, not for plain, New England spinsters.

Spinster. It was an old-fashioned word that rang true.

Jack had his reasons for indulging her tonight, getting her to talk about the night her father found her on the church doorstep, her conviction that she was Colt and Frannie's daughter.

God, what a fool she'd made of herself. What a fool!

She sobbed, the tears flowing hard. She jumped out of the chair, fled to her bedroom and threw herself on her bed. She sank into the down comforter. She grabbed a pillow and cried into it, not wanting anyone to hear, especially Jack. Did private investigators have better hearing? Would he be listening for her, suspecting she would fall apart?

Oh God oh God oh God...I'm such a fool...

He had been so kind. Curious. Polite. Charming and sexy, yet tough. He'd asked the kind of questions a private investigator should ask. Did she have any proof Frannie and Colt were her biological parents? Any real clues or evidence *suggesting* they were her biological parents? How far was she willing to go to get the proof she needed?

She'd behaved impulsively, stupidly. She'd gotten into her head the idea of telling him about her theory and couldn't rest until she'd acted on it. This was the sort of behavior she expected of Penelope, not herself. She was the analytical one, careful, rational, never acting until she'd examined all her options.

She'd done very little digging into her origins. Her parents had been open about what had happened, and they'd told her all the steps they and the authorities had taken to find out how she'd come to be in an apple basket at the side door of the Cold Spring First Congregational Church.

Since they'd found nothing, not even the slightest clue, Harriet never expected she might find anything herself. And so she hadn't bothered. Passivity reigned. Instead of taking action, she wove her fantasy about Frannie Beaudine and Colt Sinclair, fancied herself an heiress, a woman with a zest for adventure and daring in her genes even if she didn't act upon it.

Jack said he would talk to Brandon Sinclair if she wanted him to. He'd touched her hair—just a brush of his fingertips—and told her the Sinclairs all had dark hair and fair skin, like hers. It had been a simple act of kindness, she knew. Now that she'd seen a Sinclair in person, she wasn't so positive. She looked nothing like Wyatt. Nothing at all.

She made herself sit up. She tucked her knees under her chin and wrapped her arms around her ankles, holding herself tight. She could feel that her eyes were red and swollen, and her cheeks burned from the tears. Such silliness. People had real problems, and here she was crying over nonsense. What difference did it make who her biological parents were? Why did she need to know who had put her into a basket and left her?

The couple who'd adopted her were more than anyone could ever ask for or want in parents. Kind, loving, devoted—and so funny. She smiled, remembering sitting around the dinner table with her parents and brother, laughing, just howling at something one of them had said. They'd be together this summer, when her parents came from Florida and her brother from Boston. She knew she could call any of them and they would talk to her, tell her to do what she felt was right, perhaps even make her laugh.

But this wasn't their problem. As much as they could imagine and empathize, it wasn't something they could understand. The maddening curiosity. The wondering. The awful fear that her birth—her existence—had caused, somehow, the deaths of two people. That her life was forever entangled in tragedy, scandal, death.

That was what she had to know. Not that she was an heiress, but that she wasn't a curse, however innocent, however unwitting.

She cleared her throat and slipped out of bed, pushing back tear-drenched strands of hair as she walked unsteadily to the bathroom. Pink towels, little shell-shaped soaps, bottles of essential oils and scented creams. She found the lavender oil and turned on the tub, added a few drops to the steaming water. Lavender to enhance feelings of well-being. That was what she needed. She would take charge, like Penelope.

As she stepped into the tub, Harriet glanced at her body. Thick through her hips and thighs, a bit of a belly, gravity having its dragging effect on her breasts. She didn't delude herself into thinking she was Rubenesque. She was reasonably fit, just a few pounds over her ideal weight. Well, ten.

She smiled, easing herself slowly into the hot water, her eyelids heavy from crying and fatigue. *You're a healthy, attractive woman in your mid-forties.*

Suddenly she laughed out loud, so hard it echoed in her pretty bathroom. "And you're an heiress, too."

* * *

When Penelope woke up and saw the loaded Winchester at her bedside, she was so startled she screamed and fell out of bed. That brought Wyatt. She'd forgotten about him, too. Her door banged open, and all she saw was dark hair, legs, chest and underwear. Every bit of it male.

Bleary-eyed, not quite sure what was real and what was a dream, she went for the rifle, and he said, "Whoa, sweetheart. It was just a bad dream."

"Sinclair?"

"Will it get me shot if I say yes?"

She eased her fingers from the rifle. "Relax. I always know what I'm shooting at before I pull the trigger."

"Are you a good shot?"

"Not particularly."

"Dare I ask—"

"What and when I shot last? A target. Andy McNally took Rebecca, Jane and me out for some target shooting. Rebecca's a nice shot. I don't hunt," she added, as if that mattered, and got to her feet, uncrumpling her nightshirt. It was flannel, blue plaid, snug and about as feminine as most everything else in her place. She ruffled her hair with one hand, waking up the rest of the way, aware of Wyatt's dark, wide-awake gaze on her. "The only reason I keep the rifle is because it was my grandfather's. Otherwise I'd get rid of it."

Her vision cleared, and she realized the precariousness of her situation. Wyatt didn't have the look of a man who'd be kept at bay by a loaded gun for long. Her gaze drifted from the hard set of his jaw until it came to the impossible-to-hide bulge. Her head jerked up. "Oh, dear. Coffee?"

"Penelope."

In half a second he'd crossed the room, and in another half second he had her on the bed, and his mouth was on hers. Her response was instantaneous and total, all the pent-up frustration and aching bursting to the surface, demanding relief. He pushed up the hem of her nightshirt, his palms hot on her skin, and she supposed she could have stopped him if she wanted to—she did have a loaded rifle. But she didn't want to, and when he cupped her bottom and deepened their kiss, she knew this was right. She eased her palms over his hips, boldly slipped his undershorts down until she could feel the hot, firm muscles under her hands.

He was ready. She already knew that from when he was standing in the doorway. But still she eased her hand around him, testing, measuring, even as he pushed her nightshirt up higher as his mouth and tongue moved lower, doing a bit of testing and measuring of their own.

When she was spinning with desire, veering out of control, she reached with one hand into her bedside table and tossed him a foil packet, managing a quick smile. "I'm a natural optimist."

He gave a ragged laugh, dealt with protection swiftly and efficiently, and when he came to her, he held back. There was no lessening of urgency, only a black look in his eyes that said if they were to go wild and mad this once, it was going to last. He gazed at her, trailed one hand from her throat across her breasts, down her stomach and between her legs, lingering there, probing, thrusting, circling. Then he followed that same trail with mouth, tongue and teeth until she was quivering, aching

with want. But he'd reached his limit, too, and in another moment, they came together, hard and fast,
nothing to stop them but their release. Hers came
first, and she cried out with the quaking in her body,
with abandon, as he kept on until, finally, they collapsed together.

"I'm glad I didn't shoot you," she managed to
say, her breathing ragged.

He grinned crookedly. "I don't know, I'd swear
you did."

Impossibly, miraculously, a few minutes later
they did it again. Just as hard, just as fast, just as
wildly, until they were panting and raw and beyond
thought and reason.

Penelope could have stayed in bed, just pretended
all was well in her world. She wouldn't have to
think about the plane in the woods, the lies, the
strange messages or what to do about the man she'd
just made love with twice. But she whispered, "You
should get back to the inn before Harriet discovers
you're missing and all hell breaks loose."

"I don't know," he said with a deliberate, rakish
wink, "I think it just did."

But he rolled out of bed and slipped to the
shower. Penelope didn't move until she heard his
car clear her driveway. She wasn't one to sleep with
a man first and then get to know him. But here she
was. In a way, she felt as if she'd known Wyatt all
her life.

"Well, isn't that a rationalization," she muttered,
got out of bed and dove for the shower before her
thoughts could get too far ahead of her.

When she arrived at the airport, her father presented her with a list of planes to wash, floors to

sweep and paperwork to do. He'd changed his mind about her cooling her heels at home and wanted her putting in regular hours. Penelope saw it for what it was—a transparent attempt to keep her out of trouble. Little did he know he was way too late.

Her first job was to clean the small, functional classroom that served as his flight school. She'd logged enough hours in the metal chairs. Becoming a flight instructor was on her list of goals. She had a full list of challenging goals—falling for Wyatt Sinclair was not among them. Marriage, children, a new house with lots of wood and glass to replace her grandfather's old cabin would be nice, not that she had anyone in mind for husband, father and co-carpenter.

Wyatt wasn't even close as a candidate. Obviously, he didn't regard her as a sister or one of the guys, but he didn't want the same things out of life she did. A town like Cold Spring, New Hampshire, and a life like hers would never contain him. As notorious as she was within the boundaries of her hometown, she didn't compare to Wyatt when it came to a taste for drama and adventure. It was one thing to get lost in the back forty once in a while and get a little distracted flying home from Plattsburgh. He'd watched a friend die and had nearly died himself on one of his expeditions. *That* was pushing the envelope.

Penelope had no illusions about Wyatt's eighteen months in New York. They were a kind of penance, a self-imposed version of washing planes and sweeping out hangars. The demon was still inside him, biding its time. She'd had a little feel for it this morning, she thought uncomfortably but, to her surprise, without regret or embarrassment. She supposed she had a few demons of her own to exorcise.

Harriet caught up with her between jobs. She looked out of breath, her cheeks rosy. She had on her boots, her parka and her matching mittens and hat that she'd knitted out of fuzzy white yarn. Penelope frowned. "Harriet, it's forty-five degrees out. You're dressed to hike the Himalayas."

She gulped for air. "I want you to take me to see Bubba Johns."

"Bubba? Why?"

"I've been doing a lot of thinking." She paused, agitated yet focused on what she had to do. "And I just do."

Penelope sighed. "Harriet, if it's because I stirred up things for you by bringing the Sinclair family to town—"

She cut her off with a tight shake of the head. "Things are always stirred up for me, Penelope, at some level. I just don't always show it. Look, I know Bubba wasn't here when Colt and Frannie disappeared. I just want to talk to him. If you can't take me, I'll go alone. I'm sure I can find his place. It's not as if I've never hiked these woods."

"Of course, I'll take you." Penelope leaned her big broom against the wall. "Let me tell Pop. He's keeping me under his thumb, but I'm allowed a lunch break."

Five minutes later, they were in Penelope's truck, Harriet tight-lipped and tense. She wasn't an outdoorswoman. She loved her gardens and an annual swim or two in the lake, but treks over hill and dale weren't for her. She tucked stray hairs into her hat. The white emphasized her paleness, the fatigue and fine lines around her eyes. She wasn't wearing any makeup today, and her freckles stood out against her pale skin. Wyatt Sinclair and Jack Dunning had pushed fantasy into the realm of reality—or sheer foolishness. Yet if Harriet was private and often hard to gauge, she was no fool. Penelope knew that, although sometimes she had to remind herself she needn't be protective of her cousin.

With the warm temperatures, evaporating snow and gray skies, there was a haze in the air, hovering over the lake and woods, everything damp and drippy with melting. The snow was heavier and wetter today, good for snowballs and snow forts and tough on electrical wires. Penelope and Harriet set off without benefit of snowshoes or supplies.

"I don't know about you, Harriet," Penelope said as they trudged along the path, "but I'm ready for daffodils."

"Oh, me, too! But it's so beautiful, isn't it?" She beamed, breathless, and smiled at Penelope. She was more relaxed now that she'd gotten her way. "I really should get out here more often."

"Any time."

As they followed the trail, Penelope noticed fresh tracks. Both snowshoes and boots. She'd worn her day hikers and anorak. "I wonder where our Sinclair and PI are today."

Harriet was breathing hard as they crossed onto Sinclair land. Penelope stayed a yard behind her, trying not to lose patience with her cousin's slow pace.

"I don't think they like each other," Harriet said. "They certainly don't seem to be coordinating their efforts."

"That's for sure. Well, they can spin their wheels until they give up and go home. I get the feeling the Sinclair family doesn't operate the way we do. And that's an observation," she added quickly, before her cousin could spring to their defense, "not a criticism."

Harriet made no comment. She was huffing and red-faced from walking at a fairly fast clip through snow from four to eight inches deep. But it was melting fast, and before long, the woods would be filled with ferns and wildflowers.

When they reached Bubba's little homestead, all was quiet and still. Not even a curl of smoke was coming out of the chimney. Harriet sucked in a deep breath, surveying the place with her serious eyes. "It's just what you'd expect, isn't it? What a simple life."

"Provided the Sinclairs don't kick him off their land. I guess it's a lot easier to give up the rat race when you can build yourself a little place on someone else's land—not that I care. He must be out. Doesn't look as if his dogs are around, either. He doesn't always take them with him, but I think they'd be out growling and barking by now."

"Look," Harriet said, pointing, "he has bird feeders. It reminds you the best things in life are free, doesn't it?"

"I guess so." Penelope scooped up a handful of snow and fashioned it into a snowball, just to give herself something to do. Without gloves, her fingers got cold fast. She tossed the snowball against a tree. It hit with a soft thud. "Well, we've seen it—"

Harriet averted her gaze. "Maybe we could take a look inside."

"You mean just walk in?"

Her cousin spun around to her, her eyes a little wild, her intensity palpable. "Why not? Penelope, what if he knows where Colt and Frannie's plane is? If it's out here, he *must* have found it. I'm not saying you did—I don't know—but it's all got me thinking."

"Harriet, we can't just walk into Bubba's house and have a look around."

She pursed her lips, her only indication she didn't like Penelope's tone. "What if he looted the wreckage? You know what a scavenger he is."

"I can't imagine he'd find anything of use in an old plane wreck."

Harriet didn't give up. "What if he's in there, dead?"

"His dogs would be out here chewing our legs off."

Her cousin spun around and focused on the shack, her arms folded on her chest. She was fast going into a snit. Her moods could last days. She didn't indulge them often, but when she did, she wouldn't say a word or argue. She'd just get silent and what Aunt Mary called pissy.

Penelope started around her. "Come on, we can at least take a look at his garden."

"You think I'm ridiculous," Harriet said behind her.

Penelope stifled a groan. Her cousin's tendency toward self-pity was the one trait that irritated her. "No, Harriet, I just don't want to be a party to searching Bubba's place. That's all. We can wait for him, if you'd like."

"He could be gone for hours. I've got scones to

make." Her arms sagged to her sides, and her eyes shone with tears. She went from stubborn determination to whiny self-pity to remorse in a flash. She sniffled. "I'm just so...so...I don't know! I can't think straight. Sometimes it's as if I can't breathe."

Seeing how she'd made love with a Sinclair that morning, Penelope could be sympathetic. "You don't have to explain or apologize to me, Harriet. I'm not trying to climb on my moral high horse—"

"Hey, kids."

They both jumped, and Jack Dunning stepped from behind the rickety garden shed and tipped his cowboy hat. "I thought I heard something." He grinned. "Afraid it might be the bogeyman."

Harriet blushed fiercely. "We were just—I just—"

She was so flustered she couldn't finish, but Jack spared her. "Our old hermit seems to have cleared out for the day. I took a peek inside his place here. Neat as a pin, chives on the windowsills. Quite the stack of books."

"Once or twice a year he trades at yard sales," Penelope said. She was unreasonably irritated with Dunning for committing the invasion of privacy Harriet had considered. It wasn't as if Bubba Johns was her responsibility. "I can't believe you just walked right in."

He shrugged. "No locks."

"Aren't private investigators supposed to uphold the law?"

"Sure, and I do." He walked on Bubba's icy path to join her and Harriet. "Private investigators are also supposed to find answers to gnatty questions, such as whether or not our hermit friend had anything to do with why you changed your story. I

think he did. I didn't find any souvenirs from a
Piper Cub in there, but I bet he found that plane long
before you did."

"Jack," Harriet said, "Penelope is the most honest
person I've ever known."

He shook his head, and Penelope was glad he
couldn't read minds, because she was thinking that
if Harriet turned over a rock in Bubba's brook, she'd
find Penelope slithering there. Dunning seemed
mercifully oblivious. "I didn't have time to do a
thorough search. I heard you two coming over the
hill and slipped behind the shed."

Penelope had heard enough. She about-faced and
started up the trail. "I'm going back to work. My
lunch hour's over." She stopped abruptly, looking
at Dunning. The sun tried to burn through the haze,
and she squinted against the glare. "I didn't see
your car at my place."

"I parked on the main road and walked in from
there. Apparently it's Bubba's route to town."

His tone was steady, but there was a not-that-it's-
any-of-your-business edge to it. Penelope could feel
her jaw clenching. This man worked for Wyatt's father, and she didn't want to alienate him. But she
wasn't going to let him roll her, either. She turned to
Harriet. "You coming?"

Dunning stepped next to her. "Harriet, you can go
with me if you want, and I'll drive you to town. Let
Penelope get to work."

Harriet smiled almost giddily, and Penelope wondered if she looked as dopey-eyed around Sinclair
as her cousin around this PI. "Are you sure you
don't mind?"

"It'd be my pleasure," he said, the wannabe

southern gentleman and New York detective all mixed into a disconcerting, charming package Penelope wasn't sure she or her cousin should trust.

But there was no stopping Harriet, and Penelope wasted no time getting to her house. She didn't even check her taps. She *had* to get these two out of town, Wyatt and Dunning both. But how to satisfy them short of taking them to the wreckage?

It was an option. A serious option. She didn't want to not do it out of a sense of defiance. She needed to be practical and focus, as her father had said, on doing the right thing.

But what about whoever had sent the messages? What was *their* point? And Bubba and Harriet— she'd confused their lives enough as it was.

She'd think over her options—and their consequences—while she washed planes this afternoon.

TWELVE

Wyatt couldn't believe what he was thinking.

He stood in front of Penelope's cabin, her sap-boiling woodpile charred and cold, and debated the pros and cons of slipping inside for a thorough search. He'd start with her computer. He wondered what secrets it might dish up. Then he'd work his way through her closets and drawers.

"What a bastard you are."

Last night, sprawled on her lumpy, ancient couch with the smell of mothballs in his nostrils and thoughts of her snuggled under her comforter in the next room, he'd stared at ol' Willard and contemplated how to get Penelope to trust and confide in him. After all, the woman kept a dead moose on the wall and lived alone in a place not much better than Bubba Johns's shack.

He'd had no such yearnings for intimacy and trust with Madge. She was content to feng-shui his apartment, spend his money and share his bed. No demands from her, none from him.

The air was damp and chilly, the kind that got into the bones. Wyatt forced himself to acknowledge a certain uneasiness regarding his motives toward Penelope Chestnut. He'd acted on blind instinct this morning, but he wondered if, deep down, making love to her had been a cynical ploy to get the truth out of her. She'd become a challenge, and there was nothing he liked better than a good challenge.

He wondered what would happen if he did succeed in earning her trust. Would he throw it back in her face? He did not have a sterling record in that regard. When it came to love and trust, he was more Sinclair than he liked to admit.

He swore under his breath. He was a man of action. Introspection bored the hell out of him. What he wanted from Penelope was clear enough—answers and sex. The rest was self-delusion. Love, romance and intimacy were not part of this particular equation.

He heard a car negotiating the ruts and bumps and quicksand of the dirt road, and in another minute it rolled in behind him. A black sedan with Andy McNally behind the wheel. He got out, his demeanor all cop. The terrible facial scar only added to his air of authority. "How long have you been here?"

"Five minutes, tops. Something up?"

"I got a call to come check things out up here. Anonymous. It came on my private cell phone, so we didn't get it on tape. Cute, huh? If someone's jerking my chain—" He started across the driveway, a mix of melting snow, mud and gravel. "Let's just say I'm not amused."

"You think it's a prank call?"

"I'll find out. Wouldn't be the first. Penelope's got her name in the papers, stirred folks up. I wouldn't put it past someone to drag me out here just for grins." He narrowed his eyes at Wyatt. "Or to harass you."

"Me? Why?"

"You probably have a damned good idea why. You're a Sinclair, you don't believe our sweet Penelope's story—a lot of reasons." He mounted the steps to her side entrance and peered inside. "Shit."

Wyatt stood on the bottom step. "What is it?"

"Goddamn it, it wasn't a crank call. Looks as if someone's been through her place." He glared at Wyatt. "If it was you, Sinclair, I'm going to find out and nail your ass. Understood?"

"It wasn't me," he replied calmly.

"Door's still locked. A miracle she bothered. She must be more spooked having you in town than I realized. Whoever it was probably came in from the deck. Less chance of being seen this time of year—no boats on the lake." McNally was grinding out his words, growling, thoroughly annoyed by the turn of events. "I've got to get a detective up here. Goddamn it, Sinclair, don't touch anything while I call this in."

"I can go around and look at the deck—"

He shook his head. "There might be footprints." He clomped down the steps and looked at the lake. A neatly shoveled path led to the deck. "Penelope would get ambitious and shovel. I swear, I'm beginning to think we're all safer with her in the air. Scariest thought I've had in a month."

Since it was his fourth day in Cold Spring, Wyatt had a fair understanding of how the chief of police could be irritated with Penelope because her house had been broken into. Things tended to happen to her, and people tended to blame her because they did. She was a catalyst for action and drama in her small hometown.

As if reading his mind, McNally glowered at him. "This is vintage Penelope Chestnut, I want you to know. Damn it, even when she said it was a dump she found and not Frannie Beaudine's plane, I knew we were still in for trouble."

"Are you going to notify her?"

"I'll call her father after I get a detective up here. You," he said, glancing back en route to his car, "stay put."

Wyatt gave him a thin smile. He had no intention of going anywhere.

While they waited for the sole detective on the Cold Spring police department to arrive, McNally studied the driveway and the woods across the road for tire marks and footprints. "Looks as if Penelope's been out checking her taps," he said. "Lyman was trying to keep her busy today, but I heard Harriet and she took off for a noontime jaunt." He paused, frowning as he stared down the quiet, narrow road. "I wonder if they came up here, saw anything."

Wyatt debated telling McNally about the fax and the instant message. Then again, Penelope was on her way, and *she* could tell him. Some snake pits he managed to skirt.

The detective rolled in, a young guy named Pete who seemed to share his boss's opinion of the victim of the break-in. Before McNally could follow him up the steps, Penelope bounced down the road in her mud-splattered hunter green truck. Her father jumped out at the same time she did, cigar stuck in his mouth, repressed agitation adding more lines to his face.

"He insisted on coming," Penelope told McNally.

She looked pale but in control, and Wyatt tried not to think about how he'd left her that morning. "What's up?"

"Looks like your place has been ransacked. Whoever did it broke in from the deck. Pete's up there now."

She glared past him to Wyatt, her jaw set, fear—possibly unacknowledged—etched in every angle of her face. "It wasn't you?"

Wyatt had expected as much. Considering his earlier quandary, her suspicion was hardly out of place. "It wasn't me," he told her, as he'd told the police chief. "And I didn't see who it was."

Lyman Chestnut removed his cigar from his mouth, noxious fumes drifting into the damp air. "Let's not get ahead of ourselves. Andy, you said you got an anonymous tip?"

The chief nodded grimly. "I thought it was a crank call."

"Do you think it was whoever did this," Lyman went on, "or just a passerby who saw something and didn't want to get involved?"

"Damned if I know, but it's not like Penelope gets many passersby out here."

Penelope clearly hated having them discuss her as if she weren't standing there. Before she could make her displeasure known, Pete pushed open the kitchen door. "Jesus Christ, Penelope, you keep a Winchester in your goddamned bedroom?"

Andy McNally and her father turned to glare at her. She sputtered. "It's not loaded. I've got all the cartridges in my pocketbook. Look, I'm the *victim* here. Mind if I go in and see if anything's missing?"

"Do what Pete tells you," McNally warned her. "I'm not kidding around here."

"Who the hell's kidding?" she snapped.

Wyatt figured her father's patience had to be exhausted, but Lyman tossed his cigar into a snowbank. "Penelope, you sure you want to keep saying it was a dump out in the woods on Sunday and you can't find it?"

She stopped on the mushy, icy walk and thrust her hands on her hips as she looked at her father. She was clear-eyed and more scared than she'd want to admit. "It was a dump site out in the woods on Sunday and I can't find it."

Wyatt had to give her credit for holding her own against her father, the chief of police, a detective and him. Four men, and not one of them believed her. She knew it, and she didn't give a damn. She was hanging on to the shreds of her lie as if they were a lifeline.

She trotted up the steps as if she were going in to open a can of soup.

"Damned stubborn—" Lyman cut himself off with a growl. "She's always been that way, even before she could walk."

"You want to call Robby?" Andy asked.

"No, she's a nervous wreck as it is. She still hasn't gotten over having to call out a search party when Penelope missed Sunday dinner. That girl's worried her mother for years."

Andy sighed, nodding. "I'll tell Harriet myself."

Lyman attempted a feeble grin. "You do that."

Wyatt stood back, not wanting to interfere with relationships forged long before he waltzed into town. He noted that, while Lyman had insisted on accompanying his daughter, he was standing back, not interfering or trying to take charge. On some level, he seemed to understand that she was her own woman, even if he didn't like her choices or trust her decisions—and worried about her and loved her. There were no conditions on their father-daughter relationship. It just was what it was, something Wyatt found rather amazing to witness.

McNally went inside, and Lyman paced in the driveway. Finally he glanced at Wyatt. "Where's your buddy the PI?"

"I don't know. I haven't seen him since this morning."

"Think he did this?"

Wyatt had already considered that scenario. "It's possible."

Lyman's gaze was steady. "It's possible you did it, too."

"From your point of view, I imagine it is. From mine, no."

"Penelope's my only kid. My wife and I lost two before we had her, and one after. We spoiled her, I admit it. We wanted her to have a mind of her own—" He took a breath, asserting his natural stoicism. "And by God, she does."

Wyatt smiled. "That's obvious."

She emerged from her kitchen a little paler, a lot shakier. She had to grab the handrail on the way down, and it wasn't because the steps were icy. Wyatt could see the unsteadiness, the shock registering of someone breaking into her place, searching her things. "Jeez," she said, "the bastard even went through my underwear drawer."

"We'll catch him," her father said, leaving it at

that. She nodded, looking somewhat reassured. He wasn't minimizing her fears—she was accustomed to his taciturn nature. If her father had fallen apart or gone into a rage, Wyatt thought, Penelope would have really worried. She expected that stoicism, was comforted by it.

"Anything taken?" Wyatt asked.

She shook her head. "Not that I can see. Grand-dad's rifle, my gold jewelry—everything's still there."

Lyman frowned, jerked a thumb at her house. "They going to be in there long?"

"Pete's debating whether or not to dust for prints. He doesn't think he'll find any, and since nothing's been stolen and no one was hurt, it's not that high a priority."

Lyman drew his mouth into a straight line. "I don't want you staying here by yourself. Go down to the inn and stay with Harriet or come up to the house and stay with your mother and me. And why the hell did you get your grandfather's rifle out? You going to tell us that?"

McNally's brows drew together. "Good point, Lyman."

Penelope, however, wasn't going to tell them about the vaguely threatening messages—yet. Wyatt would talk to her and perhaps insist. But right now, with the police and her father breathing down her neck, she focused on where she'd sleep. "I'm not going to be run out of my own home."

Her father bit off an annoyed huff, one more in a long series of toe-to-toe battles with his daughter. "You want to be asleep in your bed next time this guy comes around? Eh? Is that what you want?"

Wyatt shook his head in amazement. "The more scared and worried you two are, the more you yell at each other." They both turned and glared at him, and he laughed. "I knew that'd unite you. Penelope, if your police pals are finished with you, I'd be happy to drive you to town for something to eat before your blood sugar bottoms out. Your father can take your truck to the airport, and I'll drop you off when we're finished. How does that sound?"

She opened her mouth to protest—just because she was in the protesting mode—but shut it and nodded. "That sounds fine."

Her father's eyes widened. "Just like that?" He turned to Wyatt and gave a short laugh. "You Sinclairs."

"I'd like to wait here a little longer," she said, more subdued but far from meek.

Wyatt nodded. "I'm not going anywhere."

She attempted a smile. "Why don't I find that comforting?"

Oh, but you do, he thought. If her father wasn't standing there, he'd have said it. But it didn't matter—he'd tell her later. Because what worried her right now, maybe more than having her house broken into and someone sending her peculiar messages, was how comforting she found his presence to be.

Penelope couldn't stop shaking. It was almost like the time Andy McNally had pulled her out of the lake and she shivered so badly she loosened a tooth. But she was twelve then, and she'd had hypothermia. To his credit, Wyatt didn't comment.

When they arrived at the Sunrise Inn, they found

Jack Dunning chatting with Harriet at the front desk.

"Harriet just told me about the break-in," Jack said.

He'd addressed Penelope, but Wyatt said, "I hope it wasn't your doing."

Jack shrugged. "I'm not that subtle." He gave Penelope an unsubtle wink. "Maybe you ought to come clean about what you found in the woods."

"The break-in wasn't necessarily related—"

"Bullshit. You know it was. So do the police and everyone else in town."

His tone was matter-of-fact and very certain, the professional at work. Penelope didn't take offense. "It might be indirectly related. My name's been all over the media—it could have prompted someone to see what they could find of interest in my home."

"But they didn't steal anything," Jack pointed out.

Penelope figured Harriet must have gotten the whole story from Andy, then told Dunning. She said, "That's because I'm not a rich woman. I don't have anything worth stealing."

Dunning leaned toward her, his gaze direct and unflinchingly to the point. "That's because they didn't find directions to Frannie and Colt's plane. Think about taking Wyatt or me out to the crash site, Miss Chestnut. Take your father, take a friend. I don't think you want to be the only person around here who knows where that plane went down. Whoever ransacked your house today could be ready to play hardball. Who knows what he'll do next."

She swallowed, her throat dry, tight. A quick glance at Wyatt told her he agreed with his father's hired detective, if not his rough tactics. She inhaled through her nose, tilted her head. "You mean he might put a gun to my head and force me into the woods?"

"That's one scenario. There are others. Put a gun to Harriet's head, your father's, your mother's. I'm sure there are a variety of ways to motivate you."

"*Why?* It's just a missing plane. I know two people were killed, but it's not as if they robbed a bank before they took off!"

"That's enough, Jack," Wyatt said quietly.

"Just want to be clear here."

"You were clear."

Harriet had gone pale. She said to Penelope, "I'm keeping a room available for you tonight. Your mother—she's gone up to your house—"

"Good, she'll see Pop and he'll calm her down before I have to deal with her. How'd she take it?"

"With her usual stiff upper lip."

Jack grinned. "You Yankees," he said and rolled toward the side door. "I think I'll take a ride out to your place, Miss Penelope, and see if I can be of any service." His humor reached his eyes. "No charge."

He headed out the door, and Penelope turned to Wyatt. "If you want to go with him, go ahead. I'll be fine here. Harriet can drive me out to the airport later on. I kind of like the idea of you keeping an eye on that guy."

"You don't trust him?"

"I don't like him. There's a difference."

Wyatt laughed. "No one likes Jack. That's one of his charms."

Harriet made a mew of protest. "He's been nothing but a gentleman toward me."

"That's because you're not lying to him," Wyatt said.

Harriet looked awkward and uncomfortable, but Penelope didn't come down on Wyatt for his implication that she was a liar. She *was* a liar. But she'd waffled before. She was convinced she needed to be extra careful about changing her story a second time. She needed to think things through, not react to whatever was being thrown at her. The messages, the break-in, Wyatt, Jack—together, they compelled caution, thinking before she acted. She wanted to be deliberate and do what was right when it was right, not leap from impulse to impulse.

And what was this morning, she asked herself, if not responding to an impulse?

It was doing what was right when it was right.

"You look as if you have a lot on your mind," Wyatt said. "I'd like to talk to Jack. You'll be all right?"

She attempted a quick smile. "If Harriet has any Indian pudding left, I'll be just fine."

Harriet touched her arm. "Do you want it warmed up with a scoop of vanilla ice cream?"

"Sounds like lunch to me."

After Wyatt left, Harriet whispered to Penelope, as if someone might hear, "You sure you don't want to follow Jack and Wyatt? You don't seem to trust them—"

"It's not a question of trust, Harriet. Right now I just want food. Besides, Pop has my truck. I'll let all the menfolk do their thing. Dust for fingerprints, examine footprints, pontificate on the peculiarities of my life-style. They'll give up after a while. Then I'll go back up and make sure they didn't miss anything."

Harriet peered at her. "You don't seem very upset for someone whose house was just ransacked."

"Oh, I'm upset. I'm just not going to give Pop, McNally, Pete, Sinclair and that jerk Jack Dunning the satisfaction of falling apart in front of them, which I would do if I don't get my Indian pudding and a few quiet minutes to think this thing through."

"I don't know why you have such a strong negative reaction to Jack. He's been nothing but a gentleman to me. Of course, he has a job to do, and if he perceives you as being in the way, I can understand if he gets a little impatient. Well, I suppose there's nothing you can do, provided you're not lying—"

"Ah," she said, "there's the rub."

Harriet snapped her mouth shut. After a few seconds she inhaled through her nostrils and said, "I'll put two helpings of Indian pudding in the microwave."

THIRTEEN

"So what did you do, Jack," Wyatt said, "ransack Penelope's house to put the fear of God into her?"

"Wish I'd thought of it. I think some little creep's got it in for her. Either he's having fun or there's a larger purpose." He eyed Wyatt. "There's more, isn't there?"

Jack didn't know about the threats. Neither did the police. Wyatt debated how long he'd give Penelope to come to her senses and tell all before he took the bull by the horns. "It's not my place to say. Jack—this may be nothing, but I'm fairly certain my father hasn't told me everything about my uncle's plane crash or his affair with Frannie Beaudine. Do you think he's holding back on you, as well?"

"I always work from that assumption."

They were in Jack's car, driving fast over the bumps, ruts, potholes and frost heaves. The sun and snow had done a job on Penelope's dirt road, making it almost impassable. Wyatt decided he shouldn't believe nine-tenths of what Jack told him.

"The girl's in over her head," Jack said.

Wyatt sighed. "I know it."

Jack pulled in behind Penelope's truck. Her father was still pacing in her driveway. He'd pulled his cigar out of the snow and had it lit, his wife waving a

hand, batting away the smoke as she talked to him.
Wyatt quickly got the gist of what she was telling
him. Their daughter was a menace to herself and
everyone else and needed therapy, peace, quiet.
What she *didn't* need was a Sinclair and a private detective badgering her. "And put that thing out,
you're going to get cancer of the lip."

"These people," Jack muttered beside Wyatt.

When she came up for air and noticed them,
Robby Chestnut had the self-possession not to look
embarrassed, if not happy, either. "The police
would like to talk to both of you."

"Good," Jack said, "I want to talk to them."

Lyman regarded Wyatt, cigar stump still in his
mouth. "Where's my daughter?"

"Having Indian pudding with Harriet. Any news
here?"

"No. Andy's checking up the road for witnesses.
This time of year, you don't get many people up this
way. He's got it in his head that a few hours later his
daughters could have been here helping Penelope
with her maple sugaring and they'd all have gotten
themselves killed."

"That's a leap."

"He'll get over it. Right now he's not a happy
man." He turned to his wife, his expression softening. "Robby, I've got to get back to the airport. You
sticking around?"

"For a few minutes," she said tightly. "I hate this,
Lyman. If she really did find that plane, or if someone refuses to believe she made a mistake—" She
shuddered, obviously thinking things she didn't
want to be thinking. "But I don't know what difference it could possibly make. It's not as if Colt and

Frannie robbed a bank and there's a million dollars sitting up in their plane. It was a tragedy. All anyone will find is the wreckage and human remains." She caught herself, winced at Wyatt. "I'm sorry. I forget Colt was your uncle."

Wyatt acknowledged her apology with a nod. "Did you know him?"

She took a sharp breath, and suddenly he could see some of her daughter in her. "I knew Frannie, too, although not well. She had such energy and optimism—it was contagious. Her death touched us all. Now, if you'll excuse me..." She skirted past him, making her way ably through snow, ice and mud to her car, which she'd parked alongside the road, not on the driveway.

"Your family weren't the only ones left bereaved," Lyman said, watching his wife's retreating figure. He leveled his green eyes on Wyatt. "Frannie Beaudine had her faults, but she was well-regarded around here. A lot of people mourned her passing."

"I understand."

"Yep. I figure you do."

Without further comment, he climbed into his daughter's truck. Jack and the Cold Spring detective came out of the house, walked down the steps and around front. Wyatt went in the opposite direction, across the muddy dirt road. In one spot he sank to his ankles. He passed between two old maples with sap buckets hanging from taps and made his way into Penelope's woods.

He had no trouble finding his way to Bubba Johns's shack. This wasn't the Amazon rainforest. There was no sign of the hermit, and Wyatt stood on the path, squinting against the brightening light and debating whether to have a look around the place. Under normal circumstances he wouldn't consider it. But Bubba Johns had been spotted lurking around Penelope's cabin, and Wyatt wanted to know why.

How the hell did an old man get away with living in the woods? Never mind that he'd set up house-keeping on Sinclair land—what about zoning, the IRS, the Census Bureau, the Board of Health?

Then again, this was Live Free or Die country, and Cold Spring was a small town where the people were willing to bend the rules for one of their own. Although they didn't seem to know much about him, they obviously considered Bubba Johns one of their own.

Instead of going straight to the shack, Wyatt followed a footpath to the brook. He needed to think. Snow clung to rocks, clear water spilling around them. That was all he could hear, the sound of water. He closed his eyes a moment, listening, clearing his mind, breathing in the cool, clean air. He could smell the pungent evergreens, the wet, dead leaves along the edges of the brook where the snow had melted.

When he opened his eyes, a tall, thin, white-haired and white-bearded old man had materialized on the opposite bank. He wore overalls and a frayed wool shirt, and he leaned against a walking stick that was taller than he was. His gray eyes were level, neutral. Two big mutts panted at his side.

Bubba Johns.

Wyatt decided to be formal and straightforward. "Mr. Johns, my name's Wyatt Sinclair. I came up from New York after Penelope Chestnut said she'd found my uncle's plane."

"That's got nothing to do with me."

The hell it didn't. Whatever happened in these woods, Wyatt instinctively suspected this old man would know about it. "She's received threats—she hasn't told the police yet, which makes me think she suspects you and wants to protect you, prove to you she's going to keep her mouth shut." But how could a hermit handle a computer, a fax machine? "Right now the police are at her house. Someone broke in and took a look around."

"And you think that was me?"

"I don't know. I'm keeping an open mind. No one believes her story about finding a dump. They think she found my uncle's plane."

Wyatt paused, but the old man said nothing, just stared at him with those penetrating eyes.

"My family owns this land. We have no quarrel with you staying here, provided you haven't committed a crime."

"And how would I prove that to you?"

"I figure you must know these woods pretty well. Even if you haven't found the plane wreckage yourself, I bet you have a good idea where Penelope was on Sunday." Using his toe, Wyatt rubbed the snow off a rock. "I'd like you to take me out there and let me see for myself. Maybe I can take some of the heat off her. I suspect someone's trying to keep her off balance while they search for the wreckage. She's not going to change her story again until she's sure it won't hurt anyone."

"You're a suspicious sort, Wyatt Sinclair," the old man said.

Wyatt grinned. "Hell, you sound like half the women in my life."

Bubba Johns smiled slightly and straightened, holding on to his walking stick with one hand. "I first saw Penelope stepping stones in this brook on a hot summer day. She'd wandered up from the lake—she was about ten. She was so caught up in what she was doing she didn't realize how far she'd come." The probing gray eyes fastened on Wyatt. "Sometimes she doesn't realize the dangers around her, and she forgets how far she's gone into the wilderness. Once, I had to lead her home."

"Meaning?"

The old man grinned. "I'll take you to the wreckage."

Wyatt went still. He didn't want to jump to any premature conclusions. The old hermit could be lying, exaggerating, mistaken. But before Wyatt could ask him any questions, Penelope shouted, *"Bubba!"* from above them, bolted from behind a hemlock and charged down the hill, undeterred by snow that was almost knee-deep in places and brush whipping against her legs and torso.

She stopped at the brook's edge, and for a second Wyatt thought she might walk right through the water to get to Bubba Johns.

"Bubba," she said, "look at the mess we've got when it's a *dump* I found in the woods. Can you imagine what'll happen if I change my story again? You'll have reporters crawling through the woods. They'll film your house, they'll scare your dogs. You'll have investigators and historians and more Sinclairs and—and—and God knows what kinds of cretins. You should see this private detective, Jack Dunning, already skulking around here."

Bubba had no visible reaction to this tirade. "He searched my house this morning."

"There, you see what I mean?"

"Perhaps truth is our best recourse."

"Bubba, trust me. Our best recourse is to say I didn't see anything on Sunday."

"But you did," the old man said.

She groaned.

Wyatt had the feeling Bubba didn't have much use for people. But he did like Penelope. He turned to Wyatt. "It's too far to go today, and I'm tired. Be here in the morning." He added, "Early."

Penelope threw up her hands in frustration. "Give this thing a few more days to die down."

But two people, one of them Penelope Chestnut, were apparently more than Bubba Johns could handle at one time. He motioned to his dogs, and they jumped up and trotted at his side as he turned his back on Wyatt and Penelope and walked up the hill.

"Let him go," Wyatt said.

Naturally Penelope turned on him. "I *knew* you'd sneak out here."

"Starting to think like a Sinclair, are you?"

"You don't trust me."

"Apparently with good reason. You found Colt and Frannie's plane."

She had the good grace to squirm. "I was trying to do the right thing."

"How is it right to lie to Colt's family? His body must be in the wreckage."

Her eyes met his. "I'm sorry. I didn't fully consider your family's feelings. I figured if Frannie and your uncle had been dead all these years—well, they could rest in peace. The plane's in a beautiful loca-

tion, quiet, isolated. As graves go—but that's not my
call. I realize that now. I didn't think about closure
for your family…what you must have gone through
all these years."

"Because we're Sinclairs?"

She didn't duck the question. "Maybe."

"People around here demonize us, blame us for
Frannie's death. If Colt hadn't swept her off her feet,
she'd still be alive."

"Frankly, I think people see it that Frannie got
killed. They assume Colt would have died young,
anyway. He just took Frannie with him. I'm not saying that's what I think—I don't know what went on
between Colt and Frannie. I just thought it'd be best
if I found a dump on Sunday instead of a plane
wreck."

"The threats didn't play a role in changing your
mind?"

She shook her head. "They didn't start until afterward."

They walked up the icy path to Bubba Johns's
shack. He had a neat woodpile under a tarp, an ax
on his chopping block, a homemade wheelbarrow.
Everything was rustic and functional. Wyatt noticed
plants in his windows—chives and parsley. The hermit had marked out a vegetable garden in a small
clearing.

"Bubba's big on bartering," Penelope said. "He's
doing sap now—he'll collect fiddleheads later in the
spring."

"He's an enterprising fellow for someone who
lives at a subsistence level. Is there any evidence of
mental illness?"

"Beyond living alone in the middle of the woods?

He keeps to himself, and he's never bothered anyone. He's not violent, he doesn't peek in people's windows, he doesn't run naked down Main Street. I guess we still believe in harmless eccentrics."

"Do you know what brought him out here?"

She shook her head. "I think he's shy, introverted—a gentle soul in a fast-paced, violent world. He's awkward around people, but I don't think of him as a misanthrope. I guess he's more like a monk."

"Your own Saint Francis of Assisi?"

"Well, I don't know about his religious convictions. I just mean his sensibilities. He's careful out here. He gets his water from an above-ground spring nearby, and he doesn't dump his garbage in the woods or use chemicals on his garden. He's old for a hippie, but he's more of your crunchy-granola type than your Unabomber type."

Wyatt gave her a penetrating look. "How long do you think he's known about the plane wreckage?"

"I can't even hazard a guess. He wouldn't consider it any of his business, and it's not as if he knew Colt and Frannie. He might not have realized the plane's been missing all these years."

"Unlike yours, his curiosity is limited."

She smiled, taking no offense. "I guess you could say that."

"The plane—when you saw it on Sunday—"

"I'm not positive it was their plane, Wyatt, or even that it *was* a plane, although there doesn't seem to be much doubt. It's on a very steep, rocky hill, and with the snow and ice and the late hour, I didn't risk a close look."

"Did you go back?"

"No. I made that up. I didn't want more tracks for someone else to follow. As it was, even with the snow we've had I've been concerned that someone knowledgeable and determined could have found my tracks and followed them—not that it's a direct route. I *was* lost."

"That part was true?"

"Everything was true except the stuff about the dump, which no one believes, anyway. I've always been such a lousy liar. You? Are you much of a liar?"

"I've never had much call to lie."

"A do-as-you-please Sinclair," she said airily, without criticism, and cut a smile at him.

When they arrived at her cabin, only Andy McNally remained. He informed Penelope that they'd finished their investigation and she was free to go inside. "I don't think I want Jane and Rebecca up here until we know more about what's going on."

"I understand. Sap's been slow the last couple of days, anyway."

"You spending the night at the inn?"

She shrugged, and Wyatt could see how much she hated being run out of her own home. "Probably."

McNally grinned, cuffing her on the shoulder reassuringly. "We'll get to the bottom of this mess. I'll have a beer with you tonight."

"Thanks, Andy."

"Don't thank me. I still want to know everything you haven't told me."

He climbed into his car, but before he shut the door, he said, "You're not in this thing alone, even if you're trying to be. You take the world out to that plane wreck, this nutcase might stop pestering you." She opened her mouth to protest, but McNally cut her off. "I'll make sure a car drives up here a few times tonight."

After the police chief left, Wyatt noticed Penelope had developed a little shiver. She saw him watching her and said, "Low blood sugar. It's that stupid Indian pudding I ate for lunch. Gave me a sugar high, and now I'm paying for it. I need a piece of cheese."

"You're not just cold and a little unnerved?"

"Not me," she said and headed inside.

Wyatt followed her. The place wasn't torn apart—it had been searched, not vandalized—but things were not neat. Drawers opened, stuff hanging out, some of it scattered on the floor, couch and chair cushions askew. He checked her study and bedroom, saw that they, too, had been thoroughly explored. Penelope, however, was bent on food. She tore open her refrigerator, dug out a hunk of Vermont cheddar, and smacked it on the counter. With a paring knife from a drawer, she hacked off a piece of cheese. "Want some?" she asked. He shook his head, and she ate. "I love cheese, even if it's not lowfat. Okay. So, what now? I need to water my plants and pack. One night at the inn should sufficiently calm everyone's nerves."

Wyatt helped her water her plants in the study. He noticed her hands, her long fingers, the delicate way she handled the tender green shoots, no sign of the restlessness or bridled energy he'd witnessed when he saw her after her troubled landing. It wasn't anything that had happened in the past few days, he felt certain—it was simply the task at hand, the incongruities of her life.

"I'll clean this mess up later," she said, and went into her bedroom to pack. She emerged a few minutes later with a backpack slung over one shoulder. "Are you going to tell Jack Dunning about the plane?"

"I'm still debating. I might want to see it first before I tell him or my father."

"Your father trust Dunning?"

"As much as he can trust anyone, I suppose. You see, I'm used to people who aren't long on trust. I always look for the undercurrent, the unspoken."

"So if our pal Jack seems to have taken a shine to Harriet, it could be a ploy to get something out of her?"

"That would be my suspicion."

Penelope thought a moment. "Well, Harriet's heart's been broken by bigger bastards than Jack Dunning. Not that he's any prize, but it's not as if she really knows him. She's just smitten."

"She's known Jack as long as we've known each other."

Her green eyes fastened on him. "Who says I'm not just smitten?"

Penelope drove her truck, when her father had returned to the cabin, Wyatt his car, to the inn, where he went upstairs to make a few calls and she joined Harriet and her mother in the kitchen. She thought she heard sighs of relief when they saw her backpack and realized she was staying. She made her own pot of tea and warmed up two cinnamon nut scones while her mother tore spinach into a pitted aluminum colander, saying nothing. Harriet fluttered around with cloths and sponges. Penelope didn't know if it would be a good thing or a bad thing to tell them she'd reformulated her plane wreck story. Probably best to keep her mouth shut.

"Harriet's handling dinner tonight," her mother said, still tearing furiously. "I'm just doing some of the prep work. We only have four guests, including Wyatt and Jack."

"That doesn't include me, does it? I'm staying, but I wouldn't want to be considered a guest. But of course I'll pay."

"You don't have to pay," Harriet said.

"I paid when I stayed those two nights after the flea infestation." She'd taken in a stray dog for a few days, fed him, cleaned him up and found him a home. He'd left her fleas. It reminded her of one of her mother's favorite sayings—*Lie down with dogs, come up with fleas.* Penelope wondered if that was what she was thinking now. "Which room are you putting me in?"

Her cousin floated by with her sponge. "The Tower Room."

Her and Ann Boleyn. Penelope wasn't fooled. The Tower Room was in an odd nook on the third floor, just down the hall from Harriet's suite. Harriet was a light sleeper. One creak of the floorboard and she'd be poking her head out the door.

"Penelope," her mother said, "I'm going out to the sugar house in a little while. Would you care to join me?"

It was the *last* thing she wanted to do. "Do you need my help?"

"I could use someone to keep the fire going. Rebecca and Jane are stopping by, too."

Good. At least she and her mother wouldn't be alone. If things were hopping at the sugar house, it could be a pleasant diversion. Her, her mother, friends, all that heat and boiling sap. If things were slow, it could be deadly. Her, her mother, all that gaping silence. She said she'd go, and, tea and scones consumed, apple in one hand, she grabbed the key to the Tower Room at the front desk and headed up the stairs.

Her room was the most unusual in the inn, with its dormer and slanted ceilings and odd little corners. It was done in shades of dark blue, with lots of wood and a touch of green. A window seat piled with pillows looked out on the lake. Penelope felt herself drawn to it, ready to just flop out and read a book, listen to music, forget the questions and fears and longings that had plagued her for days. Instead she made herself unpack, change into a fresh turtleneck and sweater, and scoot down to meet her mother.

Except she got distracted at Wyatt's room.

She could hear him talking through the door but was unable to make out words. Leaning closer, she clearly distinguished, "All right, I'll call you tomorrow," and suddenly the door opened, throwing her off balance. She jerked back, but before she could make good her escape, Wyatt grabbed her wrist and dragged her inside.

"Listening at keyholes, are we?"

"I was just about to knock when the door opened—"

"You are the worst liar."

He kicked the door shut with one foot, and his arm went around her, pulling her close. In that half second before his mouth found hers, she could have protested, bolted or otherwise said no, but she didn't. The kiss was long, tender, the urgency of this morning banked back, and she felt herself melting into him, wanting nothing more than what that moment offered.

But her mother was waiting downstairs, and for once Penelope exercised prudence. "Who were you talking to on the phone?" she asked, straightening her shirt and sweater.

"My office in New York."

"Is being here costing you money?"

"Millions," he said, "billions."

"Here I've slept with you and I barely know what you do. I don't usually do that, you know. Sleep with a man and then get to know him." She went still, all the way down deep, and studied him. The dark hair, the dark eyes, the slices and hard angles of his face. "Of course, I thought I already knew you."

He smiled, a twitch of amusement at one corner of his mouth. "Is that an admission that you've fantasized about having sex with a Sinclair?"

"It's nothing of the kind, and you're a horrible man for suggesting such a thing," she said airily, stifling a laugh. "Lucky for you my mother's waiting downstairs. We're off to the sugar house. What will you do?"

"Have dinner and fantasize about having sex with a blond Yankee pilot."

"I'm serious."

He laughed. "So am I."

The man was impossible. Irresistible. And she had no expectations about where their attraction would land them down the road. "Have you decided what to tell Jack?"

"I haven't decided anything except I'm trying Harriet's Indian pudding for dessert."

FOURTEEN

"The Sinclairs didn't buy their land in Cold Spring until the nineteen thirties," Harriet said as she and Jack Dunning walked up Main Street after dinner. It was dark, not too cold. "My mother's family came here in the seventeen hundreds. My father's family came in the mid-eighteen hundreds. Robby moved here from Massachusetts when she was ten."

Jack smiled. "I can't imagine sitting in the same town for two or three hundred years. I knew my grandparents on my father's side. That's it."

"Are you interested in finding out about your ancestors?"

"Don't know what difference it'd make. I consider Texas my home now, but I don't expect I think about home the same way you do, Harriet. When I've put aside enough money, I'm going back to Texas, buying a piece of land, building a house. I'd like to own a ranch."

"Why did you move back to New York?"

He walked close to her, close enough that she could smell his sharp cologne and occasionally brushed against his arm. He wore his shearling-lined jacket, his cowboy hat and boots. He couldn't have looked more out of place on Main Street in a small New England village if he'd been naked. He said, "I pissed off a lot of people in Dallas. Figured I could make some money in New York, let things cool off. Brandon Sinclair's not my only client, but he's got the kind of dough that if he says hop, I hop."

"I've never met him. Wyatt's the first Sinclair to come to Cold Spring since Frannie and Colt disappeared."

"Wyatt's a throwback," Jack said. "Except for not making a marriage stick, Brandon's a gentleman. He doesn't seem to need to slay dragons and climb tall mountains. I think losing his brother sucked most of that Sinclair bullshit right out of him."

Harriet hunched her shoulders against a sudden stiff breeze. She hadn't worn a hat or gloves. She'd have red ears by the time they returned to the inn. "The Sinclairs have always been considered outsiders here. Owning land didn't make a difference. Willard Sinclair—Brandon's father—used to hunt and fish with my uncle, Penelope's grandfather, but it's not as if they were friends. Willard was the rich outsider, my uncle was the local."

"Then Frannie Beaudine crossed the big divide," Jack said.

"Yes, she did. But so did Colt. They both broke the rules."

"The forbidden relationship."

Harriet gave him a sharp look but saw that he wasn't mocking her or Frannie and Colt. They kept walking, crossing a side street, moving away from the village shops. "I suppose Frannie might not have considered herself a local anymore, but she was hardly in the Sinclairs' league. She was an adventurer herself, and a scholar—she just wasn't rich."

"Who do you think was in charge? Colt or Frannie? He was the rich boy, but she was older."

"I'm not sure either was in charge. It could have been a partnership."

"That's nowadays. In the fifties—"

"My parents have always had a partnership, and they're almost eighty."

"Then they're lucky."

He walked a few paces, his boots clicking on the pavement. The street sweepers would be out before too long, clearing the roads of the sand that had accumulated over the winter. Harriet felt a sudden, deep yearning for spring. She would dig in her garden and serve tea and scones on the porch.

"Okay," Jack said. "Let me put it another way. Who took the lead? Who was the first to let the other know the interest was there? Frannie or Colt?"

"It could have been mutual, one of those moments where you just don't know…"

Jack shook his head, holding back a laugh that somehow wasn't patronizing. "For a Yankee innkeeper, Harriet, you're a hell of a romantic."

She glanced at him. "Has your work made you cynical?"

He shrugged. "I think of myself as a realist."

"That's what all cynics say."

"All right, in my work I've found that to unravel a crime, you have to unravel the relationships of the people involved. Sometimes it's easy—sometimes it's dicey."

"But there was no crime. Frannie and Colt took off, presumably to elope or at least be together, and their plane went down. That's a tragedy. It's not criminal."

Jack paused at a corner. Across the street, partially lit, was the First Congregational Church of Cold Spring, a pristine, traditional, white New England church built in the early nineteenth century. His face was lost in the dark shadows. "We don't know why their plane went down. We don't know why they picked that particular night. Until we have the plane and the bodies, it's an open investigation as far as I'm concerned."

Harriet felt a chill. "You can't believe—you can't think their plane was sabotaged or anything of the sort!"

"I don't believe or disbelieve anything. I could tick off an easy dozen possibilities for what happened that night. Until I know what *did* happen, I don't rule anything in or out."

"I suppose that's sensible, from your point of view. After all, you're a detective. You're not a participant."

"That's right." His voice had softened, its deep tone like warm liquid down her spine. He touched her arm. "This is the church where you were found? Come on, show me that doorstep."

They crossed the street, and Harriet brought him to the side entrance. The main entrance was reserved for Sundays and major church functions. "I was found right here," she said, pointing to the welcome mat. "I was in an apple basket, sleeping."

"What were you wearing?"

"A warm sleeper. It was red. And I was wrapped in a white blanket."

"Store-bought?"

She nodded. "My parents still have it. The police took everything as potential evidence—but none of it helped. They never had any credible leads."

"Incredible ones?"

"Just that I turned up the night after Colt and Frannie disappeared."

"Hell of a thing, leaving a baby on a doorstep. You still a member of the church?"

His question caught her by surprise. She nodded. "Yes, although I'm not very active."

"Is it tough, being the daughter of the retired minister?"

"It could be awkward—my father cast a long shadow. But I try to stay out of the way. I think by now people realize that anything I say isn't necessarily the voice of my father."

"He's a good man?"

She smiled. "The best."

"You're a good woman yourself, Harriet. Come on, let's head back before I freeze my ass off. Damned northern springs. In Texas, the bluebonnets are blooming."

She smiled. He was a Texan at heart, but with a New York upbringing.

"They must be beautiful."

He shot her a quick look, the streetlight catching his face, and she saw the spark in his eyes, the sudden warmth. "You're right. They are. You should see them sometime."

"Maybe I will," she said, and they walked to the inn.

Wyatt was almost finished with his second martini, which, under the circumstances, was two martinis too many. His head was spinning, his ability to function impaired. He didn't need alcohol. But he wasn't going anywhere, not tonight. He was the sole patron at the Victorian bar at the Sunrise Inn. The only other occupant was the bartender, who made a hell of a martini.

For the past hour, Wyatt had replayed the conversation he'd had with his father after dinner. It had been difficult and revealing, and Wyatt had been unrelenting, brutal in his determination to get to the truth.

He was not proud of himself. He was not proud of his father. Tonight, not for the first time in his life, he didn't much like being a Sinclair.

"Tell me what Jack Dunning knows that I don't know. Goddamn it, tell me what you've been holding back all these years."

His father had taken in a short breath, said quietly, "You don't trust me."

"This isn't a question of trust. You dispatched Jack up here, not me. He's paid, I'm not. He's not family, I am. Therefore, I presume you've told him things you haven't told me."

Brandon Sinclair's enviable reserve had snapped. "You think you're such a smart son of a bitch, Wyatt. You throw my money in my face and go out and make your own. You throw my sensibility in my face and go off and have your goddamned adventures, get this family's name in the papers again for their recklessness."

"And that I did on purpose. I killed Hal and almost killed myself just to embarrass you."

Even with two martinis swimming inside him, Wyatt regretted that comment. The pettiness of it.

Letting his father get to him. Playing out the father-son battles all over again when they were both adults now. It was time to let go of their past failings and transgressions.

"Whether you like it or not, Wyatt," his father had said, tight, clipped, "you're a part of this family."

"Father, I need to know the truth. Even before I came up here, I sensed you were holding back. Now I'm convinced of it."

They'd gone back and forth like that, his father not budging. He didn't persist in making denials, but simply, in effect, told Wyatt to mind his own business, pointing out that nobody had asked him to go to New Hampshire. But it was too late for him to pull back. He was here, and he was in deep.

Finally, he gave up. He couldn't compel his father to talk. He could only do what he thought was right. And what was right, he knew, was to tell Brandon Sinclair that Penelope Chestnut had found a plane on Sunday, not an old dump.

"There's no guarantee it's Colt and Frannie's plane," Wyatt said, "but I don't know what else it would be. She's taking me out there tomorrow."

"Have you told Jack?" His father's voice was calm. The only indication Wyatt's news had any impact was a slightly strangled quality to it. "I'd like you to take him with you. I don't trust that girl."

"I'd rather wait until I see what's out there before I tell anyone. And Jack's not my employee or my partner. Whatever you want him to know, you can tell him yourself."

"Goddamn it, Wyatt."

He'd hung up. On his own father. It wasn't done in his family. He thought of Penelope going toe-to-

toe with her father, sticking her tongue out, arguing openly and vigorously. But there was affection there, respect, trust. Wyatt had never known what there was between him and his father beyond tension and mutual suspicion. If his parents hadn't divorced, if they'd spent more time together when he was growing up, maybe they'd have worked things out. But Wyatt didn't think so.

Two minutes after his son hung up on him, Brandon Sinclair called back. Without preamble, he said, "Colt and Frannie left that night with a fortune in cut diamonds. Frannie found them in the warehouse when she was putting together the collection your grandfather donated to the Met. In today's market, they'd be worth in the neighborhood of ten million dollars."

"Jesus," Wyatt had breathed. "A hell of a nest egg."

"The family decided—my father decided—to keep the theft a secret. It wasn't pride. He blamed Frannie entirely and assumed Colt was an unwitting participant. He and Colt..." He hesitated, reluctant to speak of a beloved, long mourned older brother. To Brandon Sinclair, it was unseemly to speak of personal matters. "They had a difficult relationship. The public perception of Colt aside, my father didn't consider him capable of engineering anything that happened that night. In any case, he kept quiet about the diamonds in an effort to discourage treasure seekers. He didn't want someone to find the plane, loot it and then not report it as a way of covering their tracks."

"They'd be the prime suspect."

"Precisely. Also, if Frannie and Colt were still by

some miracle alive—" He took a breath, almost as if he were eleven again, praying his brother was still alive.

"Revealing the missing diamonds could have put them at risk. My father was a tough, unemotional man, but Colt's death shook him to his core. He never got over it."

"You?" Wyatt asked quietly.

"I worshiped my older brother, but I'm not sure I ever really knew him. Losing him has left a hole in me, an emptiness that I've learned to live with." He stopped abruptly, and Wyatt could feel his embarrassment. "Well, that's not important at the moment."

Wyatt didn't push him. "How did you find out about the diamonds? Did your father tell you?"

"No, oh, no," Brandon said, as if that were unimaginable. "I was a boy in a repressed household that was nonetheless filled with high emotion and drama. I was adept at listening at keyholes. When he was dying, I confronted my father, and he admitted everything—he seemed relieved to tell me. But he asked me not to speak of the diamonds, and I promised I wouldn't."

"And Jack? What does he know?"

"I told him it's probable something of tremendous monetary value is in the wreckage. I couldn't—" He sighed, sounding tired. "I suppose it's splitting hairs, but I didn't want to break that promise to my father prematurely. Well, then. You have your information, Wyatt. If this girl found the plane, she could have helped herself to the diamonds. I'd keep up my guard if I were you."

"I will." Then he added, "Thanks."

"I only want to know what happened to Colt. I don't give a damn about the diamonds. If Penelope Chestnut or anyone else stole them, so be it. Just let me bury my brother."

Wyatt drank the last of his martini. Stolen diamonds. Ten million dollars. Definitely not on his list of what his father had been keeping from him. He had no idea what he'd have done in his father's place. Maybe the whole damned mess *was* none of his business, and he should just go home.

Ten million. That was a hell of a lot of money.

Penelope materialized at his table and dropped onto the chair opposite him. "Do I smell like maple syrup?"

"You smell...steamy."

"That sounds suggestive. I helped at the sugar shack. We all had biscuits and maple syrup for supper. I'm going to have to reform after the way I've been eating the past few days." She peered at him, frowning. "Are you all right?"

He smiled. "It's been a long day, and the dark New Hampshire nights are getting to me."

She took him seriously. "No city lights. But this is nothing—you should be here in January. Zero degrees out, darker than the pits of hell at four-thirty. Eek. I have friends who swear by Saint-John's-wort for SAD. Seasonal Affected Disorder. I think my flying keeps me from getting too squirrelly."

"You're in a good mood for someone who had her house broken into today."

"Well, I've had a pleasant couple of hours. There's something about a sugar shack. Mother doesn't have a huge operation, but it's way bigger than my fire by the driveway. I love sugaring. You know winter's ending, and while I love snowshoeing and cross-country skiing and reading by the fire, by March I'm ready for buds on the trees and crocuses popping up."

She sighed, smug and pleased. Wyatt was just perverse enough to wonder if this morning's festivities in bed had anything to do with her mood. She ordered a Kahlúa and cream—she needed the protein, she said—and stifled a satisfied yawn. Wyatt decided he wasn't going to throw her into a funk by telling her about the ten million in diamonds sitting in Frannie and Colt's plane. Or not. He thought of the forty-five years it had been missing, the old hermit, the locals, the nasty messages Penelope had received—those diamonds could be long gone.

"Any leads on who broke into my house?" she asked after her drink had arrived.

"Not that anyone's shared with me."

"McNally usually comes around for a beer by now. Did you tell your father about the wreckage?"

He nodded. "He's still absorbing it."

"He'll tell Dunning," she said.

"That's possible. He wants us to take Jack with us tomorrow. He doesn't trust you."

"Me? Why not, because I tried to protect the privacy of a hermit and an eccentric cousin?"

Wyatt suspected that was part of his father's reasoning. But mainly his father thought Penelope Chestnut might have helped herself to a fortune in diamonds. "My father doesn't know you. Are you going to tell McNally you fibbed about the dump?"

She sipped her rich drink, and after what she'd eaten that day, Wyatt half expected her to keel over. "He never believed me, anyway. I'll wait until we check out the wreckage tomorrow. Maybe it's a different plane—a less famous missing plane, one we didn't even realize had gone down here. No point creating another tempest."

"Whatever's out there, I think you should tell the world about it tomorrow after we get back. It could discourage whoever's harassing you."

"That would be nice, but I don't want him discouraged, I want him caught. Heck of a week." She worked on an ice cube, as relaxed as he'd seen her. Her cheeks were still rosy from the heat of the sugar shack. "Grounded, a Sinclair in town, followed, weird anonymous messages, house ransacked. No wonder I slept with you. I'm addled."

Wyatt grinned. "Now you're sleeping one floor up from me."

"With Harriet down the hall," she reminded him, and cut him a quick smile. "She's a light sleeper."

"A pity."

Andy McNally arrived later than usual, and he didn't look pleased to see Penelope and Wyatt having a drink together. She leaned over and whispered, "I think we're a poor substitute for Harriet."

"She and Jack went for a walk."

"I know. I saw them on my way back."

"Jack's not—" Wyatt hesitated, then said, "He's here on a job. Harriet would be wise to keep that in mind. I could ask my father to rein him in, but I don't know that it would do any good. He doesn't control how Jack conducts his business."

"Harriet's a lot stronger than people give her credit for," Penelope said, as if convincing herself, too. "Just because she's single doesn't mean she's naive about men. In fact, quite the contrary. She probably knows more about men than a lot of women who've been married a million years. Besides, she's kissed her share of frogs."

Wyatt didn't relax. "I hope to hell she doesn't think Jack's going to turn into Prince Charming."

Penelope's cheerful expression clouded, and she nodded. "I talk a good game, don't I? She and Dunning—well, right now I'm having enough trouble living my own life, never mind hers. I suppose I should talk to Andy, tell him about the fax and the instant message. Get it over with. You sticking around?"

"No, I think I'd only complicate your discussion with McNally. I'll head on up."

"Stagger up, from the looks of you. How many martinis?"

"Just two."

Her happy, irreverent mood reasserted itself. She grinned at him as she got to her feet. "There's hope for you yet, Sinclair. If it took six martinis to get to you, I'd want more than one floor between us."

She went to the bar, and Wyatt slid unsteadily to his feet, his stomach, his head, everything swooshing and spinning. He didn't exactly stagger, but he wasn't in top form. At least he wouldn't have to contend with Penelope's lumpy couch, her moose head, the thought of her in the very next room. A good night's sleep was what he needed, one floor down from her or not. He glanced at her, saw her smiling at McNally as if that would soften the blow of withholding the messages from him, and he had his doubts about getting any sleep at all.

FIFTEEN

Penelope awoke to the sun streaming through translucent curtains, the sounds of birds outside the window and the scent of the unlit lemon candle on the bed stand. Life could be good, she thought, then rolled over and called Steve, a guy she knew from high school who worked at the local hardware store. He liked to come to her cabin to go fishing. "I need new locks for my doors," she told him.

"Penelope, you need new doors. That slider belongs in a museum."

"I could use a new house to go with the new doors, too, but today I'll have to make do with locks. Can you stop by and see what you can do?"

"Yeah, yeah. No promises."

"Today?"

He sighed. "I'll try."

"Good. I probably won't be around. If anyone asks, just say I sent you."

"No, I'll tell them I'm breaking in. I've always wanted Andy McNally and the Sinclair family on my case. You owe me, Chestnut."

The thought of fresh locks made her feel more in control of her life. She showered, put on her hiking clothes—trail pants, expedition shirt, good socks—and slipped downstairs and out the main door without being seen. Wyatt might manage on the inn's continental breakfast, but after yesterday's carbo load, she needed eggs and bacon. Listening to the birds and exulting in the springlike temperature, she scooted up Main Street to Jeannie's Diner.

Wyatt was at one of the booths, digging into a ham and cheese omelette and Jeannie's incomparable, decadent home fries. He had on his hikers, jeans and a canvas shirt. No leather jacket to be seen. He must be acclimating, Penelope thought with amusement.

She slid onto the bench opposite him. "I'm surprised Jeannie let you sit here by yourself. Usually it's a minimum of two people to a booth."

"There's not exactly a crowd."

"This is Jeannie's empire. You live by her rules."

"Jeannie would be my waitress?"

"And the co-owner with her grandfather, Ed, who only comes around to make sure she's keeping the grill to his cleanliness standards. He was always a maniac about a clean grill."

He studied her. "You're in a good mood this morning."

"It's the thrill of getting into the woods. I can only stand staying in one spot so long. And it's a gorgeous day. The brooks will be full, the water rushing over the rocks, everything melting. A good hike's the only thing that comes close to flying." At that remark, his eyebrows rose provocatively, and she laughed. "Well, not the only thing."

Jeannie, rail-thin and moving fast, flipped over Penelope's mug and splashed in coffee. "Heard your place got broken into yesterday. Can't be anyone from around here. We all know you don't have anything worth stealing, except my grandfather. He's always kind of had an eye for that moose head of yours." Ed had been known to stop at her place with his fishing pole. Jeannie set the coffeepot on her skinny hip and leaned back, eyeing Penelope. "You okay?"

"I'm fine. Thanks. Just hungry."

"Good, because I've got a mess of food to get rid of. I put in an extra order with all those reporters crawling around. They stayed ten minutes and went home. I sold out of pies, and that was that."

"I'm sorry—"

"Not your fault. What can I get you?"

Penelope ordered scrambled eggs, toast and orange juice, and Jeannie added an order of sausage to it and tore off behind the counter. "She never does anything at a leisurely pace," Penelope said. "You know, if you weren't here, she'd have interrogated me about you and Jack Dunning. Nothing happens in this town that she doesn't know about."

"You seem well-informed yourself."

"Only by default. I don't ask. Jeannie asks. Trust me, everyone who comes in here today will have to fill her in on what they know about you and me now that we've had breakfast together."

"You could have pretended you didn't know me."

"Uh-uh. She'd have made me sit at the counter, and I really like a booth."

After breakfast, they took Penelope's truck to her place. Steve had been by and put a perfunctory new lock on her side door. He left an envelope with the key inside and a note saying the slider was totaled. She examined the lock. "It doesn't look like much, does it? It's shiny, anyway. Of course, all anyone has to do is walk around to the deck and come in through the slider. Maybe I'll get a big dog."

She and Wyatt loaded two hip packs with food, water, cell phone and her wilderness day-trip medical kit, complete with its own little instruction manual. "After Sunday," she told him, "I'm not taking any chances."

As she'd predicted, the snow was melting fast, the sap was flowing, and the brooks were running high. All around were the sounds of birds and water. With the soft snow, much of it melted already, they didn't bother with snowshoes and just trekked along in their boots. Penelope noticed that Wyatt's hiking was smooth and strong, totally confident. She debated bringing it up and finally asked, "Have you missed hiking?"

He glanced at her, the sunlight catching the ends of his dark hair. "Often."

"Will you go back to it?"

"Not at the same level. I'm not as restless and driven as I was ten years ago, and not just because of Hal. He was my hiking buddy, and I miss him—I'll never get over what happened to us in Tasmania. I don't want to. I intend to remember every second of our ordeal for as long as I live." He paused, his gaze settling on Penelope, and she had no idea if he was seeing her or his dead friend. "It's a part of who I am."

"But he's not the only reason—"

"No. He's not. I don't have to keep climbing tall mountains. I don't have to keep proving myself. For better or for worse, I'm comfortable in my own skin. I choose not to be my grandfather, or Sinclairs before him, always needing the next challenge, the next enemy to conquer."

"Then why did you come up here?"

He stopped, stared at her. "Because Colt's my uncle, and no matter how much he pretends otherwise, I know my father is still haunted by not knowing what happened to him."

"But Jack Dunning could have handled the situation," Penelope said, ignoring the sense this was none of her business. "You didn't need to get involved. Why did you?"

He gave her a quick, irreverent, unexpected smile. "Karma. I needed to meet you."

She shook her head, staying on her point. "I just think you were bored."

With that in-your-face remark, she pushed ahead on the path. She could feel his black eyes boring into her. He hadn't liked what she'd said—probably because it had cut too close to the bone. The man was bored stiff on Wall Street with his numbers and money. Ebenezer Scrooge he was not.

Behind her, he said, "You're feeling damned smug, aren't you?"

She turned to face him, walking backward. "You just hate it because I'm right. You might not need to climb Everest, but you needed to confront a nice, hardworking New Hampshire woman you thought was lying through her teeth."

"Which I was right about," he reminded her.

She shrugged. "As comfortable as you might be in your own skin, Sinclair, you need a little adventure once in a while." She grinned at him, suddenly feeling energetic in spite of the grim task ahead. "You just got more than you bargained for when you headed north."

"And you got more than you bargained for when you lied."

With a rush of awareness, she remembered yesterday morning. "Checkmate," she said, and about-faced.

There was no sign of Bubba Johns at his hillside shack. One of his mutts charged out of the shadows, barking and panting, foam around his mouth from running. The other dog didn't seem to be around. They checked outside, but no Bubba, no second dog.

"I'll take a look inside," Wyatt said, "just in case."

He opened the door and, without leaving the threshold, peered inside the small shack. "Anything?" Penelope asked.

He shook his head.

She tried to ignore her growing uneasiness. "Bubba usually takes both dogs with him, but maybe this one's out of sorts for some reason. Well, I'm no expert on hermits or dogs. I expect Bubba changed his mind about taking you to the wreckage or figured I would and he was off the hook."

"You're probably right."

But she could sense his continued uneasiness.

They made their way down the hill and crossed the brook deeper into the Sinclair woods. Although, prior to Sunday, she'd never been to the ravine where she found the Piper Cub, Penelope was confident she could find it. On her way home on Sunday, she'd thrashed around in the woods for an hour before hitting familiar landmarks. Then it was a straight shot back.

Once they left the main trail and familiar ground,

she had to stop several times to think, orient herself, remember. "It'd be a damned dirty trick if I can't find my way back, after all." She glanced around her. Wyatt said nothing, obviously not wanting to break her concentration, and in another second, she had it. "Left and over that rise."

Soon they were at the rock where she'd paused to catch her breath and wish she'd had another Nutri-Grain bar. Directly below them was the ravine. To their right and down the steep hillside was the twisted heap of metal she'd found Sunday, presumably the wreckage of Colt Sinclair and Frannie Beaudine's plane.

"Over there." Penelope pointed, out of breath more from anticipation than exertion. "The sun's not hitting it—*there.* I see it."

Wyatt didn't. He squinted, following her pointed finger. Then he went rigid, his jaw setting hard, and he nodded. "I've got it."

Penelope's mouth had gone dry, but she didn't reach for her water bottle. "You can see why I didn't risk getting close to it on Sunday. It's rough going, and it was late, and I was already lost. The last thing I needed was to slip down the hill and bang my head on a rock." She swallowed, her throat tight with tension. "Wyatt—I could be wrong."

"We'll know soon. We can make our way along the top of the hill a few more yards and work our way down at an angle. It shouldn't be too difficult."

"I agree."

He glanced at her, everything about him contained, controlled. "It must have been a hell of a thing, spotting the wreckage out here by yourself, lost."

"It was definitely eerie. Everything was so quiet that day. Now..." She paused, listening. "I can hear birds, and there's a breeze. On Sunday it was as if I'd stumbled into a tomb. Afterward—I saw Bubba's footprints. I didn't know for sure he'd seen the wreckage or me, but it was a good bet."

"I wonder why he's been silent all these years."

"Because it was none of his business," Penelope said.

"Maybe."

Wyatt abruptly jumped off the boulder and pushed through the tangle of brush, whiplike without its foliage. He didn't say a word. Penelope followed, trying not to let his rigid self-control get to her. This was his uncle, she reminded herself. His family. They were on the verge of writing the last chapter on the most stubborn and mysterious Sinclair scandal of the past century. If Wyatt had to go inside himself to get through it, she could at least cut him some slack.

The soft, wet snow was deeper on the steep, north-facing hill, and their clothes—Wyatt's in particular—weren't especially suitable for the conditions. Soon they were soaked to the knees. But with temperatures in the low fifties, Penelope wasn't too worried about hypothermia. They pushed and ducked through skinny birches and evergreens, climbed over granite boulders, then made their way carefully, at an angle, down and across the steep hillside, over more rocks, ice and patches of slippery, wet leaves left by the melted snow.

They reached the main body of the wreckage. It was in the shadows at this time of day, and Penelope could feel the isolation, as if she'd stepped into a grave.

There wasn't much left of the vintage Piper Cub. Time and the elements had done their work. Yet the frame was still clearly visible, rusted engine parts, sections of the wings. One wing was farther down the hill, a possible indication of how the crash had occurred. Even forty-five years ago, this would have been a tree-covered hill. The plane could have clipped a wing on a tree, on its approach, gotten hung up in another tree, then smashed into the rocks.

Whatever happened, it hadn't been pretty.

Wyatt's slow, methodical movements gave way once they were upon the wreckage. He leaped over several rocks and stood in the midst of the twisted metal. Penelope followed cautiously, giving him time. She was on the last boulder when he turned to her, his face white. A surge of adrenaline boosted her heart rate. "What is it?"

"Penelope—my God. There aren't any bodies."

She gasped. *"What?"*

Wyatt remained grim-faced, in control. "No remains. Nothing. They're not here."

Penelope's stomach lurched. "Maybe animals..."

He made no reply.

There would have been *something*, Penelope realized. Bits of clothing. Bones. Evidence that two people had died here. She shuddered, feeling nauseous.

Wyatt squatted on a small boulder and surveyed the wreckage. "It seems so damned small, doesn't it? You get it in your head that all the questions will be answered if only you find the plane itself.

Now..." He sighed, rising. "Hell, we could just end up with more questions. Tougher ones."

"There must be an explanation about the bodies. Maybe Colt and Frannie fell out of the plane, or jumped. Their bodies could be somewhere on the hill. We might have to wait until spring, when the snow's melted, to get a good look." She paused, having to catch her breath, although she hadn't moved in several minutes. "I'm sure your family will want a thorough investigation."

A dog barked, startling her and Wyatt. They could see it at the bottom of the hill, staying close to a hemlock.

"I think it's Bubba's other mutt," Penelope said. "I don't know his name. I wonder where—" She stopped when she saw a figure in the snow, partially hidden by the sweeping branches of the hemlock. "Oh, God. It's Bubba."

She spun to Wyatt, saw that he'd seen Bubba, too. He said, "Careful, Penelope," and she didn't know if he meant be careful not to jump to conclusions or be careful racing down the hill, because she was on her way, her legs moving before she had consciously decided that was what she needed to do. Instincts, impulse, fear for Bubba—they all came together to propel her off her rock.

She could hear Wyatt behind her, muttering, "Hell," as he started down the hill after her. She was half slipping, half sliding, leaping over rocks and fallen limbs, branches and brush slapping her legs, arms, face. There was no caution, no careful negotiating of the terrain. She raced pell-mell down the hill.

"Bubba!" she yelled. "Bubba, are you all right?"

The old hermit lay on his side in the snow, his agitated mutt panting and pacing between his master's head and his toes. When Penelope moved toward Bubba, the dog growled and snarled at her. "Easy, poochie," she said in her most cajoling voice. The dog snapped, not letting her get close.

Wyatt eased in next to her. "Try a piece of ham or something."

She dug in her hip pack and located a chunk of cob-smoked ham. She flipped it into the snow a few feet from Bubba, said a few more cajoling words, and the dog stopped barking, eyed the meat, eyed her, then pounced on the ham.

Wyatt, who had a better position, eased between Penelope and the dog and knelt beside Bubba. He took the old man's wrist and felt his pulse.

Penelope could feel her heart skipping, her knees threatening to go out from under her. "Is he alive?"

Wyatt nodded. He leaned over Bubba's thin body and examined his face, lifting his scraggly white hair and beard. "It looks as if he took a hit on the back of his head. He could have slipped and fallen." He glanced at Penelope. "Or not."

"My cell phone—" She could almost not get the words out. "I'll get help."

As she fumbled in her hip pack, Wyatt stayed beside the unconscious hermit. "Bubba—it's Wyatt Sinclair and Penelope Chestnut. We're going to get help."

The dog, finished with his ham, resumed pacing and growling. He didn't make a move on the two people helping his master, and Penelope dialed, told the dispatcher Bubba Johns was hurt, she didn't know the extent of his injuries, but they were deep on Sinclair land. "It's going to be tough to find us. I didn't bring flares. Look, why don't we do this. Get a rescue crew to follow the main trail from Bubba's place. I'll leave now and meet them. *Don't leave the trail.* You'll never find us if you do. We're way the hell out in God's country."

Bubba moaned, barely conscious.

"Wait—he might be coming around."

Wyatt said softly, "Easy, Bubba. We're here to help. Can you talk?"

Bubba groaned, a foot moving, his eyes screwing up in pain.

"What happened?" Wyatt asked. "How badly are you hurt?"

But the old man couldn't answer.

"Never mind," Penelope told the dispatcher. "Just get someone up here and let's hope in the meantime he comes around and walks out himself."

She disconnected and knelt in the snow beside Wyatt for a better look. "I don't dare move him," Wyatt said. "I don't know if he has any broken bones. I don't want to end up paralyzing the poor bastard."

"If I start now, I should meet up with the rescue crew before they run out of trail."

He nodded, grim, but she could see him mentally clicking off their options. He wasn't one to panic. "It's impossible to get a helicopter in here. I'll stay with him." He turned to her, his dark gaze holding hers. "Be careful, Penelope. Whoever did this might still be out there."

"You don't think he just slipped and hit his head?"

"No, I don't. The bump's on the back of his head,

which means his feet would have had to go out from under him. Otherwise he'd have disturbed more snow, taken out some brush on his way down. It looks as if he just dropped here."

Penelope threw up her hands. "I just don't get *any* of it. The messages, my house, *this*. Over a missing plane! It doesn't make any sense." But something in Wyatt's gaze made her pause, and she narrowed her eyes on him. "What? Wyatt, for God's sake, tell me."

"Frannie Beaudine made off with ten million in diamonds the night she and my uncle disappeared." His words were clipped, unemotional. "She stole them from the warehouse when she was helping to pull together the collection my family donated to the Met. I don't know if Colt was involved."

Penelope tried to absorb this new twist. "Holy shit. Frannie and Colt had diamonds with them? That changes everything. No one ever said—"

"I know. Even I didn't know until last night."

"Your grandfather knew?"

"Yes. He didn't want to encourage looters." Wyatt spoke as if this sort of thing happened among Sinclairs all the time. "He didn't tell my father until he was dying, and he asked him to keep it a secret. Which he did, until I dragged it out of him last night."

"Does Dunning know?"

"He doesn't have the specifics. My father told him he believed there was something of value in the wreckage and wanted Jack to make sure you hadn't changed your story because you'd tucked the goodies into your fanny pack. If you had found the wreckage but hadn't touched anything, he was supposed to secure it before it could be looted."

Penelope bit the inside of her cheek to stop herself from going to pieces. Wyatt had had time to tell her this little tidbit about ten million in diamonds last night, this morning over breakfast, at any point during their three-hour trek to the plane wreck. Of course, she'd had *days* to tell him she'd found the Piper Cub.

"And these diamonds—they're not in the wreckage, either?"

"As far as I could see they and the bodies are gone."

"Did you tell Jack or your father I was taking you here?"

"My father," Wyatt said. "Not Jack."

Penelope inhaled a sharp breath. "This is one hell of a turn of events. Diamonds. When were you going to tell me?"

His expression didn't change. "I didn't know if I'd tell you at all."

"Damn," she breathed. She straightened, cleared her throat, focused on the immediate problem of Bubba Johns. "Okay, I need to get moving if I'm to meet the rescue crew before they get impatient and get themselves lost. You'll be here when we get back?"

"I'll be here."

She wanted to believe him. This morning, she had started to believe she could trust him, that they had a bit of a partnership going. But he hadn't told her about a quaint little thing like ten million in stolen diamonds—and never mind that she'd taken days to come clean about the wreckage. That was different. He knew all along she was lying. She hadn't had a clue he was holding something back.

She left him the water and her wilderness medical kit and charged up the hill, retracing her steps, moving fast, trying hard not to think.

It was ninety minutes before Penelope returned with the rescue team. Wyatt did what he could for Bubba Johns, and every time his mind conjured up images of Hal dying at his side, shivering, cold, beyond pain but lucid until the end, he pushed them back. This wasn't the same thing. This was New Hampshire, they weren't that far into the woods, the weather was good, help was on its way, and it was a remarkably fit old man who'd just been bonked on the head—not two thirty-two-year-olds who'd stepped off the edge of a mountain in the frigid Tasmanian wilds.

By the time they heard the rescue team thrashing through the brush, Bubba Johns had regained consciousness and was sitting up. He was ashen, nauseous and incoherent enough that Wyatt didn't try to interrogate him. He asked for his dogs, and the one mutt licked his face while Wyatt explained the other had made its way to his shack. The old man shut his eyes and collapsed against a rock, not complaining but clearly in pain.

Wyatt stood out of the paramedics' way. They descended on the old man, and for the first time he understood Penelope's protectiveness of him. Bubba Johns was a stringy, harmless old hermit who apparently wanted nothing more than to live his life in solitude. That he'd been sucked into a decades-old mystery didn't seem fair.

The two paramedics treated his head injury with extreme caution, bracing his neck and doing the whole routine despite their semiconscious patient's moaning protests. They and the young cop who'd tagged along knew Penelope and groused about expecting to be strapping her to a stretcher sled. She kept asking them if they thought Bubba would be okay. Finally, one, a heavyset woman, told her she didn't think he was severely injured. He'd taken a good hit to the back of the head, but it looked like a concussion, not a fracture.

"Still," she added, "we need to get him to the hospital for the doctors to take a look."

"I don't need a doctor," Bubba muttered, barely understandable. "I just need my dogs."

They ignored him. The cop informed Penelope that Andy McNally and Pete were en route, and she and Wyatt were to stay there until they arrived. As an incentive, he was staying, too.

Since his comments weren't directed at him, Wyatt kept quiet.

After the rescue team set off with Bubba, his mutt trotting alongside him, the cop grinned at Penelope. "We had a pool going for when your dump story would come apart. I lost. I was giving it through the weekend."

She scowled at him, and he grinned. He was young, probably in his mid-twenties, and he, like most males in Cold Spring, treated Penelope like a recalcitrant sister or a fishing buddy. Wyatt found this odd. He wondered how this penchant for being one of the guys affected her attitude toward him. Now that they'd slept together, was she figuring he'd gotten his sexual interest in her out of his system? Was she expecting him to offer to split a six-pack with her and fish off her dock?

It was the only slightly amusing thought he'd had in the last hour. His sexual interest in her was not out of his system. Making love to her had only made him want her more. He found himself contending with a romantic interest, the lies and distrust between them notwithstanding. He was neither optimistic nor pessimistic about their prospects. He was simply determined to know this woman better.

Ten minutes later, the chief of police arrived with his sole detective at his side. McNally must have been working up a good head of steam the entire trip. He was out of breath and out of sorts. He immediately pointed a finger at Penelope. "Goddamn it, I knew you were lying!"

She sniffed at him. Wyatt stayed out of it. She and McNally had been going toe-to-toe long before he'd wandered into Cold Spring, New Hampshire. He expected Penelope to launch into tales of stolen diamonds and missing bodies, but she didn't, keeping her mouth shut while the cops got their bearings. McNally listened to the young cop's report, then checked around the area where they'd found Bubba while Pete went up the hill and examined the wreckage, calling down to his boss, "Andy, there aren't any bodies."

McNally shifted to Penelope. "You've got some explaining to do. First you hold back on those messages, now I'm out here with a possible assault and a plane wreck with no Colt Sinclair and no Frannie Beaudine."

"What, do you think *I* took the bodies? Come on, Andy. I didn't even get close to the wreckage until today, and I had Wyatt with me the whole time."

But Wyatt could see that saying she'd struck off

into the wilderness with him wasn't any better than saying she'd struck off on her own. McNally gritted his teeth, his scar turning redder as he took in the complications of this latest chapter in Penelope Chestnut's week-long troubles. An unconscious hermit. A forty-five-year-old plane wreck with no bodies.

Pete made his way down the steep hill, and McNally stepped aside to let his detective question Penelope and Wyatt about how they'd come to be here. The police chief seemed of a mind to find a reason to lock them up for the night.

Wyatt didn't mention the diamonds. Neither did Penelope.

Pete told them they were free to go, and he, his boss and the young cop started to the wreckage. Wyatt didn't blame McNally for his foul mood. It was a long, arduous trek to the downed plane, and the circumstances of it could have been avoided if Penelope had been straight with him from the beginning. The man was flat out of patience.

As they made their way through the woods, Penelope peeled off her anorak and tied it around her waist. She'd already done her share of hiking for one day. She said, "I didn't tell him about the diamonds because I think it complicates things. They could have been stolen years ago. Frannie might have gotten rid of them before she got on the plane—we don't have enough information at this point." She squinted at him. "I wasn't trying to spare you or your father."

Wyatt ignored her cool tone. "I wouldn't expect you to."

"Besides, McNally's irritated enough with a plane

wreck and an unconscious hermit. He doesn't need ten million in missing diamonds on top of it."

"Penelope..."

She held up a hand. "I'm upset, Wyatt. I'm tired, and I'm upset. I know you were caught between a rock and a hard place and just did what you thought was right. Believe me, I understand how difficult that can be."

"But you're still pissed," he said.

A faint smile. "Yeah."

He understood. Even if she had withheld the truth about the plane crash past any point he considered reasonable, he'd learned about the diamonds *after* she'd confided in him. She'd made the gesture of trust, and in effect, he'd thrown it in her face.

But right now, they had more immediate concerns. Bubba's scroungy dog trotted out to greet them before they reached his shack. He wasn't barking and growling, but he seemed confused.

"The rescue team must have managed to get rid of him," Penelope said. "Give me a minute, and I'll put out water and food for both dogs."

The second dog—older and more independent—joined them, and both mutts followed her to the brook, where she dipped two pans of water, and to the garden shed, where she found a big barrel of dog food and scooped some into another two pans.

"I guess I should just leave them out here," she said tentatively, looking around the isolated homestead. "I can check on them later, in case Bubba has to stay at the hospital."

"If they're used to Bubba, they'll be able to fend for themselves."

Her green eyes focused on Wyatt, and he noticed

her cheeks were pale in spite of all her hiking, the last few hours taking their toll. "What do you think Bubba was doing out there?"

Wyatt shook his head. "I don't know. He must have been hit before we arrived. Otherwise we'd have heard something."

"That seems logical, but right now I don't know if logic holds. I see three possibilities. One, he went out on his own and tripped. Two, he went out on his own and someone hit him on the back of the head, which leads to another series of questions and possibilities. Or, three, he was forced to take someone to the wreckage and was bonked on the head for his trouble."

"The third scenario would mean he definitely knows who hit him. The second one, he might or might not." Wyatt paused, welcoming the gusting, cooling breeze. "I still don't buy the first scenario."

She squeezed her eyes shut. "God. We need to talk to Bubba and get him to tell us what he knows, if anything."

They made their way to her house and drove to the hospital in Laconia. Jack Dunning met them in the emergency room. He had on his jacket, his jeans, his cowboy boots. No hat. "The old bastard checked himself out. He got a nurse to give him a ride back to town."

"He's okay?" Penelope asked.

"He's got a bitch of a concussion, but he shook it off. He'll be fine in a day or two." The flat eyes settled on her. "He says he slipped. No one pushed him."

"That's bullshit," Wyatt said calmly.

"Well, it's not the first bit of bullshit we've heard

around here, is it?" Jack kept his gaze on Penelope, but she wasn't one to squirm. "So, you found the wreckage, after all."

She shrugged. "Changing my story seemed like a good idea at the time. All things considered, if I had to do it over again I'd just come up with a better story. The turn-of-the-century dump was pretty lame."

"The wreck's picked clean, Jack," Wyatt said. "No remains, no personal effects, nothing. It might have fallen out of the sky by itself without a damned soul in it."

Dunning's expression didn't change. "I'll take a look myself."

"I can draw you a map," Penelope said, adding none too subtly, "unless you don't need one."

Jack grinned. "I like how your mind works, Miss Chestnut. It's almost as devious as my own."

But she didn't grin back. She was pale, shaken and very serious. "Did you follow Bubba? Did you force him take you out to the wreckage? Did you leave him for dead?"

Ignoring her, Jack turned to Wyatt. "This thing's going to hit the news wires before too long. Do you want me to call your father about the plane?"

"No, I'll do it. If you have anything to add—"

"If I have anything to add, I'll call him myself. Don't worry, Sinclair. I'll do my job."

Behind him, Penelope said, "You didn't answer my questions."

Jack shifted to her, winked. "Sorry, toots. It's not my job to answer your questions."

He walked out of the emergency room, and when Penelope started after him, Wyatt scooped one arm around her middle and stopped her. "It won't change a thing. He'll just make you madder."

Her jaw was set, and even as she glared after Dunning, she said, "Bubba can't stay out at his place alone."

"He's been there alone for more than twenty years."

"But not in this condition—"

"How do you know he hasn't had worse concussions? Penelope, let the man live his life the way he sees fit."

She turned to him, her eyes gleaming with fear and more unspent energy than she had a right to. "What if someone did attack him today and comes back? Wyatt, I couldn't stand it if something happened to him."

He nodded. "I'll go over there this evening and check on him."

"I'll go, too."

"Haven't you done enough hiking for one day?"

She managed a smile. "I'm just getting started."

When they arrived at the inn, Lyman was pacing in the parlor, an unlit cigar in his mouth, his wife and cousin nowhere in evidence. He paid Wyatt no attention and pounced on his daughter. "Goddamn it, Penelope, this is just what got you grounded. You're reckless. You don't think. What the hell were you doing, going off into the woods with Sinclair? You don't know his motives!"

She thrust her chin out at him. "I don't? Money, adventure, thrills. A Sinclair's motives are easy. It's everybody else's motives I don't get, like whoever would hit an old man on the back of the head and leave him for dead."

Lyman growled at her. "This has all gone too damned far."

"No kidding."

He sighed. "You're okay?"

She nodded, and Wyatt could see her biting her lower lip, could sense her determination not to fall apart now that the worst was over. "Bubba—"

"Bubba's a crusty old goat. He'll be fine."

Wyatt turned to Lyman, who was visibly calmer now that he'd seen his daughter face-to-face. "Is word out yet about the wreckage?"

"It's starting to go around town. Won't be long before it's on CNN and the damned wires."

"I need to talk to Harriet," Penelope said, suddenly white-faced.

Her father nodded. "She's making scones."

"Is she mad at me for lying about the plane?"

"You can't tell with Harriet. One thing, though." He gave Penelope's hand a quick squeeze. "Be straight with her, kid. She's a big girl. You don't need to take her problems onto your shoulders."

"I wouldn't patronize her—"

"No, but you'd go to the ends of the earth for her. Go on. You two talk."

After Penelope charged off, Wyatt said something about going to call his father, but as he started for the stairs, Lyman said quietly, "My daughter's only problem before you came to town was distractibility and a touch of recklessness. Now she's got a half-dead hermit in the woods, she's getting threats, her place has been ransacked." He paused and sighed audibly. His taciturn nature made such conversations difficult for him. "I'm thinking you're bad luck at best, Sinclair. Same as your uncle was for Frannie Beaudine."

"You could be right."

"I don't want to be right. I want my daughter to stay safe."

"If it's any consolation, so do I."

SIXTEEN

Penelope found Harriet chopping nuts on a wooden cutting board with a huge butcher knife. She liked the control of a knife, she'd often said, and preferred the texture of the nuts when cut with a knife instead of a machine. She'd heard about the plane, about Bubba. When Penelope pulled up a chair at the kitchen table and started to apologize about lying, Harriet cut her off, her eyes widening, making her look a little crazy. "If there were no bodies, then Colt and Frannie might still be alive."

Penelope shook her head before things could get out of hand. "I think that's far-fetched, Harriet. From the condition of the plane, I'd have to say this was no soft landing."

Harriet hacked at the hazelnuts, her knife gleaming in the waning late afternoon light. "Then where are their bodies?"

"There's still a lot of snow out on the hill where they crashed. We might find them when the weather warms up. It's just too early—"

"Why didn't you tell me you'd found their plane? Didn't you think you could trust me?"

"Harriet…"

"No," she said moodily, "obviously you didn't."

"It was never a question of trust. It was just a

question of judgment—*my* judgment. I was in a sticky situation, and I did the best I could."

"I don't see what's sticky about it. It seems straightforward to me. You either found Colt and Frannie's plane or you didn't."

"The reporters—"

She stopped, her knife poised in midair. It was a sharp, eight-inch deal. Harriet kept all the knives scrupulously clean and sharp. "Were you afraid I'd make a fool of myself?"

Penelope sensed this conversation was going nowhere fast. She was tired, more than she'd realized. "No, I was afraid they'd try to make a fool out of you, or they'd just upset you—and Bubba. It wasn't just you. To be honest, I didn't see what it would accomplish to have the whole world parade out to the site of a tragic, forty-five-year-old plane crash. Frankly, I still don't."

Harriet pursed her lips, going snappish and pissy—her defense, Penelope knew, when she was feeling hurt and frightened. "Well, it seems you've only made things worse for everyone."

"I suppose I have. I'm sorry."

Harriet's eyes filled with tears, and she carefully set down her knife and collapsed onto a chair. She stared at the pile of nuts on her cutting board. "I know you were just doing your best, Penelope. Really, I do."

"But you expected when Colt and Frannie's plane was discovered, you'd have an answer, one way or another, about whether or not they were involved with leaving you on the church doorstep—if they really were your birth parents. Now...I don't know."

Penelope heaved out a breath, wanting nothing

more than a hot bath, a peanut butter and jelly sandwich—and Wyatt, she thought. In spite of everything. The ten million in stolen diamonds, the fact
that he was everything she'd told her father he was.
A man of action, adventure, thrills, drive. "Well, at
least we know their plane went down, and we know
it went down here in Cold Spring."

Harriet nodded dully, staring at her little pile of
hazelnuts.

"The Sinclairs will have investigators comb
through the wreckage. Maybe they'll find out how
the plane went down. That might lead to clues about
what Colt and Frannie's relationship was really like.
It's too early to jump to any conclusions."

"I suppose. I'm not sure..." Harriet took a quiet
breath, calmer. "I always thought I'd want to know
the truth, one way or the other. But I'm not sure I
do." She picked up a tiny hazelnut, placed it carefully on her tongue. "Jack will be here soon. He
called after he left the hospital."

"What's your take on him?"

She blushed, but her eyes brightened, warmed.
"He's independent and defiant, a rule-breaker." She
smiled at her cousin, some of her moodiness dissi-
pating. "He reminds me of a male version of you in
some ways. He's harder-edged, of course, because
of the work he does."

Penelope frowned. "He doesn't remind me of me
at all."

"You're both dedicated, determined, a little stubborn."

"But you're not attracted to me—"

She gasped, laughing. "Penelope, you're awful."

"And you're just saying I'm like Dunning so I

won't think he's such an arrogant bastard. He doesn't like me, you know." She grinned, pleased to see the spark in Harriet's eyes. "I don't see how you can fall for someone who doesn't like me."

"Well, if that's my criteria, I'm doomed to stay a spinster."

"Harriet!"

Her cousin waved a hand in dismissal. "I know 'spinster' isn't politically correct, but *I* like it. It conjures up images of Katharine Hepburn and Humphrey Bogart."

"I was thinking more along the lines of wicked stepsisters."

"We're getting giddy," Harriet said. "It feels good, doesn't it? But I should warn you—your mother's on her way over from the sugar shack."

Penelope scooped an apple out of the fruit bowl. "Then I'll clear out now. I'm sure that'll be easier on both of us."

"Are you staying here tonight?"

"I don't know yet. I'll call, okay?"

She met Wyatt as he was coming down the stairs. He'd changed clothes, washed up. He wasn't really handsome, she realized. He was memorable, sexy, striking in an edgy, hard way, especially for one born with the proverbial silver spoon in his mouth. "How'd it go with your father?" she asked.

"I didn't reach him. He's on the golf course. I talked to my sisters, but they're too young for tales of old plane wrecks."

"Ellen and Beatrix. They're good kids?"

He smiled. "They're perfect."

"And I suppose they adore you."

He came to the bottom step. "Of course. I'm their big brother, and I have a cat."

"You don't strike me as the cat type."

"I'm not. Pill was left by Madge, with whom I had a brief fling—just long enough for her to feng-shui my apartment and decide we were not compatible, which I'd discovered through more ordinary means."

"Ah."

He smiled. "Madge and I never were. Not to worry."

"I'm not worried. I was just thinking—you have a whole life I know very little about. Little sisters, New York, Wall Street, a cat named Pill."

"His real name's Sarsaparilla."

"You're kidding. Well, my point is—" She sighed, giving herself a mental shake. "I guess it doesn't matter. It's not as if you and I ever 'were,' either."

He pushed open the door, held it for her with a mock bow of chivalry. "I'm letting that one go," he said, "but only for now."

They drove her truck to her place, grabbed crackers and cheese and made their way to Bubba's one more time. It was getting close to dusk, the sun low in the sky, the temperature starting to drop. Penelope could hear Bubba's two dogs barking and picked up her pace, eager to see how the old hermit was doing. Wyatt had no trouble matching her pace, and she tried not to think about how much she appreciated having him along. That was dangerous thinking. Harriet thinking. The Scarlet Pimpernel, Scaramouche, D'Artagnan. Wyatt was a *Sinclair*. He wasn't Spiderman. But she liked having him walking beside her, solid, capable and just *there*.

Instead of finding Bubba, they found Andy Mc-
Nally, the two dogs circling him and growling.
Andy ignored them. "Pete and I stopped up here after we heard Bubba checked himself out. Figured
we'd make sure he's all right and ask him what the
hell happened up in the woods—but he's cleared
out. Pete's looking around."

"You're sure?" Penelope asked. "He wouldn't
just up and leave his dogs."

"What makes you think you know Bubba any better than the rest of us? We don't know what he'd do
and wouldn't do. Door was open to his shack. You
just got the feeling he'd left. No sign of him. Probably figures someone'll look after the dogs."

"He must be scared," Penelope said.

McNally frowned, all cop. "Or hiding something."

"Come on, Andy, he didn't beat himself over the
head."

"Could have been a setup. He *wanted* you to think
he'd had his head knocked in."

She groaned. Wyatt, who'd been listening patiently, said, "Do you have evidence or are you just
keeping an open mind?"

"We don't have evidence of jack shit. Which isn't
official police talk, but there you have it. We'll take a
good look at the wreckage tomorrow, see if there's
any sign Bubba's been through it. If there is, or if he
doesn't show up soon, we'll get a warrant and
search his place here. If he stole anything, he could
have panicked and tried to get the heat off him."

"The heat wasn't on him," Penelope interjected.

"All depends how you look at it. You and Wyatt
were by here yesterday, weren't you?"

Her mouth snapped shut. She spun up the trail, but Wyatt didn't follow. He said to McNally, "I didn't get the impression when I talked to Bubba yesterday that he was paranoid or worried."

"A man like that, living out here alone—he likes to stay in control. So, we'll see. I hope the old guy has a warm place to stay tonight. He's not in great shape. I'd hate to see this thing escalate if he's just worried because he stripped a forty-five-year-old plane wreck."

"Do you think he could have buried Colt and Frannie's remains?"

"I'd like to ask him."

Penelope stopped dead and turned to the two men. The dogs had quieted and were at her heels, and she stood still, sensing Andy's suspicion.

"Sinclair—if there's anything you need to tell me, do it now. Don't make me wait. You don't want me to have to drag it out of you. I'm a small-town cop, but I know my job."

Wyatt looked him straight in the eye and said, "There's nothing."

"Penelope?"

"If I knew anything I thought would help you find Bubba or whoever left him for dead this morning, I'd tell you." There, that wasn't an outright lie. "Is it okay if I take these dogs home with me? They seem to have taken a shine to me, and I'd hate to leave them out here without Bubba."

McNally sighed, nodding. "Ten to one that's what he figured you'd do."

Pete came up the hill from the brook and shook his head. "I can't find a thing. With so many people out in the woods today and the warm temps, there's not much for tracks."

"All right, Pete, thanks. Bubba knows these woods better than any of us. I guess if he doesn't want us to find him, we're not going to find him. I just hope he's in his right head."

McNally and Pete returned by the trail that led to the main road, Penelope and Wyatt by the trail that led to her house. The two mutts trotted amiably at her side. "I have it," she said. "They can be my protection tonight. I've got new locks on the side door, and I can block off the slider with a chair. With Granddad's Winchester and Bubba's mutts, I'll be fine."

They came to the first of her tapped trees, and she quickly checked the buckets, aware of Wyatt's dark eyes on her, of her out-of-control reaction to him. "And where do I fit into that scenario?" he asked.

"Well, I figure you'll be safe and snug in your bed at the inn."

"Just think of how safe and snug you'll feel if you have not only your Winchester and Bubba's dogs, but a Sinclair to—"

"To what?" she broke in. "Protect me?"

He grinned, sliding in behind her, touching her hair, lightly kissing the corner of her mouth. "To make love to you."

Andy McNally came for his nightly beer a half hour later than usual. Somehow, his scar made his moods seem that much easier to read, although he wasn't a complicated man. Harriet could see his fatigue, his worry. She was against the wall at the far end of the bar with her glass of wine, and she felt ashamed for her self-absorption.

She smiled at him. "Hard day?"

"It could have been harder. Bubba could have been dead." He glanced at her. "Or your cousin. She's got to get herself under control, Harriet."

"I know. So do her parents. But she's not a child—"

"That's the hell of it. She's a grown woman."

"She was with Wyatt—"

His gaze bored into her. "You trust him?"

She shrugged, amazed at Andy's curtness. He was usually so calm and tough to rile. His wife's death and his work had given him an unusual perspective on life. He wasn't driven or restless, and he understood life's hardships and how they could affect people. Even when he groused about Penelope, which he did often, Harriet seldom detected the kind of soul-deep frustration and concern she did now.

"I have no reason not to trust him," she said.

"Penelope's fallen for him, you know."

She nodded, saying nothing.

Andy heaved a sigh and drank some of his beer. "And old Bubba. I don't know what to hell to make of him. He had to know that wreck was out there. He's probably known it for years."

Harriet shifted on the bar stool, her wine barely touched. Her eyes burned. It took so little to turn her thoughts inward.

"What is it, Harriet?" Andy asked, some of the curtness going out of him.

"You've been through a lot, Andy. Maybe you'd understand…" She took a gulp of wine, suddenly

breathless. She didn't look at him. "When I have
something I don't want to think about—a memory,
something I've done that I'm not proud of—it's like
I put it into a little closet in the back of my mind and
shut the door. Most of the time I don't think about it,
it doesn't bother me. But sometimes the door pops
open all by itself, or something happens, and it's as
if a tornado comes through and tears open all the
doors of all my little closets…"

She stopped herself, her eyes filling with tears.
She stared at her wine, and beside her Andy didn't
speak. There was no bartender tonight. She'd sent
him home. And no Jack Dunning, no Wyatt Sinclair.
Wyatt would be with Penelope. She didn't know
about Jack. She hadn't seen him all day. Last night's
walk might have been a mirage.

"I'm not making any sense," she said, her voice
croaking.

"No, Harriet. You're making a lot of sense. You
can't let the bad memories eat away at you forever.
You have to find a way to buck up and carry on."

She turned to him, knew her stupid mascara
would be bleeding. "It's not denial?"

He shrugged his big shoulders. "I don't know, I
suppose it could be. Does it matter? I know I can't be
thinking about every bad thing that's happened to
me all the time or I'd never get up in the morning.
The stuff's there, I just don't let it control me. I guess
that's the acceptance part the grief counselors talk
about. I mean, you get to a point where you can deal
with it."

"All of the time?"

"Most of the time. There are those times…" He
raised his glass, swirled the amber liquid. "There are

those times it gets control of you." He shifted his gaze to her. "I guess that's when a door pops open or gets sucked off by a tornado, and all the bad shit leaks out of the closet."

She smiled, embarrassed. "It's the only analogy I could come up with."

"It's a good one, Harriet. I'm just wondering what on earth you could need to stuff into a closet."

"Ah, the minister's daughter, the spinster inn-keeper." She could hear her sarcasm, her cracking voice, but couldn't seem to stop herself. "How could she have any skeletons in her closets? She hasn't lived."

Andy looked stricken. "Harriet, that's not what I meant. You know—"

She held up a hand before he could say anything he regretted. "I know, Andy. I'm sorry."

"It's been a rough day for everyone." He slid off the bar stool, his beer not quite finished. "I'm turn-ing in. Tramping through the woods this time of year takes its toll."

"Good night, Andy. Say hi to Rebecca and Jane for me."

After he left, Harriet topped up her wineglass. She'd only taken three or four sips, but it seemed to be the thing to do. She wasn't ready to go to her suite yet. She could feel the long, dark night ahead of her, feel it crawling in around her, and she took a quick gulp of wine, forced herself to breathe.

"Well, at least this damned miserable day's going to end right."

Jack. His gravelly, half Texas, half New York voice. She spun, and he was at the bar. He was so lean, so good-looking in a rough, masculine way.

He grinned at her. "I hate to drink alone. What about you, Harriet? Does an innkeeper like it when she can sit here and drink alone?"

She decided not to mention Andy. "I like people," she said.

"That's your weakness, Miss Harriet," he said, teasing her, but his gray eyes warmed suddenly. "And it's your strength. Mind if I pour myself a whiskey?"

She smiled, all the struggle and self-loathing of a few minutes ago sliding away. "Pour ahead."

The night was dark, cool and windy, and Wyatt stayed awake for a long time after he and Penelope had made love. He held her, her body warm against his, her hair smelling of chamomile shampoo. Bubba's dogs were konked out by the wood stove, the fire in it dying. They'd sniffed everything in the cabin and paced, agitated and out of sorts, until Penelope thawed some waffles she had in the freezer and tossed them into a couple of pitted old frying pans. She said she'd buy Dog Chow in the morning.

While the dogs ate and Penelope heated a can of vegetable soup and grilled a couple of cheese sandwiches for dinner, Wyatt called his father again. He was back from the golf course, and when he heard the day's events—his brother's plane found without bodies or diamonds, the local hermit unconscious at the bottom of the ravine and now missing—he said, "I'll get a flight out in the morning."

And that was pretty much that. Wyatt refused to dwell on his father's uncommunicativeness. It was different, he knew, from Lyman Chestnut's taciturn

manner. He and his daughter managed to commu-
nicate quite effectively.

During dinner, Wyatt and Penelope went over
every fact and detail of the events since her discovery of the Piper Cub on Sunday. They considered
suspects, motives, alibis. And they acknowledged
their own biases. He was a Sinclair, she was a native
of Cold Spring. They'd both grown up with the mystery, the scandal, the tragedy of Colt and Frannie's
disappearance, and they had their points of view,
their blind spots.

She moved against him, her breasts skimming his
forearm. She said nothing, but he sensed she was
awake. "Tell me how you ended up grounded for
three weeks," he whispered.

She rolled over, facing him. "Is that what you've
been lying awake here wondering?"

"It didn't come about just since Sunday. Your father's been fed up for a while."

"Weeks," she said.

"Why?"

"Because he's an old grouch."

"Penelope..."

She sighed, easing one leg over him, stroking one
finger along the edge of his jaw. He didn't relent. He
wanted to know. Deep down, he knew he needed to
know. Finally, she said, "I've always been restless.
Even as a little kid I'd go my own way—and I always wanted to fly. I'm centered in the air, totally
focused and professional. I don't get distracted."

"That's not what your father says."

"I know." She shifted, and Wyatt could sense her
discomfort. She would distrust introspection as self-
indulgence, no matter how clear-eyed her view of

herself. "It's hard to explain. The kind of thinking and distractions that propel me on the ground suddenly have been haunting me in the air. Not dangerously so. It's not as if I'm even close to hurting myself or anyone else."

"Just close enough to close," Wyatt said.

"At least as far as my father's concerned. I love flying, I love my work. But lately it's as if I've been caught between the life I've been living and the life I'm going to live. Does that make sense? I really put my family and friends through their paces when I was younger. I'd get lost, fall through the ice, get stuck up in trees, swim out too far in the lake. It wasn't for thrills—it was just from not paying close attention. Then I started paying close attention. I've tried hard in the last few years to be more... predictable."

"But you let the pendulum swing too far in that direction?"

She sighed. "And maybe now I'm overcorrecting. If I could press the rewind button, I don't know if I'd let myself get lost on Sunday. Then I'd never have found Colt and Frannie's plane, and you never would have come to Cold Spring." She smiled at him in the darkness. "Maybe it's all some master plan, and I should just relax."

"You know what I think?" He smoothed a palm down her side, over her hip. "I think running out of gas at five thousand feet and getting lost in the woods are a damned poor substitute for sex."

She gasped in mock-horror. "Spoken like a man! I'll have you know what I've been experiencing the past few weeks is a restlessness of the soul, not of the body—"

"But they're connected," he said. He let his hand drift lower, feeling how hot she was, knowing her mind and body were very in tune at the moment. "What do you want, Penelope?"

She eased closer to him, letting her hand drift over his hip, lower. "I want to feel like I did two hours ago," she whispered, her mouth finding his, their bodies coming together, not with the speed and urgency and heat of their earlier lovemaking, but with a searching and deliberateness and power that tested both body and mind. Every time he felt her on the verge of release, he pulled back, prolonged it, probed deeper, gave and demanded more. The darkness of her little room was so complete that he couldn't see her under him, could only feel her as she held him tight, her body rigid with the aching need for relief, her mind focused, until he couldn't pull back, couldn't think or feel anything except his need for release, and they came together.

Afterward, in the stillness of body and spirit, Wyatt tried to listen to the wind and the rhythmic breathing of the woman beside him, but his thoughts kept drifting to the bodyless crash site in the woods, the missing hermit, the senseless loss of a brother, the senseless death of a friend. Nothing in life was certain, he reminded himself. And where a Sinclair was concerned, love was never enough.

SEVENTEEN

In the morning, there was still no sign of Bubba Johns. Penelope got word from her mother, who'd had a mother-to-cop talk with Andy McNally, when she dropped Wyatt at the inn and tried to pretend they hadn't spent the night together. Her mother, of course, asked no questions. But she knew. Penelope grabbed a couple of warm wild blueberry muffins and scooted to her truck.

Word of yesterday's events was leaking out, but she sensed that this time everyone was exercising more caution. Not that she had any illusions. Once they learned the local hermit had gone missing and Brandon Sinclair was en route, the media would be back.

Wyatt had already left to pick up his father at the Manchester airport, an hour to the south.

Penelope drove to her own little airport. It was another gorgeous, sugaring-season kind of day, the potholes and streams filling with runoff from the melting snow. She found her father alone in a hangar, going over her favorite Beechcraft.

She stood behind him at the nose of the plane. "Tell me about Bubba Johns, Pop."

"There's not much to tell." He rubbed his palm

along the nose, as if he could feel any flaws. "You know more about him than I do."

Penelope shoved her hands into the pockets of her fleece pullover. She didn't know how else to say it, except straight out. "Do you think he could be Colt Sinclair?"

Her father wasn't as surprised by her question as she'd expected. He shrugged. "You said it didn't look as if anyone could have survived that crash."

"I know, but there aren't any bodies. What if he and Frannie had parachutes? They could have bailed before the plane went down. Frannie could have died, Colt lived. He's guilt-ridden and decides to become a hermit." She made herself stop for air. Everything was just tumbling out, all the scenarios and suspicions. "The whole thing could have been a setup. Maybe Frannie and Colt planned and executed it all to a T."

"Anything's possible. Every theory you can imagine was floated in the first weeks after they disappeared. I look at the practicalities. They had no money, except through Colt's trust fund. How'd they plan to live?"

Probably on ten million in stolen diamonds, Penelope thought. But that wasn't her information to divulge.

"Look," her father went on, "I don't know what the hell happened to that plane. As for Bubba—he didn't show up around here until twenty years later. As far as I'm concerned, he's just some recluse from up north."

"But it's possible—"

"I just said anything's possible. He's probably afraid, Penelope. He saw something, maybe he did something—he sees his life coming apart and takes off."

She found that her father's inherent reasonableness helped to calm her. "I used to think he was an escaped convict."

"On Andy McNally's turf?" Her father gave a short, incredulous laugh. "That'd be the day. Whatever else he might be, Bubba Johns isn't a violent man. That much I know."

"So do I. I guess. I don't know sometimes—I've been wrong about so much. I never should have made up the story about the dump."

"Did you do it for Bubba," her father asked, adding pointedly, "or for Harriet?"

"Both. And now I think I've only made things worse for them." She smiled at her father. "I'll bet when you grounded me you never thought I'd get mixed up in something like this."

"Damned straight I didn't. You holding up?"

She nodded. "Yesterday was pretty awful, but today should be better. I need to see this through. You know Brandon Sinclair's on his way to town?"

"I heard."

"Do you remember much about him?"

"Yeah. He was just a little kid when Colt disappeared. Their father tried to protect him from the scandal, even the mourning, I expect. Willard was a good man, but he was rigid. He thought if emotions weren't displayed, they weren't felt." His eyes met hers. "I have that tendency myself."

"But you're not rigid," Penelope said, struck by his almost apologetic tone. "It's not as if you don't expect other people to express their emotions."

"Fat lot of good it'd do me if I did." But his

strange mood hadn't lifted, and he added, "I blow my top from time to time."

She smiled. "Daily, if necessary."

"Penelope—" He paused, seeming to war with himself over what to say, how much. "I was fifteen when Frannie and Colt disappeared—I didn't understand much of what was going on myself. I might have run away from home, too, if I had Willard for a father. Like I've said, he and your grandfather got along. I guess Willard was a different man when he was in the country, but I can remember him—" Another pause, his discomfort almost palpable. "Willard would push Colt into doing things when the poor kid would rather sit on the beach and read a book."

"Colt? I thought he was a big adventurer."

"That's mostly myth, from what I saw—not that we were friends. In my opinion, Frannie was more the natural adventurer. She was a born daredevil. She was innocent and in over her head with the Sinclairs in a lot of ways, but not in sheer recklessness."

"I never knew that's what you thought. Why haven't you said anything before now?"

He gave her a small smile. "Didn't want to end up on some damned tape recording in the town library. Penelope, this was none of my business forty-five years ago. Maybe it's none of yours now."

"What about Harriet?"

"Harriet's Harriet." He moved out of the hangar, whatever he'd been doing with the Beechcraft finished or gone out of his mind. "She doesn't want to know the truth, and you won't be doing her any favors by digging it up for her."

Penelope gaped at him, stunned. "Pop—Jesus, Pop, do you know something?"

He spun around. "Of course not. Where'd you get that idea?"

"All of a sudden you're like a worm in hot ashes—"

"That's because I've got work to do. Unlike some people, I don't come and go around here as I please. Now, here's one thing I know—if Harriet was a Sinclair, she wouldn't have been left on a church doorstep."

Penelope narrowed her eyes on him, still suspicious. "You were fifteen. Your uncle found her. Teenagers often know and sense stuff that the adults miss—"

"Not in the nineteen fifties they didn't. Are you going to get some work done today or stand here jabbering?"

She started for a huge push broom, but turned abruptly to her father. He was staring at the sky as if it were about to rain or he had a plane coming in, which he didn't. He was simply pulling himself together in the best way he knew how. Penelope hesitated, doubting she was making any sense. But she couldn't stop herself. "Pop—the fax I received. Was it you?"

He pivoted toward her, his expression grim but in control. "You think I'd send an anonymous message to my own daughter?"

"To deter me. To keep me from doing something stupid."

"If I thought it'd work, I might have done it. I haven't liked the way you've dived headfirst into this mess. But I know you, Penelope. I know damned well a halfhearted warning like that would just stiffen your neck. If I wanted to discourage you from something, I'd find a better way."

"Like grounding me."

"A lot of good it did."

"Are you mad at me for asking?"

He shook his head. "In fact, it's reassuring. If you can suspect your own father, maybe you can suspect everyone else. Keep your eyes open, kid."

"I will."

He headed to the office in the next building. Penelope tried sweeping, but couldn't concentrate and finally got into her truck and drove to town. No one—not even Harriet—was at the inn. Several reporters had gathered in front of Jeannie's Diner, and Penelope passed a television truck on her way to her cabin. Two cars had it staked out.

So, the sentries had arrived, and the swarm would soon follow. A wounded, missing hermit, Sinclairs and a famous plane crash with no bodies were just too much to resist—and, she had to acknowledge, they were news. Provided they didn't trespass and harass her, Penelope didn't object to the media doing their job.

But she had no intention of embracing them. She slipped into the woods and checked her taps. The milk bottles were almost overflowing, and the buckets needed emptying. She closed her eyes, envisioning the late winter and early spring ritual of maple sugaring. She could smell the bubbling syrup, feel the heat and steam on her face. She needed closure on the plane, the threats, Bubba. She wanted to get back to her life.

When she opened her eyes, she thought of Wyatt, and she knew her life would never be the same.

Pushing that thought aside, she found herself on the path to Bubba's shack. Huge amounts of snow had melted, the small patches of ground visible just two days ago spreading rapidly in the warm, springlike air. She didn't want to lose the cold nights until she had enough sap, but she loved the sense that spring was upon her little corner of northern New England.

Amazingly, no one was at Bubba's place. No police, no reporters, no Sinclairs. Penelope wandered around, stood on the hillside listening to the brook and the birds, imagining the life Bubba had lived for more than two decades. What if he had cleared out altogether? What if he'd decided to start over somewhere else, the way he had here?

She heard a noise near his little garden shed and went to investigate. It couldn't be Bubba's dogs. They were still at her place. She called his name, then noticed the shed's rickety wooden door was ajar. There were no knobs or handles, just a crude wooden latch that was down. She started to push it up. It wouldn't take much more than a good, strong wind to rip the door off its hinges.

A shuffling sound came from inside the shed, and before she could react, the door opened hard. She jumped back, slipping in the mud, the door hitting her in the face and shoulder. She went sprawling, smacking her back hard against the garden fence. Her feet went out from under her. She screamed and swore as she crashed to the ground on her rear end, her momentum carrying her until she was face first on the hard ground, mud and snow going up her nose and into her mouth.

She got to her knees, coughing, the wind knocked out of her, but by the time she was upright, whoever had knocked her silly had vanished. She listened for sounds of thrashing in the woods, but heard nothing except for the rushing of the brook at the bottom of the hill.

Which could mean whoever it was could be lurking nearby.

"Bubba—it's me, Penelope."

Her heart was pounding, the fence had scratched and bruised her back, and she had a bloody scrape on her face. Little sticks clung to her hair. Adrenaline surged painfully through her, and she had to fight for air. Trembling, she checked in the garden shed. Old tools, clay pots, organic gardening supplies—no bag of diamonds tucked in with the bonemeal.

She touched a finger to her cheek, and it came away bloody.

That was enough investigating for now. Wobbly and unnerved, she headed through the woods. She grabbed two sap buckets and crossed the dirt road with them. Let the media sentries report her as a disheveled, eccentric New Hampshire sap collector.

Once inside her house, she dialed the inn. Bubba's dogs paced between the couch and the kitchen table, restless and agitated. She knew how they felt. They needed a good run, and they needed Bubba.

Harriet answered, and without preamble, Penelope said, "Who's there? At the inn, right now. Jack, Wyatt, anyone?"

"No one at the moment. Brandon Sinclair is taking a room here, though. He and Wyatt stopped in for a few minutes earlier."

"When?"

"I don't remember the exact time. An hour ago? Ninety minutes? Penelope—"

"And Jack Dunning? Have you seen him?"

"He left early this morning. He didn't tell me where he was going."

There was something in her cousin's voice. Penelope could hear it despite her absorption in her own trauma. Her cheek stung, her body ached. "Harriet?"

"It's nothing," she said briskly. "Penelope, I don't know—I just don't know what's going on. More reporters are arriving in town every minute."

Harriet seemed on the verge of falling apart. Penelope flipped on the cold water in her kitchen sink. She had to pull herself together—she couldn't indulge her fears. "Don't worry about a thing, Harriet. I'm on my way. What kind of scones are you whipping up today?"

"Peach, but they're not ready—"

"I like to think ahead."

She could hear her cousin's feeble attempt at a laugh. "Since when?"

Penelope hung up. She didn't have time to wipe the blood off her face, much less walk the dogs, before the Sinclairs were at her door. Wyatt and his father, a tall, gray-haired, gray-eyed, handsome man in a dark sweater and trousers. Not that Wyatt introduced him. He took one look at Penelope and said, "What happened to you?"

"I had a run-in with someone at Bubba's."

The dogs had erupted, and she yelled at them to

be still. Wyatt studied her, not a muscle moving. "Who?"

"I didn't see who. Whoever it was pushed the garden shed door in my face and ran off. Unless it was the wind, I expect someone was snooping around and didn't want to be seen."

"Perhaps it was a reporter," Brandon Sinclair said, concerned.

"Or Bubba," Wyatt added.

Penelope went to her kitchen sink. "Or whoever left Bubba for dead."

"Assuming that wasn't a ruse."

She ran the water, wetting a facecloth, which she applied to her cheek. It was just a superficial scratch, but she could see Wyatt going all black-eyed and suspicious on her. "Where's Jack Dunning?" she asked.

"He's gone out to the crash site," Wyatt said. "He's making sure the investigators haven't missed anything."

Penelope turned to Brandon Sinclair, remembered his brother had lost his life in that plane crash and tried to control some of her manic, wild energy. She had the urge to grab Bubba's dogs and run into the woods, let them pick up his trail. But she reined all that in. "Are you going out to see the plane?"

"Eventually. I haven't been to New Hampshire in a long time." His tone was polite and well-bred, as if they were discussing the stock market. Her earlier speculation that Bubba could be Colt Sinclair now seemed crazy. "I don't think there's any rush at this point."

With one finger, Wyatt turned Penelope's cheek and examined it. "You should see a doctor."

"For what?"

"You might have a concussion."

"I don't have a concussion. My shoulder took the brunt of the hit, and I cut my cheek. It'll be fine."

But Wyatt wasn't finished. "You need to get Andy McNally up here."

As if two Sinclairs weren't enough, she needed the chief of police, too. Andy had thought she was reckless and out of control since she was twelve. She waved a hand at Wyatt and his father. "Don't let me keep you two from doing whatever you planned to do."

"We planned to see you," Brandon said simply.

Despite their very different mannerisms, father and son seemed to be more alike than either would want to admit. They were both used to getting their own way. Penelope's head was throbbing, the scrapes on her cheek and back stung, and she needed food. She tore open the fridge, grabbed a piece of cheese and tried to ignore the two sets of Sinclair eyes on her.

"The phone," Wyatt said.

"Okay, okay."

She dialed McNally's private number. His assistant told her he was out. "I can radio him. Do you need an ambulance?"

"No, just a couple of aspirin. Be sure to tell him that, okay? I don't need the cavalry swooping up my road."

Just in case the Cold Spring police department couldn't resist flashing lights and sirens racing in her direction, she called the inn to have Harriet warn her mother. But Harriet wasn't around. Apparently she'd left not long after their conversation, without saying where she was going or when she'd be back. It wasn't like her, and Penelope immediately blamed herself for tossing her cousin's life into a boiling cauldron.

She called Aunt Mary at the airport and gave her the rundown of her morning activities. Her aunt was uncharacteristically calm. "Your father's not here. He left a little while after you did—I think he knew you were up to no good."

"Gee, maybe he's the one who knocked me on my behind."

"No one would blame him if he was. You okay?"

"Fine. Just a few scratches and bruises."

She grunted. "I hope the bastard at least knocked some sense into you. You've got those two Sinclairs there?"

"At my kitchen table. You'll call Mother?"

"I always get the dirty work, but I suppose it's better she should hear this from me than in the streets."

Duty done, Penelope staggered to the couch with her second piece of cheese. The Sinclairs were watching her as if she were an exotic specimen in the collection they'd donated to the Museum of Natural History. She leaned against the musty, lumpy couch and glanced at Willard. A moose shot by their two grandfathers was about all she and Wyatt had in common. It was an unsettling thought, but true. She'd always prided herself on looking reality square in the eye.

"She needs some tea," Brandon said. "I'll put on a kettle."

Wyatt nodded. "Good idea. You know, Penelope,

if whoever smacked you in the face meant for you to be dead, you'd be dead."

"Could have fooled me."

Brandon didn't wait for the water to come to a full boil. He tossed a tea bag into one of her grandfather's vintage mugs, splashed in hot water and thrust it at her. "Use both hands."

She eyed the older Sinclair, an interesting mix of charm and arrogance. Yet she sensed he was out of his element, and he knew it. "I'm thinking someone's decided Bubba Johns must have looted the wreckage and made off with the diamonds Frannie Beaudine stole."

Brandon Sinclair didn't even flinch. His self-control was impeccable. "That's possible. I never knew of a hermit living on my family's land. I also just learned your cousin was found on a church doorstep soon after Colt and Frannie disappeared."

"Everyone thinks that's just a coincidence—at best someone taking advantage of the uproar."

"Your cousin doesn't think so."

Penelope shot Wyatt a look, but he shook his head. It wasn't him. That meant Jack Dunning must have filled his boss in on Harriet's fantasy. Before Penelope could rise to her cousin's defense, Andy McNally arrived, without fanfare. He couldn't get two words out before Lyman Chestnut clomped up her side steps and filled her little house with his fury and the noxious smoke of his cigar.

"Andy, what're you doing here? Penelope—Jesus Christ, what happened to you?"

"Didn't Aunt Mary get in touch with you?" Penelope asked.

"She was attacked at Bubba's," Andy told him. "She went out there alone."

"I'm fine, Pop, and I don't know if I was really *attacked*. I was just sort of pushed out of the way—and there's no smoking inside."

Her father glared at her and tossed his cigar into the sink. Andy took her statement, her father paced, Bubba's dogs paced, the Sinclairs stayed out of it, and when Penelope finished, her mother arrived.

"I hope you're all satisfied," Robby Chestnut said, beside herself with worry and irritation. "Now Harriet's missing."

EIGHTEEN

Harriet didn't stop running until she tripped over a fallen tree and the branch of a pine whipped her in the face. Her cheek stung, and she stayed on all fours, the snow melting into her knees, her hands and wrists aching from the cold. It wasn't soft, fluffy snow, it was sugar snow, and it bit into her skin. She could smell pine pitch and the rich, acidic smell of wet, dead leaves. She wondered if this was what death would be like, if somehow she'd smell the earth as she was lowered into her grave.

"Oh, God, you're pathetic," she breathed, and she got upright and sat on a tree trunk. It was another pine. Split down the middle. It must have happened during one of the brutal storms over the winter.

She needed spring. Tiny new leaves on the trees, green grass, daffodils, her early rhodies. She wanted to dig in her garden and feel the dirt in her cuticles, have an earthworm wriggle over her hand. She planned to plant more perennials. Foxglove, bleeding heart, evening primrose, lots and lots of hosta. She liked her life. She was happy. It wasn't as if she wanted to do anything else. Run away. Buy a mansion. Anything like that. She had no intention of picking up and whisking herself off to Texas or New

York with Jack—not that he'd want her to, would ever ask.

Jack wasn't an innkeeper, and the lakes region wouldn't keep him in the kind of work he did. And it wasn't Texas. Texas was home for him—not New York where he'd grown up, not New Hampshire where she'd grown up. She could see his eyes soften when he spoke of the ranch he wanted to buy. Brandon Sinclair paid him well, and one day he would have his ranch.

Her cheeks burned at the thought of Brandon Sinclair. Could he be her uncle? Her father's brother? She was embarrassed by her thinking, and yet she couldn't stop herself. He'd looked so patrician, such a gentleman. But he was the head of the Sinclair family, perhaps not one to tolerate false claims against his family. He wouldn't indulge her fantasies. He would insist she prove her claim, could even bring legal action against her if she said anything about Colt being her biological father. He hadn't said so, but it was clear to her. She was a threat. A *ridiculous* threat, but one nonetheless.

Andy had warned her to be more circumspect about being a Sinclair. For years, it had never occurred to her that anyone would think her odd. Even the police had looked for a connection between her arrival on the church doorstep and Colt Sinclair and Frannie Beaudine's disappearance.

But they hadn't found one, of course, and reporters were crowding into Cold Spring, wanting to know more about the quaint intrigues of the spinster innkeeper and her fantasies of being an heiress. Harriet felt claustrophobic, overwhelmed.

The sounds of a woodpecker tapping on a nearby

tree dragged her into the moment, out of her obsessing. She'd had to get away from the inn, away from anything to do with Sinclairs and reporters. At first she thought she'd drive into the mountains, but she'd found herself at Robby and Lyman's place outside town, on one of the smaller lakes, and she'd parked her car and launched into the woods.

She'd never been much of a hiker. When she hit a stream, instead of stepping stones across it, she plunged in and ran right through it. The water was frigid, numbing her toes, making her socks all squishy. She kept running until she fell. She didn't quite know where she was. She wondered if this was how Penelope felt last Sunday when she realized she was lost. Harriet wasn't dressed properly, she had no food or water, and her feet were cold and wet.

Well, she didn't care. She could sit out here a while longer and let matters take care of themselves. Her fantasy had hit the hard wall of reality. She wasn't a Sinclair. She wasn't anyone.

"You're a Chestnut," she whispered. "They're your family."

And they *were*. She loved her parents, Lyman and Robby, Mary and her brood, Penelope. That wasn't the point.

The point was that she was a fool. A laughing-stock.

She got stiffly to her feet, a breeze stirring, chilling her. She shivered, her teeth chattering, her feet aching from their dunking in the cold stream. Even with the warm temperature, when the sun darted behind a cloud, the air felt cool—a reminder it wasn't spring. She wondered what would happen if she didn't find her way before dark.

Robby would be beside herself by now. The inn was almost at capacity. So many reporters to feed, as well as Brandon Sinclair, Wyatt, Jack. There was dinner to prepare, work to do with so many guests. She had a responsibility to them, and to Robby and their small off-season staff. This was no time for her to be absent.

"You're being self-indulgent."

She kept her voice to a whisper, although there was no one to hear her. She thrashed her way down a gentle slope, stumbled on a lane flanked by stone walls. It would have to lead somewhere.

Ahead, she could hear people talking, and she picked up her pace. "Hello? Hello—is anyone there?"

"Harriet?"

Penelope rounded a bend, Wyatt right behind her. The sun struck her hair, and Harriet suddenly realized how pretty her cousin was with her blond curls, her creamy skin, her green eyes. She'd always focused on Penelope's skills as a pilot, her penchant for action and adventure—not on how attractive she was, how kind. Harriet's eyes filled with tears, and she felt stupid.

"Hey, Harriet," Penelope said, "I hope you weren't running away, because you're easy to find. Mr. Wilderness here was able to pick out your tracks every few yards or so. We found your car and figured you had to be out here somewhere."

Harriet sniffled. "I was just out walking—"

"It's okay, Harriet. I've run away a few times myself this week."

"Your cheek—I didn't notice. What happened? Penelope—"

"I'm fine, I'm fine. We should get going. Mother's down at the inn changing all the dinner specials around to the way she likes them."

Harriet attempted a smile. Penelope's energy was so addictive. It was strange how perfect she and Wyatt looked together. Did they realize it? But Harriet knew Penelope wouldn't easily let herself fall for a man who was just as strong, driven and smart as she was. And a Sinclair, no less.

They headed out of the woods, and Harriet saw she hadn't gone that far or been that lost. Penelope insisted on riding with her to the inn, while Wyatt took his car.

Several reporters had gathered before the fireplace at the front desk. As Harriet had feared, they'd learned she was found on the church doorstep by the local minister forty-eight hours after Colt and Frannie had disappeared. It was a fresh angle, it would add texture—a current human interest element—to their stories. A small-town spinster who thought she was the long-lost daughter of two missing adventurers. It was improbable, of course. The timing, the plausibility. Harriet had done the math herself. Even if by some miracle Frannie Beaudine was her mother, Harriet was at least six weeks old when George Chestnut found her. Someone must have known about her, cared for her when she was a newborn.

"The police still haven't recovered any bodies at the crash site," one reporter said. "What do you think, Harriet?"

"I think I want to have a cup of tea before starting

dinner." Her stomach ached. She wasn't as brazen as Penelope. "Are you joining us this evening?"

"Sure. Wouldn't miss it."

She ran upstairs and washed her face. If she were Colt and Frannie's daughter, she would be beautiful and adventurous. She was neither. She was a plain, forty-five-year-old woman with a lovely inn, a wonderful family she'd hurt with her questioning and fantasizing. Yet they'd never said anything—they were stoic, taciturn, loving in their own quiet way.

She looked at herself in the mirror, and she hated herself for wanting to be anything but Harriet Chestnut.

Penelope got a ride home with Andy McNally, who remained unconvinced that whatever had happened to her at Bubba's wasn't an attack. He lectured her on personal safety before he dropped her off. "It was probably just a reporter out there who got spooked and ran off, but watch yourself. I don't like not knowing where Bubba is."

"I've got new locks and Bubba's dogs."

"And Wyatt Sinclair, from what I hear," he said without enthusiasm.

"He's powwowing at the inn with his father and Jack Dunning. I expect they'll be consulting various lawyers and advisers about what to do next, how to handle the investigation of the crash site, the media."

Andy eyed her from across his car. "Might not be a bad idea for you to think about some of those things."

"Already have. I plan on unplugging my phone."

He shook his head. "Christ, you're a pain in the ass."

She grinned at him. "Deep down, Andy, I know you're on my side."

"It's chief to you. Why don't you have dinner with your parents?"

"Because they think I'm having dinner with the Sinclairs. The Sinclairs think I'm having dinner with my parents, so it's working out. What I need," she added as he turned into her driveway, "is a little time alone so I can think."

Andy didn't like that idea. "You want me to sit out in your driveway until you're done thinking?"

"That would defeat the purpose, Andy. I need to be alone as in *a-l-o-n-e.*"

"You're sure?"

"I'm sure."

"If you need me, you've got my number."

She smiled. "Thanks."

He gripped the wheel, suddenly looking awkward. "Penelope..." He grimaced, out of his element. "I'm worried about Harriet."

"We all are." She swallowed, remembering how terrible her cousin had looked when they'd found her in the woods. Her hair a wreck, her clothes soaked and muddy, her hands red and scraped. If they hadn't found her, if she'd stumbled around in the woods for much longer, she'd have gone into hypothermia. "If I could undo what I've done, Andy, I would. I'd leave that plane out there. I'd pretend I never saw a thing. It's just not worth what it's doing to her. And Bubba."

"Don't beat yourself up, Penelope. Hell, even I don't blame you for this one. Harriet was going to have to deal with this Sinclair thing one of these days."

Inside, Penelope fashioned a couple of makeshift leashes out of rope for the two mutts and walked them up and down her driveway a few times. What they needed was one of their treks with Bubba Johns. They were already going soft on her. All they wanted was food. She tossed Dog Chow into their pans and watched them go at it, growling and snapping at each other until every morsel was gone.

Her message machine was full, all messages from reporters. Her fax machine was empty. She had no unread e-mail. At least her anonymous nut had stopped pestering her.

While frozen bean soup heated on the stove, Penelope ducked into her bedroom to change. Her various treks into the woods had left her muddy, wet, sweaty and bruised. A hot bath was definitely in order. She'd had enough of the wilds for a while. She couldn't wait to get in the air.

She returned to the kitchen and got down a bowl, her soup bubbling on the front burner. For no reason her eyes filled with tears, and it was all she could do to keep from crying. Maybe solitude wasn't such a good idea, after all.

The dogs suddenly jumped up, howling and carrying on, racing to the sliding glass door. Penelope forgot all about her Winchester and grabbed a butcher knife. One of the dogs, the scroungy black one, bared his teeth.

The dogs flopped and started whining.

Penelope lowered her butcher knife. "What is it, guys?"

But she knew. It had to be their master, Bubba

Johns. She set the knife on the counter, pulled the chair from in front of the slider and peered onto the deck. It was right after sunset, not yet really dark. Eerie shadows shifted with the wind. There was nothing there. Maybe the dogs only thought they'd heard Bubba.

He materialized in front of the sliding glass door, startling her. She screamed and got the dogs going again. Bubba held one finger to his lips, and they quieted. Steve had done what he could to fix the door temporarily, but it needed to be replaced. Penelope managed to open it about six inches. "That's the best I can do, Bubba. If you want to come in, you'll have to go around—"

He shook his head. "Reporters."

"I understand." She squinted at him, taking in his scraggly beard and hair, his grayish, ghostly skin. "Jeez, Bubba, you look like Jacob Marley. All you need is the ball and chain. You okay? Your dogs have missed you."

"They're good dogs."

His voice had a rasping, Marley quality to it, too. Penelope used both hands to try to open the door wider. "You should come on in. I've got hot soup."

"No soup. Penelope, you need to know. The diamonds—"

She stared at him. "You know about the diamonds?"

He nodded. "They were in the plane wreckage. They've been gone for more than twenty years."

She was so stunned she couldn't answer.

"If someone's after them, it's too late. They're gone."

"You didn't take them?"

"I didn't want them. The woods are already filled with beautiful stones. I don't need more."

"Yeah, but New Hampshire granite isn't worth ten million."

The frosty eyes bored into her. "What is ten million worth to me?"

Penelope remembered she was dealing with hermit logic. "You don't know who took them?"

He shook his head.

"Bubba, you didn't attack me out at your place today, did you? I didn't startle you in the garden shed—"

"No."

"Did you see who did?"

"No."

Straightforward enough, not that Bubba would elaborate without a lot of prodding. "Where are you staying? The police want to talk to you. I never meant for any of this to disrupt your life—"

"It disrupted my life long before you came along."

Penelope went still. Blood rushed to her ears. "Bubba—are you Colt Sinclair?"

The eyes, the ghostly skin, the wild beard and hair. She had to be crazy. Bubba didn't answer her. A car sounded in her driveway. The dogs jumped up, barking. Bubba took a step toward the edge of the deck. Penelope tried to squeeze through the opening in the slider to go after him, but she didn't fit. "What about the bodies?" she asked him. "Did you bury Colt and Frannie? Bubba, if you tell me what you know, maybe I can explain to the police—"

But he was gone, and Wyatt was at the side door.

He walked right in. Her new locks were useless if she didn't use them. She swung around, tried to ignore the instant knot in her stomach that told her she'd hoped he'd come. "I hate people who don't knock," she snapped.

"I wanted to see who was out on your deck. Bubba Johns, I take it?"

"And know-it-alls. I hate know-it-alls."

Wyatt grinned at her. "You get cranky when you're caught. It's not your best trait." He moved to her side at the stove, touched her cheek. "Still hurt?"

"Not that much." She scooped soup into her bowl, relieved he wasn't going to press her about Bubba. For now. "Have you eaten?"

He shook his head. "I'm having dinner with my father later. You sure you don't want to join us?"

"Thanks, but no thanks. There's just too much going on at the inn. Reporters, police, Sinclairs, Harriet. My mother. I need a quiet evening. How'd it go with your meeting?"

"Nothing new. An aviation expert is going to take a look at the wreckage and try to determine a cause. Meanwhile, the family strategy will be—as expected—to stay above the fray."

"That makes sense, doesn't it?"

"I suppose. Your father comes by his reticence naturally. My father is calculating and deliberate about everything he says."

Penelope sat at the table with her bowl of soup. She was so stiff, her muscles aching—and not just from being knocked on her behind at Bubba's. There was last night, too. She felt warm thinking about it, and a little self-conscious. She told Wyatt, "I haven't noticed you fretting over every word. Seems to me you speak your mind."

He shrugged. "One of my rebellions."

"But you and your father love each other—"

"That's one thing you don't seem to know about my family, Penelope." He pulled out a chair, sat down. "Love is never enough for a Sinclair."

"Is that another of your rebellions?"

His black eyes held her. "I could only wish."

She put her spoon down and leaned over the table, her mouth finding his. She didn't give a damn if love wasn't enough for a Sinclair, if tomorrow he'd pack up and head to New York. All that mattered was feeling his mouth on hers, touching his hair, his jaw. If he didn't have dinner plans with his father, she was certain they'd have ended up in her bedroom.

Finally, she sat down to her soup. "It was Bubba on my deck," she said.

As demonstrations of love and trust, it wasn't much. But Wyatt's dark eyes flashed. "And?"

"The diamonds have been gone for twenty years or more."

Wyatt went very still. "Anything else?"

She shook her head.

"All right. You have two choices. Either I come back here tonight or you stay at the inn. You can't stay here alone, Penelope—hell, I wouldn't stay here alone myself."

"I'm used to it. It's my home." She sighed, glancing at the little kitchen and the living room with their mix of old-man lakeside cabin and her. She hadn't bothered with a fire in the wood stove. The dogs had settled next to it, anyway. Her gaze shifted to Wyatt, and she smiled. "I guess it's a weird home, isn't it?"

His gaze softened. "It's a little eccentric."

"Oh, God. *Harriet's* eccentric. I'm just a pilot who can't afford to tear this place down and build my dream house." Without thinking, she shot to her feet and grabbed her fleece pullover off the back of the chair. "Dinner at the inn sounds good, after all. If you and your father want to have a private dinner, that's fine by me. I can eat in the kitchen with Harriet and my mother—or help out. With all these reporters in town, they must be swamped."

"And tonight?"

"I have to come back here. This place isn't much, but it's all I've got. I'm not leaving it to Bubba's dogs and a bunch of reporters."

Wyatt got to his feet. "Then I'll pack my toothbrush and razor and join you."

She smiled, nodded. "That would be nice."

As he observed her during dinner with his father and Jack, Wyatt came to understand something about Penelope Chestnut. He wasn't sure she would agree with or approve of his insight. He didn't care, either. Because he knew he was right. She was a woman who'd put herself out there—say anything, do anything—for the people she loved. That was one thing. That gave her an air of determination, courage, impulsiveness, even stubbornness. But when it came to asking for or accepting help, she was uneasy. She didn't like other people to see her vulnerabilities, her fears, her deepest longings. She preferred to be the rescuer, not the rescued.

Wyatt understood. It had taken a tragedy in the

southwest Tasmanian mountains to get him to acknowledge that he wasn't invulnerable, that his body and soul could break. His body had mended just fine. He wasn't so sure about his soul. But that was another problem for another time. Now it was enough to have his insight into Penelope.

Her mother had seated them up in a small, private sitting room off the front room that looked out on the porch and lake. Reporters and a few curiosity-seekers occupied the Octagon Room. Robby winced at the bruise blossoming on her daughter's cheek but said nothing about her choice of dinner companions.

Jack had already lectured Penelope on her recklessness, which from his tone was another word for stupidity. She was a woman not accustomed to being chewed out. She let Jack have his say while she buttered a small slice of warm pumpkin bread. Wyatt's father seemed more ill at ease with Jack's tirade than she did. That, Wyatt assumed, was because he didn't yet know Penelope.

They discussed the situation in broad terms. Anything specific Brandon Sinclair would have considered a breach of etiquette. Neither Wyatt nor Penelope mentioned Bubba Johns's visit to her deck, although Wyatt wasn't sure why. "I want you people to let me do my job," Jack said over dessert. "If I need to question the old man and tear his place apart inch by inch, that's what I'm going to do. It won't help if you get in my way."

Brandon Sinclair regarded his investigator with a calm that, from long experience, Wyatt knew he wasn't feeling. "Jack, I won't have you doing anything illegal on my behalf."

Dunning turned to him, the muscles in his neck and jaw visibly tense. "I was speaking figuratively. I know my parameters."

Penelope cut through the awkwardness with a bright smile. "You boys can discuss tactics. I think I'll go say good-night to Mother and Harriet in the kitchen."

"Thank them," Brandon said, "for the lovely meal and for allowing us to dine in here. It's worked out beautifully."

Wyatt could see Penelope was smitten. Now he'd have to hear what a charming man his father was and what a beast he, the only son, was. It had happened with women before. They seemed to ignore the history of three wives and many lovers, the undercurrent of repressed emotion that Wyatt had sensed even as a child. His father seemed happy enough with his third marriage and two daughters, but Wyatt knew there was a yawning abyss in him, a cavern of unrecognized dreams and deep pain that, he suspected, went back to the abandonment of an older brother when he was just eleven.

After Penelope left, Jack filled his wineglass and said coolly, "You need to be careful with that woman, Wyatt. We don't know how much of her story holds up. She could have found the plane years ago and made off with the diamonds."

"And done what with them?" Wyatt asked. "Stuffed them in her moose head? Come on, Jack. Penelope's not living the life-style of someone with ten million dollars in diamonds at her disposal."

Jack didn't back off. "You know these people up here. They don't trust money."

"The Chestnuts are frugal," Wyatt said. "That

doesn't make them cheap or anti-money. If Penelope could, she'd build her dream house, buy a plane, probably make a bid for the Sinclair acreage."

"You're biased. But that's neither here nor there." Jack got to his feet, nodded to his boss. "I'll let you know if anything develops."

After he left, Wyatt studied his father across the table. There was a tightness around his eyes, but otherwise no indication of the stress of the past twenty-four hours. "Bubba Johns stopped at Penelope's earlier this evening. He told her the diamonds have been missing for more than twenty years and then took off."

His father lifted his wineglass, a slight tremble in his hand. "Will she tell the police?"

"Probably, but that's just a guess. She's protective of Bubba. She doesn't want to violate any trust he's developed for her. That's why I didn't mention it with her there. Also, frankly, I'm not sure I want Jack to know."

"This hermit's life could be at risk," Brandon said simply.

Wyatt nodded. "I know. Father, could he be Colt?"

"Good God, no. Colt had a family. Whatever happened, whatever he did, he would know he could come back to his family."

"Would he?"

His father was silent a moment, his eyes narrowed to slits. "What are you saying?"

"I'm saying your father was not a forgiving man. If Colt didn't measure up to his standards of a Sinclair, I'm not sure he'd expect to have all forgiven and forgotten." Wyatt shifted in his chair, debated having more wine, then rejected the idea. "Everyone believes Colt was an adventurer and scoundrel. But I'm not so sure."

"He would read to me." His father's voice was quiet, the emotion buried deep, but there. "He loved adventure novels. Jack London, Alexander Dumas. And he loved to draw. I remember once he took me to the Museum of Natural History and showed me a stuffed eagle and how he'd done a charcoal drawing of it. He wasn't…" He paused, whatever battle he was fighting within himself brought under control. "My brother wasn't a man of action."

"But he felt as if he should be," Wyatt said.

The smallest, driest of smiles. "Don't all Sinclairs?"

"You did?"

"Of course. But I made a conscious choice to honor Colt's memory by not giving in to my impulses. My father knew what I was doing. He was ambivalent. He wanted me to take physical risks—to have the grand adventures. He'd have respected me more if I had." He finished the last of his wine, set the glass down, gazed at it. "But he also wanted me to live."

"It took courage to carve out your own identity against that kind of pressure."

"Ah, yes. The pressures of family tradition and a man who measures another man's worth by the physical risks he's willing to take. My brother knew he fell short. I was determined to prove to our father that what Colt wanted to be—what he was—was every bit as good and worthy as the Sinclairs before him."

Wyatt saw it. "So you sacrificed your own de-sires."

"Yes, I did. I'd have climbed Everest, Wyatt. I'd have explored the Amazon. I'd have put together expeditions to support scholarship and research. I chose not to because I knew—I *know*—that my brother was every bit as good and courageous as any Sinclair. It was my personal, private rebellion."

"Father..."

But that was the end of the discussion. His father snapped to his feet, his back straight, his patrician reserve in place. "You should see to Penelope before she lands herself in another tight spot." He gave his son a faint smile. "For years, Wyatt, I've hoped you'd end up with a woman who's just as reckless and high-spirited as you are, just so you could begin to understand what your mother and I have en-dured. It seems that's one wish of mine that's come true."

"I'll be staying at her place tonight."

"Yes. You should."

His father started across the small, pretty parlor. Wyatt turned in his chair and said, "What do you think Colt would have done if Frannie Beaudine duped him and played him for a fool, if she stole the diamonds without his knowledge and then she died when their plane crashed and he lived? You knew him. Could he have faced your father?"

"I don't know. But it's been forty-five years, and Father's been dead for ten. He had to know he could have faced me."

NINETEEN

First thing in the morning Penelope went onto her deck and looked at the mushy ground and patches of snow for Bubba's tracks. He couldn't have materialized out there. He had to have come from somewhere.

Wyatt joined her, thrusting a mug of coffee at her. "Anything?"

She shook her head. She felt tight, keyed up, as if she'd slept two inches above her bed. "I've made such a mess of things. Harriet's a wreck, and Bubba's been run out of his home. If I was trying to protect anyone, it was them." She added bitterly, "I'm sure they're very grateful."

"Your intentions—"

"Oh, my intentions be damned. As my mother is fond of telling me, the road to hell is paved with good intentions."

"No, it's not." His eyes were distant, even blacker in the morning sun. "It's paved with neglect, inattention and thoughtlessness."

"I didn't think."

"But you're not thoughtless."

She smiled at him, welcoming the feel of the hot mug in her hands, the briskness of the morning air.

A high in the fifties today. "You're not a bad guy to wake up with in the morning."

He leaned over the deck rail, listening to the birds on the quiet lake. "This is a nice spot."

"It's very different in the summer. I often get up early and take my kayak out for a spin before I head to work. There are camps all up the road. You can hear kids and smell the barbecues from here."

"You don't mind?"

"I love it—it's a refreshing change from winter. I'm not a recluse. I can understand Bubba on one level, the peace and satisfaction he must feel at living such a simple, independent life." She sipped her coffee, staring across the lake. "But I'm more of a people person. As much as my family and friends can get on my nerves—and vice versa—I have no desire to run away from them."

"Do you think that's what Bubba did?"

"One way or another, I expect so. Who knows, maybe he needed to run away in order to survive. We don't know what his family and friends were like."

Wyatt was silent, and Penelope knew that he, too, suspected Bubba Johns of being his uncle. The age, the lean physique, the gray eyes. He could be a Sinclair.

"I've been thinking," she said. "Since we've got ten million dollars worth of missing diamonds and a hermit, I figure why not a secret baby? It's all so flipping far-fetched right now. Let's say Harriet *is* Colt and Frannie's daughter. It means Frannie would have to have given birth to her here, in Cold Spring."

Wyatt digested that one. "Why not New York?"

"Too complicated. She'd have to tuck her away somewhere, pick her up en route to the airport—and then somehow the baby survived the crash and so on and so on." Penelope drank more coffee, her heart thumping, not from caffeine but from thinking too damned much. "But here in Cold Spring, Frannie had friends."

"Careful, Penelope. You don't want to leap too far ahead of the facts."

She raised her eyes to him, said quietly, "You're right. Look, I should go out to the airport. I want to talk to my father. If reporters have his kingdom staked out, too, he's going to be fit to be tied. Are you going to see your father and Dunning?"

"They'll keep. I'll tag along with you."

"Because you're being protective or don't exactly trust me?"

He grinned, and with two fingers snatched a few stray hairs and tucked them into her hasty braid. "How about because I enjoy your company?"

"I think I'll go with 'all of the above.'"

They found her father drinking coffee with his older sister, complaining about the taste. "If I can put up with your cigars," she told him, "you can put up with my coffee."

Penelope sat in a metal chair with a vinyl seat. Wyatt wandered around outside, looking at Jack Dunning's plane and generally making himself scarce. She shook her head at Aunt Mary's offer of coffee and said, "Pop, did you know that Frannie made off with ten million dollars worth of stolen diamonds?"

"Oh, good Lord," her aunt breathed.

Her father, in his flannel shirt and work pants,

drank some of his coffee, made a face, and said, "I expected something like that. Maybe not ten million, maybe not diamonds. But money had to be involved somewhere—the way Willard Sinclair acted at the time and with what's been going on the past few days. It wouldn't happen for a couple of people who've been dead for almost fifty years."

"If they are dead," Penelope corrected.

He shrugged. "All right. If they are dead."

"So, if Frannie stole diamonds, the question is, why? I have a hypothesis. Do you want to hear it?"

"I have a choice?"

She tried to smile, couldn't. "Let's say Frannie Beaudine is also Harriet's birth mother. If that's the case, someone in Cold Spring must have helped her deliver her baby. It doesn't make sense she'd have had the baby in New York. Once the baby was delivered, someone had to take care of her while Harriet went back to New York."

Her aunt jumped up. "I have errands to run. I'll leave you two to talk. I've listened to every possible scenerio for forty-five years. If you want my opinion, not every mystery needs to be unraveled."

Neither Penelope nor her father made an attempt to stop her. Aunt Mary had no patience for this kind of talk. When she had gone, Penelope resumed, her father steely-eyed, listening with apparent patience. "So Frannie's back in New York, and she and Colt come forward with their relationship. It's met with hostility—she's not the sort of woman Willard Sinclair wants to marry his eldest son. Frannie's pissed. She knows she has this baby and she feels entitled to a share of the Sinclair fortune. And she can't count on a future with Colt. So she helps herself to some diamonds."

She paused, hoping her father would tell her she was making sense or no sense at all, but he merely said, "Go on."

"Let's say Colt finds out, or guesses—something happens that makes him agree to run away with Frannie. He knows he'll be disinherited or whatever it is Sinclairs do to their own who stray, but she's not worried."

"Because she has the diamonds."

"Exactly. So they fly off to reunite with their baby. Only the plane goes down, and they're lost. Meanwhile, her helpers here on the ground in Cold Spring have this tiny baby and no knowledge of the diamonds. When it's clear Colt and Frannie can't have survived the crash, they have no choice."

"So they leave the baby on the church doorstep for my uncle to find."

"That's my hypothesis."

He nodded thoughtfully. "Do you have a hypothesis about the helpers on the ground?"

"I do."

"And?"

She met his clear, unswerving gaze. "I think it was you and Granddad."

"Why? Because we wouldn't sit for one of your interviews?"

"Partly. Also because if I were twenty-five and in trouble, I would go to someone like you and Granddad for help. I would know I could trust you, and I would know you'd do the right thing. And in my hypothesis," she went on, hanging on to the last shreds of self-control, "the right thing clearly would be to make sure the baby had a chance at a good life and happiness. With Frannie and Colt dead, nothing else mattered."

Her father rubbed a hand over his jaw and sighed heavily, shaking his head. "You had to work hard to come up with that one, I'll say that much."

"It wasn't hard, Pop. It was easy."

He got to his feet. "I've got work to do."

"Pop—"

He turned to her with none of the aggravation she'd expected. "I don't know much, kid. But I do know what's mine to tell and what's not mine to tell. Now, you up to pushing a broom?"

Penelope attempted a smile. She'd pushed her father as far as he'd be pushed. Let him digest what she'd said. "You know how to get rid of me, don't you? I'll go see what Wyatt's up to."

She stood outside the office and looked out at the windswept airport, not seeing him at first. Then she spotted him at the farthest of the three hangars. He didn't notice her, and she headed over, a stiff, cold wind blowing in her face. She could feel her scrapes and bruises this morning. She caught up with Wyatt, the wind catching the ends of his hair. With the drop in temperature, he had on his leather jacket. "You should take flying lessons," she told him. "You'd fit right in."

He smiled. "I can see myself in the front row of one of your father's classes."

"He put up with me, he can put up with you. What're you up to?"

"Just looking around."

"There's not much out here. We don't really use this hangar until warm weather, when it's busier.

Pop brings in more staff, and this place really hums."

"You love it, don't you?"

"I do."

But there was something in his expression. Pretending she hadn't noticed it, she crossed her arms against the cold and walked to a corner of the hangar as if to get out of the wind. She glanced around for what had gotten his attention. And there, in the blackened remnants of snow and the frozen mud, she saw distinct footprints.

She swung around to Wyatt. "You weren't going to tell me? Where do they lead—did you follow them? It's not reporters, they'd have no reason to be way out here..." She stopped, catching her breath, *knowing*. "It has to be Bubba. My father's hiding him."

"There's a side door to the hangar, way at the end. It's locked. Penelope, we can't let ourselves jump to conclusions—"

But she was already marching over the frozen snow and mud along the isolated far side of the hangar, the chain-link security fence a couple of yards to her left. She could hear Wyatt's hiss of irritation behind her. Impulsive. Reckless. But not distracted, she thought. She was focused and she was mad—and she was certain.

She came to the door. It was windowless, locked. Because of its location, it was never used. It led to a small storage room that was generally accessed from an inside door in the main part of the hangar. Its huge doors, too, were locked this time of year.

If she wanted to hide someone, or hide herself, this would be a good choice.

She raised her fist to knock, then changed her mind and gave the door a good kick.

"Penelope!"

It was her father, with Wyatt right behind him. She ignored them both and kicked the door again. She thought of the creepy messages, her ransacked house, her broken door, her new locks, her terror yesterday when Bubba's shed door banged into her face. It was all too damned much. If she'd changed her story from finding a plane wreck to finding a dump, it was done on impulse, out of fear for an innocent old man and a woman she cared about. It wasn't calculated, it wasn't deliberate. And it hadn't gone on for *years*. Not like her father. He'd been lying to her forever.

"Penelope, goddamn it, you're going to bust the door!"

"Good."

Her father was huffing, out of breath. Wyatt, standing behind him, looked remarkably calm. All that Sinclair control kicking into gear. She was suddenly unreasonably irritated with him. He wouldn't have told her about the footprints. He'd have found an excuse and snuck back here, even talked to her father behind her back.

And wasn't that the pot calling the kettle black? She remembered how hard she'd tried to keep him from noticing Bubba's footprints when they were collecting sap. When was that? Wednesday? It seemed ages ago.

"Jesus," her father said. "Stop. He's not here."

She gaped at him, and her eyes clouded. "You lied to me."

His mouth snapped shut, and he nodded. "All I can say is that it's not about you."

"Pop—my God—I can't believe—"

But he and Wyatt were looking at something behind her. She pivoted, and Bubba was there, as if he'd materialized out of thin air. He must have been hiding around the corner of the hangar, heard her kicking the door, acting like a maniac. She gulped in air, and her father said, "Bubba, you have to tell them. It's time."

The old man nodded. He looked at Penelope, and then he looked at Wyatt, and he said, "My real name isn't Bubba Johns. I made that up. My real name—" and he paused, swallowing, the frosty eyes filling with unexpected tears "—I'm Colt Sinclair."

Lyman Chestnut, the taciturn New Englander, and Colt Sinclair, the scraggly hermit, made an odd pair in the chief of police's office. They wanted to make a clean breast of it. How Colt had survived the plane crash, what had happened to Frannie, what he knew about the diamonds, how Lyman had come to be involved. Everything. And they wanted to do it properly, to the police, before anything else could happen.

This did not please Penelope. She wanted answers, and she wanted them now. Wyatt could see her bursting with impatience, almost losing it when Andy McNally, curt but professional, asked the two of them to leave. But Wyatt touched her hand, felt some of the stiffness go out of her, and she followed him.

The wind had died down, but the air was more winter than spring. They took his car to the inn, where the reporters had gotten word about Bubba Johns showing up at the police station and were on their way. Penelope was not of a mind to worry about the old hermit. "He and Pop deserve what they get."

Her mother, fussing with the fireplace, was of like mind with her daughter, which Wyatt didn't expect happened often. "I always knew Lyman would get himself arrested over a Sinclair one of these days."

"He hasn't been arrested," Penelope said. "What would Andy charge him with, keeping secrets from his wife and daughter?"

Robby Chestnut paled, and Wyatt felt for her. Her husband was sitting in the police chief's office, and her daughter was bruised, bloodied and standing with a Sinclair. And all she wanted was a pretty inn, a nice life. She said, "He and Frannie—God, he adored her. We all did. She was so full of life, so determined to make her mark in the world. He'd have gone to the ends of the earth for her."

Penelope grabbed her mother's arm. "Mother— you're not saying Pop and Frannie…"

"*No!*" If possible, she paled even more. "Oh, good heavens, no. He was just fifteen. He wasn't…" She shook her head, adamant. "No."

"I didn't think so. But with the way things are going—"

"You don't have to explain."

Robby stuck a log on the fire, and it almost fell onto her foot. Penelope said, "Not that way, Mother, you'll burn yourself," and Wyatt left the two of them alone.

He found his father on the front porch, staring at Lake Winnipesaukee. He wore no coat, just a heavy

Scottish knit sweater. Before Wyatt had come beside him, he said, "It looks remarkably the same up here. It's more populated, of course, and this was just a dying, isolated little village in the fifties. Now it's got an active, vital, year-round population, as well as a thriving tourist business. This inn—" He paused, glanced at the covered furniture, the wide, quiet porch. "It was just a crumbling old lake house when I was a boy."

"You were so young when you were here last. It must be strange coming back."

"I wanted to help find Colt. I remember—I was so desperate to find him. It was all I could think about for weeks, months. But my father forbid it. He didn't even allow me up here. I stayed in New York with Mother, attended my classes. I did what was expected of me, but all I wanted to do was run away from home and find my brother."

"Father—"

He shook his head, cutting Wyatt off. "I did run away. Three times. All in the first eighteen months after Colt left. Once I got as far as Massachusetts, the other two times I was picked up at Port Authority." He inhaled sharply, containing his emotions. "I think, secretly, Father was pleased."

"This must be very painful for you," Wyatt said lamely, feeling helpless.

"I heard about the hermit on our land years ago. I suppose I suspected it might be Colt. I never could bring myself to make a serious effort to find out." He looked at Wyatt, his gaze hardening. "He walked away from his family, not once, but twice. He ran off with Frannie Beaudine without saying goodbye. And he survived the plane crash and became this Bubba Johns character. He's had forty-five years, Wyatt. If he'd wanted to see me, to know you, he knew where to find us."

As much as Brandon thought he might be burying his emotions, coping with them, triumphing over them, his mix of anger, betrayal, loss and confusion was right there at the surface, raw and impossible to ignore. Wyatt felt no relief, no satisfaction. Inside this fifty-six-year-old man was a boy trying to come to terms with what his big brother had done, the choices he'd made that left his little brother alone.

It was so searingly simple. He'd loved his big brother, and it wasn't enough.

"I've failed you in a thousand ways, Wyatt," his father said. "I know that. But I've never abandoned you—I've always tried in my perhaps inadequate way to be there for you."

"I know."

"Do you?"

His tone was almost harsh. Wyatt nodded. "You love all of us. Ellen, Beatrix, me. It's all we could ask, and it's enough."

Colt Sinclair was alive.

Harriet stood at her bay window overlooking the lake. She was stricken, hardly able to breathe. Her chest hurt. Her heart raced. She thought she might collapse.

If Colt was alive, he couldn't be her father. He would never have left his own child on a doorstep. He would have taken her and raised her.

He was only twenty-one. Not much more than a boy himself.

Still, she knew he wouldn't have abandoned his own child.

She'd never figured out who'd done the leaving. Who'd wrapped her in a blanket and put her in an apple basket and tucked her onto the church doorstep that cold, dark April night. Now it looked as if it must have been Lyman. Her own cousin, a man she'd known all her life. He'd known their town hermit was really Colt Sinclair. What other secrets did he have?

She didn't want to see him, speak to him. Not right now. Right now, she only wanted to breathe.

There was a quiet knock at her door. She shrieked and jumped, knocking over her needlework stand.

"Harriet? It's me, Jack."

Ridiculously, she pushed back her hair, checked her dresser mirror to see if she was at all presentable. She wasn't. Hair dank and gray-looking, eyes wild, and so pale. She was too stunned to cry. It wasn't as if she hadn't considered Bubba Johns might be Colt. She hadn't ever expected it to be *real*.

"Harriet—"

"I'm here!"

She pulled open the door, inhaled at the shock of his sexiness. It was there every time she saw him, thought of him. "Jack—what can I do for you?"

"May I come in?"

"Of course."

He shut the door behind him. Harriet felt a rush of excitement that did nothing to steady her breathing. Jack walked around, checking out her three rooms, and she bit the insides of her cheeks to keep from passing out. She was so self-conscious. She couldn't remember when she'd had anyone besides Robby

and Penelope to her rooms. Most of her friends she
met downstairs in one of the common rooms. She'd
never had a man up here. He looked so out of place
amidst her laces and flowers and frills, and yet he
didn't seem to mind.

He smiled at her. "This is just what I pictured."

"It's especially nice in the summer, when there's a
breeze off the lake—" She stopped, stunned, when
he pulled open one of her dresser drawers. "What
are you doing?"

"I'm just wondering what you did with the diamonds."

She didn't speak. Couldn't.

"Good," he said. "At least you're not going to
pretend you don't know."

"Jack, don't. Please."

He sat on the edge of her bed, his flat eyes taking
her in. She had on navy chinos and a white button-
down shirt, just her watch for jewelry. She didn't
have Robby's flare for clothes, Penelope's natural
good looks—she had to work at her appearance.
And most often she didn't. This morning she'd
given up on makeup and washed it all off.

"Harriet—" He sighed audibly, shaking his head.
"Hell, you're my weakness. But I think you know
that." His gaze narrowed on her, the detective at
work. "I figure you found the wreckage a long time
ago. How long?"

Her mouth was parched, and she almost couldn't
get the words out. "I was sixteen."

"Sixteen. A hell of an age to find the plane you believed your parents died in."

"My birth parents," she amended in a whisper.

"Birth parents. Right. Christ, what a quaint term.

So, you've kept quiet for almost thirty years. That's damned impressive, Harriet. Damned impressive."

"I never—I never looked in the wreckage. I didn't want to see the bodies. I stumbled on it by accident. A friend and I had gotten separated...." She shut her eyes, the door to that long-locked closet in the recesses of her mind popping open, a tornado ripping through everything she'd buried, denied even to herself. "I found the diamonds on the hill a few yards below the wreckage, lodged against a rock. They were in a small artist's case. It must have tumbled down the hill during the crash."

"Serendipity," Jack said, amused, sarcastic.

Harriet looked at him, and for that split second she saw what he might have been—what they could have been together—and what he was. A gentle man with a dream of owning a Texas ranch, and a tough, competitive man who would burn anything in his path—including her—now that his dream was within his reach.

"I didn't take them at first," she said. "I wasn't sure what they were—if they were real. I didn't think I was supposed to find them. I left them with the wreckage. Later, after Bubba Johns built his shack, I got them."

"Why didn't you tell anyone you'd found Colt and Frannie's plane?"

She licked her lips, but there was no moisture left in her mouth, on her tongue. "I wasn't ready to know the truth, whatever it was. I loved my parents. My real parents. And I just didn't—"

"Where are the diamonds now?"

There was no point in lying. He would tear her room apart if he felt he had to. She was on the third floor. No one would hear. If she started to scream, he'd gag her. "They're here."

She showed him. She opened the antique trunk in her sitting room, and inside, down at the bottom, was the artist's case filled with diamonds. She'd made a black velvet bag for them, with red ribbon ties. She opened it and gave the diamonds to Jack.

"Fuck, Harriet." His voice was a hoarse whisper, his eyes pinned on her. "I wish things could be different."

"I know."

He touched her cheek, let his fingers drift into her hair. "You want me to be your knight in shining armor. I'd like to be, maybe more than you know. But I'm just a rough Brooklyn boy who's getting his the only way he knows how—the only way he can. I want my ranch, Harriet. I wish I could explain—"

"You don't have to explain, Jack. I understand. When Robby and I were transforming this falling-down old house into an inn, I could imagine it all done up with needlepoint pillows and pretty wall-papers and potpourri. There were days we'd be working, down on our hands and knees, so bone-tired and discouraged that we just wanted to give up, and I'd watch the sun glow orange on the lake—" She stopped herself, swallowed in her dry, tight throat. "I know what it is to have a dream."

"I thought being a Sinclair was your dream."

She smiled sadly. "No, that was just a silly fantasy. I'm a Chestnut. I belong right here where I am. It's a little late to realize that...." She shrugged. "But it's true."

Jack tilted his head and appraised her. "Holy hell.

Harriet, you're the one who's been trying to scare Penelope."

She lowered her head. Another door popped open, another terrible truth fell out. She was so ashamed. She couldn't cry. Tears were too easy.

"What the hell was your point?"

"I don't know," she whispered, her voice barely audible. "I just don't know. I guess I wanted to be the only one who knew where Colt and Frannie's plane went down. I was afraid of the truth, and Penelope—" She gulped for air, unable to stand the strain. "Penelope isn't afraid of anything. I sent her the e-mail, the fax—but I never hurt her. That was you, Jack. I know it was."

"Believe in me, Harriet." Jack reached over, took her hand in his. "Come with me. We'll make this work, you and me. I don't know what it is about you. I never thought I'd fall for someone like you, but I have."

She squeezed his hand. It was warm and strong, callused in the right places. "Did you leave Bubba out there to die?"

"Hell, no. I knew Wyatt and Penelope would find him. I followed the old bastard to the wreckage, but he knew I was there all along. He tried to get the drop on me. I hit him on the head, he dropped like a rock, and I checked out the plane wreck. No bodies, no booty."

"Did you know there were diamonds?"

"I guessed it was something like diamonds that wouldn't get ruined from exposure. I finally dragged it out of Brandon Sinclair. It's taken me a while to put it together that it was you. Harriet, I'm not a murderer. I've worked hard my whole life.

You don't know how it is—I can't slice honor and integrity and put it on my plate. I can't buy a ranch with it. I can't watch it from my front porch. I came back to New York for a fighting chance at the good life. I've spent three years saving Brandon Sinclair from his own paranoia. It's my turn now. I *deserve* this chance."

"And what do I deserve, Jack?" she asked quietly.

His expression was unreadable. He got to his feet. "I doubt even the hermit knows you took the diamonds. I only figured it out because I fell in love with you. If I hadn't—" He shrugged. "Who knows?"

"It's wrong."

He didn't look at her. "I just need time to clear out."

"What about me?"

"You won't talk." His gaze fell to her, his eyes flat and dead, any warmth that had been there turned cold. "Your silence and what you've done to Penelope have already doomed you."

TWENTY

Penelope hit every pothole and frost heave on the road to the airport. She knew her driving wasn't safe, but she had to find Harriet and Jack Dunning, and she had to find them now. She didn't trust Dunning, and she was worried about Harriet.

The story was out. On the wires, on CNN, in all the Boston and New Hampshire media. Every reporter in Cold Spring wanted a shot of the heir-turned-hermit. Bubba Johns—Colt Sinclair—and Lyman Chestnut, however, weren't cooperating. When they emerged from Andy McNally's office, they went to the Sunrise Inn.

Robby Chestnut brought them into the kitchen, warned the reporters it was off-limits per order of the board of health, and fed them sandwiches and coffee. Penelope had never been so proud of her mother. As enraged as Robby was at the secrets her husband had kept from her, she loved him, and she was going to let him eat lunch with his friend in peace. She did ask Bubba if she needed to spray after he'd sat in her kitchen.

No one offered to fetch his brother and nephew for him. That was for him to request, and he didn't.

"So," she said, pouring more coffee, "what happened to Frannie?"

"She died a few hours after the crash," Colt Sinclair said. "There was nothing I could do. We were supposed to have flown to Canada, but she insisted we detour to Cold Spring. Lyman and his father were going to be waiting at the airfield. It wasn't much in those days. But I..." His old gray eyes clouded. "Something went wrong, and we didn't make it."

Lyman took over from there. "My father started looking immediately. He had a pretty good idea of where they went down. He met up with Colt on the way—Frannie had dragged herself off, wouldn't keep still. She was bleeding internally. Pop did everything he could. There was just no saving her."

"All she wanted to do," Colt said quietly, "was to get to her baby."

"Jesus Christ in heaven," Robby breathed.

"I had the baby up at Pop's cabin on the lake," Lyman said. "Pop and I took turns for weeks watching her. Mother got suspicious—and I caught Mary following me once or twice. Frannie had come home to have her baby. She didn't realize I knew she was expecting. I guess you don't realize what a teenager knows until it's too late. We kept it our secret as long as we could."

Penelope was stunned. "Did you help deliver her baby?"

He nodded. "My father arrived right in the middle of it. First thing, he figured I was the father. That was a rough moment, I can tell you. When we got that straightened out, he rolled up his sleeves, and we did our best."

"Why, Pop? Why not take her to the hospital? I don't get it."

"In those days an illegitimate child wasn't the same as it is now. And Frannie—Frannie had her own ideas about doing things. She didn't want anyone to know about the baby. She was afraid."

Colt, his sandwich untouched, clasped his big, scarred, bony hands on the table and shook his head. "I didn't know. Not until that night in the plane. I never even guessed she was pregnant that whole winter. She was—" He shut his eyes, swallowed. "She was the most wonderful woman I'd ever known."

"And his old man was the father of her baby," Lyman said with brutal clarity.

Penelope gasped.

Her mother was horrified. "Willard Sinclair? That rotten son of a bitch!"

"He'd seduced her the previous summer," Lyman went on painfully. "Frannie didn't know what to do. She knew Willard would never admit to being the father. He was finished with her, acted like nothing had happened. And Frannie—Frannie wanted her cake and to eat it, too. When he offered her the job in New York, she took it. She hid her pregnancy from everyone, then came home and had the baby here, among friends."

"Then went back to New York?" Penelope asked.

"She promised to be in touch when she figured out what to do. Pop and I took turns tending to the baby."

"To Harriet," Robby said stiffly.

Her husband nodded. "She was six weeks old when Frannie called to say she'd made arrangements to fly to Cold Spring. Only she didn't make it."

"How awful," Penelope breathed. "To have been seduced by one man and then fall in love with his son—"

Colt shook his head. "Frannie was never in love with me. She needed me to help her start her new life. She was desperate. She stole the diamonds—my father owed her that much, she said—and planned to take her baby up to Canada and start fresh."

"With you," Penelope said.

"No. Before she died, she told me I belonged with my family—with my brother. She intended to send me back to New York."

Robby scowled. "Frannie didn't think that one through very well, did she?"

But Colt refused to speak ill of her. "She was desperate. She knew my father would never acknowledge their child."

Robby was unmoved. "I don't care. She used her child's brother and a fifteen-year-old boy to save her skin." She swung to her husband. "And your father, Lyman. What in God's name was he thinking going along with this scheme?"

"He was thinking of the baby," Lyman said simply. "He thought she should be with her mother, and he didn't know any way of making that happen besides doing what Frannie asked. We didn't know about the diamonds, of course. We assumed she'd just been saving her money."

"So when Frannie died," Penelope said, trying to sort it all out in her mind, "you and Granddad came up with the apple basket and left her on the church doorstep for Uncle George to find."

Lyman nodded. "That's right."

Robby thrust a finger at him. "If Harriet wants to

slice your heart out, by damn it, I'm not going to stop her. Keeping such a thing secret all these years!"

"It wasn't my secret to tell. My father and I made a promise to Frannie, and to Colt. And we kept that promise. What else would you have had me do? Turn Harriet over to Willard Sinclair? He'd have tossed her back in a heartbeat."

Robby snorted in disgust, but Penelope could tell her mother's anger wouldn't last. She wasn't sure about her own. She turned to Colt, sitting quietly with his untouched coffee, his untouched sandwich. "What about your family? Why didn't you go back?"

The gray eyes were so clear. "I couldn't."

"I don't understand."

He almost smiled. "Be glad you don't. I buried Frannie under a mountain laurel. I struck off into the woods. I meant to go back to the plane and get the diamonds, but I just kept walking. I ended up on the Canadian border. I stayed there for a while, then came back down here and built my place near the spot where I'd buried Frannie. I guess I just started thinking about how I'd explain everything to my father and never could find a way."

"But your brother—"

"I believed my brother would be better off without me. I thought of myself as an incompetent fool, a dupe. Because of me, Frannie was dead and her baby was being raised by someone else. I wanted Brandon to look up to me, but I knew my father would never let him—and I knew I didn't deserve it."

It was only then, and only because of Andy

McNally's arrival, that they realized Wyatt and Brandon Sinclair had been listening at the door behind them. Robby must have seen them but had said nothing. She tried to get Andy's attention and stop him, but he said, "Why don't you two pull up a chair?"

A white-faced Brandon Sinclair abruptly turned on his heels and walked out. Wyatt, clearly torn, went after him.

Penelope did nothing. She could feel her connection with Wyatt slipping away, and yet she wanted it more than she'd ever wanted anything. Andy didn't seem to understand what he'd done wrong. He'd come for Harriet, and that was all that was on his mind. He was still ashen over what he'd learned from Colt and Lyman, his scar the only color in his face.

"Someone needs to tell Harriet what's going on."

"I will," Lyman said. "And I'll call George and tell him and Rachel. They'll want to come up here, I expect."

"Do they know?"

Lyman shook his head.

Andy couldn't contain his impatience. "I know you all are caught up with what happened forty-five years ago. But let's not forget that just yesterday someone smacked the hell out of Penelope—and there's still the matter of ten million in diamonds missing."

"That could be anyone," Robby said. "Colt says they've been missing for years. If I stumbled on a fortune in diamonds in a plane wreck, I'd keep my mouth shut about it."

"I don't think that's what happened," Andy said.

And everyone in the room knew. Penelope could feel the energy change.

Harriet.

Robby paled. "Andy, you can't think—"

"It explains a lot of things, Robby. Think about it. I'm not saying she fenced them or anything like that—but they've been her little secret for a long, long time. I'd stake my reputation on it."

"I'll help you find her," Penelope said quietly.

Someone had reported seeing Harriet with Jack Dunning. Someone else reported seeing Dunning driving to the airport. Penelope volunteered to check the airport, which her father had shut down for the day. No traffic in, no traffic out. It was truth-telling time in Cold Spring, New Hampshire.

She left without a word to Wyatt. Harriet was his half-sister. Bubba Johns was his uncle. And Lyman had known it all for years. It was too much to expect Wyatt and his father to digest it over tea and scones.

Penelope bounced over the pits and ruts of the dirt parking lot. Jack Dunning's rented car was there. Indulging in a small surge of hope, she jumped out of her truck and charged across the parking lot, breaking into a run when she saw his plane sitting on the runway. At least he hadn't left.

But no one was in the cockpit. She climbed in and sat in the right pilot's seat. It was a very nice plane. A custom interior, plush, state-of-the-art. She was used to planes she and her father kept together with duct tape and bailing wire. Unless the Sinclairs owned his plane, Jack Dunning had expensive tastes.

If she were a New York private detective and

wannabe Texan and had made off with ten million in diamonds, where would she put them?

"Christ, you're like a bad penny." Penelope jumped as Jack Dunning materialized in the open door and climbed into the left seat, shaking his head. "You keep turning up when I don't want you."

She kept her cool. This did not bode well. And she was without dogs, rifle or Wyatt. "You're clearing out?"

"I have business in New York."

"Kind of taking off in midstream, aren't you? We've found Bubba but there's still some nasty bastard on the loose."

"I don't think so." He turned to her, and she realized his expressions had a very narrow range, from none to barely none. "I think everything will turn out to be Harriet and your hermit. Harriet sent you that cute little instant message and the fax, then shot over here and messed up your aunt's machine to throw suspicion off herself."

"That's ridiculous—"

"Oh, no, it's not. It's quite true. And our hermit-heir Bubba—he did everything else."

"Including hit himself over the head, I presume."

"To draw attention away from himself. So, yes, you presume correctly."

Penelope calculated her options, which were few. Scream, pray, make a run for it, brazen it out. "Where's Harriet now?"

He averted his gaze. "I have no idea."

"She fell for you, you know. But of course you know. You used her to get the diamonds from her."

He didn't look at her. "I know you people up here like life in black and white, but here's the thing. I love your cousin. I didn't make her do anything. She made her choice, that's all."

"She didn't—" Penelope stopped herself, the thought like a white-hot knife in her stomach. "She's not going to kill herself."

"I don't know what she's going to do. It's none of my business anymore. You, however, are."

She saw what was coming. The gun, the flat eyes. She swore and reached madly for the door, but the blow came hard and fast to the side of her head. She could feel herself collapsing, and in the split second before unconsciousness claimed her, she knew she was in very serious trouble.

If he went over all his moves during the past week, Wyatt was fairly certain he could find alternative choices that would have prevented him from being in his current predicament. He could have stayed in New York with Pill. He could have thrown Jack Dunning out his office window. He could have believed Penelope's story about the turn-of-the-century dump and decided to visit his father in the Bahamas.

Instead he'd done all the things he'd done, and now he was stuck in the back of a plane with the woman he was fast falling in love with tied and gagged and a larcenous, murderous son of a bitch at the controls.

They were in the air. Dunning had taken off seconds after dispatching Penelope, and Wyatt forced himself to stay cool and time his move. Jack was armed, and he was a professional. Wyatt had only the element of surprise at his disposal—and raw anger.

His father, in shock at what they'd overheard in the inn's kitchen, had asked him to find Jack. Seeing Colt again had sucked everything out of Brandon, and he wanted to update Dunning and call him off. He'd said nothing, but Wyatt knew they both suspected the same thing—his private investigator was out of control, responsible for turning an emotional situation into a dangerous one.

When Wyatt arrived at the little airport, it was shut up tight. No Jack, not even a security guard. He drove to the hangar where his uncle had spent the past few nights, not knowing what to expect. Diamonds? Jack Dunning rustling through the old hermit's stuff? But the place was locked. He'd left his car over by the third hangar and walked around in the cold, still air, checking out the other two hangars, trying to picture Penelope's life before he'd stormed into it.

While he was investigating, Jack arrived. When Jack stepped out of his car, Wyatt decided he didn't like the looks of things and slipped into the plane, climbing out of sight in back. He expected to give the handsome, custom plane a quick once-over and sneak out before Jack returned. But then Penelope jumped aboard, and Jack right after her, and Wyatt thought it best to duck. He scrunched down behind a cargo trunk and pulled a tarp over him. He would wait for Jack to hang himself, then announce his presence.

In hindsight, not the best plan. Jack had, in fact, hung himself, but he'd also bonked Penelope on the head. Wyatt decided not to announce his presence. He didn't want to risk doing anything to further endanger Penelope. Next thing he knew, they were taking off. Seeing how he wasn't a pilot, Wyatt was biding his time. The bad guy pilot was at the controls. The good guy pilot was unconscious. He needed to be patient.

He was still under the tarp, cramped and growing more irritable by the moment. But if he acted prematurely, Jack could end up shooting Penelope, or him, or the wrong part of the plane. It seemed wise to stay put for now.

"Well, well, well," Jack said. "Look who's awake."

He must have slipped Penelope's gag off, because she said, "Bastard."

"Ooh, your head hurts, doesn't it? I could have killed you yesterday when I popped you with the shed door. That's when I figured out Harriet had the diamonds. I searched that crazy hermit's place high and low. He'd have dumped them if he'd picked them up. So it was either Harriet or they were gone."

"What did you do with her?"

"I told you. Nothing. She's not going to say anything. She's in this thing neck-deep herself."

"You think you know her. But you don't."

Penelope sounded groggy and racked with pain, her words slurring. Wyatt kept still, every muscle in his body twitching, ready to spring.

"You can't possibly think this scheme of yours is going to succeed," Penelope said.

"Sure I do. I caught you messing around with my plane and realized you were going to pin everything on me to protect your weird cousin Harriet. We struggle. You prevail momentarily and take off, not realizing my plane's low on fuel. Penelope Chestnut and her impulses, you know?''

''Far-fetched.''

''So's the idea of sweet, plain Harriet Chestnut being a Sinclair, but look at that one. Besides, I have to work with what I've got. And what I've got, sweet cheeks, is you.''

''I'll run out of fuel, crash and die.''

''That's the plan. Nothing but trees and hills ahead. You could sit out here in the boonies for fifty years yourself.''

''And you?''

''I will go back to New York and continue my work with the Sinclairs. One by one, I fence the diamonds and amass a nice fortune for myself. Then I buy my ranch in Texas. If things get too hot here, I skip to Argentina, maybe Australia. Unfortunately, you were killed in the crash, and the diamonds weren't recovered.''

''Harriet'll talk,'' Penelope said.

''If she believes her actions—or her lack of action—got everyone's favorite Chestnut killed? I don't think so. She'll just wither into a bitter, pathetic prune. Or hang herself on her front porch.''

''You're evil.''

''I'm just a guy trying to make a buck.''

Wyatt could hear a rustling sound and something like a lock snapping. Then Penelope's voice. ''You're going to jump? I hope you break your neck.''

''Lucky for you I don't break yours. But I need the autopsy to say you died in the crash.''

Next came the sickening sound of him whacking Penelope one more time. Wyatt yanked off the tarp and surged forward, but he felt a whoosh of cold air and knew what was happening. He moved over the trunk, banging his knee, catching his foot.

Jack was gone. The left pilot's seat was empty, the door flapping in the cold, clear air. With a vicious curse, Wyatt pushed himself forward and got into the vacant seat, the door next to him still open. He could feel the cold air. Having no desire to fall out of the plane, he pulled on his seat belt, then grabbed the door and yanked it shut. The plane felt steady, the airspeed felt okay. But he wasn't a pilot. He couldn't land the thing.

Penelope was slumped in her seat, unconscious. There was no time for niceties. He reached behind him for a water bottle, tore off the top and dumped the contents on her head. "Come on, sweetheart. Wake up and land the plane." He patted her cheek. "Penelope, we're in a bit of a pickle here."

She groaned, brought a hand to her head, which had to be aching. "Wyatt? Where—why am I all wet—"

"I dumped water on you. Jack's parachuted. We're about out of gas, and I'm not much on flying planes."

"Jack?"

"Jumped. He's gone. It's just us up here."

She held her head up. Progress. "That was cold water."

"Penelope, you have to land the plane."

"You don't fly?" She managed a ghostly grin. "I thought Sinclairs did everything. God, I have a headache. I think I'm going to throw up."

"You're not going to throw up. Okay, forget it. Tell me what to do. We're low on fuel." As if to prove his point, the engine sputtered. "I need to check the airspeed first, right?"

That got her with the program. She squinted at the controls. "I hate flying with a headache." The engine sputtered again. "Hell. We don't have much time. Ten to one the reserve tank's empty." She fiddled with something under her seat. "Yep. That bastard."

"Bad?"

"Lots worse than Monday when Pop grounded me. Airspeed's good—I need to get this thing on the ground before the engine stops. Look for a nice big feather bed on the ground. A field, a road."

Below them was an endless expanse of trees and hills.

Penelope was grim-faced. She focused on her task as she brought the plane lower. "What'd he do, bail in broad daylight?"

"He's arrogant enough to think he can get away with anything." Wyatt spotted the tiniest of clearings ahead and pointed. "There."

"It's not enough. We'll end up in the trees." She looked at him, her eyes wide and alert, shining with determination. She was pale, and a swollen, ugly bruise had formed on the side of her head under her left ear where Jack had clipped her. "It's going to be close."

"We'll make it."

"I have no regrets about the last week." They were low, just above the trees, and the clearing seemed even smaller. She was focused on the controls, the terrain ahead, but she said, "None."

"No goodbyes. I'm planning a long future with you."

The engine died, and they dropped, Penelope

working to keep the nose up. Wyatt checked her seatbelt, saw that it was buckled tight. Jack's doing. He wanted this to look like an accident.

"Hold on," she said.

The plane hit the ground hard, plowing through ruts and snow and fast running out of clearing. A big pine snagged a wing, spun them around.

Another tree was there in front of them. Too damned close, too damned big. Penelope swore.

Wyatt grabbed her, and they ducked.

TWENTY-ONE

Two diehard snowshoers in the back woods northeast of Lake Winnipesaukee reported seeing a small plane go down. The state authorities launched a major search effort. Lyman Chestnut got in his plane and joined the search. No one tried to stop him, and Robby sat next to him in the cockpit for the first time in at least twenty years.

That was all Harriet could digest at one time. Andy sat with her in front of the parlor fire. She was beyond trembling, beyond crying. If Penelope and Wyatt died, it would be her fault. Andy, who'd been so kind, had tried to tell her otherwise, but not very hard. He knew.

He pressed a mug of hot cocoa into her hands. "Drink up, Harriet. It'll help."

She nodded, but didn't touch the cocoa.

"Penelope's a good pilot."

Another nod. It was Andy who'd found her upstairs. She had just dialed his number at the police station. When she saw him, she told him everything. She'd found the diamonds, she'd kept them, she'd said nothing about them or the plane wreck. To deter Penelope, she'd sent her the lame instant message and the fax. She wasn't responsible for ransacking Penelope's house—that was Jack looking for the valuables he'd known were in Colt and Frannie's plane or any clues that would point to its location—and she hadn't followed her or attacked Bubba Johns or shoved the shed door into her face. All Jack.

But without her unwitting complicity, he never would have made off with the diamonds and done whatever he'd done to Wyatt and Penelope. That they were in the small plane reported to have gone down was a reasonable deduction based on the evidence at the airport—Wyatt's car, Penelope's truck, Jack's rented car and no plane.

The Sinclair brothers had borrowed Robby's car and were hunting for Brandon's errant investigator. It was the strangest thing Harriet had ever seen. Wild-haired, wild-bearded Colt Sinclair in his frayed, stained work pants, flannel shirt and suspenders, and Brandon Sinclair, suave and handsome in his pressed trousers, Scottish knit sweater and polished, expensive shoes, going off together. They were her half-brothers. Willard Sinclair was her father.

"Harriet, Jesus, don't cry." Andy sounded unbearably pained, as if he couldn't take one more thing in his life. "Everyone knows you'd never hurt a soul."

"It's not that." She brushed her tears with her fingertips, her chest so tight it felt as if it were being crushed. "My parents—my real parents—what are they going to think of me?"

"I can't speak for them, Harriet. But I have two daughters of my own, and if one of them were sitting here in your place, having done what you've done, it wouldn't change anything. She'd still be my daughter, and I'd still love her."

"You're a good man, Andy."

He nodded sadly. "Yeah. That's what they say."

Pete, Andy's detective, charged into the parlor so abruptly Harriet jumped and spilled hot cocoa down her front. Pete hardly noticed. "Andy, the Sinclairs just called in from up north. They've got Jack Dunning. The slimy son of a bitch was joining in the search for his plane!" He turned to Harriet. "Sorry about the language. That was unprofessional."

"Did they tell him I'd talked?" she asked.

"I don't know. Apparently he made a run for it and Brandon and Bubba—I mean, Colt—jumped him, tied him up, gagged him, and waited for the police." Pete grinned. "That I'd love on tape."

"What about the plane?" Andy asked.

Pete's grin faded. "Nothing yet."

After the detective left, Andy asked Harriet if she wanted to go up and change her shirt. She shook her head. At his insistence, she took a few sips of what was left of her cocoa. An air search could go on for days. Weeks.

But an hour later, they heard hoots among the reporters gathered in the Octagon Room, consuming gallons of coffee and waiting for news from the search. Many had already headed north. Andy got a call on his cell phone. He thanked the caller and hung up.

He grinned and winked at Harriet. "They've found the plane. They're alive."

By the time the rescue team reached them, Penelope had washed off most of the blood with snow. She had superficial cuts on her face and arms. She knew her parents would be right in the thick of the rescue team. She didn't want to upset her mother. Wyatt, also bloodied, declined her offer of a handful of snow. He could see the team crossing the small field and would wait for proper treatment.

She grinned at him. She wasn't feeling any pain. She knew she would. The shock would fade, and she'd hurt like hell. But right now, there was only the overwhelming sense that she was going to spend the rest of her life with this man. "Aren't you glad I saved our lives?"

Wyatt gave a short laugh. He was feeling no pain, either. He'd stayed close to her from the second they cleared Jack Dunning's mangled plane. "You'd have crashed without regaining consciousness if I hadn't dumped water on you."

"Well, there's that," she admitted. "You know what it was, don't you? What cleared my head?"

He smiled. "The thought of me making love to you?"

She shook her head. "Babies."

"Penelope?"

She grinned at him, giddy, her head swimming. "I could see these little Sinclair-Chestnut babies learning to swim in Lake Winnipesaukee, and I just knew we had to live. Of course, we'll have to put little homing devices on them. If they're like us, we're in for it."

He took her hand, which wasn't injured, and kissed her forehead, which was injured, and he whispered, "I love you."

"If I didn't have a concussion," she said, "I'd make love to you right now. How on earth did I fall in love with a Sinclair?"

But she had, she realized.

When the search team arrived, her mother went pale but stayed calm. The paramedics pounced on Penelope, asking her questions and checking her over. "Why are you doing me first? You should do Wyatt. He's not a pilot."

Wyatt leaned over the paramedics. "I didn't get smacked on the head twice with the butt of a gun."

Somehow she'd forgotten that part. "Oh. Right."

"A gun?" Her mother's voice croaked. "There was a gun?"

But her father, at the rear of the rescue team, took his wife by the hand and pulled her toward the wrecked plane. "Come on, Robby. Let me show you why flying's so safe and why Penelope's a damned good pilot when she keeps her mind on the job."

Penelope smiled, and when the paramedics laid her in the stretcher sled, she glanced at Wyatt, who was still on his feet and looking so good. He winked at her and said, "I'm walking out," rubbing it in, but it didn't even occur to her to be mad.

EPILOGUE

It was the kind of hot summer day that brought the cars from Boston and filled the Sunrise Inn with guests content to have tea in the gardens, swim in the lake or sit on the porch with the cool breeze and a good book. Harriet, finished with her day's work, sat at the bar with her glass of wine. Unlike in the off-season, the inn's small, wood-paneled tavern was filled with guests. Their laughter reminded her that the work she did was good.

Andy McNally came in and got himself a beer. He sat beside her as if it had been last night he'd been here, not three months ago. "You're looking well, Harriet," he said.

"Thank you."

She'd dyed her hair copper—one of those semi-permanent dyes—but had given up makeup. She didn't like the feel of it on her skin. But she liked her hair. Andy looked the same, although not as tired and stricken as he had that day they'd waited in her parlor for news of Penelope and Wyatt. Jack Dunning was awaiting trial. Penelope and Wyatt were hopelessly in love.

It was only her life, Harriet thought, that still seemed up in the air. She'd never been charged with a crime. Penelope insisted they'd said much worse things to each other over wallpapering the inn's rooms than Harriet had said in her little anonymous messages. They had returned the diamonds to the Sinclairs, who immediately donated them to the Sinclair Collection in Frannie Beaudine's honor. Harriet had come to a place of peace about the woman who'd given birth to her, whose last breaths were drawn in an attempt to give her baby a good life. And she *had*. That was what Harriet had finally come to realize. Whatever her faults, Frannie had done right by her daughter.

But what still haunted her and kept her awake nights was the misguided, frightening way she'd fallen for Jack Dunning.

Andy sipped his beer. "So, you're an heiress, eh?"

"I don't know about that. I'd never ask the Sinclairs for anything."

"I won ten grand in the lottery once."

She smiled. "Did you?"

"Yep. Invested it. I've done okay, but I'm no Sinclair, that's for damned sure. And I come with two daughters I'd go to the ends of the earth for, and I've got this hell of a scar." He shrugged. "I'm no catch, I guess. But if you want me, Harriet, you've got me. I think you know that."

But she didn't. She was totally taken aback. She started to shake, and she knocked her glass over. Wine spilled into her lap, and she mumbled, "I think we did this last time."

"Harriet—it's okay, I didn't mean to scare the bejesus out of you. Forget I said anything."

"No! No, Andy, that's not it." She grabbed his arm, felt her fingers digging into his flesh. "I'm just taken aback. I didn't think you'd want anything to do with me. I made such a fool of myself."

He shook his head, his eyes filled with tenderness. "We all have to find out who we are sometime, Harriet, figure out what's important. It's not always easy. I've loved you for a long time. I should have come forward and said so before now. If it's too late, so be it."

"It's not too late."

His entire body seemed to relax. He nodded. "It's a nice night. Would you like to take a walk along the lake?"

She nodded and ran upstairs to change her wine-soaked shirt. When she caught her reflection in her dresser mirror, she stopped abruptly. She touched the spray of freckles on her cheek, the fine lines at the corner of one eye, and she smiled.

Having decided it was weird to fall in love with a man and not know where he lived, Penelope had ventured to New York City three times since she and Wyatt survived their plane crash. All three times she came away thinking she liked New York—she even loved New York—but she really didn't want to live there.

It was Wyatt who pointed this out to her. "What you want to do," he said as they sat on her dock, their feet in the clear, cool water of Lake Winnipesaukee, "is to fly planes and get qualified as a flight instructor and build our house on the lake."

She liked the way he said "our." It made her feel as if they could sort out all the complications of their lives. His uncle was a hermit. His grandfather was her cousin's father. "I can compromise," she said.

He grinned at her. "I'm going to tape record that and play it for your father."

"You have a life in New York. Your parents are there, your sisters, your work. Your cat."

"Pill'd be happy anywhere."

"Pill's a city cat."

He gave her one of those appraising looks that suggested this was the mind of a man who spoke five languages. But Penelope thought he was so damned handsome and sexy with his pant legs rolled up and those black, black eyes. His little sisters had them, too. Harriet didn't. Everyone had decided she had Frannie's eyes. "So, you want to move to New York with me?" he asked.

"No!"

He laughed. "Called that bluff, didn't I?"

"I mean, I'd compromise. Really. I can drum up some kind of business that'd give me a regular route to New York so I can fly in and out. Maybe you could work out something so you could be up here for long weekends. That sort of thing."

"Can't."

"You're your own boss. You—"

"I don't have an office or a secretary. I gave them both up to a friend of mine who's putting together some kind of big money deal. I didn't ask. I've already cleaned out my desk."

She stared at him. "Wyatt?"

"I got rid of everything. The office, the secretary, the apartment. A couple of bank accounts is about all I have."

His idea of a "couple of bank accounts" and hers, she knew, would be two different things. "The cat?"

"Madge is keeping him until I can pick him up."

"What will you do?"

"Your little business with your father and Aunt Mary could use a Sinclair mind. I've talked to them about it already. They said if it's okay with you, it's okay with them. Plus there are a few things I could do from a computer. New York was a healing time for me," he added. "A between time."

"But your family—"

"My family has roots here, too. Colt isn't going anywhere. He and my father have a long, long way to go. My father's coming up next weekend. He and Colt are going to play cards and swat mosquitoes, like they did when they were boys. I doubt we'll ever get Colt to New York, but it's something. Then there's our land. I figure with it and your acreage here, and this lot on the lake, we can have a good life."

Penelope swallowed. "You're giving up everything for me. What can I give you?"

"I'm giving up nothing, and all you have to give me is your love."

"You have it."

"I know." He smiled. "And it's enough."

From the bestselling author of
Shocking Pink and *Fortune*

ERICA SPINDLER

THEY OPENED THEIR DOOR TO A STRANGER...AND THEIR DREAM BECAME A NIGHTMARE

Julianna Starr has chosen Kate and Richard Ryan to be *more* than the parents of her child. Obsessed with Richard, Julianna molds herself in Kate's image and insinuates herself into the couple's life, determined to tear their perfect marriage apart. But the nightmare has only begun. Because Julianna is not alone. From her dark past comes a man of unspeakable evil....
Now no one is safe — not even the innocent child Kate and Richard call their own.

CAUSE FOR ALARM

New York Times bestselling author

LINDA LAEL MILLER

Escape from Cabriz

Kristen Meyers's impulsive decision to marry the exotic
prince of Cabriz is beginning to seem like a very bad idea.
On the eve of their wedding, the palace is under attack by
angry rebels, and her fiancé has suddenly become a
coldhearted stranger. There doesn't appear to be any
escape from the complicated mess.

Then Zachary Harmon arrives. Kristen and the secret
agent were once lovers. Now he's risking his life to rescue
her. All the old chemistry is still there, but now they must
survive something even more explosive—escaping from
Cabriz alive.

> **"Linda Lael Miller is one of the hottest romance
> authors writing today."**
> **—*Romantic Times***

On sale in mid-March 1999 wherever paperbacks are sold!

MIRA

If you enjoyed this novel from
bestselling author

CARLA NEGGERS

Don't miss the opportunity to pick up her previous
title from MIRA® Books:

#66266   CLAIM THE CROWN $5.50 U.S.☐ $6.50 CAN.☐
(limited quantities available)

TOTAL AMOUNT	$
POSTAGE & HANDLING	$
($1.00 for one book, 50¢ for each additional)	
APPLICABLE TAXES*	$ _____
<u>**TOTAL PAYABLE**</u>	$ _____
(check or money order—please do not send cash)	

To order, complete this form and send it, along with a check or money order for the
total above, payable to MIRA Books, to: **In the U.S.:** 3010 Walden Avenue, P.O. Box
9077, Buffalo, NY 14269-9077; **In Canada:** P.O. Box 636, Fort Erie, Ontario L2A 5X3.

Name: _____

Address: _____ City: _____

State/Prov.: _____ Zip/Postal Code: _____

Account Number: _____ (If applicable)   075 CSAS

   *New York residents remit applicable sales taxes.
    Canadian residents remit applicable GST and provincial taxes.

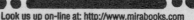